# PEOPLE
## of the MASKS

# KATHLEEN O'NEAL GEAR
# AND W. MICHAEL GEAR

TOR®

A TOM DOHERTY ASSOCIATES BOOK
NEW YORK

This is a work of fiction. All the characters and events portrayed in this book are either products of the author's imagination or are used fictitiously.

PEOPLE OF THE MASKS

Maps and interior illustrations by Ellisa Mitchell

A Tor Book
Published by Tom Doherty Associates, LLC
175 Fifth Avenue
New York, NY 10010

www.tor.com

Tor® is a registered trademark of Tom Doherty Associates, LLC.

ISBN: 0-812-51561-7
Library of Congress Catalog Card Number: 98-8695

First edition: November 1998
First mass market edition: June 2000

Printed in the United States of America

0  9  8  7  6  5  4

To Harold and Sylvia Fenn

And the remarkable H. B. Fenn staff across Canada

In gratitude for their warm friendship, and their dedication
to publishing books about Canada's rich archaeological
and historical heritage

| 13,000 B.C. | 10,000 B.C. | 6000 B.C. | 5000 B.C. |
|---|---|---|---|

*Paleo Indian*

*Early Archaic*

**People of the Wolf**
Alaska & Canadian
Northwest

**People of the Fire**
Central Rockies &
Great Plains

**People of the Sea**
Pacific Coast &
Great Basin

**People of the Lightning**
Florida

*Paleo Indian*

*Archaic*

| 3000 B.C. | 100 A.D. | 800 A.D. | 1000 A.D. | 1300 A.D. |
|---|---|---|---|---|

*Archaic*    *Woodland*         *Mississippian*

**People of the Earth**
Northern Plains
& Basins

**People of the Mist**
Chesapeake Bay

**People of the River**
Mississippi Valley

**People of the Masks**
Ontario &
Upstate New York

**People of the Lakes**
East-Central Woodlands
& Great Lakes

**People of the Silence**
Southwest Anasazi

*Basketmaker*         *Pueblo*

People of the Masks

North

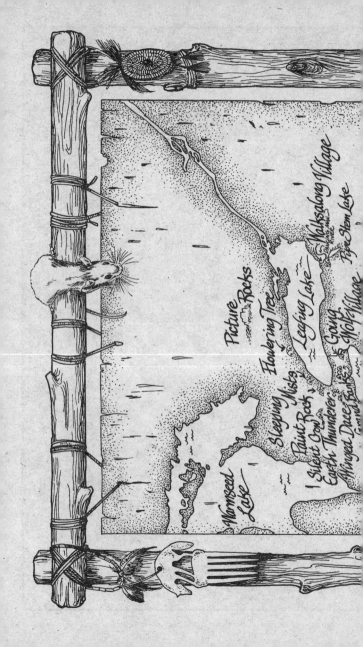

# Acknowledgments

None of the books in this series would be possible without the in-depth research of field archaeologists, historians, and specialists in Native American religions and culture. We would especially like to thank William Fox, Ronald F. Williamson, David G. Smith, Gary W. Crawford, Dean R. Snow, W. A. Ritchie, Bruce Trigger, Francis Jennings, for their superb research into what constitutes "Iroquoian" culture, and Cara E. Richards, Laura Klein, Lillian Ackerman, and Joy Bilharz, for their work on the changing roles of women in Native American societies.

Lastly, we offer our deepest thanks to Harriet McDougal. She has been a spring of renewal for us. Whenever we've felt tired or suddenly alone, she's always been there to straighten reality for us.

Thanks, Harriet.

# Foreword

For most people living in what is now the northeastern United States, and southeastern Canada, the word "Iroquois" conjures a number of romantic images: large palisaded villages composed of longhouses; magnificent warriors fighting colonial armies; flourishing fields of corn, beans, and squash. The Iroquois are seen as a strongly matrilineal and matrilocal people, meaning they traced their descent through the women, and when a man married, he went to live in his wife's village.

The truth, however, is that Iroquoian culture was a great deal more varied and interesting. It is only over the last one thousand five hundred years that the Iroquois have moved from being patrilineal hunter-gatherers to the grand matrilineal agricultural people that we know today.

This transition was not a quick one. The Iroquois are a classic case demonstrating that matrilineages can and do develop slowly over time.

Historical documents from the sixteenth through the nineteenth centuries demonstrate that closely related groups of Iroquoian peoples often handled matters of descent, marriage, and divorce quite differently.

For example, in 1624, Father Gabriel Sagard reported that before an Iroquois couple could marry, the man had to seek the consent of *both parents,* and that a father had complained to him about the obstinacy of his daughter with regard to one young man. Sagard also said that in the event of divorce, all children, except for unweaned infants, stayed with the father. (A patrilineal trait.)

In 1724, Father Joseph François Lafitau wrote that while men were only allowed one wife, Seneca women took more than one husband. He also said that after divorce husbands claimed to have the right to the male children, and often came great distances to try to take them, but that women had the final say as to whether to let the children go or to keep them. (Apparently a time of transition between the old patrilineal system and an evolving matrilineal one.)

By 1851, Lewis Henry Morgan, in his book *League of the Iroquois,* reported that marriage was under maternal control, and that the Iroquois rejected all claims made by a father with regard to his children, either "to the custody of their persons or to their nurture." (A matrilineal trait.) In fact, anthropologists use this classic "Iroquoian" kinship system as a model for evaluating other cultures.

We can see the roots of these changes in prehistory. *People of the Masks* is set at approximately A.D. 1000. This is a pivotal and very complex period of northeastern prehistory. We will be focusing on three different cultural traditions: the Princess Point (A.D. 500–1000) and Glen Meyer (A.D. 900–1250) traditions, in southern Ontario, and the Carpenter Brook phase of the Owasco tradition in New York State (A.D. 1000–1100).

House styles at this time show a great deal of variety, ranging from circular lodges, roughly fifteen feet across, to early forms of longhouses.

This period may mark the beginnings of the first matrilineages, for pottery styles are fairly homogeneous. When pottery styles stay the same for an extended time, the fact suggests that this knowledge is being passed from grandmother to granddaughter, and on down the line. A woman's female descendants, then, are not leaving after marriage, but seem to be staying in the village where they were born. These people are, therefore, probably matri-local, and matrilocal peoples are almost always matrilin-eal.

Distinctive pottery styles may also survive in the long term because of internecine warfare, which isolates vil-lages from one another.

This is certainly a time of expanding populations. Vil-lages are becoming larger and more compact. Between A.D. 900 and 1000 the first palisades were constructed. When people start building walls around their villages, archaeologists ask: "Are they trying to keep something in, or something out?"

We know that historically many peoples built earthen walls or palisades to define the boundaries of holy ground, as in *People of the Lakes*—in such cases, then, the walls keep something in; they preserve sacred space. More often, however, palisades were erected to keep something out. Namely, enemy warriors.

Let's look at what might have frightened them.

By A.D. 1000, Early Iroquoian peoples had been grow-ing corn for at least four hundred years and maybe longer. They were in the middle of a warm, rainy climatic episode called the Neo-Atlantic. Whenever crops flour-ish, population generally follows. But these were not ag-ricultural peoples, they did not plant vast fields and live year-round in one village. They were horticulturalists. That is, they planted small fields, and some villagers may have stayed behind to watch them through the growing season, but other members of the village were undoubt-edly out hunting, fishing, and collecting wild foods to supplement the cultigens.

Northeastern North America is a rich environment. We know the Early Iroquoian peoples hunted deer, raccoon, black bear, red fox, skunk, woodchuck, rabbits, muskrat, beaver, squirrel, chipmunk, passenger pigeons, ducks, shorebirds, bald eagles, geese, snakes, turtles, frogs, as well as fishing and collecting freshwater mollusks, to name a few of the species utilized. They also gathered blueberries, raspberries, sumac and strawberries, wild rice, elderberries, wild plums, wild grapes, marsh-elder seeds, goosefoot, sunflower seeds, lamb's quarter, gourds, walnuts, hickory nuts, and acorns.

Despite the variety and abundance of these resources, as the population base increased, each of these cultures would have found themselves surrounded by people who also needed land for crops, as well as fishing, hunting, and gathering grounds. It must have created tension, but may also have spurred the establishment of some of the earliest alliances. On top of many Princess Point and Glen Meyer sites we see new house styles joining the old, and new types of pottery being used alongside the traditional pottery.

These early village mergers would set the stage for one of the most extraordinary alliances in history, the League of the Iroquois, established around A.D. 1450.

We will talk more about the League of the Iroquois in the afterword of this book. For now, suffice it to say that the foundations for our modern democratic world originated, not in Europe, but in the northeastern corner of North America.

# Prologue

Maureen Cole sat on the old-fashioned porch that wrapped around three sides of her small house in Niagara on the Lake. At the age of thirty-five, she looked ten years younger, or so she'd been told. No wrinkles marred her face, and her long straight hair shone a glossy black. Her traditional aquiline features, straight nose, dark eyes, full lips, came from her mother, a full-blooded Seneca. She wore a pair of faded button-front Levi's and a white T-shirt.

She propped her moccasin-clad feet on the porch railing and leaned back in her big wicker chair. To the north, in front of her, Lake Ontario spread vast and blue. A glass of iced mint tea sat on the table beside her, the cubes melting. She had poured the glass an hour ago, and hadn't yet taken a sip.

John, her husband, and best friend, had died on this day one year before. Of a heart attack. He'd been thirty-eight. She longed for a stiff scotch, preferably a twenty-five-year-old McCallan. Or maybe a bottle of Belgian Guinness. Belgians truly knew how to drink Irish beer. The stuff in Ireland couldn't hold a candle to the rich creamy stout they served under the Guinness label in Belgium.

But she'd stopped drinking six months ago.

After John's death she'd gotten herself into real trouble, learning firsthand what the phrase "drowning in the bottle'' meant. She had no desire to find herself there again.

She studied the hands laced in her lap. The nails were broken and uneven. John used to tease her about them. She'd never had paintable fingernails. Not even as a child. Though her mother was a devout Catholic, and had raised Maureen in the ways of the church, she had also insisted Maureen learn traditional Seneca skills, making pottery, doing porcupine quillwork, beadwork, basketry, even hunting, skinning, and tanning the hides she harvested. As her mother often reminded her: *"Puny white women have perfect hands because everything living and dying frightens them. You, my daughter, will remember that your great-great-grandmothers were hunters and warriors. Five Iroquois women warriors received military pensions for heroic service during the American War of 1812. One of them, Julia John, is a relative of yours. Our women were leaders, not followers. If I ever find one of your moccasin prints inside someone else's, you'll be scraping fresh hides for the rest of your life."*

Having scraped dozens of fresh hides, and with the traditional stone tools, Maureen had vowed never to set foot in someone else's moccasin prints.

She frowned at her nails, wondering if she *could* paint them. Probably not. If she got close to a bottle of pink nail polish, she would undoubtedly start clicking her heels to get out of there.

Maureen lifted her watered-down tea and took a sip. It went down cool and naturally sweet. She grew the mint in her own garden. The stuff they sold in Canada was an artificially sweet, lemony horror.

The United States didn't have much going for it, but it did have iced tea. Now that she thought of it, the U.S. actually had two great assets: iced tea, and Dodger dogs.

She suspected that the rest, however, could be nuked and nobody would notice.

She swirled her tea, watching the pale green liquid wash the sides of the clear glass, then set it back down on the table.

Her wedding ring shimmered in the tree-filtered summer sunlight that streamed across the porch. Plain and gold, she'd never had it off. John had given it to her before their marriage, in the dark days when they'd been struggling to eat while they finished their Ph.D.s at McGill University in Montreal. It had been both an engagement and a wedding ring, a huge extravagance, and she cherished it more now than she had then.

Maureen covered the ring with her right hand and held it against her heart.

Around the west side of the house, to her left, the old floorboards creaked. Maureen knew from long experience what that meant: she had an unexpected visitor.

She turned, and saw a medium-sized man with thick gray hair come around the corner. He wore dusty clothing and a battered 1940s-style fedora. His gray mustache and bushy eyebrows quirked when he saw her.

"Dr. Cole, are you always sitting here on summer afternoons? I would think that the head of the anthropology department at McMaster University would have better things to do."

Maureen smiled. "It's July, Dale. Summer vacation? Ever heard of that?"

"No. That's when we archaeologists work the hardest."

"Well, we physical anthropologists need more time for lofty thoughts. You know, to contemplate the nature of reality, and the future of the human species. . . . What are you doing in Canada?"

He took off his hat and batted the dust off on his jeans. He walked forward. "Working."

Maureen gestured to the wicker chair beside hers. "Have a seat. Working where? I thought it would take an AK-47—of which you have plenty in the U.S., for home defense, of course—to get you out of the American Southwest."

Dale Emerson Robertson, the grand old man of American Southwestern archaeology, sank onto the soft pillows of Maureen's wicker chair, and propped his dirty boots on the railing beside her moccasins. Almost seventy, his brown face bore deep wrinkles from the scorching sunlight in Arizona, New Mexico, Utah, and southern Colorado.

"Why don't you let me have a sip of your iced tea?" he said.

She handed it to him, and watched him drink half the glass in four swallows. "I can get you one of your own, you know. We have refrigerators in Canada. The best of them all was invented in Yellowknife one December."

"No, thanks. This is fine."

Dale was a small-town western boy who didn't know how to get down to business unless you provoked him, so Maureen said, "What happened? Have all the Anasazi sites in the Four Corners region succumbed to bulldozers?"

Dale's wrinkles rearranged into a scowl. "Bite your tongue. Bulldozers are the least of our worries. Congress, along with several oil companies, are doing everything they can to undermine the preservation of our glorious American heritage." He finished her iced tea and handed the glass back. Maureen set it on the table. "But that's not why I'm here."

"I didn't think so. What's up?"

Dale's brushy brows lowered over his blue eyes. "I have a site I want you to take a look at."

"Really? Where?"

"Across the border, south of Buffalo, New York."

Maureen tipped her chair back on two legs, and said, "I've been to the American Association of Physical Anthropologists meetings. It's crawling with bone people. Why do you need me?"

"Well," he said and gazed out at the shimmering vastness of Lake Ontario. A quacking flock of ducks circled the water, landing in a series of splashes. "For one thing, you're the best damned physical anthropologist in North America—"

"Flattery will get you everywhere."

"—and for another thing, you're Iroquois."

She set her chair down hard, and gave him an unfriendly smile. "I do hope you're not suggesting I play the 'token Indian' role to give you a way out of your screwed-up American cultural resources policies. What did you find? A burial? Who's screaming about it?"

Dale turned in his chair and gave her his most charming smile. "Would you take a look at it? It's an hour's drive. I'll have you back by supper."

They passed through the Gestapo boxes at the border, showing their passports, answering inane questions, and Dale headed south on Highway 62. Just north of Eden, New York, he pulled onto a side road.

Towering beech and sugar maple trees lined the way, dappling the windshield with a patchwork of warm sunlight and cool shadows.

Maureen knew when they'd arrived. She saw the archaeological field school, around thirty students, hard at work in the meadow. They'd dug at least eight two-by-two meter units, which meant they'd been here for a while. All wore shorts, T-shirts, hiking boots, and hats. Except one bareheaded hedonist. Tall and blond, he knelt looking down into an excavation unit where two female crew members dug. From the smile on his face, it seemed to be more ogling than business, however. He had broad shoulders, and a killer tan. He reminded her of one of Michelangelo's visions of the perfect male, which annoyed her. She'd never felt comfortable around blond-god types. This one, fortunately, was also filthy. Which made her feel a little better.

Dale pulled to a stop in the cool shade of a pecan tree, and Maureen opened her door and stepped out. To her moccasined feet, last year's pecans felt like small rocks. She hobbled out into the sunlit meadow, and waited for Dale.

He grabbed some notes off the dash, slammed the car door, and came to meet her. After he'd tugged his hat down over his eyes, he said, "Welcome to the Paradise Site."

"Is that a play on the fact that the town of Eden is just down the road?"

"I can't imagine how you guessed."

"I've worked with archaeologists before, Dale. I've never met one who was particularly creative when it came to naming sites. Beers, yes. Sites, no."

Dale's mustache twitched as he smiled. "Well, let me deliver these notes to our crew chief, Myra Linn, and I'll escort you to the burial."

"Where is it?"

Dale pointed. "Over there at the edge of that grove of flowering dogwood trees."

"Okay. Before you go, I assume you're the project director, who's in charge—"

"I'm one of the project directors. My partner . . ." Dale squinted, gestured to the blond god, and said, "There he is. That's William Stewart, he's actually heading up the fieldwork. I've known him for years. Mostly in the Southwest. He's here on a one-year appointment, teaching in Buffalo—"

"Wait." Maureen held up a hand, and gave Dale an askance look. "You don't mean Dusty Stewart? The Madman of New Mexico?"

Dale wiped his sweating brow. "You've heard of him."

Her mouth gaped. "Heard of him! What I've heard is petrifying! Donita Rodriguez told me he was a womanizer, a scoundrel, a glorified pothunter—"

"Yes, well, everyone is entitled to their opinion," Dale said with a casual wave of his hand. "I admit he's a colorful character. He's also fluent in Navajo, Hopi, Zuni, Apache, and Arapaho. He's one of the few archaeologists in America whom strong traditionalists trust, and—well—he's a fine archaeologist, too. Give him a chance."

Maureen propped her hands on her hips. "All right, Dale. For you. But I'll only give him one."

"Fair enough. Now, let me deliver these notes, and I'll show you around."

Dale walked to the far southern edge of the site, to Maureen's right, and stood talking with a woman wearing reflective sunglasses. After five or ten minutes, Maureen got antsy. She headed in the direction Dale had pointed, toward the burial site.

As she passed excavation units, she peered in, smiled at the students, and proceeded on her way. It didn't look as though they'd found anything particularly impressive yet. A couple of fire hearths, some lithic debitage—the chips of stone left over after someone made a stone tool—and what looked to be a living floor. At this point, the students had only begun to reveal a roughly circular soil discoloration. She didn't see any post holes, or associated artifacts, but it might be a small lodge.

Maureen continued through the tall green grass. As she approached, she could see that the two-by-three-meter excavation was relatively shallow, about a meter in depth. She hadn't seen this one from the road. It sat in the shade near the cluster of flowering dogwood trees. Fragrant white blossoms covered the branches and scented the air. For centuries her people had boiled flowering dogwood roots to make a magnificent red dye. Historically, the powdered bark was used as a quinine substitute.

She knelt beside the unit and looked down. What she saw filled her with awe. "My . . . God," she whispered.

"Excuse me!" someone called. "Who are you? What are you doing there?"

She looked up to see Dusty Stewart trotting toward her with a sour expression on his face. "Ma'am? Do you have a reason to be here? This dig is not open to the public!"

"Really?" she called back. "I didn't see a sign saying Keep Out!"

He stopped on the other side of the excavation unit from her, breathing hard. Around his hairy, tanned legs, Maureen saw Dale striding through the field school as fast as he could, calling "Dusty? Dusty!"

Maureen stood up and faced Stewart. "I'm here with Dr. Robertson."

"Are you?" he said and propped his hands on his hips. "Well, I wasn't informed."

"Gee. Do you think maybe Dr. Robertson doesn't trust your judgment? Why would that be?"

His bright blue eyes narrowed, then he stabbed a finger at her. "Listen. I don't know who you are—"

"She's Dr. Maureen Cole," Dale said, panting as he stopped at Stewart's side. Sweat sheened his wrinkled face.

"Oh." Stewart slowly lowered his finger. "Uh. Hi."

Maureen said, "I hope your vocabulary improves when it comes to the archaeology."

Dale tugged his fedora down over his forehead. He said, "Allow me to properly introduce you two. Maureen, this is Dusty Stewart. Dusty, this is Dr. Maureen Cole."

"Nice to meet you," Stewart said, but he shoved his hands into the pockets of his shorts as though he didn't mean it. "What do ordinary people call you? Maury?"

In her haste to get to his throat, she almost stumbled into the pit. "No," she said, "ordinary people call me Dr. Cole. What do people call you?" *Asshole?*

He smiled, as if reading her thoughts, and showed her a row of perfect pearly whites. "You mean to my face?"

"Not necessarily."

Dale put a hand on Stewart's shoulder. "Why don't we get down to business. I promised I'd have Maureen back to her home by supper."

"Sure, Dale. I'm all business. You know that."

Stewart crouched at the head of the two-by-three-meter unit. Both burials had been nicely pedestaled, meaning the dirt had been cleared away around the bodies, and associated artifacts. Over the female's head a triangular arrow point nested inside a ring of broken pot shards. The male had been wearing a cowl embroidered with olivella and marginella shells, and two gorgets, one copper and one made of exquisitely etched shell.

Maureen sat down cross-legged, and Dale bent over and braced his hands on his knees.

She examined the remains. The artifacts dazzled her. She indicated the shell gorget. "What is that?"

Stewart responded snidely, "We call that a necklace, Doctor. Do you see that intricately etched figure in the middle? That's Bird-Man. He was very big with Mound Builder folks. A little like the Archangel Michael. He flew back and forth between heaven and earth delivering messages to doomed humans."

Maureen felt the corners of her lips tightening, and had to grit her teeth to quell the reaction. "Dale?" she said. "What is that?"

"It's a Mississippian gorget." He pushed his hat back on his head, revealing damp gray hair, and gave Stewart an irritated look. "Mississippians are the people who built the grand mounds in Cahokia, Illinois; Spiro, Oklahoma; Moundville, Alabama; and dozens of other places."

"Ah, yes, I remember," she said. Of course she did, but her ignorance seemed to provoke such interesting comments from Stewart. "I'm sure they were mentioned in the few boring archaeology classes I took."

Stewart's nostrils flared.

"And that?" She pointed to a shiny black arrow point lying inside the pot rim. "It looks like obsidian."

"Congratulations," Stewart said. "You must be a rock hound."

"I—"

"Maureen," Dale interrupted, "that's Yellowstone obsidian. From northern Wyoming."

"Wyoming?" She frowned at the two skeletons. They both rested in flexed positions, on their sides with their knees up, but the female's right arm rested under the male's ribs. Her left arm over his left arm—as if she'd been holding him. It struck an emotional chord in Maureen's soul. The woman must have loved him very much.

She squinted against the sun to look at Dale. "What are Mississippian gorgets and Yellowstone obsidian doing here in New York?"

Stewart leaned toward her, and whispered, "You mean you don't believe that aliens brought them?"

After a moment, she said, "Are you a scientist? Or a radio talk-show host?"

"Neither," he answered bluffly. "I'm an archaeologist."

Maureen's face froze. She nodded stiffly. "Good answer, Stewart."

His mouth smiled, but it didn't reach his eyes.

Maureen leaned over the pit. "Are those cord-wrapped stick markings on the pot shards?"

"Yes, they are, Doctor," Stewart replied.

Many peoples wrapped a cord around a stick, and pressed it into the clay before firing the pot to provide a simple decoration, but these looked distinctly like Princess Point ceramics. While archaeologists loved to argue about dates, the Princess Point culture had thrived between approximately A.D. 500 and A.D. 1000. Geographically, Princess Point sites encompassed an area in south-central Ontario, from Long Point to the Niagara River along the north shore of Lake Erie and around the western end of Lake Ontario, north to the Credit River.

But New York had several sites which contained Princess Point–like ceramics—theoretically copies made by other peoples. This might be one of those.

"So," Dale said, "what do you think about the remains?"

"Rather spectacular," she answered. "I've never seen an individual with such severe achondroplasia survive. Usually they die at birth. Notice the—"

"Is that English?" Stewart asked Dale.

Dale said, "Just try to listen, Dusty. I'll explain later."

Stewart's right brow arched. "For you, Dale."

"Thank you. Please, go on, Maureen."

"Well," she said, pointing, "notice the sharp lordotic angulation in the region of the lumbosacral junction, the shortness of the limbs, and bowing of the lower extremities—"

"Are you trying to say," Stewart asked with exaggerated interest, "that he was a dwarf?"

Maureen nodded. "Yes."

Stewart threw up his arms. "Jesus Christ, Dale, I could have told you that! You had to bring in an outside specialist for that stunning observation?"

Dale's mouth quirked. "What else, Maureen? Can you determine age?"

She studied the skull. At birth, the bones of the cranial vault were thin, and plastic. The sutures, the joints in the skull, remained open, to allow the brain to grow. "Well, all the cranial sutures have ossified, but not only that, look at the epiphyseal cartilage plates. I—"

"The what?" Stewart asked. "Is that in the head?"

Maureen braced her elbows on her knees. Epiphyseal cartilage grew at the ends of leg bones, and arm bones. It thinned as a person aged, until it disappeared. "Well," she answered, "that would certainly explain a lot about your head, or at least make it more interesting than it currently appears." She sighed, and tossed long black hair over her shoulder. "My point, Dale, is that they're not there. I'd guess this little guy was between fifty and fifty-five when he died."

"And the female?" Dale asked.

Maureen shook her head. "She died at around sixty, but it's amazing she lived so long. You can see fractures in the three ribs on her left side, but take a look at that lesion on her skull. Do you see the small area of bone necrosis? It's surrounded by a zone of hypervascularity. That must have happened when she was young. Part of the bone reabsorbed, but—''

''You mean somebody hit her in the head?''

''Oh, good work, Stewart,'' she said, ''you're catching on fast. The interesting thing is that all those injuries healed. She took a lot of punishment, but survived.''

''Warfare? Slavery?'' Dale smoothed his fingers over his gray mustache.

''You're the archaeologists. You tell me. The only thing I can say for sure is that somebody didn't like her very much.''

''Another *stunning* observation,'' Stewart said, with a smile.

Maureen smiled, too. ''Don't you have a student you can annoy? Preferably somebody male. I'm sure the females are tired of pretending they have to pee every time you show up.''

She'd never known a man whose mouth could curl down as quickly as up. He glowered at her.

Maureen looked at the male burial and said, ''Several of the male's phalanges are missing. Did you recover them?''

''The finger bones?'' Stewart said. ''No.''

''Not even one of them?''

''I'll expand the excavation unit and keep looking, all right? Can I have ice cream, now?''

She gave him a stony look, and turned to Dale. ''Given the exotic trade goods, I'd say these two were extraordinary traders. Is that your assessment?''

''Possibly. If so, they traveled over half the continent. But this may just be an example of down-the-line trade. You know, the arrow point and gorget traveled a few miles at a time, being traded from one hand to the next.''

She frowned at the shell gorget. It shimmered in the sunlight. "What's your guess for cultural affiliation?"

Dale opened his mouth, but Stewart responded, "Princess Point."

"Really?" she said. "Why? Other than the pot shards I see no—"

"We've collected and analyzed seven C-14 dates for the site. They all come out to between A.D. 900 and A.D. 1050."

"Yes," Maureen said with practiced reserve. "There are many cultures in this region which date to that time period, why—"

"Call it a hunch," Stewart said.

"A . . . hunch?" She cocked her head. "Is that a scientific term?"

"Yea. It's a scientific term. *My* kind of science," he said hostilely.

Maureen smiled. "Which is a lot like military intelligence, I suppose."

His face went blank. He propped his hands on his hips again. "Just wait," he said with authority, "when all this is finished, your theories are going to be dog meat, sweetheart."

"My people have always been very fond of dog meat. It has to be a puppy, of course, and cooked slowly in the coals, but—"

"I'm telling you," Stewart insisted, "these two are early Iroquoian people. They—"

"I thought you said they were Princess Point?"

"I did."

"Then they're Algonquian." She rose to her feet and crossed her arms. The issue had been debated long and hard in Ontario, and she'd always liked the "migration" hypothesis, which presumed that Iroquoian peoples had moved out of the United States around A.D. 900 and migrated northward, conquering the Algonquian-speaking peoples who'd lived there.

Stewart shook his head. "You need to get out of the laboratory, dear. Hunches come from dirty hands. And hunches are the very heart of good *solid* science."

"Solid science is based on facts, Mr. Stewart, not conjecture. Something you archaeologists have never really learned."

He pointed a finger at her again, but this time he didn't stab it like a dagger. "It *will* turn out that these two people belonged to the early Iroquoian cultural tradition. I *will* show you."

"Oh, please," she said. "*Do* show me."

# The Winter of Crying Rocks.
# Moon of Frozen Leaves.

*Dreams. Strange Dreams...*

*I hear a child's footsteps running through deep sand. The pace is halting, erratic, as if the child turns frequently to look over his shoulder.*

*I see the grains sink beneath his weight as he approaches.*

*Sand blows.*

*But there is no child.*

*There is only blood red sunlight falling through gaps in the clouds.*

*The steps run up to me, and I reach out, desperate to touch him.*

*But my hands find air.*

*Cold. Unbearably red.*

*My wife... my former wife... told me that when a child dies, somewhere in the world, the desert grows. The sand takes another step.*

*From the moment of my young son's death, the sand has been walking in my heart. Relentless. Tramping out every spark of life that dares to flicker.*

*The more I struggle against the sand, the stronger it grows, sucking me down into some unfathomable darkness that lives in my heart.*

*Gods, I miss my son.*

*And my wife.*

*It makes it harder that she is alive, breathing, her heart beating.*

*Even worse . . .*

*I know that somewhere in the terrible smothering darkness lies a well of strength.*

*But to find it I will have to leap into the abyss, and gaze nakedly upon the darkness.*

*What a coward I am.*

*A broken miserable coward.*

*So . . .*

*All day, every day, the desert walks in me.*

*And I walk in the desert.*

# One

Pale Cloud Giants sailed westward, their bellies gilded with the hues of morning. Against the sere blue winter sky, they seemed to be huge animals fleeing the newborn glare cast by Grandfather Day Maker's face.

Silver Sparrow glanced at them, and followed their lead, heading west. The cool air carried the scents of wet earth and frozen bark. He inhaled deeply as he tramped up the frosty trail through the forest.

Huge hickory trees towered above him, their bare limbs stark. Among the branches birds flitted and sang, creating a pleasant serenade. When he reached the top of the hill, he turned to look back at the black tracery of shadows painting the forest. The filigree wavered, rushing toward him when the wind blew, then flying away before he could reach out to touch it. His knees shook badly. He'd seen fifty-three winters, and felt each one this morning. Long white hair swayed around his owlish face as he braced his feet to keep standing. Three days of fasting and praying had weakened his body, but his souls floated in euphoria, like bits of cattail down sailing on a warm autumn breeze.

He started to turn back to the trail, but movement caught his eye. He squinted. Something blue flashed through the trees.

Sparrow stood quietly, waiting.

A man emerged. He wore a pack on his back, beneath

his cape, and it made him look like a hunchback. Their people made a variety of winter garments: capes, heavy coats, short jackets. Each person had their own preferences.

"Oh, no," Sparrow whispered to himself. "Blessed ancestors, not today. Not when I so desperately need to be alone."

Tall Blue climbed the hill. His waist-length black hair gleamed with each step. The blue designs painted around the hem of his buckskin cape flashed as he walked through the streaks of sunlight. Twenty-seven winters old, he had a long straight nose and wide mouth. He also had a reputation for valor. No doubt the reason he'd been chosen for this task.

"I am seeking a vision!" Sparrow shouted at the top of his lungs, startling the birds into silence. "I don't care what's happened, Blue!"

Sparrow turned and forced his rubbery legs to carry him down the trail and across a meadow, hoping to outdistance the young man dogging his steps. Voles and mice leaped through the grass at the sound of his moccasins, scurrying for cover.

Sparrow shook his head in disgust. He hadn't the strength to engage in a lengthy conversation about anything. This had to be Dust Moon's doing. She was forever trying to sabotage his vision quests. The worst part was, as matron of Earth Thunderer Village, she had the right.

"Elder?" Tall Blue called in a deep apologetic voice. "Wait. Please?"

Sparrow pushed his legs harder, crunching over frozen leaves.

"Go home, Blue!"

Tall Blue spread his arms, as if helpless to comply.

Legs wobbling, Sparrow went to a fallen log and

slumped down atop it, yelling, "The Spirits are watching you, Tall Blue. Do you know this? They are watching and saying, 'Look at that young war leader annoying his elders. What shall we do with him?' "

Tall Blue smiled. Sparrow had said similar words to him many times when Tall Blue had been a gangly growing boy.

"I am not here of my own choice, Elder. You must know this."

"Yes, of course. But for the sake of your great-grandmother's ghost, Blue, you also know I need to be alone! Why did you allow Dust Moon to bully you into coming?"

"Patron Buffalo Skull also asked me to speak with you, Elder."

A pinecone rested on the log a short distance away. Sparrow picked it up and threw it at the war leader. Tall Blue dodged the cone, gave Sparrow an indignant look, and continued walking.

He stopped ten paces in front of Sparrow. "Forgive me, Elder. I really do carry important news from our clan leaders."

Sparrow folded his arms. "But mostly from Dust Moon, correct? What happened? Did she discover a boil and wishes me to come and Dance over it?"

Embarrassed by the lightness with which Sparrow took their clan matron's wishes, Tall Blue lowered his gaze and blinked at the ground. "A passing Trader stopped and told us some terrible things."

Sparrow heaved a breath, but didn't answer. It was always something.

Tall Blue shifted his weight from one foot to the other. "I know this is a distraction, Elder, but I must speak with you."

Sparrow's chest tightened. A distraction! Dust Moon

must have told him that. Tall Blue would never think of something so ridiculous by himself. For the Earth Thunderer Clan, nothing was more important than seeking guidance from the Spirit World. Including impending warfare . . . which was surely why Tall Blue had come.

Sparrow closed his eyes, grumbled something unpleasant, then gestured to the log. "Sit down, Blue. What is it?"

Tall Blue sat down beside Sparrow, and his young face turned grim. "It's the Walksalong Clan, Elder."

"Of course it is. What's Jumping Badger done now?"

For five winters, Jumping Badger, the war leader of Walksalong Village, had been terrorizing people for a moon's walk.

"He attacked Sleeping Mist Village. At most that's—"

"Three days' run from here." Sparrow knotted his fists and shook them at nothing. "And Dust Moon is afraid we will be next. Yes?"

"Yes, Elder."

"I don't know what she expects me to do about it, Blue. Curse them and pray they turn on each other instead of us?"

Earth Thunderer Clan was part of the Turtle Nation. Peaceful hunters and gatherers, the Turtle clans moved their small villages often, following the game, or visiting different root grounds or nut groves. Their distant relatives, the Bear Nation, saw this as a weakness. They'd started openly attacking Turtle villages, pushing the people farther and farther away from the animals and plants they needed to survive, taking the land for themselves.

The Turtle clans had to fight back. Soon. And Sparrow had to give them his best advice. He couldn't do that until he'd spoken to his Spirit Helper. This was not a matter for human beings. They had done all they could.

Only the Spirits could resolve this problem.

Tall Blue's moccasins crunched the frozen snow at the base of the log. "Elder?" he said. "You have been in the forest for three nights. Has your Spirit Helper appeared?"

"No."

"No?"

"*No!*"

The truth had been eating at him. Ordinarily his Helper came to him on the second day of questing. This was the beginning of the fourth day, and he hadn't even—

"Matron Dust Moon said he probably hadn't," Tall Blue glibly informed him. "That's why she felt it would be all right to disturb your quest."

Idly, Sparrow wondered what would happen if he marched into Earth Thunderer Village and bashed Dust in the head with a war club.

"So." Tall Blue slapped his palms on his knees. "I have come to ask you to return to the village. Matron Dust Moon said that right after you've given words in council you can return to your quest."

Sparrow just stared.

Dust had never undertaken a vision quest. She did not know the bitter cold that settled in the soul, or the effect that going without food or water for days had on the body. She could not even imagine the wrenching despair that consumed a Dreamer who feared he might fail.

Sparrow wet his chapped lips. They tasted of dried blood and salty tears. "Do you have any notion what Matron Dust Moon would say if you'd just brought her this message after she'd been praying and fasting for days?"

Tall Blue tilted his head. "I—"

"She'd tell you to go throw yourself off a cliff, which is what I ought to do."

"Elder," Tall Blue said in exasperation. "The matron is not as horrible as you suppose."

"Don't tell me that." He narrowed his eyes. "I lived with her for thirty-five winters, Blue. I *know* the twisted paths her thoughts take."

Wind Mother whistled above Sparrow, and a shower of snowflakes fell from the trees, glittering, onto his white hair and cape. He feebly brushed at them. "You may tell my former wife that I will be home as soon as I've finished my quest. Not before."

Tall Blue nodded dejectedly. "I will, of course, do as you say, Elder. I just hope she doesn't come looking for you herself."

Blue shrugged out of his pack and pulled it onto the log between them. As he loosened the laces and began to dig around inside, the sweet scent of roasted corn rose. "Forgive me, Elder. I'll leave as soon as I've eaten. I've been searching for you since early yesterday."

Sparrow's belly groaned at the sweet aroma of corn cakes filled with roasted hickory nuts. It occurred to him that the scent was achingly familiar. He lifted a brow. "Dust Moon made those for you, didn't she?"

"Why, yes, Elder," Tall Blue said around a bite. "How did you know?"

"Because they're my favorites, that's why." Through gritted teeth, Sparrow said, "I swear she's the spawn of witches."

Tall Blue finished his first cake, and started on a second. Crumbs fell down the front of his cape.

Sparrow should have known Dust would do something like this.

Only five nights before she had arrived at his house, and announced that she'd just spoken to a runner who'd told her he'd seen Bear Nation warriors massing—as if preparing for a major attack. Dust had informed Sparrow that, in this time of uncertainty, he ought to strive to be useful: "Go seek a vision. Your people need good advice. Not the sort of pathetic drivel you usually give."

Sparrow slitted one eye and studied Tall Blue. "She's trying to shove me into madness, Blue. First she orders me to seek a vision, then she sends you to interrupt my efforts. What's next? Water hemlock in my food?"

"I am sorry, Elder," Tall Blue said as he chewed his corn cake. "I knew you would not be happy to see me. I have so often heard you speak of the difficulties of the quest: the hunger, the thirst and loneliness. Are you lonely?"

Sparrow lifted a shoulder noncommittally. He was, of course. Desperately.

Tall Blue finished his cake, let out a satisfied sigh, and pulled the laces closed on his pack. "I'm leaving now, Elder. Are you certain you will not come with me?"

Sparrow stuffed his fists into the pockets of his beautifully painted elkhide coat. Its red spirals and dark green trees gleamed in the branch-filtered sunlight. "If I give in to the temptation, my Helper will be angry. He may never appear to me again."

Tall Blue slipped the pack straps over his shoulders and shrugged it into position. "Perhaps that's why he hasn't come to speak with you yet. He's already angry with you."

"Really? What would make you think so?"

"Well, I—I don't know, of course," Tall Blue stammered, "but Matron Dust Moon said—"

"Blessed Spirits! If you wish to know something about me, ask *me*!"

Tall Blue wiped the crumbs from his hands, and watched them drop onto the forest floor. "I should have, Elder. You are right."

Sparrow shifted to look at Blue. "What did she say?"

Tall Blue gazed at him askance. "Well, Elder, you . . . you do realize that you've wakened the village many times over the past moon, do you not?"

"Yes."

"Your cries have frightened people, Elder. You always sound as if you are in great torment. Matron Dust Moon said your wicked Spirit Helper was probably torturing you again."

Sparrow squeezed his eyes closed. He often jerked awake at night, drenched in sweat, moaning, and in excruciating pain. He wakened feeling physically exhausted, as if warriors had been beating him with clubs all night. He knew what it meant. It was his Helper's way of issuing a call. One that Sparrow could not refuse.

Sparrow opened his eyes and squinted at the bare branches over his head. "Not the spawn of witches," he said. "The spawn of bird droppings, of snake semen, of—"

"Elder." Tall Blue studied the tight line of Sparrow's mouth. "Please return with me. If you wish to begin your quest again after the council meeting, you are free to do so."

In the sudden silence, the chirping of the birds seemed louder, the wind through the bare branches more shrill. The forest smelled rich and pungent this morning.

"Very well." Tall Blue sighed. "Perhaps you might give me a possible time when your quest will end?"

"I am too terrified to guess."

"You? Terrified? You are a great holy man. What could frighten you?"

"Well—" Sparrow made an airy gesture. "To begin with, Blue, I'm afraid that I'll finish my vision quest without seeing a Spirit Helper, and it will prove Matron Dust Moon's theory that I'm just demented, not a Dreamer. I'm also worried that we might have to go to war soon. And, if you really want to know, I'm very frightened by this pain in my chest." Sparrow touched the spot between his breasts.

Tall Blue said, "Your heart?"

"I don't know."

Blue sat down on the log again, and examined Sparrow more closely. "Does it hurt all the time?"

"No."

"Does it hurt now?"

Sparrow shook his head.

Tall Blue murmured, "Have you been witched? Should we call a shaman?"

Sparrow smiled, and his chapped lips broke open. Blood trickled warmly down his chin. "No," he said as he wiped it away. "I actually think it's a good thing, that the pain comes from my Spirit Helper."

Tall Blue seemed to relax a little. "I've heard that elders often suffer curious pains. My great-grandfather used to wince every time he—"

"I doubt that it's the same thing, Blue. Did his pain have golden eyes?"

Tall Blue closed his mouth. He didn't answer for a time. "I don't think so."

"My pain has eyes. They sparkle at me in my dreams."

"How long have you been seeing these eyes?"

"About seven moons."

A swallow went down Blue's throat. He seemed to be nerving himself to ask his next question. "Elder, perhaps we should send a runner for Rumbler. I'm certain the False Face Child could tell you if this 'thing' is good or bad."

Rumbler, the dwarf boy who lived two nights to the north in Paint Rock Village, had great Power. He terrified most people, including Sparrow, and Sparrow loved the little boy with all his heart and souls.

"I'm sure Rumbler has more important things to do than worry about an old man's pains." To emphasize his point, Sparrow groaned as he stretched his aching back muscles. "Go home now, Blue. I'm having a difficult vision quest. I need to concentrate."

Tall Blue rose to his feet. "Very well, Elder."

But the young war leader stood with his brows lowered, peering worriedly at Sparrow.

Sparrow pointed. "Just follow your own footprints in the snow, Blue."

Blue gave him an irritated look, as though that were not news to him. "I pray your Spirit Helper arrives soon, Elder."

"So do I."

Tall Blue nodded, and walked away. Sparrow watched him wade through the frosty meadow grass, toward the trail back to Earth Thunderer Village.

Sparrow braced his shaking arms on his knees. The past three days had taken a greater toll on his strength than he'd thought. He inhaled several deep breaths and let them out slowly while he scanned the forest. The slant of sunlight had changed. Its flaxen veils fell through the trees, glittering and twinkling. Where they struck the ground, it steamed.

Sparrow forced his legs to hold him as he rose, and headed toward the crest of the hill.

Pines flanked the way, their fragrance heavy on the breeze. The trail curved around a boulder, then wove through a tangle of deadfall and onto a flat stone ledge. Sparrow made it to the ledge and bent over to catch his breath. Lungs heaving, he barely heard the change in the timbre of Wind Mother's voice. It had gone from a faint whimper to a deep-throated growl. When the distant cry of a wolf carried to him, Sparrow turned, his long white hair whipping around his wrinkled face. High-pitched and haunting, the mournful call tingled his spine.

Deadfall cracked behind Sparrow.

He turned, expecting to see Tall Blue again, but only flailing tree limbs met his gaze. Frigid wind flapped his collar around his throat.

He heard it again, to his left, twigs snapping beneath heavy feet, closer this time.

*Blessed gods, I didn't lure a cougar, did I? Or a disgruntled moose?* He slowly turned around. The brown leaves that clung to the hardwoods fluttered, creating a gorgeous interplay of light and shadow. *Maybe it's just a deer, or . . .*

A new sound reached his ears, low, rhythmic, like the panting of an animal, rushing toward him.

The hair on Sparrow's neck prickled. He backed away.

The breathing seemed to come from everywhere at once, as though it lived in Wind Mother's heart.

His gaze darted from one shadow to the next. "There's nothing there!" he roughly told himself. "Nothing. Look around! You're just—"

Branches exploded over his head. Sparrow hit the ground on his belly, crawling for cover. When he'd made it into a shelter of tangled limbs, he looked up.

Near the pointed top of the pine, a squirrel sat, working its jaws. Bits of debris floated down. Sparrow struggled to see what the little animal was eating, then a pinecone fell, producing a breathy sound as it tumbled through the air, and cracks when it struck lower limbs.

The forest had gone quiet, the sunlight almost too brilliant to bear. Sparrow wanted to laugh. He rolled to his back, and took a few moments to satisfy his starving lungs. "Blessed gods," he cried, "I can be such a fool."

From the air around him, an eerie childish voice whispered, *"Yes, you can."*

Sparrow's blood turned to ice.

# Two

Lamedeer's silver-streaked black hair fell around his square-jawed face as he leaned forward to warm his hands before the fire. The patriarch of Paint Rock Village sat on a log across from him, his wrinkled face dour. The old man hadn't said a word in over a finger of time. Lamedeer longed to rise and go about his duties as war leader, but the clan patron had called him here, and he had to stay until dismissed. Red Pipe's gaunt face looked shriveled. The few gray hairs left on his freckled scalp clustered around his ears. He wore a beautifully tanned buffalo cape, the fur turned inward where it rested warmly against his skin. Starbursts of blue and yellow porcupine quills encircled his collar.

"So," Red Pipe finally murmured. "What do we do? Wait and see? Or burden our sister villages by asking for their help?"

"These rumors have been flying for half a moon, Patron. Yet we are still safe, our village prosperous."

Red Pipe's wrinkled lips sank inward over his toothless gums. He nodded, and went silent again, thinking.

Eight small bark-covered lodges nestled at the edge of

the trees to Lamedeer's left. Curls of blue smoke rose from the rounded roofs, twined through the dark oak branches and drifted into the late afternoon sky. Lamedeer could not see Grandfather Day Maker, but knew he must be sitting on the western horizon. The heavens had a bronze sheen. Most of the villagers had retreated inside their lodges to cook supper, leaving Lamedeer and Red Pipe alone in the plaza.

"You are not frightened?" Red Pipe asked.

Lamedeer fiddled with a twig that had dropped by the side of the firepit, twirling it in his fingers. His twenty-eight winters had given him a face as wrinkled and rough as an eroded cliff's. He could feel those lines deepening. "No."

"Why is that, War Leader? I would expect you to be the most cautious of all."

"Ordinarily, yes. But Cornhusk is a liar. He exaggerates to add drama to his stories."

"And to make himself appear more knowledgeable than he is. I know this." Red Pipe stared for a long moment into the wavering flames. His eyes had an odd opaque sheen. "What I do not know, is how we can ignore his warning. Will you be able to sleep at night if we do not call out for help to our sister villages?"

Lamedeer tossed the twig into the fire. "Patron, do you recall the Deep Water Village battle ten winters ago? It happened because of lies spread by a Trader. I'm sure the man thought he was just enlivening conversation, but his words resulted in fifty deaths. Villagers are suspicious of each other these days. It doesn't take much to build a fire in our hearts. A Trader has only to mention that a Bear Nation village hates us, or that their warriors are making new weapons, and that they were seen in the forest nearby. We send out search parties looking for battle, and in an instant of uncertainty, somebody shoots an arrow.'' Lamedeer spread his hands. ''Then we are lost.''

''Yes,'' Red Pipe agreed. ''All of these things are true.''

''I do not trust Traders, Patron. It is just my way, but I tend to think they are all spies.''

Firelight flickered over the old man's scalp as he leaned forward. ''But you did not answer my question, War Leader. Less than five hands of time ago, Cornhusk reported that he'd seen Jumping Badger in the forest with at least eighty warriors. He said the war party seemed to be moving our way. Will you be able to sleep at night if we do not ask for help from our sister villages?''

''If we *do* ask them to send warriors, and there is no attack, will they send them next time, when we really need help? When we have reliable information and know for certain that we are in danger?''

Red Pipe hesitated. ''I do not know.''

''Would you, Patron? If you had sent warriors to Earth Thunderer Village, leaving your own village vulnerable for nights, and your warriors returned saying nothing had happened, what would you do the next time Earth Thunderer Village requested your help?''

Red Pipe ran his tongue over his sunken lips. ''It would depend, but most likely, I would decline.''

''That is why we should wait, Patron. Until we know more.''

''Perhaps you are right. I suspect Cornhusk spread these same rumors to the other Turtle Nation villages, and none of them have asked us for our help. At least not yet. I . . .''

He paused when Briar-of-the-Lake, the village holy woman, came down the trail from the forest with a load of wood in her arms. She wore a white doeskin cape, and her long hair looked startlingly black against that background. Tiny, frailly built, she had a green tree tattooed

on her forehead. He and she had been raised for a few
winters in the same lodge. His mother and her father had
both died when they were very young. After the death
of Lamedeer's mother, his father had remarried, taking
Briar's mother, Evening Star, as his wife.

Lamedeer could see Briar's lips moving, but couldn't
hear her words. Her son, Rumbler, walked in a swinging
gait at her side. On his heels, his black dog, Stonecoat,
trotted with his tongue out. Rumbler's round face had an
unearthly sheen, like moonlight off water. Though he'd
seen nine winters, he stood only the height of a boy in
his fourth winter. Thick black hair hung to his chin. Their
people called him the False Face Child because after his
birth they had been terrified he might be a Forest Spirit,
like his father. The Disowned, as the boy's father was
known, often disguised himself in human form. They'd
actually cast Rumbler and his mother out of the clan for
a short time.

"Yes," Red Pipe said, his gaze on the boy. "Jumping
Badger would have to be very foolish to attack us."

Lamedeer studied Rumbler. The dwarf child had made
Paint Rock the most feared village in the Turtle Nation.
A person had only to look into the boy's eyes to understand why. Power lived and breathed in those bottomless
black wells.

Lamedeer said, "Jumping Badger must know that the
False Face Child would foresee his coming, and warn
us."

"If I were Jumping Badger, I would be terrified that
the False Face Child would call out to his father, and the
whole forest would rally against me and annihilate my
war party."

From the time Rumbler had been readmitted to the clan
at the age of two winters, the elders had pampered and
coddled him, treating him like an adult. They asked for

Rumbler's opinion before making any major clan decisions, and spent a great deal of time teaching the boy about plants and animals, telling him the old stories over and over, and showing him how to draw Power from the earth and sky. The Turtle Nation had many stories about great dwarfs and their miraculous deeds. Most of those dwarfs had risked their lives to save their people. Rumbler knew that the Paint Rock elders expected no less of him.

"Besides," Lamedeer added, "Cornhusk made no sense. If Jumping Badger were planning to attack us, why bring eighty warriors? He could overwhelm us with fifty. Our village is small. We have forty-two warriors when everyone is healthy, and no one is away hunting, or fishing. Why would Jumping Badger pull eighty warriors away from Walksalong Village for us?"

Red Pipe seemed to be pondering this. After several moments, he said, "It does seem unlikely. Taking so many warriors would leave his village, Walksalong village, almost defenseless."

"Yes, Patron."

Red Pipe reached down, took a piece of wood from the woodpile to his left, and placed it on the fire. Sparks crackled and spat. Golden glitters lifted into the sky. "I have spoken many times with old Starflower, one of the Walksalong matrons. She is too smart to do this."

Lamedeer folded his arms around his knees, relieved that he would not have to send runners to nearby villages begging for help. Such begging embarrassed him, but more than that, he did not wish to use up favors before they truly needed them. Certainly not on the words of a notorious Trader like Cornhusk.

"Good day to you," Briar said with a smile. Her youth and beauty always touched Lamedeer's heart. Her long black hair shimmered in the wavering light of the flames.

"Good day, my sister," Lamedeer said. "I see you have been out gathering wood. I hope you collected some for my fire, too. I have been engaged all day long with these silly rumors—"

Red Pipe interrupted, asking Rumbler, "How are you, my child?"

Rumbler's black eyes seemed to expand. He stepped forward like a cat after prey, his moccasins silent. "What is it you wish to ask me, Patron?"

Red Pipe hesitated, then said, "We have heard some frightening news this day. We were wondering if you have Dreamed anything. Perhaps about an attack?"

Rumbler did not seem to breathe. After several moments, his head turned and his gaze fixed on his mother's lodge. His dog, Stonecoat, dropped to his belly at Rumbler's feet, whining softly.

Rumbler whispered, *"Look."*

Red Pipe's faded old eyes narrowed. He followed the boy's gaze.

Briar dumped her load of wood, and brushed at the duff coating the front of her white cape. "What is it, Rumbler? What do you—"

*"Who is he?"*

Stonecoat barked.

Lamedeer, pulse pounding, rose to his feet and rested his hand on the deerbone stiletto tied to his belt. "Who?"

"That boy," Rumbler said, almost too low to hear. "That little boy."

Lamedeer stepped away from the fire, and circled around behind Red Pipe, guarding the old man's back. "I see no one." He looked questioningly at Red Pipe.

The patron shook his head. "Nor do I."

Briar frowned and touched her son's hair. "Rumbler, where is the boy?"

Rumbler just stared at nothing.

Red Pipe's wrinkled lips worked. "Where does the boy come from, Rumbler? Is he one of the blessed ancestors? Or a Forest Spirit?"

Rumbler slowly lifted a foot and put it down a step closer to his mother's lodge. "He says you mustn't send runners, Patron. There will be no attack."

Relief and fear mixed in Lamedeer's chest. He and Red Pipe turned in unison to peer at each other. Briar studied their expressions.

"Who did you think would be attacking us?" Briar asked.

Lamedeer started to answer, but Rumbler let out a small dreadful, *"No!"*

Stonecoat yipped and jumped up to put his paws on Rumbler's chest, peering intently into the dwarf boy's wide eyes.

Rumbler did not even seem to see the dog. He stood like a carved wooden statue, his short arms and legs rigid, as if bracing for a hurricane. He whispered, "Why?," and seemed to be listening to someone they could not hear.

Lamedeer gazed at the empty space between two lodges. Not even a breath of wind stirred the dead winter grasses.

"Rumbler?" Briar knelt beside her son. "What's happening? Tell me."

"Oh, Mother!" he wept. "They're coming for us. It's us they want!"

"Who? Who wants us?" she asked in panic.

Lamedeer's guts suddenly went runny. The boy had inhuman eyes, blacker than black, and old, as if the souls that inhabited that small malformed body had lived for more centuries than Lamedeer could conceive. He clenched his fists to nerve himself, and said, "Who's coming for us, Rumbler? Jumping Badger?"

Rumbler's tears ran in silent streams down his round face. "No. No, it's Grandfather Day Maker's children. *They're hunting us.*"

"What? Grandfather Day Maker's children?" Lamedeer gazed at the western horizon. The drifting clouds had turned pink. "Why would the sun . . ."

Rumbler ran away, across the plaza, and ducked beneath the leather door curtain of his mother's lodge. Stonecoat dutifully trotted after him.

Red Pipe gripped Briar by the arm, and said, "Find out what he meant, cousin. We *must* know."

"Yes, I—I will." Briar left Lamedeer and Red Pipe alone in the cold windy plaza.

The wrinkles around Red Pipe's eyes deepened. "What do you make of that?"

Lamedeer shook his head. "I cannot say. The boy often sees and hears things we do not. It may have been a message only for him, or Briar, and have nothing to do with us."

The leather curtain of Briar's lodge swung as she ducked inside, revealing glimpses of her and her son, the colored baskets on the walls, a pot lit by the glowing embers in the firepit. Rumbler had his back to the door. A strange sound, like the keening of distant wolves, rode the wind.

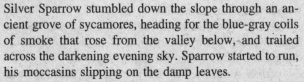

Silver Sparrow stumbled down the slope through an ancient grove of sycamores, heading for the blue-gray coils of smoke that rose from the valley below, and trailed across the darkening evening sky. Sparrow started to run, his moccasins slipping on the damp leaves.

Within a hand of time, he saw the gigantic oaks that

overhung Paint Rock Village. As he ran the well-worn trail toward the plaza, the fragrance of roasting beaver filled the air. He could almost taste the sweet, fatty meat. His starved belly whined. He had not eaten in five nights.

"Blessed Ancestors, give me the strength to keep going. Just a little farther."

The trail seemed to go on forever, winding around rocks and fallen timbers. Owl eyes blinked at him from the treetops, and he heard a faint *hoo—hooo*.

Panic warmed Sparrow's veins. They might be owl calls. Probably, they were. But they could also be warriors signaling each other in the darkness.

He had been a warrior once, many winters ago. He knew the tricks men used to stay in contact while sneaking up on their victims.

As night deepened, more and more Cloud Giants gathered overhead, blotting out the white feathered lodges of the ancestors in the Up-Above-World. Sparrow had the feeling they had come just to watch him, to see if he had the courage to race into a doomed village, a village where they disdained him and his Dreams, and tell the people what he'd seen.

He almost tripped over the guard. The burly man sat on the low hill overlooking the village, his back propped against the thick trunk of an oak. When he saw Sparrow, he let out a cry, and leaped to his feet with his bow drawn.

"Wait! Don't shoot! I am Silver Sparrow of Earth Thunderer Village. I have run for two nights to speak with War Leader Lamedeer."

The man lowered the bow slightly and squinted at Sparrow, as if trying to discern his features in the dwindling light. "Come forward. Show yourself."

Sparrow walked toward the man. He appeared to have seen around thirty-five winters. A braided leather headband held his shoulder-length black hair held in place, and he stood a head shorter than Sparrow.

"I am Calling Hawk," the man said, introducing himself. "What business does the famed madman of Earth Thunderer Village have with War Leader Lamedeer?"

"My words are for Lamedeer. I must see him. Now."

Calling Hawk released the tension on the bowstring, but he did not remove his arrow. "You should have sent a runner ahead, to let Lamedeer know you would be coming."

"Why?" he asked, his voice shaking. "Don't tell me he's gone. He can't be gone! I must—"

"I did not say that. He's here. But he hates to be disturbed when he's asleep. Not only that, I have orders never to let you set foot in this village. Red Pipe hasn't forgotten the time you told him he was going to contract a terrible disease. He wandered through blizzards for three weeks in fear that he might give the disease to the rest of the village. The whole time he was gone, he never even had a sniffle."

Sparrow had been a new Dreamer at the time, and not yet adept at interpreting the curious images that plagued him. He said, "Lamedeer is asleep? It's barely past sunset."

"The war leader will be taking my place at midnight, as he did last night. He needs his rest." Calling Hawk slung his bow and slipped his arrow back into the quiver over his shoulder. "Tell me what news you bring, and I will decide if it is important enough to wake him."

Sparrow contemplated asking to see one of the village elders, but figured Calling Hawk would view that request with even more suspicion. He said, "Tell Lamedeer that I Dreamed his death. Paint Rock Village is going to be attacked. I saw it—"

Calling Hawk laughed, actually threw back his head

and roared. The sound echoed through the stillness.

Sparrow mustered the courage to say, "That amuses you?"

"No." Calling Hawk shook his head, chuckling. "No, it's just that the False Face Child recently told us we were not going to be attacked. He said that Paint Rock Village is as safe as a child in its mother's womb. But do not fear." He held up a hand. "I will deliver your message. Lamedeer will want to hear it. A little merriment is better than sleep, eh? But you stay here." He added, "Understand?"

"Of course."

Calling Hawk marched across the village, and Sparrow sank down in the spot the short warrior had vacated at the base of the tree.

"Oh, gods," he whispered to himself. "Rumbler Dreamed Paint Rock was safe . . ." He leaned back and vented a deep exhausted breath. "I'm not wrong again, am I?"

"Lamedeer?"

Lamedeer roused at the sound of Calling Hawk's voice. He rolled to his side and braced himself on one elbow. The embers in his fire pit threw a bloody light over his lodge, gleaming in the empty eye sockets of the skulls that hung from his roof. Trophies taken in war, he'd polished them until they shone like slate mirrors. He called, "Enter."

Calling Hawk ducked his head beneath the door curtain. "Forgive me for waking you, but I thought you'd want to hear this."

Lamedeer yawned. "It had better be important. What is it?"

"Old Silver Sparrow just ran into the village. I swear he looks like an outcast. His clothes are filthy, his white hair is all tangled and filled with leaves. He—"

"What does he want?"

"He said to tell you that Paint Rock Village is about to be attacked and you're going to die." Calling Hawk chuckled.

Lamedeer smiled. "Did you ask him if he got this news from Cornhusk?"

"He said he'd Dreamed it, and run for two nights to tell you."

Lamedeer shook his head. Silver Sparrow's reputation for spouting nonsense ranged far and wide. "Tell the old man that the False Face Child says our village is safe. We—"

"I did tell him. He looked a little ill at the news."

Lamedeer shoved his hides down around his waist, and sat up. "But he wanted you to tell me his Dream anyway?"

"Yes."

"What do you make of it? Did he tell you anything that would make you believe the False Face Child might have been mistaken?"

Calling Hawk shifted. "No. I mean, I'm sure he's just an old fool. Everyone says so. But I must admit I've been wondering about the False Face Child's vision. Did he ever explain the Spirit Boy's words about Grandfather Day Maker's children hunting us?"

Lamedeer heaved a breath. His thoughts didn't seem to want to congeal. "Rumbler told his mother that the message was for his ears alone. That we did not need to concern ourselves with it."

Calling Hawk considered that for a while, then the

smile returned to his face. "I knew it was nothing. Shall I drive Silver Sparrow away?"

"Yes. Perhaps you should also suggest that he go home and see if Earth Thunderer Village is still there, eh?"

Calling Hawk laughed. Sparrow's former wife, Dust Moon, the matron of the Earth Thunderer Village, took every opportunity to evade the madman, moving her village anytime he was away. Rumor had it that once she'd even managed it while Sparrow slept.

Lamedeer lay back down and pillowed his head on his arm. "Be quick about it, Calling Hawk. We do not want Red Pipe to discover Silver Sparrow has been here, or we will all face the consequences. Every time Red Pipe hears that Sparrow is nearby, he sleeps with his bow, and hatchet."

"I'm going," Calling Hawk said and let the curtain drop.

Lamedeer lay back down, and listened to Calling Hawk's steps growing fainter. He closed his eyes. . . .

Four hands of time later, Lamedeer woke.

Utter darkness filled the lodge. He gazed up at the smoke hole in the roof, but couldn't see any of the Night Walker's feathered lodges. Cloud Giants must have swallowed them.

Lamedeer pulled on his heaviest cape and moccasins, and reached for his bow and quiver.

When he ducked outside, the night air stung his lungs. As his eyes adjusted, he could make out the small rounded shapes of the lodges. Paint Rock Village lay quiet and peaceful. A few sparks escaped through smoke holes and winked in the cold breeze. Lamedeer shivered as he walked across the frozen plaza.

Wind Mother whimpered through the towering oaks, and tousled his graying black hair around his face. Cold leeching from the ground ate into his moccasins. Though snow had not yet started to fall, he could smell it in the air.

He quietly passed Briar's lodge, and continued up the trail.

He'd slept fitfully, spending much of his time with old ghosts. The dead had come to twine their icy bodies around his like mating snakes. Lamedeer had never had the gift of Dream guessing, though many among his clan did. A person could recite his worst, most complicated nightmare to Red Pipe, for instance, and in less than thirty heartbeats he would have deciphered the meaning, and told the person what he had to do to appease the Spirits.

*Tomorrow. I'll go to Red Pipe. Perhaps he can help me understand the images.*

Before he reached the trunk of the old oak, he could see that Calling Hawk was not there. Yet every warrior in the village knew it meant death to leave his post without authorization.

Angry, Lamedeer started up the trail, his moccasins crunching the frozen leaves. He halted when he noticed a strange shadow clinging to a sycamore trunk. Against the white bark, the shadow looked vaguely human. Lamedeer stepped closer. A man stood there, his head bowed as if in shame.

"Calling Hawk?" Lamedeer said. "What are you doing out here? I should carve you alive!"

The man said nothing, and Lamedeer lifted his bow, nocked an arrow, and eased forward until, in the dim light spilling through the clouds, he could see the arrow that pinioned Calling Hawk's body to the tree. A stone ax had been used to split his skull. Blood had soaked his cape and pants. The coppery tang clawed at the back of Lamedeer's throat.

Lamedeer stumbled backward.

Warriors oozed from the trees like ghosts. In shock, Lamedeer watched. *No. This can't be happening. The False Face Child said we were safe. He told us not to send runners. He—*

He shouted, "Awaken! Everyone! Get up. Hurry! We must—"

War cries split the night, and dogs scrambled from lodges, barking, racing out to meet the intruders. Red Pipe staggered from his lodge, his wrinkled mouth agape as he ran. A woman warrior shot him in the back, knocking the old man facedown in the dirt. Everywhere, people flooded from their lodges and raced across the plaza. Mothers clutched infants to their breasts. Men threw themselves at the intruders. Old people and children scurried for cover.

Deafening cries rose. They climbed Lamedeer's spine like a lightning bolt. He charged into the chaos, shooting his bow wildly.

People shrieked and fell all around Lamedeer. He saw two men duck out of Briar's lodge. One carried Rumbler in his arms. Briar's shrieks of *"No! No, please!"* pierced the din. There had to be a hundred warriors! They couldn't fight this many! A tiny dagger of flame flared in his heart and built to an insane blaze.

Lamedeer screamed hoarsely, "Follow me! Don't try to fight! Follow me before we are all killed!"

Elk Ivory lowered her bow. A half a hand of time had passed since they'd first entered the plaza. In the glare of the burning lodges, she could see there would be no more fighting this night. Bodies scattered the ground, mouths gaping in silent cries. A tall, muscular woman with shoulder-length black hair, she had seen thirty-eight winters . . . but she had never witnessed anything like this. What the men did to the dead sickened her. She straightened to her full height, and sucked a breath in through her broad flat nose. Smoke and the odor of burning flesh filled the firelit darkness.

Jumping Badger stalked up the trail toward her, his beaver-hide coat covered with blood, his long black braid tangled and matted with gore. He'd slung his bow and quiver over his right shoulder. At the age of twenty-four winters, he was one of the youngest war leaders in the history of the Walksalong Clan. A handsome man, he had finely chiseled features and dark eerie eyes.

As he passed by her, Elk Ivory gripped his arm, and stared at him. "You ordered the men to rape the dead? To cut unborn children from their mothers' wombs? *Why?*"

He leaned closer to her, hissing in her face, "Because I wished it."

He shook off her hand. In the lurid gleam, his eyes shone. "Stay here. Watch over the men until they have finished carrying out my orders, then bring them."

She clutched her bow hard, knowing she could not refuse. "Bring them where, War Leader?"

"We will make camp up this trail—"

"To the north? But our war canoes are to the east, on the shore of Leafing Lake."

"We are not going home. Tomorrow, at dawn, we will start tracking down the survivors. I want Lamedeer."

"We have no orders to track down survivors!" Elk

Ivory objected. ''The matrons told you to—''

''Do not argue with me, old woman!'' he shouted, and his voice rang above the roaring fires. The dreadful laughter of the men ceased. Heads lifted across the plaza. Jumping Badger pointed at Elk Ivory with his fist. *''Just obey my orders. Or you will suffer the consequences.''* He opened his fist to the bloody plaza, and a small cruel smile curled his lips.

He turned and walked away up the trail. Firelit shadows fluttered around him.

Elk Ivory glared at his back until he vanished over the crest of the hill, then she let out the breath she'd been holding, and fought to quell her anger.

Gods, she wished Blue Raven were here. He could stop this. He *would* stop this.

She bowed her head and shook it.

If only he had remained a warrior.

But he hadn't. He had become the village Headman. She still found that fact strange. As a boy, he'd longed to be a great warrior, to marry and have many children . . . as she had.

He'd done none of those things—though he'd been a good warrior for a few winters.

Her thoughts drifted to the warm days of her youth, to lazy afternoons of love on the soft newborn grass near Walksalong Village. The thrill of his eyes upon her had been intoxicating. Blessed Spirits, she had loved Blue Raven with all her strength.

A raucous laugh went up from the plaza.

Elk Ivory's eyes narrowed as she watched a man fling a dead baby into the darkness.

She folded her arms tightly across her breasts, and braced her feet. Her thoughts turned bitter as hate filled her up inside. Hatred for Jumping Badger.

Soon, she would not be able to obey him, despite his position as war leader.

When that moment came, she would have to kill him.

Mossybill threw out his blankets beneath the same blackened, lightning-riven hickory where Skullcap sat, his eyes fixed on the False Face Child. Skullcap had unbraided his hair and the waves framed his narrow face, accentuating the size of his bulbous nose. The young warrior looked stunned, as if he'd been struck in the head with a tree limb.

Mossybill massaged his aching kidney, then stretched out on his blankets. Just after they'd run out of Paint Rock Village, a snarling, barking dog had leaped for Mossybill's throat. He'd turned quickly, but the dog had crashed into his back, and knocked him flat. Fortunately he'd been able to draw his knife, and kill it before it really hurt anyone, but he'd been peeing blood all day.

Irritably, Mossybill said, "Skullcap, what are you looking at? He's just a boy. Nothing more. If he were as powerful as his people claimed, would we have been able to capture him? Eh? Think of that." Mossybill laughed.

Skullcap didn't even blink. Deep wrinkles etched his young forehead, and his dark eyes took on a frightening look.

Mossybill dug around in his pack for a length of venison jerky.

They could not risk lighting a fire in case survivors of the Paint Rock slaughter had followed them, and the jerky made him long all the more to be home in Walksalong Village with his family. As she did after every raid, his wife, Loon, would cook him a feast, and drape their best hides around his triumphant shoulders. His proud children would crowd around him, asking him a hundred questions about the battle.

He bit into the jerky, and chewed hard to work some juice into the dried meat. "Skullcap?" he repeated in irritation. "What's wrong with you? You've been staring at that boy for—"

Skullcap's eyes widened. *"Don't you see it?"*

Mossybill lowered his jerky. "What? I don't see anything."

The False Face Child lay curled on his side five paces away, his feet drawn up behind his back, his hands tied to them. By morning he'd be in agonizing pain, but it couldn't be helped. Jumping Badger had given strict orders that they were to take no chances that the boy might escape. The child had not made a single sound in two days.

Skullcap swallowed hard. "There's . . . something . . . in his eyes. It's alive. I swear it, Mossybill. Look! Sometimes it flashes!"

"Flashes?"

"Yes! Look!"

Mossybill made a disgusted sound, and ripped off another bite of jerky. From Mossybill's angle, the boy's face was in complete shadow. He couldn't see his eyes at all. "You've lost your wits. Try to get some sleep. You need it."

Skullcap eased down into his blankets, but his gaze remained on the False Face Child.

As though the boy knew it, he lifted his head. A smile turned his boyish lips. "I'm going to kill you," he said. *"Soon."*

Skullcap jerked his blankets over his head and curled into a tight ball on the ground.

Mossybill sharply ordered, "Don't try to frighten us,

boy! We are two of the greatest warriors of the Walks-along Clan. If we wish, we can carve out your liver and eat it for breakfast!''

Soft childish laughter echoed through the stillness.

Skullcap whimpered, and the sound enraged Mossy-bill.

He rose, tramped over to the boy, and viciously jerked on the child's ropes until they cut into his wrists and legs. The boy didn't utter a sound, but Mossybill saw him squeeze his eyes closed in pain. Mossybill grinned as he twisted and secured the ropes in their new position.

''There,'' he whispered in the boy's ear, ''learn the price of offending the Walksalong Clan. By morning, you won't be able to use your arms or legs.''

Mossybill strode back toward the charred hickory. He started to roll up in his blankets, but a strange sound made him go still. A deep-throated sound, like an animal's growl, a wolf about to attack . . .

*''You will die first, big man,''* the inhuman voice said. *''Writhing in agony.''*

Mossybill lunged to his feet, breathing hard, and looked around.

''Who said that?'' he shouted into the darkness. His gaze searched the forest and cloudy sky, then landed on the dwarf child. ''Boy? Boy, can you change your voice like that?''

A bare whisper of wind rustled the trees. Branches sawed back and forth.

''Skullcap? Did you hear that voice?''

Skullcap's blankets shook violently in response.

Mossybill backed to his blankets and sat down, then drew his quiver close. As he braced his bow on his drawn-up knees, the False Face Child lifted his head. Teeth glinted in the darkness.

Mossybill's fingernails dug into the polished wood of

his bow. "Lie down, boy, before I come over there and knock you down."

The boy gave Mossybill a smile that chilled him to the bones.

"When we get to Walksalong Village," Mossybill said, "we'll beat that arrogance out of you, boy."

But as he rolled up in his blankets, Mossybill pulled his bow very close.

# Three

Lamedeer drew back his bowstring and aimed out the cave entrance. Dawn Woman moved in the narrow valley below, the pale blue hem of her skirt trailing through the forest as she walked. His release came smooth and silent. The arrow sailed out.

Throughout the tangle of trees, shadows leaped as men dove for cover.

"Blessed Falling Woman," he whispered, and sank back against the stone wall. He lifted a shaking hand to wipe long silver-streaked black hair away from his brown eyes. Sweat pooled in his deepest wrinkles, and trickled coldly down his square jaw.

From the cave's darkness, a timid voice asked, "Are the Walksalongs still there?"

It sounded like one of the younger warriors, and Lamedeer couldn't find it in him to answer. When he'd led his people into the ambush last night, they'd split into three groups, trying to fight their way out. His group of fifteen had been forced back against the cliff on the north side of this valley. Most of the women and children had died as they'd scrambled up the rocky slope trying to reach the shelter of this small cave.

"Lamedeer?" the boy called again.

"Try to rest," he forced himself to say. "You will need it."

He squinted into the cave's dim recesses. During the night people had shifted, hunting for comfortable sleeping positions. Lamedeer no longer knew who lay or sat where. Or, for that matter, which of his relatives lived, and which had died. One wounded man had been panting for over a hand of time, panting as if he couldn't get enough air.

"Lamedeer? Are there very many? Can you tell?"

He hesitated, and people stirred. A cloud of dust filled the cave.

"Lamedeer, please!" the youth begged. "Tell us. What's to see out there? Are we to fight, or—"

"You will fight," Lamedeer answered, and gazed into the darkness to his left. He thought the speaker was young Crowfire. Barely sixteen winters old, the youth was probably too frightened to rise and look for himself into the faces of death that filled the forest below. "But not for a time yet. Drink the last water in your gut bag— if you have any—and rest."

Three of Lamedeer's seasoned warriors came forward, among them his oldest friend, Blackstone. The men joined him in the entry, silently surveying the valley. Down the slope below the cave, and along the narrow creek that cut a winding swath through the meadow, the dead lay sprawled. The frozen eyes of women and little children stared up at them, their gaping mouths rimmed with frost. The scene paralyzed Lamedeer's souls.

*My fault. All mine.*

"What are we going to do?" Crowfire asked. "We must escape! Tell us how, Lamedeer. What have you planned?"

Blackstone turned to Lamedeer. Short and burly, he had the stoutness of a tree stump. Forgiveness filled his eyes. He put a hand on Lamedeer's shoulder, whispering, "The ancestors chose our time for us. That is all."

"Is it, my friend?"

Blackstone searched his face. "There is no blame here. Not for you. Not for any of us. We just ... lost our Power." He exhaled hard and looked out the cave entrance. The lines crisscrossing his face deepened. "The False Face Child was wrong. It was the first time. You could not have known."

Blackstone studied Lamedeer's grim expression, let his hand drop, and walked to the opposite side of the cave's mouth, where he slumped against the cold limestone.

"Lamedeer?"

As Dawn Woman strode closer, more light streamed into the cave, and he could make out Crowfire's plain, almost austere face, round and framed with shoulder-length black hair. Desperate hope shone in the youth's dark eyes.

"What is it, Crowfire?"

"You can accomplish anything, Lamedeer. We all know it. You have but to give us your orders!"

Even now, after he'd led his people to their deaths, Lamedeer could not escape the fabric of legends that clothed him. For twelve winters he had been the greatest warrior of the Paint Rock Clan. People told winter stories about his adventures, turning his hard-fought battles into sacred acts. Until three nights ago, they had all believed that just by lifting his bow, he could conquer their enemies.

The destruction of Paint Rock Village had changed that. For all except the most naïve.

"Very well, Crowfire," Lamedeer answered, "I will give you an order. You and Walking Teal will stay in this cave with me until I signal you"—he raised a clenched fist—"to run. Then you will take the deer trail that winds through the boulders to the top of the cliff. We saw it last night. Do you remember?"

"Oh, yes, I do!"

"When you reach the top, you will run for Earth Thunderer Village as fast as you are able, and tell the story to Silver Sparrow. Tell him . . ." His mouth went suddenly dry. He swallowed hard. "Tell him he was right."

"Right?" Crowfire asked. "Right about what?"

Lamedeer rasped, "Just repeat my words, boy!"

Crowfire's wide eyes disappeared into the shadows again.

Lamedeer turned away. Silver Sparrow had run for two nights, and Lamedeer had laughed at him.

Though many people among the Bear Nation believed Silver Sparrow had great Spirit Power and feared him, among the Turtle Nation people whispered that the old man was deranged. Sparrow's own wife had divorced him, and told anyone who would listen what an old fool Silver Sparrow had become. Of course Lamedeer had ignored Sparrow's warning. Sparrow's words were unreliable. He—

"Lamedeer?" Crowfire pressed. "I do not wish to run. Please? I wish to fight. I am a warrior! I—"

"You will do as I tell you, Crowfire."

Crowfire's mouth hung open, then he lifted both fists and shook them—a sign of obedience.

Lamedeer looked out at the valley, trying not to see the bodies, or the enemy warriors. He wanted only to enjoy the breathtaking beauty of this last morning.

Sunlight fell across the forest in bars and streaks of bright gold, sparkling in the tendrils of mist that curled from the creek. As he watched, one tendril crept across the frosty ground, climbed the trunk of an old oak tree, and coiled languidly in its highest branches, like a serpent sleeping in the warm sunlight. The birds had wakened. They hopped from limb to limb, chirping and singing.

Lamedeer inhaled deeply and held the breath in his lungs.

"Do you think Briar is out there?" Blackstone asked. "That she is watching us even now? Perhaps conferring with her husband, laying plans to save us?"

Before he could stop himself, Lamedeer squeezed his eyes closed, his pain obvious. Whispers drifted through the cave.

"I do not see how my sister could have escaped, Blackstone. The Walksalongs struck her house first. They stole the False Face Child. Surely they must also ... have ..."

The possibility that she might be gone from his life forever left him feeling as empty as Falling Woman's heart. Briar would have fought like a she-bear to keep her child. The fact that the False Face Child had been taken meant she could fight no more.

A prickly sensation, like a swarm of biting flies, ate at his chest. As he scanned the faces of the people in the cave, he could feel her. Pieces of Briar hid in each of them. Breathing, smiling, gazing out through their eyes. The meekest and yet most self-confident woman he had ever known, Briar had treated everyone with reverence, adults, children, animals, even the wing-seeds that spiraled through the summer air. An admired holy woman, she'd also had a reputation for being flighty. When a village meeting was called, everyone knew she would dash in late, breathing hard, and spend the next quarter hand of time apologizing to the elders. There was always one more person who'd needed her. She had lived her teachings, believing in charity and, above all else, love, which she gave without question. At night, when the rest of Paint Rock Village slept, Briar could be found before her fire, offering consolation to the lost or bereaved, reminding them of what they already knew but—in their loneliness—had forgotten.

She had given both her souls to the Paint Rock Clan.

And she had suffered so much at their hands.

Many winters ago Briar had told him that her son protected Paint Rock Village. It seemed true. After the dwarf boy's birth they had triumphed, winning not just battles, but ball games, running matches, spear-throwing contests. Lamedeer had believed with every sinew in his body. Perhaps because he'd so desperately needed to.

Silver Sparrow had tried to shatter that belief, and Lamedeer had treated the old man like a child.

Crowfire jerked suddenly. "Did you hear that?"

Lamedeer stiffened as Jumping Badger called, "Nock your bows!"

*We are not really here,* Lamedeer longed to tell his people. *We are on a hunt. It's autumn and the trembling leaves are crimson and gold. Deer are bounding through the forest before us. . . .* The sweet scent of roasting venison rose so clearly in his souls that for an instant he thought he truly smelled it.

"Make ready!" Jumping Badger shouted.

The words leaped from man to man, echoing back and forth across the valley.

It had taken five winters, but Jumping Badger had finally trapped Lamedeer. He must be light-headed with joy, slapping his warriors on the backs, promising them great honor if they succeeded today.

The shadows filtered through the trees and coalesced

into a black line at the periphery of the meadow.

Lamedeer straightened, and grains of sand cascaded from his blood-stiff war shirt, playing a soft serenade on the cave floor.

"They're coming," he said.

Breathed words slipped through the darkness. Longhorn said, "I have no arrows. I didn't wish to tell you. I used them last night."

Eyes glinted as people turned toward her.

"You will have plenty of arrows soon enough, Longhorn," he told the young woman. "They will be shooting uphill. Many of their arrows will sail over our heads and strike the rear and ceiling of the cave. We will collect them and use them against the Walksalongs."

Dark shapes collided in the back of the cave, people struggling to their feet, or dragging wounded limbs across the floor searching for a safer place. Muffled moans and gasps rose. Lamedeer saw a hand moving spiderlike in the darkness, reaching for a bow.

"Kingfisher, Sapling," he called, "stand with Blackstone and me." He searched the remaining faces. "Sorrel, be prepared to take the place of the first man that falls. Willow, I know your leg is injured, but you must rise after him. Understand?"

Heads nodded.

The wounded man started panting again, like a dying beast running for its life. An arm detached from the shadows along the rear wall, and the man's hand fell limply to clutch at his belly. A muffled groan replaced the panting. Yarrow. He was barely a man. Fifteen winters. Lamedeer clutched his bow more tightly.

Blackstone, Kingfisher, and Sapling lined up in the entry. The quivers over their right shoulders carried two or three arrows. Lamedeer had one left. He nocked it and turned to stand with his men.

From the edge of his vision, he saw Yarrow's twin brother, Walking Teal, crawl across the floor and slump down beside Crowfire. The youth must have stood witness to his brother's draining strength, and intensifying pain, all night long. He looked terrified. Crowfire wrapped his arm around Walking Teal's shoulders, and hugged him.

"Look," Blackstone whispered.

Lamedeer swung around.

Like an oncoming wave, the Walksalongs rushed across the valley, their arrows gleaming in the slanting sunlight. They leaped the creek and raced for the cliff. When they started up the slope, the taste of victory turned their war cries shrill.

"Remember," Lamedeer said in a strong voice, "they must climb the slope to get to us. Do not waste arrows on questionable targets. Let them come close. When you are sure of striking the enemy, then, and only then, should you fire."

A flock of arrows arced through the golden morning.

"Fall to your knees!" he ordered, and watched his archers smoothly drop.

Arrows shot into the cave, clattering against the ceiling. Curses rang out as stone chips flew.

Near the creek, Jumping Badger stood with his arms folded, studying the progress of his warriors. Handsome and arrogant, he had a reputation for brutality. Villages for a moon's walk spoke of the grisly acts he'd committed. Though his hide shirt and pants were grimy with blood and dirt, he had greased his hair into a tight bun for this occasion. It gleamed with a blue-black fire.

As they came on, five warriors fanned out, taking the lead. Lamedeer gripped his bow and forced himself to wait. *Wait!* Sweat ran coldly down his chest.

"They are going to rush us!" Blackstone warned.

Arrows rattled from the cliff, and tumbled end over end when they hit the ground, bouncing from the rocks.

The first man shrieked a war cry and dashed for the cave.

"Blacksto—"

Before Lamedeer had finished the name, his friend let fly. The arrow took the warrior in the stomach. The enemy staggered, clawing at the protruding shaft before he screamed and fell.

An eerie, horrifying sound erupted in the cave, like a dying rabbit's squeal. Lamedeer killed the next warrior climbing the slope. Two more rushed them, howling like wild dogs, their eyes blazing.

Out of arrows, Lamedeer fell to his knees to search the floor . . . and landed beside Kingfisher. He lay curled on his side. The squealing came from his throat. Without thinking, Lamedeer started to reach out, to comfort his friend, but quickly grabbed the last arrow from Kingfisher's quiver, and lunged to his feet.

Blackstone screamed, *"He's coming in!"* as he stumbled backward, almost knocking Lamedeer over. The enemy warrior burst into the cave with a deerbone stiletto in his hand, and leaped for Blackstone.

Lamedeer grabbed the enemy's shoulders from behind, pulling him off, while Blackstone took the man's weapon, and plunged it into his chest and belly. When he went limp, Lamedeer thrust the enemy warrior aside, nocked his bow with Kingfisher's arrow, and spun. . . .

His drawn bow quivered as his eyes examined the slope.

The Walksalongs had taken cover. Arrow points gleamed in the sunlight, appearing strangely disconnected from the jeering faces near the boulders. In the foreground, men writhed in a haze of sunlit dust, some twisting round and round, like dying serpents, others jerking and yipping in the voices of clubbed dogs.

As understanding tingled through him, Lamedeer's gaze traced the outline of the cave entrance. *Blessed gods, Jumping Badger planned this. He lured us into this valley knowing I had only one refuge. Just now, he sacrificed a few warriors to get the rest into position. . . .*

Jumping Badger's deep-throated laughter climbed the slope. Lamedeer watched his enemy leap the creek, a grin splitting his handsome face as he trotted to join his forces.

The fire of battle, the rage to survive, all drained from Lamedeer's heart like water from a broken pot. He lifted a trembling hand to brush hair from his eyes.

"Why aren't they shooting?" Crowfire quavered. His deeply set eyes shone with hope. "Did they leave? Have they had enough?"

"Yes!" Young Walking Teal shouted. "That's it! We've beaten them!"

For several heartbeats stunned silence filled the cave.

Then Blackstone chuckled dryly, and several other warriors laughed. A nervous sound, like ancient bones rattling in the wind.

Soft pearlescent sunlight streamed into the cave, glinting in the pools of blood on the floor. Shapes within them shifted, bright and indistinct.

"Count your arrows," Lamedeer ordered. "How many have we left?"

Blackstone's mouth fell open. "You can't believe that even with arrows we—"

"I have one," Lamedeer interrupted. "Who else?"

"Lamedeer!" Blackstone shouted. "We have three choices: We can slit our own throats while we have the strength; wait until desperation sends us running into Jumping Badger's arms for a sip of water; or, when we become too weak to resist, the Walksalongs will simply walk up and carry us down to the torture rituals. Fighting is pointless!''

Lamedeer didn't even look at his friend. He repeated, "Who else has arrows?''

"I have two,'' Sorrel said, and lifted them for Lamedeer to see.

Longhorn, who had just become a woman last moon, called, "I found two unbroken ones on the floor!''

"Bring them forward.''

He gave each person a confident nod as they placed the arrows in his palm.

Blackstone gaped. "What madness is this? We're beaten, Lamedeer. If we were wise we would take out our knives and end this before Jumping Badger makes sport of—''

"You're beaten. Not I.''

Smiles curled the lips of the Paint Rock survivors.

Voices murmured, *"Lamedeer has a plan . . . won't let us die . . . kill them yet . . ."*

Crowfire gazed at Lamedeer as though he knew more than Falling Woman herself. "What shall we do, Lamedeer? Rush them?''

When Lamedeer answered, "Yes, Crowfire. That's exactly what we're going to do,'' Blackstone swung around as if he'd been slapped.

*"What?"*

"Blackstone, I want you to take Sapling, Willow, Sorrel, and . . .'' He searched the cave. "And Longhorn. The five of you will go first. Head west. Run hard. Draw them away if you can. I will give you ten heartbeats, then I will take Walking Teal and Crowfire eastward, up the deertrail through the boulders. I will cover both youths for as long as I can. Maybe, if Falling Woman smiles upon us, one will make it to the top of the cliff.''

Blackstone said, "What possible purpose—''

"There is only *one* purpose now, Blackstone."

Prisoners would be tortured for days. Jumping Badger would make certain of it. He would force-feed his victims to give them the strength to last. Only one course of action remained: They had to teach the cowardly Walksalongs the meaning of courage.

Lamedeer divided his arrows, keeping two, handing three to Blackstone.

Blackstone stared at them. A curious calm had settled over him. "Yes," he said. "You are right. At least this way, we . . ." The words faded. He slipped the arrows into his quiver, and in a sudden powerful voice, called, "Let us show them how Paint Rock warriors die! Come forward!"

Young Longhorn came first, shaking badly. Sorrel and Sapling flanked her. Willow hobbled to stand behind her, his bandaged leg leaking blood down his hide pants. The men towered over Longhorn, making her appear unnaturally short and as thin as a newly sprouted reed.

Blackstone moved closer to Lamedeer, whispering, "What of the wounded? Do you wish me—"

"No," Lamedeer answered. "That is my responsibility."

Blackstone stood for a long moment looking into Lamedeer's eyes, then he backed away, nodded, and shrieked a blood-chilling war cry. He charged from the cave with his warriors on his heels. Dust flew up behind them as they stormed down the slope.

A cry of disbelief rose from the Walksalongs. They cursed, hastily nocking their bows. Several leaped up to pursue.

Lamedeer pulled his knife from his belt and ran for the back of the cave where Yarrow lay. The wounded man stared at him with huge eyes.

"Hurry," Yarrow said. "Please . . . hurry."

Lamedeer searched that brave young face, then slit Yarrow's throat, quickly, cleanly.

Walking Teal's hoarse scream rang in the narrow confines of the cave: *"What have you done?"* The youth lunged for his brother, sobbing as Yarrow's head lolled to the side.

Lamedeer ran for Kingfisher. The man stared unblinking at the stone ceiling. Dust and bits of old leaves covered his wide dead eyes. Lamedeer touched his friend gently, then sprang to his feet.

"Crowfire? Walking Teal?" He gave the youths the clenched-fist sign. "Follow me!"

Lamedeer sprinted out of the cave into the blinding morning light. Westward, only Blackstone remained on his feet. At least twenty warriors chased him. Lamedeer ran eastward.

Over his shoulder, he shouted, "Crowfire! Run to my left. Walking Teal, stay close behind me!"

Lamedeer pounded up the deertrail through the maze of wind-smoothed boulders. Brush and lichen grew in the cracks, giving them a mottled appearance. Excited war cries rent the air. Lamedeer ran faster. Rounding a curve in the trail, he glanced back, and stumbled. *"Walking Teal! Where—"*

Crowfire yelled, "He would not leave his dead brother! I left him sitting on the floor of the cave beside Yarrow!"

Sickness welled in Lamedeer's throat. He bounded ahead. Had he known in advance, he would have spared Walking Teal the horrifying consequences of his decision. Instead, the youth would face his torturers alone.

*"Run, cowards! Run!"* Jumping Badger shouted, and laughed shrilly.

As the deertrail climbed higher, boulders thrust up on

the south side. The cliff rose on the north. Lamedeer ordered, "Crowfire, get in front of me!"

The youth raced ahead, his legs pumping.

Arrows clattered on the rimrock. Lamedeer did not waste time turning to shoot at his pursuers, he had to shield Crowfire's back.

"Hurry, Crowfire. Run hard!" Lamedeer's feet beat the trail behind the boy, forcing Crowfire to run as fast as he could.

One hundred hands away, the trail climbed onto the top of the cliff. It would be a miracle if Crowfire made it, and even more a miracle if he managed to reach Silver Sparrow . . . but, by the ancestors, Lamedeer *would* give him that chance.

A hoarse cry wavered. "Help! Someone? *Lamedeer, help me!*"

Crowfire's pace faltered, and Lamedeer shouted, "Do not turn around! Walking Teal chose his death himself! You must not let the same happen to you! Run, boy! Run!"

Crowfire sprinted the last distance in less than fifteen heartbeats, and scrambled over the rimrock.

Elation seared Lamedeer's veins.

He whirled, pulled an arrow from his quiver, and shot the first man on the trail. Six others, including Jumping Badger, dove for cover in the boulders.

"Jumping Badger!" Lamedeer cried, trying to gain more time. "You are a cursed man! Do you hear me? Four nights ago, old Silver Sparrow came to see me. He told me you would attack Paint Rock Village and steal the False Face Child, and he said it would cost you your souls! He cursed you! *Do you hear?* Silver Sparrow said your Power would drain away until you are like a camp dog, kicked by everyone! When you can no longer defend yourself, the False Face Child will kill you. If you don't release him now, he will be your death!''

He could hear the Walksalong warriors gasp.

A man leaped onto the trail fifty hands away, and let fly. The arrow struck Lamedeer in the thigh, staggering him. Lamedeer pulled his last arrow, nocked his bow and killed the man.

Two more arrows flew. One splintered the rock wall to his right, the other struck Lamedeer squarely in the chest, driving him back against the cliff. He clawed at the rocky crevices to stay on his feet.

Enemy warriors whooped. Twenty men, and one tall woman warrior, the woman who'd killed Red Pipe, rushed up the trail.

*Blessed gods, did I give Crowfire enough time?* He tried to look up the trail, but blood welled in his throat, cutting off his air. Terror overwhelmed him when he toppled backward into the trail, writhing, his body waging a battle of its own. The sensation melted to a warm weightlessness. Lamedeer blinked at the brightening sky. Gray mist, like a thousand dove-colored butterfly wings, fluttered at the edges of his vision. He struggled to imagine Briar's face, the way her brows lifted when she laughed, the gleam in her soft brown eyes.

Jumping Badger straddled him, grabbed Lamedeer by the shirtfront and shook him hard, shouting ''Liar! I haven't done anything to that old man! Why would Silver Sparrow curse me?''

With his last strength . . . Lamedeer smiled.

Silver Sparrow walked the trail that led to Earth Thunderer Village. He'd traveled all night after they'd thrown him out of Paint Rock Village, too embarrassed to stop anywhere close, too agitated to rest if he had stopped. He'd eaten a handful of shriveled rose hips yesterday afternoon, and drunk a handful of water this morning. He felt better, though every now and then his legs unexpectedly gave out on him, and he found himself sprawled in the dirt. He wanted to be home. His wounded heart needed the soothing sights of his family, and his gaunt belly needed a thick slice of venison.

He passed through a copse of red plum trees. Standing five or six body lengths tall, the highest limbs grew together, creating a canopy over the trail. Sunlight scattered the ground like strewn chips of amber. As he stepped over a fallen log, he braced a hand on one of the plum trees. It felt cool. The thin gray-brown bark had peeled away in places, revealing the darker inner bark, and the buds on the branch tips had turned chestnut-colored with winter. In less than three moons, however, he knew those buds would be bright green, and a wealth of white blossoms would cover the trees.

Sparrow longed for spring. Actually, he longed for any place and time other than where he was. He kept hearing the sound of Calling Hawk's laughter, and the chuckles that had come from Lamedeer's lodge.

"What's the matter with my Spirit Helper? Can't he get anything right?"

Or did the mischievous boy just like tricking Sparrow to teach him humility? The boy had never directly lied to him, not that Sparrow knew of, but he often presented the Dream images in such a way that Sparrow had trouble determining their meaning. When Sparrow got it wrong, people roared with laughter and reviled him, calling him either a simpleton or a madman.

Sparrow kicked at a squirrel-gnawed plum pit that lay in the trail.

While most of the fault for his curious reputation belonged to Sparrow alone, Dust Moon hadn't helped matters. Every time Sparrow made a mistake, she made sure everyone for three moons' walk knew about it.

He strode out onto a grassy hilltop and followed the trail beside a brook. The clear water burbled over rocks, splashing and sparkling in the glory of Grandfather Day Maker's face. Three crows cawed above him. Sparrow glanced up. The big birds flapped southward, their bodies jet-black against the azure sky.

"You can't blame Dust," he chastised himself. "This is your problem, not hers."

The pain that had lived in Sparrow's heart for almost two winters tingled to life. He missed her. So much that sometimes he could barely stand it. In the thirty-five winters they had loved each other, she had become part of him—the part he liked best. Together they had made fourteen children, and grieved over the deaths of thirteen of them. Sparrow had loved her with all his heart—until eleven moons ago, when she'd cast him out of the lodge he'd built.

The rift had sprung from many sources. Each time one of their children grew ill, Dust spent all of her time working to heal that child. Sparrow had never thought about it until recently, but while she'd emptied herself into her children, she'd left him alone. Desperately alone. The more children they had, the more they lost, and the less time she could spare for him. Toward the end, he'd felt hopeless, like a starving man locked in a cage, waiting for her scraps.

When his Spirit Helper had come to him, Dust had refused to believe it. She'd treated Sparrow like a stranger.

He'd hated her for that . . . for a time.

But he'd gotten over it.

He reached up to touch the shell-bead necklace around

his throat. He'd restrung it ten times over the past thirty-seven winters. About to leave on his first war raid, he'd been afraid, and filled with longings he could not explain. He'd gone to Dust to say goodbye. She'd held him tightly, and told him how proud she was of him, how much faith she had in his abilities as a warrior. When she'd draped the necklace over his head, he'd felt strength flow into his veins. . . . He'd never let the necklace out of his sight.

Yearning settled in the pit of his empty stomach. He started to run, heading home to her and his grandchildren. He especially longed to see Planter, his daughter. Sparrow might not be able to do anything else right, but he could help her and his grandchildren.

He neared the crest of the hill overlooking Earth Thunderer Village, and slowed to a walk. The crows had circled. They sailed over his head, diving playfully, cawing to each other. Sparrow forced his wobbling knees onward and up.

Strange. By now he ought to hear voices, and see smoke rising from the village fires. The dogs ought to be barking. . . .

Sparrow followed the trail over the hill and came to an abrupt halt. The sapling lodge frames stood naked; the bark coverings had been carefully rolled up and carried away. Not even a whiff of smoke spiraled up from the cold fire pits. Earth Thunderer Village had been gone for days.

Anger mixed nauseatingly with despair.

"Oh, Dust Moon," he said through gritted teeth.

To track them down might take days.

His shaking knees went out from under him. He collapsed into the dirt, and the rich scent of damp soil filled his nostrils.

Rather than rising, and beginning his pursuit, he rolled to his side and tried to sleep.

*The Dream rolls in like thunder over the lake.*

*I am cold. Freezing cold. Running . . .*

*Pale light streams down through the winter-bare branches to dapple the shining face of the Boy. He Dances through collapsed piles of burned bark, jumbles of charred roof beams, standing skeletons of walls—all that is left of Paint Rock Village.*

*His laughter is like the melodious call of the finch. Sweet. Joyous.*

*He climbs upon a smoldering roof beam, spins on one foot and leaps to the ground, landing as soft and silent as mist.*

*No delicate ash puffs beneath his moccasined feet. The smoke spiraling up from the beam does not even waver as he Dances alongside it.*

*All is still.*

*No one knows he is there.*

*Except you. And me.*

*And the dead who watch with ash-caked eyes.*

*The shell beads on his hide shirt glimmer as he skips through an ocean of torn bodies. Some have arrows sticking from their chests. Others have crushed skulls.*

*The Boy opens his arms to the sun-drenched sky, and calls:*

*"Wake up, my shadows! Hurry! Grandfather Day Maker's children are hunting you. If they catch you, I will lose the endless eyes you have opened in me."*

*The Boy turns and stares. His eyes have changed. They are no longer wide and dark; they are glowing embers.*

*Bright gold. Fiery. He fills his lungs with the smoky air, and shouts, "Have you no ears? Hurry! You are being hunted!"*

*The Boy spins around, laughing, and the ash from the burned village whirls up, growing blacker, forming a deep dark hole in the face of the world.*

*It is the gaping maw of oblivion.*

*Inside it, I see millions of gaunt, stricken faces, crying out for help. . . .*

# Four

*"Blue Raven? Blue Raven, they are here!"*

Plume threw back the hide door curtain to the longhouse, and peered inside. Ten winters old, the boy had a broad flat face. He wet his lips nervously and used a grimy hand to shove shoulder-length black hair away from his eyes. "They just arrived! Starflower says you must hurry. But just you! No one else. They are taking the False Face Child to the council house!"

The longhouse went silent.

They had been waiting for this, most like children expecting an enchanted gift from the Spirit World, some as if dreading the terrible punishment they deserved for the crime. Blue Raven's gaze drifted down the house's hundred-hand length, studying his relatives' taut faces. He had opposed this raid. They knew it. All forty sat perfectly still, horn spoons of food halted halfway to their mouths.

"Let me gather my things." Blue Raven set down his freshly poured cup of fir-needle tea. Tall, with long graying black hair and an oval face, he had seen forty-one winters. He reached for his cape.

His aging mother and young niece sat across the fire from him. Both appeared to be in shock. His mother, Frost-in-the-Willows, had her head down, face blank, but her breathing had gone shallow. The triangles of pounded copper encircling the collar of her tan dress shimmered with each swift exhalation.

His niece, Little Wren, gazed at him in awe. Twelve winters old, Wren had a slender angular face, as if carved from a fine golden-brown wood. She wore her long hair in a single braid which fell over her left shoulder. Her parents and younger brother had died in a canoeing accident eight moons ago. Their bodies had never been found. Since then, Wren had grown unruly and bold. She had been averaging one nasty fistfight each moon. Perhaps even worse, certainly more dangerous, Wren was absolutely fearless. She might chase a wolf into the forest just to watch its fur shine. Blue Raven never knew what the gangly girl might say or do next.

Wren set her teacup on the floor and leaned forward to whisper, "The False Face Child is here? Truly?"

As he swung his beaver-hide cape around his broad shoulders, Blue Raven said, "Did you doubt your cousin's abilities as war leader, Wren?"

"Yes," she answered blithely, and her frankness made him suppress a smile. "And I thought the child had more Power than to *let* himself be caught," she added. "May I go see the boy, Uncle? Just to look? I don't have to touch him, I just wish to—"

"No!" Plume threw the curtain aside, leaped into the house like a small ferocious bear, and blurted, "Matron Starflower told me that only Blue Raven could come!"

Blue Raven patted his niece on the head. "I thought you were going to visit Trickster today?"

"Oh, yes, I must. I promised him I would." Wren's hand dropped to touch the knotted strip of rawhide that hung from her cord belt. One end showed teeth marks. She petted the toy as if it soothed her. "But Trickster will understand, Uncle, if I go to visit him after I see the Power child."

"I know, but not now, Wren. Later."

Wren scowled at Plume, and the boy grinned.

"And I had best not discover you sneaking through the brush after me, Wren," Blue Raven warned.

She blinked owlishly, trying to convey innocence. "You won't, Uncle."

Blue Raven gave her a skeptical look. "If I see you, I'll turn you over to Starflower."

Matron Starflower showed disobedient children no mercy. She forced them to fetch water, grind corn, and carry wood, until they pleaded for pardon.

Wren slumped dejectedly. "I will remain here, Uncle. You have my oath."

The longhouse seemed to stir to life. Murmuring broke out. As people shifted, their brilliantly colored clothing became a sea of rich reds, greens, yellows, and the palest of blues. Shell earrings danced. Though hides covered the hard-packed dirt floor, it required four evenly spaced fires to heat the longhouse. The orange light from the flames flickered over the baskets, bows, and lances that hung along the bark walls, and played among the dried vegetables suspended from the high arching ceiling. After moons of hanging in the rising smoke, the corn, beans, squash, sunflowers, and other plants had obtained a shiny patina of black creosote.

"What will you do, Blue Raven?" a man from the

opposite end of the longhouse called. "Will you bring the child here? To live among us?"

"I will make no decisions until I see him."

Red porcupine-quill chevrons ran down the sleeves of his cape. They flashed as he rose from his place by the fire.

People stared, their apprehension palpable.

"Continue eating," he said calmly. "The worst is done. We have stolen the child."

Frost-in-the-Willows pursed her withered lips, but did not comment.

"Mother," he said. "I will return soon. Don't fret about me."

As she tipped her brown face up, firelight flowed like honey into her deep wrinkles, making her seem a thousand winters old. Her white hair gleamed. "It is very dangerous, my son."

"He is nine winters old, Mother."

"It is an abomination!"

Blue Raven knotted the laces of his cape. "Perhaps. I will wait to judge."

"Why is he an abomination?" Wren asked. She balanced on her knees as if preparing to spring into a run. "I thought he was a Power child?"

"He is," Blue Raven said. "For now, that is all we know."

Frost-in-the-Willows lifted a thin white brow. "You would call the Paint Rock elders liars? They say it is *very* dangerous."

"Yes, and their words have kept us frightened, haven't they, Mother? Just as they planned."

Frost-in-the-Willows used the authoritative tone that had trembled Blue Raven's heart as a child. "Those elders say that by the time the False Face Child could run, it was hunting, not little birds and chipmunks, like other boys its age, but wolves and bobcats. At the age of four, it no longer needed a bow or arrows. It could kill by calling out to an animal in its own tongue. Old Silver Sparrow has seen it sit upon a rock all day long, as if deaf and blind, and when he asked what it had been doing, the boy answered, 'Listening to my father's people talk.' ''

Wren gasped. ''His father was a Forest Spirit! Is that not right? That's what Beavertail told me!''

*''Hush, girl!''* Frost-in-the-Willows shouted and Wren almost bit her tongue off closing her mouth. Frost-in-the-Willows turned back to Blue Raven. ''For the sake of the ancestors, my son, the child went on its first vision quest at the age of five winters. You cannot treat it—''

''I know the stories, Mother,'' Blue Raven replied shortly. He had met Silver Sparrow once, and liked the old man. But he hadn't been a Dreamer then, just a Trader. ''Your nephew, Jumping Badger, has made certain everyone knows them. I wish that you would trust me.''

Plume glanced back and forth between them. His broad face shone orange. ''Elder, Starflower said for you to come *now*.''

''I'm almost ready.'' Blue Raven picked up his mittens from where they warmed at the edge of the hearthstones. ''Tell Jumping Badger—''

''He is not here, Elder,'' Plume replied. ''Jumping Badger sent two runners ahead with the boy. Mossybill and Skullcap said Jumping Badger should return tonight, then they turned the False Face Child over to the matrons, and fled for their longhouses. The runners were so ill they could scarcely walk!''

''Ill?'' Wren asked, her interest piqued. ''From what?''

"No one told me!" Plume bellowed. "I am just a boy!"

Blue Raven uneasily slipped on his mittens.

The men had been running and fighting for days, of course they would be exhausted, but . . . ill? "And why is Jumping Badger still out? Where is he?"

"He is hunting down the survivors of the Paint Rock Village battle."

Heat flushed Blue Raven's cheeks. The clan matrons had sent Jumping Badger to kidnap a child, and he had taken it upon himself to kill every last member of the child's village. For many winters Blue Raven's dislike for his arrogant cousin had been growing. Jumping Badger had been war leader for five winters. In that short span, he'd managed to antagonize nearly every village within a moon's running distance. His words, it seemed, possessed more strength than Blue Raven's. He waved a mittened hand at Plume. "Run and tell Matron Starflower I am on my way."

"Yes, Elder." Plume ducked under the curtain and dashed away.

Frost-in-the-Willows squinted at Blue Raven. "Listen, my son. Everyone knows you opposed this raid. I opposed it, too. None of that matters now. The deed is done. The False Face is here. Treat it as you would a wounded panther, a beast in pain who will do anything to escape."

"A *beast*, Mother?" Blue Raven's strained voice went low, and it seemed that the entire house swayed toward him to listen. "He is a little boy. A child who has just witnessed the destruction of his entire world. He—"

"I warn you." She lifted a gnarled hand. *"It is not human."*

Wren's mouth gaped. "It isn't? Then what is it?"

Blue Raven ignored Little Wren. He loved and respected his mother too much to challenge her words in

front of others. She sat stiffly, her white hair glimmering
with firelight. "I will be heedful, Mother. I give you my
pledge."

Lifting the door curtain, he quickly ducked outside.

The cold hit him like a fist, stinging his flesh and burning his lungs. He hurried forward.

Six longhouses encompassed the central plaza. Around
the village they had constructed a palisade of upright logs
that stood twenty hands tall—the result of Jumping
Badger's raiding. They no longer felt safe even in their
own village.

People rushed to doorways to watch him pass, breaths
puffing whitely as they whispered to each other. He could
feel their excitement and fear; the emotions prickled at
him like the first drops of a torrential rain that would
flood the rivers and send them all scrambling for their
lives. He could do nothing to stop it now.

The entry in the palisade consisted of the space between two overlapping walls. There were two entries, one
on the north side of the village, and one on the south.
He slipped through the southern entry and headed down
the hill.

His cousin had been railing about the False Face Child
from the night he'd become war leader, recounting horrifying events of murder and mutilation—describing in
detail the times the boy had saved his people from destruction. The want had grown in Jumping Badger until
it had seemed to consume him. *"We must have the boy!"*
he'd said. *"He is a False Face, a Spirit being! Paint
Rock Village has not been attacked since the day of the
child's birth, while we have been raided once every two
or three winters! Every battle that the Paint Rock war
leader has waged he has won! Think. Think what would
happen if we had the boy? We would be invincible! We*

*could raid where we wished, take what we wanted. We* must *have that child!''*

A quarter moon ago, new rumors of war had drifted in with the Traders. Blue Raven mused as he walked. The Walksalong Clan was part of the Bear Nation. For hundreds of winters the Bear Nation and Turtle Nation had been pushing against each other: The Bears pushing northward, then the Turtles pushing southward, and now, again, the Bears pushing northward. Ever since the Bear Nation began to cultivate crops and live in large fortified villages, they had been forcing the Turtle Nation to flee before them, or to blend their villages with Bear villages. Often this meant that longhouses existed alongside the traditional small conical lodges preferred by the Turtle elders. They all spoke similar languages, so melding was possible, but it was not easy.

Three distinctly different kinds of villages had resulted: Bear Nation villages, which generally had longhouses, like Walksalong; Bear-Turtle villages, like Grand Banks, which often had both small houses and longhouses, and Turtle villages like Paint Rock, with small conical lodges.

The Turtle Nation reckoned descent through the father, not the mother. This created great confusion when a member of the Turtle Nation wanted to marry someone from a Bear Nation clan, as often happened west of Pipe Stem Lake. In Bear-Turtle villages, a young man had to gain the permission of both the mother and the father before marrying their daughter. In Bear villages, women alone arranged marriages. In Turtle villages, fathers arranged marriages. The poor children were left to sort out the conflicting rules and taboos.

Bear-Turtle villages allowed children to choose which clan they wished to belong to, their mother's or their father's, but this compromise had resulted in chaos. If a man and woman divorced in a Bear Nation village, the children stayed with their mother's clan. Their names remained the same, as did their status and future obligations. But if a child had been born in a Bear-Turtle village, and had chosen his father's clan, he had to leave his mother's village and go to live with his father's people. Children too young to choose had their lives decided for them. Fathers generally claimed the boys, and mothers claimed the girls.

This strange mixture of customs, originally intended to maintain harmony between different clans, had become a source of mounting hostility—because people no longer agreed on how they were related.

Incest taboos had become impossible. Last summer a young woman from Walksalong Village, named Pebble, had wished to marry a man, Blackhawk, from Grand Banks Village. Because the Walksalong Clan traced descent strictly through the mother, only maternal kin were forbidden as marriage partners. The Walksalong matrons had approved the marriage. The Bear-Turtle council of Grand Banks Village, however, had refused to allow it. Blackhawk, it turned out, was Pebble's father's brother's son, and in Bear-Turtle villages both maternal and paternal kin were forbidden as marriage partners.

Just thinking about it made Blue Raven's head swim. No wonder warfare had broken out.

To complicate matters, Bear and Turtle used the land differently. Bear clans planted corn, beans, squash, sunflowers, and tobacco. While most people left the main village for hunting and fishing camps in the spring and summer, many women and children stayed to tend the crops, weeding, watering, burying fish to fertilize the tender plants, harvesting, storing, guarding the stores. As a result of constant use, every few winters, the soil gave out, and they had to move their villages to find new fields.

Bear-Turtle clans spent winters in their villages, but abandoned their villages in the summers and moved to smaller camps where they fished and hunted, gathered nuts and berries.

The Turtle Nation barely used the land at all. They threw some seeds in the ground and left, spending most of their time hunting and gathering the natural resources. They returned in the fall to harvest whatever the birds and insects had left them of their crops, then settled into their winter villages. Clearly they did not need the soil as badly as their cousins in the Bear Nation. There had been many clashes in the past; houses burnt, women and children stolen, food stores raided. Nothing unusual. Until now. The Traders claimed that the Turtles had vowed they would be pushed no more. They would band together and wage open warfare on the Bears.

Blue Raven had laughed at the very idea. The Turtles could barely get along with one another for six nights at their annual ceremonial gatherings. How, he'd asked, could they hope to band together for a long war?

Jumping Badger had connived and wheedled, using the rumor to convince the clan to vote for a raid to steal the child. When their approval came, Blue Raven had been stunned. Before he could try to reason with people, Jumping Badger had gathered his war party and disappeared into the forest.

Faint images of fleeing people and charred houses flitted across the fabric of Blue Raven's souls. His dreams last night had been tortured, filled with the screams of dying children.

He took a deep breath, and bulled forward.

Icy wind gusted up from Pipe Stem Lake, pungent with decaying leaves and wood. A light dusting of snow glistened on the winter-bare maples and birches. Blue Raven's gaze clung to that beauty. Against the golden sky, the frosted branches etched a blinding filigree.

He reached the fork in the trail, and took the path down the hill toward the council house in the small grove of red cedars. One hundred twenty hands long, and sixty wide, the rounded roof stood fifty hands tall. The bark walls had grayed with moss. It resembled a giant shaggy beast.

Blue Raven slowed. What should he say to the boy? The Paint Rocks called him the False Face Child, but surely he must have a name. A boy's name. His mother, the woman Briar, had supposedly borne him at thirteen winters, before her bleeding began. The Paint Rock elders whispered that Briar had mated with a Forest Spirit that resembled a withered tree. It had come to her for six nights in a row, to watch and court her. On the seventh night, they had coupled. The boy took after his father, the elders said, in both his frightening Powers, and his twisted appearance.

Blue Raven gazed at the council house. No sounds came from within. Curious. All captive children wept for home and lost family. Blue Raven had witnessed it a hundred times. Perhaps the clan matrons had gagged the child? Starflower could be practical to the point of cruelty.

He walked to the door, and stood outside the leather curtain. "Matron Starflower? I have come as you commanded." He leaned closer. "Matron? It is Blue Raven. Would you have me wait outside?"

A hoarse voice whispered, *"Enter. Hurry!"*

Blue Raven threw the curtain back and lunged inside. As the curtain swayed behind him, light flashed over the gray heads of the clan matrons. Starflower stood with her back to him, facing the corner to his right, while Kit lay on her side forty hands to his left.

"What happened? Is Kit hurt?" He started across the floor for her.

"Stop!" Starflower ordered. "Stay where you are!"

Blue Raven halted, his fists clenching and unclenching. "Why?"

Fifty-nine winters old, Starflower had lips that sank in over toothless gums, making her narrow face appear shriveled at the center. She lifted a trembling chert knife and pointed, but the tip wavered, aiming at the ceiling, then the floor, then the ceiling again. "Do you see it?"

"See what?" he demanded. "Where is the boy?"

Starflower swung around with fiery eyes. "It is not a boy. It is the Disowned! Look!"

Blue Raven surveyed the room, scanning the brightly painted ceremonial masks that hung at regular intervals along the walls. His people rubbed them with sunflower oil to keep their skins shiny and soft. Pots sat on the floor to his right, along with a stack of deerhides used for seating, and a pile of chopped wood. The Disowned? It was a very old and tragic love story told around the winter fires. He had heard people whisper that the Disowned might be the boy's true father, but not the boy himself.

"Matron," Blue Raven said, "what has happened? I do not see the boy. Did he escape? Did you . . ."

Something skittered across the roof.

Blue Raven stumbled backward at the same time that his gaze shot up, his heart thundering.

The boy seemed wedded to the darkness, little more than a black spider among the roof poles of the house. His stunted arms were spread like wings. The feet below his stubby legs, bound with rawhide straps, rested upon an oak bole. He wore a black garment that glittered with what looked like quartz crystals.

Blue Raven stood there, breathing hard, fighting the sudden terror that perhaps the boy *was* a Spirit. He whispered, "How did he get up there? His feet are bound!"

"Old White Kit . . ." Starflower's voice broke as she gestured to the matron curled on her side on the floor. "She felt sorry for him. The warriors had pulled his ropes until they'd rubbed bloody gashes in his ankles and wrists. Kit said, 'He is the size of a four-winters-old boy. If we leave his feet tied he will be no trouble to us.' She used her knife to cut his wrist bonds and the child . . . it struck without warning, Blue Raven! Like a serpent! It grabbed the knife and plunged it into Kit's heart! Then . . ." She lifted her own knife again, pointing, and this time Blue Raven saw that blood streaked the white stone blade. "It killed Kit and flew up there. I swear! It flew up there like a wingless blackbird! I—I cut him as he leaped, but he—"

He swung around to White Kit. "Then Kit—"

"Yes." Sobs choked Starflower. She lifted a hand to cover the mournful sounds coming up her throat, and nodded.

"Blessed gods. The village will explode. Everyone loved her."

Rage and hurt vied for control of his senses. Kit had been a faithful leader of the clan for thirty winters, tending the ill, feeding the hungry. She had loved children more than her own life. People would scream for retribution.

"Does the child still have the knife?" he asked.

"No!" Starflower gestured toward Kit. "He dropped it right after he realized what he'd done. Threw it down like it had burned him. The knife lies in front of Kit on the floor."

Blue Raven didn't see it. But he didn't see any blood,

either. The poor light probably kept a wealth of things hidden from him.

"Why didn't you call for help, Starflower? Someone would have heard and come running."

Starflower wiped her damp eyes on her red sleeve. "It happened only moments ago. I was too stunned to cry out. I feared that if I took my eyes from it for a single instant, it would escape, transform itself into a Forest Spirit, and destroy our village!"

Disgust built in Blue Raven's chest. Disgust with Jumping Badger because he had demanded they kidnap the boy, and with his clan because they had approved the raid. How many had died because of it?

Blue Raven backed toward the door, lifted and hooked the curtain over its peg. Light flooded the council house. He cupped a hand to his mouth and shouted, "Acorn? Springwater? Come quickly! We—"

A flutter, like the frantic batting of wings, came from the roof. Blue Raven's heart nearly burst through the cage of his ribs. He jerked around. The darkness near the boy seemed to ripple and sway, as if fanned by feathers. In the heart of the disturbance, a tiny hand grasped frantically for a roof pole.

"Starflower," Blue Raven ordered. "Leave. Now. I ask that you make certain Acorn and Springwater heard my call. Send them if they did not. I will stay—"

*"I will find them for you, Uncle Blue Raven!"* Little Wren leaped into the doorway, panting, her eyes curiously searching the council house. She wore a painted deerhide cape over her shoulders. When she saw the dark shape clinging to the roof, she went silent and as still as Mouse seeing Owl.

Blue Raven started to shout at her, but instead said, "Wren, help Matron Starflower up the trail and back to the village."

"Yes, Uncle!"

Wren ran to Starflower and gripped her elbow, helping the old woman to her feet. They passed him without a word, out into the daylight.

Wren called, "I'll fetch Acorn and Springwater, too, Uncle!"

Blue Raven shivered.

The council house had turned bitterly cold, of a sudden, as if the Thunderbirds had flown in and made nests in the walls. He rubbed his arms, and turned back toward the child.

A low hiss, like a snake slithering through the brush, slipped through the darkness.

Blue Raven's knees shook. It shamed and angered him, but he could not stop. All of the stories Jumping Badger had been telling for the past five winters came into focus, and he had the dreadful feeling that nothing he knew for certain was certain at all.

"I—I am Blue Raven, Headman of this village," he said. "You are called the False Face Child, are you not?"

He forced his feet to move. When he stood directly beneath the child, Blue Raven removed his mittens, tossed them to the floor, and spread his arms to show he held no weapons in his hands—though he did have a knife tied to his belt beneath his cape. "Do you have another name? A boy's name?"

The hiss came again, but this time it sounded more like scratching, and it clearly originated from the boy. When the scratching faded, a *click-click-click-click* rose. The sound of claws on wood. It paced back and forth, each click as carefully placed as a prowling animal's.

Blue Raven clenched his hands to hard fists. He longed to draw his knife. "Boy! I have come to help you. Do you understand this?"

A drop of water struck Blue Raven's forehead. He

blinked, startled. Another hit his shoulder. The next splatted in the dirt.

He frowned.

. . . Tears.

A little boy's tears.

Softly, he said, "I did not wish this, boy. No more than you. I'm sorry for what has happened. Please. Let me help you. The floor must look frighteningly far away from up there. May I climb up and carry you down? I—"

*"Blue Raven?"* Acorn shouted. *"Blue Raven, we are here! We've brought the whole village! We all have bows. We're—"*

A low sound, half moan and half growl, came from the False Face Child. Blue Raven's blood pounded in his ears. The cry resembled that of an animal caught in a trap.

"Acorn?" he called, but his eyes remained glued to the misshapen black silhouette on the ceiling. "Keep everyone outside. Do not come until I summon you. Do you understand?"

Panicked voices rose in questions, and dust drifted in as dozens of anxious feet shifted.

"Do you understand?" Blue Raven repeated. "Go back up the trail. Wait until I call."

"But Blue Raven, what if—"

"Do not question me now! We will speak of this later. Just do as I ask. Please!"

"Yes . . . very well," Acorn answered hesitantly. "I— I don't like it! But we will go."

People retreated, their voices dimming until only a faint buzz drifted on the wind.

Blue Raven fought to calm his labored breathing. The boy hung silently, high above, his eyes glinting.

"I'm climbing up to get you, boy."

"No!"

"I will not hurt you. I promise you this."

A pathetic whisper floated down, "You wish to kill me."

"No, no. You must believe me. I have never wished that. Nor have my people. We wish only—"

"They burned my village! I saw it!"

A muted cry filled the stillness—the sound of sobs straining against tightly closed lips.

"I vow to you that you will be safe here," Blue Raven said. "You may trust me, boy. I have never lied to a child."

Cautiously, Blue Raven made his way to the corner pole, a log about two hands in diameter. Saplings wove around the pole, giving it stability, and creating a strong ladder, which they used for repairing the walls and roof. He lifted his right foot and placed it on the first rung.

"I'm coming, boy."

The higher Blue Raven climbed the better he could see the dwarf child. Despite his stunted arms and legs, the boy had thick dark hair, cropped even with his chin, and a beautiful round face. Tears glistened in his black eyes. A wound leaked blood down his left arm. The wound Starflower had, no doubt, inflicted. Blue Raven took two more rungs. The boy's robe, which he had earlier assumed to be decorated with quartz crystals, was really speckled with pieces of exquisitely etched shell. The shapes of Thunderbird and Falling Woman adorned two of the larger discs. The boy's copper gorget, his pendant, was so large it nearly covered the Power bag he wore around his throat. The gorget bore the grotesque image of a gnarled uprooted tree.

Blue Raven stopped at the junction between wall and roof. The boy stood eight hands to his left, his back pressed to the sloping roof, his bound feet resting on the bole. Is that why Starflower thought he'd "flown" up?

The boy had used his arms to climb while his useless feet dangled behind him? The child had been holding so tightly to the roof poles that his stubby fingers had gone white.

Blue Raven reached out. "Take my hand. Please. Don't be afraid. I won't let you fall."

The boy shook his head.

Blue Raven stretched his arm out farther. "Just reach down. I'm right here."

Desperately, the boy's gaze darted over the council house, obviously searching for another way to freedom . . . and landed on one of the smoke holes in the roof.

Panic warmed Blue Raven's veins. He would surely fall to his death if he attempted it. "It's too small for you, and too far," he warned. "Please, don't!"

The False Face Child's eyes remained on the smoke hole, as if calculating the risks involved in reaching it.

"And—and our warriors are outside, boy. Even if you should make it, they would surround the house and have you the instant you climbed down."

The False Face Child gripped one of the roof's cross-poles, and appeared ready to leap.

Blue Raven shook sweaty locks of hair away from his oval face. He had to keep the boy talking, to shift his thoughts. "Boy? Please. What is your name? The name your family calls you by? Do you have a boy's name?"

The False Face Child did not answer.

"When I was a boy," Blue Raven said, "I had a special name. My parents called me Dancing Foot, because I was forever whirling around on one foot. They said I resembled a demented one-legged grouse." He smiled at the memories. "The other children used to cluck at me when I passed. Do you have a name like that?"

At first silence met his question, then, barely audible, came, "R-Rumbler."

"Rumbler? That's a shining name. I've never heard it before. Why did your mother call you that? Did she tell you?"

Rumbler lowered his gaze and tears fell from his eyes onto the distant floor of the council house. Tiny puffs of dust sprouted, spinning like tornadoes in the sunlight. "I like echoes."

Blue Raven smiled. "I know a wonderful canyon where the Echoers shout back and forth five times or more. I used to go there as a boy, to talk with them. Would you like to go?" He extended his hand again, leaning out as far as he could without risking doom. "I would be happy to take you. You will be surprised by the voices you hear. Each of the Spirits has a different tone of voice, like the unique sounds made by moving your fingers over the holes in a flute."

Rumbler bit his lip. After a long while, he slid his bound feet toward Blue Raven.

"Good. That's good. Don't look down."

The boy inched closer, his whole misshapen body trembling.

"Don't be frightened. You are doing well. I can almost reach you."

When the boy came within range, Blue Raven grabbed for his left hand, and Rumbler let out a small cry of pain or fear.

"I have you! It's all right."

As Blue Raven scanned the boy's wrists, he understood Kit's fatal decision. The ropes had cut deep gashes just above the boy's hands. Shadow Spirits had been feeding upon the flesh, leaving festering trails of infection. Rumbler's bound legs looked just as bad, bloody and swollen. The sight pained Blue Raven. How could two grown men do this to a child of nine winters? If they had been that frightened of this little boy, their presences shamed the Walksalong War Society! They should be driven out as cowards!

"I won't let you fall, Rumbler," he said gently. "Slide your feet closer a bit at a time, just work your way to me. I need to cut off those leg ropes."

Rumbler's black eyes narrowed, as if searching for trickery.

"I am reaching inside my cape to pull my knife from its sheath. I don't want you to be concerned. I am only going to use it to cut your bonds. Do you understand?"

Blue Raven moved slowly, lifting the gray chert knife toward Rumbler's legs. He sawed through the knot and the ropes fell away, plummeting toward the floor.

A small sigh of relief escaped Rumbler's throat.

"There," Blue Raven said. "Moving should be easier now. Come. We'll climb down and find a warm fire to sit by."

Rumbler tentatively reached out again, and Blue Raven grasped a tiny freezing hand.

"Good. Thank you, Rumbler."

As he came closer, Blue Raven slipped an arm around the boy's waist, and pulled Rumbler onto his hip.

"Hold tight as we climb down, you understand?"

The boy nodded.

Blue Raven began the descent. On the third rung, Rumbler buried his face in the folds of Blue Raven's cape, hiding his eyes.

"We are doing well," Blue Raven soothed. "Don't be afraid."

In response, Rumbler frantically groped through the opening in Blue Raven's cape and grabbed a fistful of blue shirt.

When he stepped onto solid ground, Blue Raven said, "You can look now. See? I told you we wouldn't fall," and he set Rumbler on the floor.

The boy's injured legs shook. He seemed to be trying to still the tremor by tightening his muscles, but it did little good. Finally, he spread his feet to brace himself. After several deep breaths, he bravely asked, "What will you do with me now?"

"I will take you to my longhouse. Where is your cape? Or did the warriors give you a blanket to keep you warm?"

Rumbler tucked a shaking finger into the corner of his mouth. As he sucked, an expression of solace slackened his features. Around his finger, he slurred, "I had only my shirt."

"Surely the men who captured you gave you something to wear for the long journey."

Rumbler shook his head. "They gave me nothing. No food, or water. They feared me. The second night, when we made camp, I told them I was going to kill them. After that, they didn't wish to touch me."

Blue Raven removed his own cape and draped it around Rumbler's shoulders. "They had orders to take good care of you, Rumbler. They will be punished for their foolishness. I assure you."

He tied the cape's laces beneath the boy's chin. "I think this will work." Two hands' worth of hem dragged the floor. "You might have to pull up the hem when you walk, so as not to trip over it, but at least you will be warm."

Rumbler clutched the cape, and stood silently, watching Blue Raven. Finally, in a soft voice, he said, "I grant you your life."

Blue Raven inclined his head in amused gratitude, but he felt oddly vulnerable. "I appreciate that, Rumbler. Are you ready?"

The boy turned to White Kit. He pulled a wet finger from his mouth and pointed. "She made sounds. Like the crackle of the night sky when the stars fall down.''

Blue Raven frowned. ''Her voice crackled, you mean? Yes. She had seen almost seventy winters—''

''No. Not her voice. The sound in her eyes.''

''In her eyes?''

''Yes. It was loud.''

Blue Raven cocked his head, not certain whether to laugh or be afraid. ''Do you often hear sounds in people's eyes?''

Rumbler tucked his finger back in his mouth. ''Just when the Night Walkers come.''

The hair on Blue Raven's arms prickled. The Night Walkers were the ghosts of the ancestors. Their lodges, sewn of white feathers, gleamed across the night sky. They only descended to earth to bring important messages, or to guide the dying to the Up-Above-World.

''Rumbler,'' Blue Raven said with an uneasy smile, ''I must return to my longhouse to call a council meeting. Do you wish to come with me?''

''I wish to go home.''

''This is your new home, Rumbler. But you do not have to come with me. If you wish, I will take you to stay with Matron Starflower, or—''

''My mother will be here soon.'' Rumbler craned his neck to look into Blue Raven's eyes. ''She will. She promised. And you will *all* die.''

''Rumbler, I—''

''She *is* coming for me. Lamedeer, my uncle, is helping her. They promised a long time ago. They said they would never let anyone hurt me.'' He nodded certainly. ''She's coming.''

Blue Raven stroked Rumbler's black hair. He didn't have the courage to tell the boy that both his mother and the Paint Rock war leader were probably dead by now.

''Well, while you wait for them,'' Blue Raven said,

"let me help you. You had a long journey. You must be starving and tired. First, we will feed you, then you may roll up in my buffalo hides and sleep by the fire for as long as you wish."

Blue Raven reached down and grasped Rumbler's hand. They walked from the longhouse and up the sunlit trail toward the crowd of people assembled near the hilltop. Blue Raven studied the boy, seeing him clearly for the first time. Though he had the girth of a normal child his age, his short arms and legs gave him a squat appearance. He swaggered oddly when he walked.

Grandfather Day Maker's light slanted through the trees and scattered golden triangles across their path, but Rumbler's gaze desperately roamed the forest.

"Rumbler, I wish you to know that my people, everyone in Walksalong Village, consider you very precious. We will treat you well, and you will be happy with us. I promise you this. I—"

A commotion rose on top of the hill. Blue Raven gripped the boy's hand more securely. People shouted, and several women raced away from the crowd white-faced. The rest turned like one huge many-headed animal to look directly at Blue Raven and Rumbler.

"What's happened?" Blue Raven whispered anxiously. He started up the trail at a fast walk. Rumbler trotted at his side to keep up.

"I told them."

Blue Raven glanced down. "Told who?"

"Them. Those men."

Acorn broke from the crowd and dashed down the hill. A burly man, he wore his hair in the warrior's cut of the Thornbush Clan, shaved on the sides with a bristly ridge down the middle of his skull. His buffalohide cape, curly and brown, flapped about him with each footfall.

Acorn halted a cautious thirty hands away, breathing

hard, his mouth hanging open. His panicked eyes focused on Rumbler.

"Well?" Blue Raven demanded. "What is it? What's happened?"

"Elder," he said breathlessly. "Mossybill, one of the runners who brought in the False Face Child . . . I think he's dying."

Blue Raven gaped, unable to speak for several moments, then he sputtered, "Wh-what? But why? Are you certain of this?"

A swallow went down Acorn's throat. He took a step backward. "I checked him myself. I know the face of death, Elder."

Blue Raven just stood there. Then, slowly, he looked down.

The False Face Child's white teeth shone, and his black eyes had turned bottomless, the darkness alive, moving.

"Rumbler, what—"

Bright childish laughter erupted from Rumbler's throat, and Blue Raven went rigid. The boy laughed again, his head thrown back.

"I *told* them."

# Five

At Starflower's shrill cry, Blue Raven whirled to look up the hill. She stood panting, her elderly face as white as birch bark. "Take it out of the village!" she screamed. "Get it away before it kills anyone else!"

"Matron, please," Blue Raven urged. "We know nothing yet. We mustn't make accusations before we—"

"Kill it!" Starflower's sticklike old legs started shaking so badly she had to grab onto the woman next to her to keep standing. "It is not human!" Her voice had turned hoarse. "Kill it!"

Blue Raven gripped Rumbler's hand harder. To Acorn he said, "What of Skullcap? Is he—"

"Alive," Acorn responded. "But I don't know for how long. He's very ill."

"I want you to find Bogbean. Tell her to get her Healer's bag and meet me at Beadfern's longhouse."

"Yes, Elder."

Blue Raven picked up the False Face Child, and rushed up the hill. When he reached the top, he handed the dwarf boy to Frost-in-the-Willows. "Please, Mother, take care of the boy until I've had a chance to—"

"I don't want it!" Frost-in-the-Willows lurched backward. "Get it away from me!"

"Mother, just until I've—"

"No!" She slapped at the boy.

Blue Raven pulled Rumbler back and turned to the assembly. "Who will care for the boy while I—"

"I will!" Wren said, shoving through the crowd. "You go and see about Mossybill, Uncle. I'll watch the False Face Child while you are gone."

Wren reached out hesitantly as if sticking her hand in a dark hole, and grasped Rumbler's tiny hand. She looked up at Blue Raven with terrified eyes, but she didn't let go.

"Thank you, Wren." Blue Raven set the boy on the ground, and touched Wren's cheek in pride. "Take him to our longhouse. I'll send four warriors with you. I will be there shortly."

"Yes, Uncle."

Blue Raven pointed to four of the older warriors and they fell in around Wren.

She started off fast, then slowed her steps to match Rumbler's shorter stride. He could hear Wren talking to the boy, her voice shaking.

Blue Raven shouldered past the onlookers and hurried for the gate in the palisade, then trotted across the plaza toward old Beadfern's longhouse, Mossybill's wife's grandmother. The entire village followed behind him, their shuffling feet like the hissing of cougars.

The longhouse sat at the opposite edge of the village, near the northern palisade gate, and the trail that led down to Pipe Stem Lake. Five shadblow trees, ten times the height of a man, created a half-moon behind the house. The short branches formed narrow round-topped heads. Birds perched in the trees, their feathers fluffed for warmth, but none dared chirp with the frenzy in the village below. Several young people and children huddled together outside the longhouse.

Blue Raven walked to the door curtain and called, "Beadfern? It's Blue Raven. May I enter?"

"Yes! Come!"

Blue Raven stepped into the house. The stench nearly overpowered him, sickly sweet, like a mixture of vomit and long-dried urine. A single fire burned in the middle of the floor, and six people crouched around it, their taut faces gleaming orange. Old Beadfern watched Blue Raven with wide eyes. Near her, two bodies lay covered with hides. Four men and one woman knelt beside the closest man, holding him down while he thrashed and groaned. Only one person sat beside the other man.

Blue Raven strode forward. "What happened?"

Mossybill let out a hoarse cry when he saw Blue Raven, and strings of saliva flew from his mouth. He struggled to sit up, but the four muscular warriors holding his arms and legs forced him down. His wife, Loon, threw herself across Mossybill's chest, clawing at his arms, weeping. "Talk to me! Mossybill, tell me what happened!"

Mossybill's glazed eyes darted feverishly, but kept coming back to Blue Raven's face. He gnashed his teeth, and tossed his head from side to side, as if trying to speak.

Blue Raven knelt by Mossybill's shoulder. "It's all right, Mossybill." He tried to soothe the man. "Bogbean is coming with her Healer's bag. She'll be here soon, but we need to know what made you ill, Mossybill. The boy said—"

Mossybill shook his head violently, as if the mention of the False Face Child terrified him. Blue Raven glanced at Loon. "Has he said anything?"

She pressed a hand to her lips to still their trembling, and nodded. "Yes. When he staggered into the longhouse, he said, 'The boy! The boy!' That's all. Then he collapsed on the floor, and I covered him with hides, and sent Acorn for you."

"Good. That's what you should have done. I only wish he'd—"

Mossybill lurched against the hands that held him, and snarled like a beast.

Blue Raven tried again. "Mossybill, if you can, tell me about the boy. Did he—"

The scream that erupted from Mossybill's throat made Blue Raven sit back. Loon started sobbing. Mossybill fought with all his strength, writhing and twisting. Garbled words accompanied the foam that dripped from his jaws: "Boy! Boy!"

"Mossybill," Blue Raven said, "did the False Face

Child do something to you? Poison you? Wound you? What—''

As if his strength had suddenly failed, Mossybill went limp. His head thumped the floor.

''Mossybill?'' Loon whispered. She leaned over him. *''Mossybill?''*

Blue Raven studied the man's chest. It still rose and fell. ''He's alive, Loon. Let him rest.''

Tears streamed down Loon's face, but she nodded. ''Yes. Of course.''

Blue Raven rose and went to kneel beside Skullcap, who lay on his side, his black hair shielding his face. To Skullcap's wife, Pretty Shield, he said, ''How is he?''

Young, with a round face, hooked nose, and full lips, she reminded Blue Raven of a bobcat with an eagle's beak. She'd plaited her long hair into a thick braid that hung over her shoulder. Her blue dress bore the faded red images of Mouse and Vole.

''I do not know, Elder,'' Pretty Shield answered. ''He crawled into his hides as soon as he entered the long-house. He has been asleep ever since. I tried to wake him, but . . .''

Blue Raven placed two fingers against the large artery in Skullcap's throat. The heartbeat fluttered weakly, but it was there.

Blue Raven let his hand drop. ''Let me know if he wakes, or if his condition changes. I must return to my longhouse to take care of the False Face Child, but I want you to send for me if Skullcap starts showing any signs of the same illness that afflicts Mossybill.''

''Yes, Elder, I will.''

Blue Raven rose, took a deep breath, and walked down the length of the house. He ducked outside into a milling crowd of over a hundred. Starflower met him at the door, gripped his arm, and tugged him toward her.

"What is it, Matron?"

"Is he dead?"

"No. He's alive."

"And Skullcap?"

"He seems to be sleeping."

Starflower's fingers bit into Blue Raven's arm. "The False Face Child must leave the village. Do you hear me? You must take it away before we are all dead!"

"Where, Matron?" he asked in exasperation. "Where shall I take him?"

Starflower thought for a moment, then blurted, "Stake it out at the roots of the Sunshine Boy! Let the False Face stare up into the golden eyes of its own death!" Starflower whirled to face the assembly. "Hear me! *No one* must go near him! We will wait until Jumping Badger returns, then we will convene a full village meeting!"

Blue Raven's veins warmed. The Sunshine Boy was a mutant Spirit, half his body dead, the other half alive. He inhabited an ancient oak south of Walksalong Village. All natural illnesses and deaths came from the Sunshine Boy.

Blue Raven found Acorn in the crowd and gestured for him to come forward. When Acorn arrived, Blue Raven said, "I will get the False Face Child, and take him to the Sunshine Boy. Please gather rope and meet me there."

"Yes, Elder."

Two guards had stationed themselves at either end of the longhouse. They stood with their arms crossed over their broad chests, and hatchets in their hands. Bows and quivers draped their shoulders. Grandmother Frost-in-the-Willows had refused to enter the house with the False Face Child inside. Bogbean had come in, ransacked her space for her Healer's bag, then left at a run.

Wren placed another stick of wood on the fire. The False Face Child sat next to her, his knees drawn up. His black eyes stared unblinking at the low flames. When sparks popped and flitted, he did not stir. He seemed to see nothing.

"Would you like a cup of tea?" she asked, forcing a strength into her voice that she did not feel.

He didn't answer.

"My grandmother mixes currants with plums and dries them. The tea is tasty."

Around the winter fires, the elders told stories about sacred dwarfs, but she'd never seen one until now. And never imagined them to be children. In all the stories, the dwarfs were adults doing wondrous deeds, healing the sick, afflicting the wicked, leading their clans to great victories. Could such a small stunted child truly be a sacred being? It didn't seem possible.

"I know you can talk," she said. "I heard you earlier."

Wren inspected his stubby arms and legs. They were half the length of hers, and she wondered why Power had stunted them. Were there things he could do better with short arms and legs? Things that had to do with the Spirits? Wren silently contemplated this. From what Uncle Blue Raven had told her, Power often required shamans to perform tasks that ordinary people found impossible. Perhaps the rope ladder that led into the skyworlds had really narrow rungs? Or maybe the entryway stood only six hands tall?

Wren tapped the False Face Child on the shoulder. When he turned to face her, she said, "I've heard there are monsters who ride the backs of the Cloud Giants. Big ones, with teeth as long as sycamores are tall. My people say that those monsters like to eat holy people journeying to the Up-Above-World. Is that why Power made you small? So you would be harder to spot?''

The boy's lips parted slightly, revealing his teeth.

''I—I was just wondering,'' she said.

Wren picked up a stick and turned over the biggest log in the pit. Sap boiled and sizzled on the underside, and a curious blue-green flame licked up. Wren threw her stick in on top of it.

''What did you do to Mossybill and Skullcap? Shoot Spirit arrows into their bodies to kill their souls?''

The boy turned away.

''I never liked either one of them,'' she admitted. ''Mossybill used to whip me with willow switches when I was little.'' She glanced at his injured wrists. ''Did he hurt you?''

The boy looked at her, and she could see the answer in his eyes.

The revelation had a curious impact on Wren. She felt suddenly indignant. The boy had many bruises on his face, but his wrists and ankles looked the worst. They oozed bloody pus.

She pointed. ''Did Mossybill tie the ropes that cut you?''

His head moved in a barely perceptible nod.

''He loves ropes,'' she said. ''I had a friend once, named Marmot. Mossybill found her sneaking some walnuts from his cache—you know, we'd all been out in the grove picking up nuts, and Mossybill had scooped up a big pile for himself. Mossybill took Marmot out into the forest, tied her to a tree and left her there all night. That was during the Moon of Brown Leaves. It was very cold.''

The False Face Child wet his lips, and whispered, "Did she die?"

"No, but Marmot's parents were crazy with fear that night. They didn't know where she was, or what had happened to her. Mossybill didn't tell them until the next morning. He said he'd left her tied to a walnut tree as punishment for stealing."

"But she—she just took a few nuts, didn't she?"

"Yes, but her parents were upset with her anyway. That's why her father didn't kill Mossybill. It ruined their friendship, though. And poor Marmot. Her hands never worked right after that. She said that Mossybill had tied the ropes so tightly it had damaged her joints."

The False Face Child raised his hands and flexed his fingers. The wounds broke open and blood trickled down his forearms.

Wren flinched. "When I was five or six, I used to wish the Thunderbirds would whack him with a bolt of lightning."

Tears sparkled in the boy's eyes, and he suddenly looked very vulnerable. His mouth quivered.

Wren bravely reached out and took his hand. "Are you sure you aren't hungry? We have some rabbit stew left from last night. It has dried onions in it, and corn flour."

Voices rose outside the longhouse, and Wren turned when Uncle Blue Raven pulled back the door curtain and stepped inside. Both guards flanked him. He came straight to Wren and crouched at her side, but his eyes were on the boy. Wind had tangled his long hair, spreading it over his shoulders in knots of gray and black.

"How is he?"

Wren got on her knees. "I think he's all right, Uncle. I tried to get him to eat or drink something, but he didn't want to."

Uncle Blue Raven's soft brown eyes tightened.

"Please, Rumbler, eat something. Quickly, before I have to take you away."

"Take him away?" Wren asked. "Where to?"

"Matron Starflower ordered that he be staked out at the roots of the Sunshine Boy—"

Wren felt herself pale.

"—until Jumping Badger returns and we can convene a village council meeting. She's also decreed that no one may go near the boy until that time." Uncle Blue Raven held out a hand to the False Face Child. "Try to eat something, Rumbler."

The boy didn't move.

Uncle Blue Raven rose, walked around the fire, and pulled Rumbler to his feet.

"I'll return soon, Wren. Please help your grandmother while I am away. You are braver than she is."

"But Uncle, don't you remember? I have to . . . I—I promised . . ."

Uncle Blue Raven strode past her, and vanished through the door.

# Six

Wren's deerhide cape whispered against the brush as she sneaked down the winding game trail behind Uncle Blue Raven and the False Face Child. Wind Mother had been blowing all day, her frigid breath tumbling old leaves through the cloudy sky, and spitting snowflakes. Hair loosened from Wren's braid and tangled with her eye-lashes. She anxiously brushed it away.

A chill always ate at her stomach when she came here. The Sunshine Boy moved with the silence of hawk's shadow, stalking the sick or the weak. If he sneaked inside someone, they withered and died. She'd seen it happen.

Stopping at a high point, Wren scanned her backtrail to make certain no one had seen her, then silently stepped into a dense stand of pines. She tiptoed forward several paces, before breaking into a run. If she hurried, she might make it there ahead of Uncle Blue Raven—and she needed to. She had promised Trickster she would come today.

Many people and animals lay buried beneath the Sunshine Boy's spreading limbs, including her own best friend. As she climbed a small hill, she saw Trickster's grave. The dirt had sunken into the hole, leaving a shallow depression at the base of the massive twisted oak. Just seeing it made her heart pound.

She felt around in her cape pocket for the gift she'd brought, then raced down the hill.

Before she had made ten paces, though, she glimpsed Uncle Blue Raven and the False Face Child entering the meadow. He was moving faster than she'd thought. Wren leaped behind a fallen log, praying she had not been seen. After Matron Starflower's warning, if she were caught, she would be grinding corn and hauling water for the rest of her life.

Scents of damp wood and frozen dirt encircled her. Her uncle walked like a man going to his own execution, his steps quick, but deliberate, leading the child toward the Sunshine Boy. The False Face Child swaggered along with his eyes on the trees that bordered the meadow. Just before they reached the oak, Acorn came sprinting down the trail behind them with a coil of rope in his hands.

It took almost no time. The men made the little boy lie down, tied his hands and feet, then staked his feet down. Next, they drew the boy's bound hands over his head, and staked them, too.

Acorn hastily backed away, wiping his palms on his red shirt as if to rid himself of the boy's feel. Uncle Blue Raven, however, knelt and spread his cape over Rumbler. He said something Wren could not hear, and the False Face Child laughed again, a high-pitched unearthly sound that made Wren's whole body sting.

He hadn't laughed like that in the longhouse—thank the Spirits.

She had not realized until this moment what a brave man Uncle Blue Raven must be. When he rose from the boy's side, he did not even seem to be shaking. He heaved a breath that condensed into a white cloud before him, and turned to walk up the trail beside Acorn.

Wren waited until they'd disappeared into the trees, then stared at Rumbler.

Wind Mother tousled his black hair around his plump face, and tugged at the edges of the cape that covered him. He was staring wide-eyed at the Sunshine Boy. The oak's right half had been charred black by a lightning strike, and in the spring the burned limbs appeared eerie beside the green leaves that covered the left half. Wren wondered if the False Face Child could see the terrible Spirit Boy with sunshine eyes who lived in the tree. The Walksalong elders said that only those with great Power could look directly into the sacred boy's blinding eyes.

Wren gathered her courage. Trickster's grave rested about twenty hands from the False Face's bound feet.

*I'm coming, Trickster.*

She checked the trail again, making sure no one saw her, then ran across the snowy meadow. The False Face

Child's black eyes glinted when he saw her coming.

She walked directly to Trickster's grave.

"It's me, Trickster," she whispered. Snow had begun to fill the depression.

The False Face Child shifted to keep his eyes on her.

Wren knelt beside the grave. "I have been worried about you, Trickster. Are you warm enough? It's such a cold day."

She brushed the snow from the hole, and sighed. The hurt that lived in her souls reared. After the deaths of her parents and brother, Trickster had been her only friend. He'd slept with her at night, keeping her warm, licking her face when she'd cried. Trickster had made her grief bearable.

"Is it a dog?" the False Face Child whispered. "A dead dog?"

Wren's throat tightened. "He was my best friend."

"I had a dog," the boy said softly. "He's dead, too."

Wren swallowed hard as she looked at the shallow depression. She knew exactly how he lay in the grave. With her eyes, she traced the point of his nose, down his back and around his tail. He had two black spots on his forehead, which looked like an extra pair of eyes. Among her people, such dogs were believed to have special Powers. Trickster had been a great hunter. He always picked up the scent of game before any other dog in the village, and he could keep a bear or cougar treed all day.

"I'm sorry, Trickster," she said. "I still love you."

"Why are you sorry?" the False Face asked. "Did you strike him down?"

Wren did not answer. She should not even be here, and definitely should not speak with the boy, not after Matron Starflower had screamed orders against it. But more than that, it hurt to talk about Trickster's death.

It had happened so fast. Trickster had been playing in

the snow all day, romping with the other village dogs, until that afternoon his nose and ears had grown fiery hot. Throughout the long night, Trickster had lain in Wren's lap, gazing up with watery eyes, occasionally wagging his tail at the sound of Wren's concerned voice.

She had fought to stay awake, to keep watch so that the Sunshine Boy couldn't sneak past and steal Trickster's wavering soul. Then, suddenly, in the middle of the night, Trickster had wakened her, barking three times—his signal to Wren that he'd scented an intruder. Wren had swung around to peer at the fluttering door curtain. By the time she'd turned back, it was too late. The Sunshine Boy was already inside him. Trickster had looked up at Wren, not with love, not to say goodbye, but with sadness and surprise, as if Wren had betrayed him by falling asleep and letting the Sunshine Boy enter. As the soul-light drained from Trickster's eyes, Wren had started shaking him with all her might, trying to dislodge the Sunshine Boy. Then she'd started screaming. She remembered because her grandmother had slapped her to make her stop.

The False Face shifted to see the grave. "My dog's name was Stonecoat."

Wren's mouth pressed into a tight line. She really ought to obey at least one of Matron Starflower's prohibitions.

Wren dug around in her cape pocket, and drew out the gift she'd brought. "Look, Trickster. I found it behind a stack of baskets." She held the stick out to her friend. Both ends had been heavily chewed. "Remember how we used to play with this? You would growl and leap, trying to tug it away from me?" Gently, she laid the toy on the frozen ground over Trickster's nose. "I was afraid the ghosts in the Up-Above-World might not know you loved such things."

Snow began to fall heavily. Huge white flakes pirouetted from the sky, coating the surrounding rolling hills, and melting on Wren's long braid. The land became so silent when it snowed. Birds sat hunched in the trees, looking miserable, while wisps of cloud scudded just above the treetops.

She tucked her hands inside her cape and let out a breath. "I gave some of your jerky to Black Nose. I hope you do not mind, Trickster. He was hungry. You know what a hard winter it's been. All the raiding has left people frightened. No one wishes to share a bite with a puppy."

The raiding had been going on for many winters, since long before Wren's birth. Her grandmother said that the Turtle people—the False Face Child's people—deserved destruction because they were ignorant and dirty. Wren did not know how she could say that. Or how anyone could deserve to die. She fumbled with the stick. Trickster hadn't deserved it.

"Something's wrong with my mother," the False Face Child whispered, "I don't know what. She promised me she would come, but"—his eyes scanned the trees again—"she hasn't."

Thoughtlessly, Wren said, "She's probably dead."

The boy's black eyes seemed to expand. "Why do you say that? Is that what it means, when the echoes die?"

"Echoes?" She swiveled to peer at him. "What echoes?"

"Of my mother's heartbeat. I have always heard them, even before I was born."

"A person can't remember things from before they were born. You did not even have a human soul then."

That's why newborns could be left out to die on Lost Hill when a Starving came upon the people. Some souls had to be returned to the earth, so that the clan might survive. Better a newborn child with only one animal soul, than an adult with two souls. The second soul, the human soul, came to a person at about age four. Everybody knew that!

"But I do remember," the False Face Child said.

Wren tenderly petted the frozen dirt over Trickster, letting his closeness soothe her fears. After a pause, she added, "My mother is dead, too. So are my father and brother."

The False Face Child strained to lift himself to look into her eyes. "How did they die?"

"There was a storm on the lake. Their canoe tipped over. They drowned." How peculiar that she could recite the event without even the slightest hesitation, as if it had been someone else's heart that had shattered and blown away like old leaves.

Rumbler let his head slowly fall to the snowy ground. "Are their echoes gone from inside you?"

Wren wondered about that. Sometimes she had trouble recalling what their voices sounded like, and it terrified her. Is that what he meant? "I don't know. I . . . I guess so."

Sobs puffed the False Face Child's chest. "Then maybe my mother is dead."

Wren let her finger trace the place where Trickster's pointed ears rested beneath the soil. The boy's cries clawed at her heart, sounding very much like her own eight moons ago. At least she'd had Uncle Blue Raven and Trickster to comfort her. This boy had no one.

"She can't be dead!" the boy sobbed. "She promised she would never leave me!"

"Well, you are a False Face, aren't you? Can't you bring her back with your Spirit Powers?"

"I don't have those kinds of Powers!"

"How do you know? Have you tried?" Wren asked.

"We have a story about a very old dwarf named Hungry Eyes. He could bring ghosts back from the Up-Above-World. He snared them, carried them home in a rawhide bag, and tied them to their bodies again."

"And the people came alive?"

"Yes. You may not be old enough to soul-fly yet, but I suppose that same Power lives inside you. Even if it doesn't, you're no worse off for trying."

He squeezed his eyes closed, and cried. Like every other stolen child who had ever come to Walksalong Village, he looked lost and hopeless.

"Thank you," he croaked, "for talking."

Wren lifted a shoulder. As she began scooping snow over Trickster's grave, covering him and his favorite toy, she said, "I have to go, Rumbler. Matron Starflower said that no one was supposed to come near you. If she catches me here, I'll be punished."

Rumbler gazed back toward Walksalong Village, which hid beyond the low pine-whiskered hill to his left. Blue smoke curled above the treetops. He frowned, apparently seeing something that Wren did not, and Wren's chest prickled. She got to her feet.

"What's wrong?" she asked.

"I will have to learn to fly fast." He breathed the words. "Your people are going to kill me."

"How do you know? We have had no council meeting yet."

Rumbler twisted his wrists against his bonds, and Wren saw the blood that dripped onto the fresh snow. Pain laced his expression. "I know."

Wren started to back away. But stopped. Rumbler was biting his lip to hold back his tears. She did not know why she did it, but she walked forward and knelt beside the Power child.

"It's going to be a bitter day," she said. "And tonight

will be worse. I can smell a bad storm on Wind Mother's breath.''

She tucked the edges of Uncle Blue Raven's cape securely beneath him, so it wouldn't blow loose. "Try not to roll around too much."

Rumbler's mouth opened, as if to thank her, but he whispered, "If you see my mother, will you tell her where I am?"

"Well . . . I don't know. That would get me into a lot of trouble.''

"I know, but will you?"

"But I—I don't even know what she looks like.''

"She is short, and thin, with long black hair and eyes the color of a buffalo's undercoat. She has my father's image, a green tree, tattooed on her forehead.''

Wren chewed her lip, trying to imagine how she'd feel if their positions were reversed, if she were the one staked out in the snow by an enemy people.

"All right, Rumbler. If I see her, I'll tell her you are here. But you can't tell anyone I did it.''

Rumbler smiled weakly, and Wren found herself smiling back. When she realized it, fear, like cold hands, gripped her throat. Blessed Spirits, if anyone found out what she'd just said, she would be flayed alive!

Turning, she walked across the meadow until she was out of his sight.

Then she ran as if wicked Spirits were diving at her head.

A little boy's cries . . .

Crowfire staggered to a stop. The cries echoed through the forest, circling him like playing falcons, sometimes loud enough to make him jump and spin around. At other times, they toyed with his souls, whispering and taunting.

"Who are you?" he shouted.

His gaze searched the glistening world. A doe stood perfectly still fifty hands away, her eyes shining like white shells, but he saw no people.

"Hallowed Spirits, has the fever stolen my wits?"

He reached for the boulder that thrust up to his left and braced his hand. Snow spun out of the ashen sky, the flakes frosting the trees, and blanketing the well-worn trail. Grandfather Day Maker had risen over a hand of time ago, but his gleam barely penetrated the clouds. This *was* the right trail. Crowfire had run it dozens of times. Matron Dust Moon always placed her village somewhere along this trail, perhaps two or three days to the east or west, but . . .

Why hadn't he reached Earth Thunderer Village yet?

He scooped a handful of snow from the boulder and put it in his mouth. The crystals tasted cool, blessedly cool.

"I cannot be lost," he whispered to the doe. "I know this trail!" She flicked her ears at him, and trotted into the trees. Twigs snapped in her wake.

At the base of the hill, a lightning-riven black stump stood. He remembered it.

He had been here with Lamedeer not more than four moons ago. Lamedeer . . . oh, Lamedeer.

Emotion choked Crowfire. He'd never known what to think about the man. Crowfire had seen five winters when Lamedeer murdered his own father for witchcraft. The fact had always left Crowfire uncertain and fearful—but Lamedeer had saved Crowfire.

He looked down at his bandaged leg. The arrow had pierced the bone just above his ankle as he'd scrambled over the crest of the bluff, but Crowfire had kept running, dashing through the forest like a madman. The first night, he'd taken his knife and tried to cut the stone point out, but it had lodged in the bone. Two nights later, the swelling had outgrown his pant leg. He'd slit the deerhide to the knee, then all the way to his hip. With every breath he took now, he could smell the taint of Shadow Spirits feeding upon his flesh. Their foulness overpowered the tangs of wet bark and dirt.

. . . Laughter wove through the trees.

"Who's there?" Crowfire shouted. "Who are you? Why do you not show yourself?"

He examined every shadow, every odd color, then he bowed his head and shook it.

For three nights voices had been speaking to him, whirling out of the air. Once, he'd heard his grandmother calling his name over and over, and followed it through the forest. Later, when he remembered that she'd been dead for more than ten winters, terror had gripped him.

A freezing gust blasted through the oaks and maples, and whipped black hair around Crowfire's face. He fought to stay on his feet.

*"Hurry!"* the child called. *"I'm over here!"*

"Who are you!"

Snow blew along the forest trails, twisting and leaping. Crowfire limped forward, the pain in his leg throbbing through his entire body. He feared that if he sat down to rest, he might not be able to rise again.

*"This way! This way!"*

Crowfire slipped on ice, and his feet skidded out from under him. A hoarse cry of agony escaped his throat when he struck the ground. Lungs panting for air, he longed to weep.

"Blessed ancestors," he whispered. When he struggled to sit up, blurs of sky, forest, and ground swirled sickeningly.

*"Stop being lazy! I'm this way! Come this way."*

A fuzzy form stood no more than seven paces away. Crowfire rubbed his eyes. It looked like a . . . a boy. One of the Paint Rock children?

Crowfire yelled, "Do I know you, boy? Did you escape the Paint Rock massacre? Come here! I need help!"

The child didn't move, and Crowfire dug his fingers into the trail and hauled himself forward. Snow mounded before him, freezing his bare hands and packing the front of his shirt.

The boy skipped away down the trail.

"Wait. Wait! Boy? Bring help! Do you hear? Bring someone to help me!" At the top of his lungs, he screamed, "For the sake of Falling Woman, I'm wounded!"

The apparition vanished into a twisting wreath of snow.

Crowfire dropped his forehead onto his hands. He longed to give in to the cold and exhaustion. If he could just sleep for a day, perhaps the swelling would go down.

Snow crunched.

*"Who is he?"* a woman asked.

"I do not know, Planter," a man answered. "But I recognize the markings on his clothing. He's from Paint Rock Village."

Crowfire looked up.

He had never seen the young woman, but he knew the old man. Long white hair framed that deeply wrinkled face, highlighting the elder's broad cheekbones and the curve of his hooked nose. Intense eyes peered into Crowfire's.

"Silver Sparrow? You . . . you are, aren't you?"

The old man knelt. He nodded solemnly. "I am. Who are you?"

"Oh, gods." Tears tightened his throat. "Silver Sparrow, Lamedeer sent me. To tell you that you were right. Jumping Badger stole the False Face Child.'' He mustered his last strength to reach out to the old man. Silver Sparrow took his hand in a strong grip. ''Lamedeer is dead. Just as you Dreamed. He's dead!''

The old man's fingers tightened around Crowfire's. ''When did it happen?''

''I—I am not certain . . . of anything. I—''

''What is your name, warrior?''

''Crowfire,'' he said and his strength vanished in a rush. He sprawled face first into the snow, sobbing like a child.

A warm hand gripped him by the shoulder and rolled him to his back; then fingers brushed the snow from his face. ''You are safe now, Crowfire,'' Silver Sparrow said, his voice strong and comforting. ''If anyone wishes to hurt you, they will have to face me to do it.''

Blue Raven heard Wren step into the council house, breathing hard, as if she'd been running, but he did not turn.

He concentrated on the blood that marked the hard-packed dirt. He had checked Kit's body just after her stricken family had carried her home to prepare her for burial, and had seen that Rumbler had not killed her. At least not with the knife. The blade had struck a rib and been deflected, that's why almost no blood soaked the floor.

''Did you hear?'' she asked. ''As I was coming across the plaza, people were talking about it.''

''Yes. I heard.''

Mossybill, and Skullcap too, had died little more than half a hand of time ago.

Wren sat down cross-legged beside him. "Do you think the False Face Child did it?"

Blue Raven glanced at her. Snowflakes dotted her hair. A generally pretty child, she had dazzling eyes. Large and dark, with long curling lashes. For the past eight moons Blue Raven had tried to be father, mother, and brother to her—and done a poor job of it. He had never married, and knew little about children, especially girls. But he was all that Wren had. The Spirits knew his own mother cared little about her granddaughter. Frost-in-the-Willows had always found children tiresome. As a boy, Blue Raven had hated her for that. But he had learned acceptance over the long winters; it was just her way.

He pointed to the blood. "How much blood do you imagine it would take to make a spot this size?"

Wren extended a dirty hand to cover the spot. "It's smaller than my palm," she said. "A horn spoon would contain more blood."

Blue Raven nodded. "Yet Matron Starflower said that Rumbler stabbed White Kit in the heart."

Wren's dark brows drew together over her pointed nose. "If he had, the floor would be drenched in blood, wouldn't it? I have seen many deer shot through the heart with an arrow. They bled a lot."

"Yes. I fear that Starflower did not really see what happened. She saw Rumbler stab Kit, then, when Kit fell and did not rise, Starflower assumed the worst. It is what I would have assumed. Wouldn't you?"

Wren touched the blood spot and hastily wiped her hand on her cape. "I would have been very scared, Uncle. I don't know what I would have thought."

"Starflower was scared, too. That's why she did not

run to examine Kit. I suspect she was too frightened to move.''

''Did you examine Kit's wound?''

''I did. The knife did not penetrate. It struck a rib, then Rumbler dropped the weapon and fled.''

Wren used her finger to draw an irregular circle around the blood. ''But Kit is dead.''

''Yes. I cannot say why. Yet.''

The snow on Wren's hair had melted, leaving shining beads of water to net her head. ''Have you examined Mossybill and Skullcap?''

''That is my next task.''

Wren leaped to her feet excitedly. ''May I go with you? I would like to—''

''No.''

Her face fell. ''But—''

''No, Wren. The families of the dead will be torn with grief, and saying many things they do not mean. It is not a time for outsiders. As Headman, I must go. It is my duty to try to understand what happened here today. If I did not have to, I would leave them to navigate their sorrows by themselves.'' He gestured to the door. ''Besides, don't you have a Teaching this afternoon with Bogbean? I heard her say this morning that she would be showing you how to make wooden bowls.''

Wren's shoulders slumped. ''I truly hate her Teachings, Uncle. She doesn't like me. She always asks me questions I can't answer, and the other children laugh at me.''

Blue Raven rose to his feet and propped his hands on his hips. ''That tells me that you are not listening very carefully, Wren. You must learn these things, for your own good, as well as the good of our clan. What would happen if our village was attacked and you were the only one left to care for the sick and injured? If you soul-float during all of your Teachings, you will not be able to help them. They will die, and whose fault do you imagine it will be?''

Wren scuffed the toe of her moccasin against the floor. "The person's who shot them."

Blue Raven's mouth quirked.

"I'm sorry, Uncle," Wren said. "I will try. I promise. But will you tell me later what you find out about Mossybill and Skullcap? I wish to know if the False Face Child is a murderer."

Blue Raven caught an odd undercurrent in her voice. "Do you have a special reason?"

"Well, it's just that he does not seem wicked to me, Uncle. That's all."

"You did not see him for more than a finger of time, Wren. He may . . ." When red mottled her cheeks, Blue Raven's brows lowered. *"Did you?"*

"Uncle, I . . . Do you remember that I promised Trickster I would go to visit him today?"

"Blessed Falling Woman!" he shouted. "Despite three deaths, and Matron Starflower's orders, you—"

"I *had* to! Trickster called to me in my dreams last night, and I promised!"

Tears moistened her eyes, and Blue Raven bit off his next words. Though their people ate dogs on special occasions, they also kept them as cherished pets. Many of their sacred stories were about great heroic dogs who had saved humans from destruction. Wren had loved Trickster. For three moons after the death of her mother—his sister—Blue Raven's own grief had prevented him from truly caring for Wren. Only Trickster had comforted her.

Blue Raven put a hand on her back. "You could have been injured, or worse, Wren. How do you think that would have made me feel? You are the warmth that keeps my heart beating. I could not bear to lose you.

Please do not go there again. Not until we know more about the False Face Child.'' He guided her toward the door, slowing his steps to match hers.

When they came out into the cold wind, Blue Raven unhooked the door curtain and let it fall closed behind him. Almost three fingers of snow had fallen in the past hand of time, and he suspected there would be much more before nightfall.

''Did the False Face Child say anything to you, Wren?''

''No,'' she answered, then apparently thought better of it, and added, ''Well, he—he said he thinks something is wrong with his mother.''

Blue Raven started up the trail toward the village with Wren beside him. Snowflakes whirled about them as they walked, as silent as delicate white feathers. ''And what did you say?''

After a long pause, she replied, ''I told him she was probably dead. But I wish I hadn't, Uncle. He cried. He cried hard. Just like a human boy.''

Blue Raven rested his hand on top of her head. Though she exasperated him by questioning every order he, or anyone else, gave her, she also spent a good deal of time thinking about the world around her. She would make a fine village matron one day, as his sister would have, if she'd lived. ''Remember that tomorrow, Wren, when you are asked to cast your voice in council.''

''I will, Uncle.''

He patted her black hair. ''Now, tell me about Trickster. What did you take him today? Another bone? Or a toy?''

She tipped her head to smile up at him. ''A toy. Do you remember the oak stick he loved so much? I found it behind a basket. I was afraid the Night Walkers might not understand about dog toys. Do you think they do?''

Blue Raven smiled. "I think so. But I'm glad you took it."

Wren turned and abruptly hugged him around the waist. "Thank you for not yelling at me, Uncle. I love you."

A huge hand seemed to tighten around his heart. He smiled. "I love you, too, Wren."

# Seven

As late afternoon changed to evening, cold wind gusted across the plaza and assaulted the fire in front of Little Wren. Ashes and smoke blew into her face. She wiped her eyes, and lowered her half-finished wooden bowl to her lap. The sweet scent of burning hickory encircled her. The two other girls, Dark Wind and Vine, who knelt across the fire, lifted their bowls to shield their faces. Firelight flickered on the rough-hewn bowl bottoms.

Building thunderheads promised more storms, but for now twilight cast pale light over the people who sat around the plaza fires. To Wren's right, a group of eleven old women huddled together, including Bogbean. Bogbean had finished her Teaching about wooden bowls, and left the girls to work while she tended her own duties, making cordage from the soft inner bark of the basswood tree. Bogbean's silver head glinted in the wavering gleam of the flames. She wore a brightly painted leather cape, covered with seashells and stitched with blue porcupine quills. The old women's laughter rang through the village. When finished, the finer cordage would be woven into scarfs, collars, and bracelets. The coarser cordage would become mats, and hanging baskets. To her left, about twenty men, mostly the very young and the very old, stood in a circle. Nearly every man of warring age, and many women, had accompanied Jumping Badger on the raid. Those who had remained were supposed to guard Walksalong Village, but like these loungers they generally spent their time boasting about war parties they'd been on, or raids they hoped to make.

Wren wondered at that. Uncle Blue Raven had been a renowned warrior, but he spoke little about his exploits, preferring, he said, to keep the terrors locked in his own souls. Yet many warriors swelled with pride during such discussions, as though the killings had been the greatest accomplishments of their lives. Her people valued bravery and battle skills, but they also cherished humility. Wren did not understand why someone would wish to boast about slaying another human being, or to recount the manners in which the enemies had died. It seemed somehow cruel to her.

"Well, I think the boy is wicked," Dark Wind said as she lowered her bowl. "When the instant comes to cast my voice, that is what I will say."

Tall and skinny, Dark Wind had her hair greased into a bun on the crown of her head. She was the prettiest girl in the village, with an oval face, broad cheekbones, and eyes the color of a golden eagle's feathers. Though in her thirteenth winter, and not yet a woman, she smiled at every boy who passed.

Wren said, "You mean you have already decided your voice, sister? Before you have heard the telling of the stories?"

In the Bear Nation, all women in a longhouse were called "mother," or "grandmother," and they might address any child as "my son," or "my daughter." In the same way, boys and girls often affectionately called each other "brother" or "sister."

"I already know the stories, Wren. I have listened to the things said by the families. They live in my long-house."

Vine, Dark Wind's best friend, snickered. She did not see very well, and was forever running into people. Pudgy, squinting, and round-faced, with two big front teeth, she resembled a fat squirrel. Her black hair hung to just below her ears. "Your uncle is not the only one with ears, Little Wren. I have heard the tales, too."

Wren held her tongue. Her uncle had taught her not to speak at all if anger touched her heart. She set her wooden bowl on the ground, next to her tools: a granite hammerstone, an antler punch, and a large gray chert scraper. Aspens rotted from the inside out, leaving a layer of hard wood around the punky decay. Once cleaned and fire-hardened, the pale wood made a beautiful container.

"Did your ears die last night, Wren?" Dark Wind taunted. "Everyone has been discussing the murders. How could you not have heard the whispers in your long-house?"

"Oh, I heard them, sister," Wren answered as she picked up her antler punch and hammerstone. Positioning the sharp antler tip against the rotten wood, as Bogbean had shown her, she pounded the top of the punch with her hammerstone. The punky wood chipped loose, and Wren dumped it onto the fire. Flames leaped and crackled. "I just do not listen to fools."

Dark Wind stiffened. "Are you calling me a fool!"

"Only if you listened."

Vine's slitted eyes went back and forth between her best friend and Little Wren, as if waiting for them to waste their words on each other before leaping. She was such a coward.

Dark Wind said, "You act just like a man, Little Wren. You appreciate neither words nor emotions. The death of your mother has stunted your growth."

Wren couldn't help it. Her eyes flooded.

Her interests *were* different. Even her mother had said so. Where other children dreamed of marriage and gaining status within the clan, Wren longed to run off adventuring. Last moon she had actually spoken with Uncle Blue Raven about studying the ways of the Trader. Her mother had suggested the profession to her, though few girls wanted to become Traders. The occupation held many dangers, but the smells and sights of distant places called to Wren. Uncle Blue Raven had given her his tentative approval, but told her that she would have to discuss it with her grandmother. Wren hadn't worked up the courage yet, but would.

Dark Wind smiled. "Why don't you try acting like a woman, even if it does not come naturally to you? It would certainly make you more acceptable to the other girls in the village."

Vine nodded, and said, "That's true, Wren. I don't see why you can't—"

"Of course not, Vine. You can't see more than two paces in front of your nose." Wren wiped her tears with the back of her hand. "As for acting like a woman, I am not a woman, and neither are you, Dark Wind."

"Well," Dark Wind said with finality, "nobody likes you."

The words stung, mostly because Wren knew them to be true. She had never been good at making friends. The only real friends she'd ever had were dead: her little brother, Skybow, and Trickster.

Her brother's round smiling face formed on the fabric of her souls, and Wren's throat ached.

She grabbed the two sticks that rested near the hearth-stones, picked up a large red coal from the fire and dropped it into her bowl. She violently crushed the coal with her hammerstone, and shook her bowl to scatter the embers. When the wood began to smoke, she dumped the embers back into the fire. The charring appeared fairly even. She reached for her hafted gray chert scraper. Rounded on the top, and about the size of her palm, the stone gleamed brightly in the last sunlight. The stick it was hafted to—tied to with deer sinew—was about as long as her hand. She tipped her bowl on end and braced it against the ground, then started scraping out the char, revealing the pale aspen wood beneath. The burning and scraping process created the bowl's basin, and the heat from the coals hardened the wood. Care had to be taken, Bogbean had said, to assure that water had not seeped into a crack in the wood. If it had, when the coals were added, steam built up in the crack and split the bowl in two. Wren had seen it happen. First came the loud crack, then flying splinters sent people diving for cover.

She said, "I don't care who you do or don't like. I think you both have caterpillar brains for condemning the False Face Child before you have heard all sides—not just the words of the gossips in your longhouse. If—"

"You would call Loon, Mossybill's wife, a gossip?" Dark Wind snapped. "Her husband is dead!"

Wren scraped more charred wood from her bowl and dumped it out. "Loon is heartsick. Her words cannot be trusted."

"It isn't just Loon. I have heard that all the people in Journeycake's house are going to cast their voices for death."

Vine grinned, and her two front teeth stuck out like boards. "I heard that, too."

"Haven't we suffered enough deaths?" Wren said, exasperated. "The least we owe White Kit, Mossybill, and Skullcap is to think about this before we take another life."

"You think." Dark Wind used the sticks to lift a coal from the firepit and toss it into her sloppy bowl. She had not even bothered, as Bogbean had shown them, to patch the tiny bug holes by pushing in sticks of the right size. "I already know my voice."

Wren went cold inside. Perhaps everyone in the village had decided. Except her. Her hand sneaked beneath her cape to touch the knotted strip of rawhide hanging from her belt. A flicker of Trickster's soul rose from the toy, and like a single flame on a dark winter night, it warmed her heart.

"What are you doing?" Dark Wind asked sharply, her gaze on the place where Wren's hand rested beneath her cape. "Stroking that filthy piece of rawhide again? You act like a five-winters-old child, Wren."

Wren drew out her hand and formed it into a fist. Getting to her feet, she walked over and held the fist in front of Dark Wind's gaping mouth. "And you act like you want a broken nose."

"You wouldn't dare—!"

"What's happening over there?" Bogbean shouted as she stamped toward Wren. Her portly body shook the ground. "Little Wren, are you fighting again?"

"Not yet."

Could she hit Dark Wind and get away before anyone caught her? She glanced at Bogbean, judging her speed, then reluctantly lowered her fist. "If you wish to stay pretty for the boys, Dark Wind," Wren advised, "you will be more careful in the future."

Bogbean lumbered up, grabbed Wren's hand and twisted it. "We do not strike each other in this village. We talk about things. Apologize to Dark Wind. Right now!"

Wren clamped her jaw, and gave Dark Wind an evil look.

Bogbean said, "What were you fighting about?"

Wren didn't answer, and Dark Wind feigned ignorance. "I never know what upsets Wren! She's like a weasel. She leaps up and down for no reason!"

Bogbean's eyes slitted. "Dark Wind," she said threateningly, "you had better tell me, or I—"

"I said that I was going to cast my voice against the False Face Child, that was all!"

Bogbean looked at Vine, who'd shrunk as low to the ground as she could, trying to avoid the elder's glare. "Vine, is that true? Is that what the fight concerned?"

Vine nodded heartily. "Oh, yes, that was it. Wren didn't like the way Dark Wind planned to cast."

If Wren disagreed, she would have to explain about Trickster's toy and how much Dark Wind had hurt her. The truth would embarrass Wren, and Dark Wind knew it. She gave Wren a knowing smile.

Bogbean shook Wren's hand. "What is your side?"

Wren replied, "I told Dark Wind we owed it to the dead to think carefully before we decided to take another life. Life is too precious."

Bogbean glowered at her. "You talked of the preciousness of life with a fist shoved in Dark Wind's face?"

"Well"—Wren shrugged—"I thought if words wouldn't work—"

"I don't wish to hear it! I am full of your excuses, girl! That's all you are, Wren. One excuse after another!" She put a fat hand against Wren's back and shoved her toward Frost-in-the-Willow's longhouse. "Go and fetch as many water bags as you can carry. You are going to haul water up from Pipe Stem Lake until it becomes too dark to walk.''

"Pipe Stem Lake!" Wren objected. "But the little pond down the hill has plenty—"

"Do not argue with me!" Bogbean bellowed. "Go!" She thrust a massive arm at the longhouse.

Wren stalked for the doorway. Behind her, she could hear Dark Wind and Vine giggling, and the sound ate her belly like tiny teeth. She wished she had broken Dark Wind's nose. At least then she would have something to smile about while she endured her punishment.

Pushing aside the leather door curtain, she ducked into the dim longhouse and reached for the gut bags that always hung on the peg by the door. *Ten* hung there! Had some slouch been hanging bags on Frost-in-the-Willow's peg, or . . . she tried to recall the last time she'd gone for water.

Guilt-ridden, she dragged the bags off the peg and slung five over each shoulder. Blessed Spirits, once she'd filled them, she'd waddle home like a dog burdened with too many packs.

She ducked out of the house, and marched down the trail toward Pipe Stem Lake. Children laughed in the plaza, and Wren knew she was the joke. She lifted her chin, and tried to convince herself she didn't care, that she didn't like them anyway. . . . But she did care. Their laughter hurt. She ran for the northern palisade gate, and the forest beyond.

Shadows had already eaten most of the underbrush, and the hickory limbs looked like dark skeletal hands opened to the graying heavens.

She trotted up the first hill, and down the other side, then stopped and pondered a while. As it was, she would not make it home until well after dark. What was her hurry? When she finally returned, her grandmother would ridicule her, and spend the rest of the evening telling people in the longhouse how much trouble Wren was. Worse, Uncle Blue Raven would sit before the fire with his head down, and his mouth tight with pain. That look always made Wren feel as if she'd been born under a rock.

She kicked a pinecone, and watched it tumble down the trail, then sauntered along behind it. The land smelled damp and earthy, and Wind Mother swayed the tops of the tallest pines. Lingering patches of snow glittered in the depths of the forest.

The trail veered around a toppled maple. Wren walked past the gigantic roots that had been torn from the ground, and examined the hole they'd left. Rocks glittered inside.

As she continued on down the hill, she could see the beach. Grandmother Moon had just risen, and her gleam silvered the waves. Wren dropped her water bags in a heap on the sand and let the sight fill her. To her right, Lost Hill rose a hundred hands tall, the top whiskered with pines and oaks. She did not even glance at it for fear that she would hear the cries of the lost children who had died there.

Instead, she gazed up longingly at Grandmother Moon. Of all the hero stories told by her people, Grandmother Moon's story fascinated Wren the most. Before the world was shaped, Grandmother Moon had lived in the Up-Above-World. One day while she was out trying to find Healing plants to cure her sick husband, she pulled a tree up by the roots and opened a hole in the sky. While she was peering over the edge to get a better look, the ground crumbled away beneath her feet, and she was sucked through the hole. Beaver saw her falling, and dove down beneath the vast waters that covered the earth, found dirt, and made a soft place for her to land. But when she landed, all manner of evil landed with her. She gave birth to twin boys, one good and one very bad. The bad one, Red Flint, forced his way out of her womb and killed her. In mourning, the good son, Sky-Holder, cast her face into the heavens where it became the moon, then he molded the mountains from her breasts. The rest of her body melted into the water and became Grandmother Earth. From her had sprouted the three Sacred Sisters, corn, beans, and pumpkins.

Wren's favorite part of the story, however, concerned Grandmother Moon's souls. Like all living beings, she'd had two souls, one that stayed with her body forever—meaning it lived in Grandmother Earth—and one that was supposed to join the Night Walkers in the sky. This second soul was called Falling Woman. Falling Woman was filled with rage at her murder. She vowed she would never return to the Up-Above-World until she'd found Red Flint and killed him. But Red Flint was crafty. He learned to hide by transforming himself into other red things, rosehips, bird eyes, stones, and blood. Unfortunately for humans, whenever Red Flint changes himself into blood and tries to hide in someone's veins, Falling Woman drives him out by sending all manner of illnesses upon the person's body. Sometimes, they even die.

But people could die from other things, too: Wicked Spirits hunted human souls; witches killed with poisons and magic arrows; powerful shamans, like the False Face Child and Silver Sparrow, could kill with a word.

In the dying light, gulls hunted the lake, diving and swooping, their guttural calls like wood scraped against gravel. Farther out, fish leaped high into the air, wriggled and fell. Silver rings bobbed outward from their splashes.

This had always been one of Wren's favorite places. She and Skybow used to play here. With Trickster. They would run up and down the beach, laughing, while Trickster chased them. Her souls could still hear his happy barks. She turned to the place where her mother always knelt to wash clothes, and Wren's insides, broken and carefully pieced back together again, suddenly cracked. She felt as if her heart and bones were falling apart before her eyes.

"Stop it," she murmured, and wiped her eyes on her sleeve. The last time she'd cried for her family, her grandmother had ordered her to sit in the corner with her back to the rest of the longhouse until she'd gotten over it. She'd stopped crying, but as for being over it . . .

Wren knelt and dunked a gut bag. Cold green water flowed inside. When it was full, she jerked the laces closed, knotted them, and slung the bag over her shoulder.

As she dipped the second bag, she heard a strange sound, like . . . laughter.

She spun around.

Sweet and high, the laughter seeped from the depths of the twilight.

"V-Vine? Is that you?"

Wren scrambled to her feet.

"Dark Wind? You coward! Come out and face me!"

Her gaze searched the trees, lingering on tangles of deadfall and dark bushes, expecting to see one of the other village children. If not Vine or Dark Wind, maybe little Toothwort. He was always doing irksome things to people. Only last moon he'd set a snare in a walking path and caught old man Marsh Elder by the right foot. After pounding dirty clothes with stones for twenty-eight days, Toothwort should have reformed a little. But perhaps not.

"Toothwort? Is that you out there? You'd better get back to your lodge before I catch you and wring your neck like a grouse!"

Stepping over the water bags, she—

*"Hello, Wren."*

—jerked her head up.

The boy leaned against the trunk of a pine, his arms folded across his bloody chest. He was a stranger, but he looked to have seen ten winters. His hide clothing hung in filthy tatters, and the deep gashes across his chest and throat leaked red down his pants. As dusk grayed into night and fires sprang to life in Walksalong Village at the top of the hill, shadows danced across his young face. He smiled at Wren.

Her pulse pounded in her ears. "Blessed gods, what happened to you? You're hurt!"

The boy stepped away from the tree. *"Yes. Hurt badly. Come and help me, Wren. I need your help."* He turned and ran into the forest.

Wren hesitated. How could anyone smile when they were draining blood like a deer with its throat slit? But perhaps the pain had taken his senses.

Cautiously, she followed him. When she entered the trees, the brittle scents of damp bark and dirt filled her nostrils. The forest giants moaned in the evening breeze.

She cupped a hand to her mouth and called, "Where are you?"

*"I'm here. Up the trail. Follow my voice."*

Wren's breathing went shallow. Grandmother Moon's silver light slanted down through the trees, shining on black spots in the snow. Drops of blood. She knelt and touched them. The odor left a tang at the back of her throat.

"Come back!" Wren yelled. "I'll take you to my village, and we'll Heal you. You're bleeding badly!"

*"I need you to come to me, Wren. It isn't far. Come, please. Help me."*

Wren's eyes widened when she saw him—Dancing—a

specter of blood and moonlight flashing between the dark trunks of the trees. He lifted his arms and spun like a summer whirlwind. Blood flew from his wounds, speckling the trees and snow.

Wren couldn't move. It was like staring into the eyes of a big cat about to pounce. . . .

"I'm not following you!" she said. "I don't know you!"

A pale ghostly face, streaked with blood, peered from behind a smoke-colored trunk. He grinned. *"Do you know why ghosts build houses, Wren?"*

"What?" Wren shook her head.

*"They build houses because they do not have enough lightning arrows, and they know it. They are afraid of us."*

"Afraid? Why? They're ghosts! We can't hurt them."

He held out a hand, and it seemed to be made of moonlight, luminous, sparkling. *"You must see the ghost houses for yourself, Wren. Our world is about to end. We have to warn people, before it's too late. Please, come with me. Help me. I cannot do this alone."*

The only feeling in her entire body was the powerful, rhythmic slamming of her heart. "I'm not going anywhere!" She took a step backward. "Except home!"

He lowered his hand to his side. *"I'm sorry, Wren. Truly. I cannot stop it now. You* will *come with me. Power has chosen."*

Fear gripped her by the throat.

The boy took a step, spread his arms to her, and his chest wounds broke open. Blood poured over his stomach and down his legs. *"It will be easier on you if you come now. Please come."*

Wren threw down her water bag and ran with all her might, screaming, "Uncle Blue Ra-a-ven!"

Blue Raven ducked into his mother's longhouse, and gazed at the central fire where Frost-in-the-Willows, Starflower, Bogbean, and Beadfern sat on thick piles of hides. Beadfern wore a buckskin cape. The other elders had blankets around their shoulders. Starflower's was red, Bogbean's had blue and black stripes, and his mother wore a solid cream-colored blanket. Jumping Badger paced before them.

Blue Raven regarded his cousin for a moment. About half Blue Raven's age, he had broad shoulders and a narrow waist. His arm muscles bulged through the finely tanned buckskin shirt he wore. Long jet-black hair hung loosely over his shoulders, glinting in the firelight. He had a strong face, with a chiseled jaw, and dark eyes. He'd been married once. Nine winters ago. The only reminder was a white ridge of scar tissue across his throat. His wife's blade had missed the major arteries. In the chaos of screams and blood, she'd fled. No one had ever heard from her again. Blue Raven had always thought that poor Hollow Hill had been the true victim. She had lost everything. Even her family.

As he strode forward, Blue Raven said, "Greetings, Matrons, cousin."

Frost-in-the-Willows turned to look at him. "Have you heard about your niece?"

Blue Raven frowned. "No. Where is she? I thought she was here with you."

"Bogbean caught her in another fight."

"Oh, not again," Blue Raven said with a deep sigh. Wren never seemed to learn. "What was her punishment?"

"Bogbean ordered her to carry all of our water bags down and fill them in Pipe Stem Lake. That should take a while. She's been lazy this quarter moon. I suspect she had eight or ten to fill."

"Well, we'll discuss it later." Blue Raven stopped and stood before the fire, across from Jumping Badger. "Are you well, cousin?"

"I am alive," Jumping Badger replied, "which is more than I can say for Mossybill and Skullcap. Where is the child?"

"Staked out beneath the Sunshine Boy, but I am not certain he is to blame for their deaths. This is something we must discuss, after we talk about Paint Rock Village."

"It was a great success," Jumping Badger said and massaged his forehead as if fatigued. "There is little to tell. We attacked, stole the child, and burned the village. I—"

"You also hunted down the survivors. Or so Mossybill said. Is it true?"

Jumping Badger turned, and his eyes narrowed. "Yes. It was a small task. There weren't very many."

A grisly head leaned on a pole at the end of the longhouse. The stench filled the air. Blue Raven's gaze locked with his cousin's. "On what authority did you do this? I do not recall the matrons telling you to kill everyone in Paint Rock Village."

"Did you want them *here,* cousin?" Jumping Badger asked. "In our village with their bows drawn? If a single person had been left to pursue us, don't you think they would have? Which of your relatives would you have dead because they tried to rescue the False Face Child? Eh? Name him, or hold your tongue!"

"I—"

Starflower held up a hand. "Please. Blue Raven, take

your seat beside your mother. Jumping Badger, sit here beside me. Have a cup of mint tea.'' She gestured to the pot hanging from the tripod at the edge of the flames. Extra cups rested near the hearthstones. ''This has been a long day for all of us.''

Blue Raven calmly lowered himself next to Frost-in-the-Willows, and watched Jumping Badger crouch beside Starflower. The man's gaze had turned icy.

Blue Raven took one of the cups and dipped it full of tea. Jumping Badger had risen to the rank of war leader by audacity. It still served him. In his first battle, after his sixteenth winter, he'd killed four enemy warriors. Since then, another twelve had fallen to his bow and warclub. He seemed fearless, even reckless, when it came to war. Each exploit fed his reputation.

''Forgive me, cousin,'' Blue Raven said. ''I should have begun differently. Your raid was successful. For that your people are grateful. Were you injured during the fight?''

Jumping Badger dipped himself a cup of tea and held it in both hands, as if to warm his cold fingers. ''Cousin, all of the creatures that dwell in the sky, forest, meadows, seas, and under the ground joined forces with us. Our triumph was stunning. We—''

Blue Raven said, ''How many warriors did we lose?''

''In the first battle at Sleeping Mist Village, we lost eight, then—''

''*Sleeping Mist?*'' Frost-in-the-Willows leaned forward. In the fire's gleam, her white hair shimmered golden. ''For what reason did you attack them? I recall no such order!''

Starflower added, ''Nor do I, War Leader. What is this?''

Bogbean, her mouth quivering, said, ''Why would you attack innocent people? They had done nothing to us.''

Jumping Badger made a calming gesture with his hand. "Please, Matrons. Hear my side. We did not *wish* to attack Sleeping Mist Village. We had no choice. I instructed half my forces to circle around to the south of Paint Rock Village, and wait for my signal. I took the other half northward in the hopes that we could surround the village—"

"To assure that the False Face Child did not escape?" Starflower surmised.

"Yes. But my forces and I ran into a Sleeping Mist war party. We obviously had to kill them before they could warn their relatives in Paint Rock Village. It so happened that we fought the war party all the way back into the village, and some of the villagers died in the battle." He shrugged casually. "I cannot say how many." He swirled his tea in his cup, and took a long sip. "We did not take a count."

"Blessed ancestors," Blue Raven said. "How could you have been clumsy enough to run into a war party? Didn't you have advance scouts out? You should have—"

Jumping Badger shouted, "Do not tell me what I should have done! You have not been a warrior in fifteen winters! What do you know of strategy? War parties sometimes meet accidentally, with no warning, and they are thrust into battle before anyone can think! We did what we had to!"

"But you—"

"Enough!" Starflower said. "I am certain you did your best, War Leader." Her faded old eyes went from Jumping Badger's enraged face to Blue Raven's tight mouth, and she set her teacup on a hearthstone. "Perhaps meeting tonight was not wise," she admitted. "We are all tired, and grieving. Let us end this. We will begin again tomorrow morning, after a good night's rest."

"Thank you," Beadfern murmured, her eyes moist. "I wish to see Kit, to tell her good-bye."

Frost-in-the-Willows nodded. His mother's wounded expression touched Blue Raven's heart. "I, too. There are things I wish to give her. To take with her to the afterlife."

Jumping Badger stood. "If you are dismissing me, I will go and find my blankets. Every muscle in my body aches."

"Of course, War Leader," Starflower said. "Rest."

Blue Raven watched his cousin stalk away, toward his bedding at the northern end of the longhouse, then he gently placed a hand on his mother's shoulder. "If you need me, mother, I—"

A shrill scream penetrated the house. Blue Raven was on his feet before he heard his name: *"Uncle Blue Raven! Uncle!"*

Little Wren flew beneath the door curtain and ran madly across the longhouse, her pretty face wild with fear. *"Uncle!"* she wailed. She threw her arms around his waist so forcefully that she almost knocked him backward into the firepit.

"Wren!" he said in shock. "What's wrong? What's happened?"

"He—he tried to g-get me!" she stuttered. "A bloody b-boy! He had crazy eyes, Uncle! Crazy! He told me I had to go with him, and when I said I wouldn't h-he told me Power had chosen me!" She looked up with swimming eyes. "Oh, Uncle, you have to hide me. Don't let him take me away! I don't want to leave you!"

"Shh, Wren," Blue Raven whispered. "I won't let anyone take you away from me." He stroked her hair for a few moments, trying to calm her, then said, "Who was the boy? I will speak to his mother about this. He has no right to frighten you this way. Tell me his name?"

Wren's mouth opened, but no words came out. Finally, she blurted, "Uncle. He wasn't *human*! He was one of the False Faces of the Forest! I know it! No human boy could have laughed that way with his body cut to pieces! He had to be a Forest Spirit! Please! Don't let him take me!"

She buried her face in his shirt, and Blue Raven glanced for help to the elders seated around the fire. Starflower's eyes had narrowed, and Bogbean and Beadfern looked genuinely worried. Only Frost-in-the-Willows appeared perturbed. She rose to her feet, hobbled forward, and shoved Wren's shoulder hard.

When Wren stood facing her, Frost-in-the-Willows poked a bony finger into Wren's chest.

"Stop this lying, girl! Did you run off to play and forget the water bags? Eh? Are they down by the lake? You forgot the bags and decided you needed a good story to cover for yourself. That's it, isn't it? You are the most insolent child I have ever known! Get into your bed and cover your head. None of your relatives wish to see your face!"

Wren's mouth gaped. "Grandmother, it's not my fault! I—"

Frost-in-the-Willows slapped her hard across the face, and Wren stumbled backward. A red handprint swelled on her cheek.

Blue Raven grabbed his mother's hand and gasped, "Blessed gods, why did you do that?"

Wren dashed for her bedding. She crawled under her hides, and pulled them over her head.

Frost-in-the-Willows jerked her hand free, and glowered at Blue Raven. "Supper is ready, my son. Come to the fire and eat."

Frost-in-the-Willows limped away.

Blue Raven felt empty, and exhausted . . . and he still

had duties to perform. Jumping Badger might not wish to speak with him tonight, but Blue Raven wagered that some of his cousin's warriors might. He knew that Elk Ivory would be honest with him, and at the thought of looking into her eyes, his tension eased.

He frowned at Wren. She lay curled silently beneath her hides.

Blue Raven went to kneel beside her. Softly, he said, "I believe you, Wren. There are many things about the ways of Spirits that mystify me. Will you speak with me more later?"

Her hand crept from beneath her hides, touched his moccasin and quickly retreated.

Blue Raven patted the place where he thought her head must be, then rose to his feet. As he passed Frost-in-the-Willows, he said, "I'm not hungry, Mother. Wren and I will eat later. When she is feeling better," and he ducked outside into the darkness.

Later, in the middle of the night, he lay awake, his head propped on his arm.

*"Mother! Mother, where are you?"*

Blue Raven did not know how anyone could sleep with those piteous cries on the wind.

He pulled up his sleeping hides. Long graying black hair spread around him. Wren huddled in her hides beside him. She'd been shaking off and on throughout the long night. She'd been asleep when he'd returned, so he'd eaten while Frost-in-the-Willows repeated her accusations about Wren: "The girl is a liar! She's always been a liar! Tomorrow you will see. Send someone down to the lake early. You will find the water bags there, I'm sure of it. Your niece just needed an excuse for her impudence!''

It was possible, he admitted it, but he didn't think so.

The fires had burned down to pits of glowing red eyes, and soft sounds filled the longhouse: a baby nursing, a boy mumbling in his sleep. Two of the brightest of the Night Walker's lodges shone through the smoke hole in the roof. From the many sleepless nights Blue Raven had spent staring at that smoke hole, he knew their gleams signaled midnight.

*''Please, Mother! Please come!''*

The cries had started about a hand of time ago. Since then, he'd been fighting the urge to rise. If he defied Starflower's command, it would shame her, and him, and encourage others to ignore her authority. Clan order would crumble into chaos. But he had to clench his hands to keep them from reaching for his cape and moccasins.

He gazed down the longhouse. No one else even seemed to hear Rumbler.

Jumping Badger's snores shook the walls, and they irritated Blue Raven more than usual.

Blue Raven had questioned many of his cousin's warriors. Most had told him nothing. Only Elk Ivory, his childhood love, had confided to Blue Raven that Jumping Badger had been particularly brutal at Paint Rock. He'd ordered his warriors to rape every woman—even the dead—then he'd personally mutilated the bodies of the male children. Elk Ivory had also told him that, on the run home, Jumping Badger had terrified them all. She'd whispered that he had risen every night, gone a short distance away from camp, and carried on long conversations with the severed head of the Paint Rock war leader, Lamedeer. He'd acted as if he no longer knew who he was, or where they were going. At the first hint of darkness, Jumping Badger had insisted that huge fires be lit. No one, not even Elk Ivory, had dared refuse.

A voice whispered, "Do you hear him, Uncle?"

Blue Raven turned. Wren's lean face peered out at him from a small round gap in her mound of hides. Her eyes had a reddish sheen.

"Yes, I hear him."

"He must be freezing. I can see my breath, and I'm inside the longhouse. How much snow do you think has fallen?"

"About three hands."

"I hope your cape has not blown loose."

"I do, too."

Wren picked at a loose thread that stuck out from her blanket.

"Are you all right?" he asked.

She nodded. "I feel sick. Deep inside. Like my bones are drying up."

"I'm sorry, Wren. Your grandmother . . . I don't think she meant to strike you, she just didn't know what else to do."

Bravely, Wren said, "It's all right, Uncle. I'm more worried about the bloody boy than Grandmother's slap. I mean, you don't think that Face would come into the longhouse to find me, do you?"

Blue Raven pondered the question. "The False Faces of the Forest don't like harming children, Wren. I don't think so."

She sat up in her bedding, and long black hair tumbled around her shoulders. "Uncle? You don't think the Face will go after Rumbler, do you? Since he couldn't get me? Rumbler is out there alone, and tied up."

"I think Rumbler has more to fear from the cold and wolves than Spirits, Wren."

She seemed to hear the bitter undercurrent in his words. She eased back down. "It isn't your fault, Uncle.

You didn't wish to steal the boy. Everyone knows that.''

Blue Raven's belly soured. "I should have done more, Wren. I wish I had.''

"Could you have? Without getting killed?''

"I think so. It is easier to ignore a calm man, than one shouting and shaking his fists. I should have shouted.''

Her brow furrowed. "But you are Headman, Uncle. Headmen do not shout. They explain. People expect War Leaders to yell and shake their fists, but if a Headman does it, they hate him.''

Wind shook the walls, and penetrated around the edges of the door curtain. The coals in the firepit flared, throwing a crimson veil over Wren's swollen face. The slap had left an ugly welt.

Blue Raven reached out to touch it gently. "Even if a Headman's actions make him the most hated man in the village, he must do whatever is necessary to assure the safety of his people. Three of our clan are dead, Wren, and I fear it is all because I was not willing to be hated. I did not have the courage.''

She studied him from beneath her long lashes. "Did you examine Skullcap and Mossybill?''

"Yes.'' He nodded. "I could find no evidence of violence. No blood. No wounds. But their families are convinced Rumbler killed them.''

"Why?''

"Because it is the only answer they have.''

Wren reached beneath the edge of her hides to pull Trickster's knotted rawhide toy from its nightly resting place. "Uncle, do you think Rumbler has family in another village? We might be able to find them. If you freed Rumbler and took him to his family . . .''

Blue Raven rolled to his side. Clearly, she had decided Rumbler was not to blame for the deaths and had been thinking about how to resolve this unpleasant situation.

"Our clan would declare me an outcast, Wren. I would be hunted down and killed for my crime. Just as you would if you did such a thing."

Wren clutched the rawhide toy more tightly. "Could we get someone else to do it for us? Pay them, maybe, twelve or thirteen beaver pelts, or a bag of seashells?"

Blue Raven whispered, "The result would be the same, Wren. Treachery never remains a secret. No, I think there is only one way to end this madness."

"What is that, Uncle?"

"Something I have been considering for many winters: an alliance with the Turtle Nation."

"An alliance?" she said in surprise.

"Yes. Just imagine what life would be like if all of our villages, and all of their villages, agreed to keep the peace. If we said, 'We won't raid you, if you don't raid us. In fact, if you are ever in trouble we will help defend your villages, if you will also help to defend ours in our times of need.'" Blue Raven sighed. "Such a thing is just a dream now, but it is worth praying for. Both of our nations would be better off. Trade would prosper."

"Then why haven't we done it already, Uncle?"

"There is too much hostility, too much distrust. But someday—"

The words dried up in his throat when Rumbler shrieked, *"Mother!"*

Tears filled Wren's eyes.

Blue Raven reached out and squeezed her hand. "Try to sleep, Wren. There's nothing we can do tonight."

She curled into a ball, and pulled her hides over her head again.

"Wren?"

Sniffles.

"I'm sorry any of this has happened. But I give you my pledge that if he is innocent, I will do my best to save him."

# Eight

Evening purpled the rolling hills, turning the fresh snow a deep amethyst. Silver Sparrow stood before his newly built lodge on the hillside overlooking the ten conical lodges of Earth Thunderer Village. Dust Moon had ordered the village be set up in a crescent moon around the southern end of Goose Down Lake. His clan did not construct clumsy big longhouses like those of the Bear Nation. They built small lodges that could be easily torn down and moved to a new location. Rounded in shape, with bark-covered walls, they stood the height of a man, and spread two to three body lengths in diameter. Delicate tendrils of smoke curled from the roofs.

People had begun to gather in front of Matron Dust Moon's lodge, all shouting at once.

Sparrow knelt to stir his stewpot. The aroma of venison heart bathed his face. A teapot, cup, and bowl rested at the edge of the hearthstones. His moss tea had been steeping for a quarter hand of time and smelled sweetly fragrant.

Dust Moon's voice split the night. *"You must speak one at a time! I can hear nothing!"*

Sparrow glanced to his right. Inside his lodge, Crowfire lay beneath a buffalohide, his lips moving, as they had for two days, in soft, incomprehensible words. The flickering light danced over the youth's face, accentuating his gaunt cheeks, and the damp, stringy hair that spread around him.

Sparrow had tended his wounds, and given him bone-set tea and meat broth, but Crowfire's fever continued to rage. If it didn't break soon, Sparrow feared his souls would fly.

"Tall Blue!" Dust Moon called.

The young war leader came forward with his shoulders hunched defensively. Dust Moon said something that Sparrow could not hear, and the war leader broke from the crowd and marched up the trail toward Sparrow. The red and yellow porcupine quills sewn along his leather sleeves glinted.

Sparrow's wrinkles rearranged themselves into tired lines. He laid his stirring paddle on the hearthstones and propped his elbows on his knees, waiting.

The closer he got the more reluctant Tall Blue's expression became.

"Good evening to you, Elder," Tall Blue said as he entered the halo of the firelight. His clamshell necklace flashed.

"A Blessed night to you, War Leader. Will you share my venison stew?"

Tall Blue held up a hand. "Thank you, no. I couldn't keep anything down."

"Yes, Dust Moon has that effect on men."

Tall Blue winced. "I never used to have such frail nerves."

Sparrow threw a chunk of hickory on the fire, and watched the sparks shoot upward into the cloud-strewn evening sky. "What message are you carrying?"

Tall Blue squatted on the opposite side of the fire. "I have been instructed to ask you if the Paint Rock warrior is well, or if his souls have flown?"

"He is not well. But I cannot answer for his souls. The

arrow point in his leg will not come out. I snapped it off even with the bone, and placed a snakeroot poultice over it, but there has been no change. Shadow Spirits have filled the wound. His souls may be inside, or outside. They may be gone forever, or return by morning.''

Tall Blue glanced through the doorway at Crowfire, then quickly looked away.

''What?'' Sparrow pressed.

Tall Blue shifted uneasily. ''This morning Matron Dust Moon said she felt a malignant presence around the village. She feared it might be the soul of the Paint Rock Dreamer, Briar, flying. The hair''—he gestured—''on top of the matron's head stood straight up. Just like that of a dog when an intruder approaches.''

''Really?'' Sparrow said with exaggerated interest. ''Well, Dust has a strange new accomplishment. What other feats did she perform?''

Tall Blue added in a hushed voice, ''She said a bitter scent rode the wind, like moldering bones.''

''Moldering bones?''

Tall Blue nodded.

Sparrow picked up his paddle and stirred his stew again. It had started to boil. ''So, her unruly hair and the odor of the garbage behind the village convinced Dust that Briar was soul-flying. How many people believed her?''

Tall Blue rested his hands on his knees and stared at them as if he'd found something he'd never seen. ''Elder, how much longer will you allow the young warrior to remain in your lodge?''

''Until he can tell me himself that he wishes to go.''

''Elder, please.'' Tall Blue spread his hands imploringly. ''A Trader came through at noon. He said that after Jumping Badger stole the dwarf boy, he hunted down and killed every member of the Paint Rock Clan that he could find. What if he discovers one survived? Do you not think he might come looking?''

''Maybe.'' Sparrow shrugged. ''But I doubt it.''

''Why?''

''Jumping Badger wipes out villages. He's worked very hard to convince people that he has a special talent for it. Killing one lone warrior would be an insult to his reputation.''

Tall Blue prodded one of the hearthstones with the toe of his moccasin. ''Not everyone agrees with you. The entire village is ready to move away and leave you, unless you—''

''Again?'' Sparrow shoved his paddle into the stewpot. ''What shall I do, Tall Blue? Take Crowfire out and abandon him in the forest? Is that what you wish?''

Crowfire's tortured voice filled the sudden silence, the words breathy, garbled. Perhaps he'd heard his name and was endeavoring to respond.

''Earlier today,'' Tall Blue said, ''Matron Dust Moon suggested that if the Forest Spirit had truly married into the Paint Rock Clan, as they claimed, he might care for this youth. The warrior is, after all, a relative of the Forest Spirit's.''

Sparrow shifted to peer around Tall Blue's broad shoulder at Dust Moon. She stood warming her hands before the bonfire, but her eyes were glued to Sparrow's camp. He longed to tramp down there and tell her just how ridiculous she was being.

Instead, he leaned toward Tall Blue, and confidentially whispered, ''Forest Spirits are the bringers of plagues and droughts, Tall Blue. I've never heard of a renegade Healer among them, have you?''

The corners of Blue's mouth turned down. ''Matron Dust Moon feared you would speak this way.''

''No, she didn't, Blue. She *knew* I would.''

"I think she was hoping you would heed her wisdom this time, so that we would not have to move in the middle of the Moon of Frozen Leaves."

"Tell my former wife that if she wishes me to heed her wisdom, she should be brave enough to share it with me herself."

Tall Blue nodded curtly. "Yes, Elder." He rose to his feet, and said, "I will do that. Good evening."

Tall Blue marched down the hill, his cape flapping in the wind.

The crowd around Dust Moon's fire fell silent as Tall Blue descended the hill. Dust Moon shouldered through the gathering to meet Blue halfway. When he arrived, they spoke, and Dust threw up her arms in a gesture of utter disgust.

Sparrow ladled stew into his bowl. Lifting his horn spoon, he gingerly tested the hot mixture. It tasted rich and tender.

Dust Moon tramped up the trail.

Despite her fifty winters, she had a lithe, supple body, and long hair the color of starglow.

When she stepped into the firelight, she gruffly asked, "Are you trying to kill us all?"

Sparrow ate another bite of stew. "No, Dust." He used his spoon to point to the opposite side of the fire. "You're the only one I've ever wanted to kill. Please, sit. Share my fire."

She threw up her arms again. "You do not even know this warrior! Why would you risk the lives of your relatives to protect him?"

Sparrow took his time chewing a large piece of succulent meat. "He's sick, Dust. I can't just let him die. You are a Healer. You should understand that."

"I don't. Your own people should come first. Besides, this young warrior is a relative of Briar's and—"

"And you go blind when it comes to relatives of Briar's, and many other things, I might add, including me. Now fluff up like a mating grouse and tell me I'm just as blind as you are, and worthless, too, and when you are finished strutting, I'll explain why I must try to Heal this boy."

She propped her hands on her hips and glared at him. "I don't care to hear it. Briar has made you—"

"That's a curious thing to say, given that Briar was your best friend for ten winters."

At one time, Dust had affectionately called Briar her "little sister." When Briar discovered she was pregnant with the Forest Spirit's child, Dust had been her only friend. Everyone else had fled as if Briar had contracted a deadly disease. Dust had run all the way to Paint Rock Village when she'd heard Briar was giving birth. Briar's relatives had refused to touch her, so Dust had brought that child into the world with her own hands.

"When our son Flintboy was dying—"

"Yes, I know," he said. "You begged Briar to come and help Heal him, and she refused. After all the love you'd given her, you felt betrayed. But she wasn't at fault, Dust, and you know it. When you called her, half of Paint Rock Village was ill with the same fever. Her own people needed her more than you did." He pointed at her with his dripping spoon. "Weren't you just speaking of how one's own people should come first? You've never been able to understand that in others. You think you and yours should be first to everyone."

The lines around Dust's eyes deepened, and Sparrow had to clamp his jaw against his own hurt. He had watched each and every wrinkle in Dust's face come into being. He knew them by heart. The long jagged line that cut down around her right eye had been formed as she'd watched their fifth son die. The son Briar had not Healed.

He'd seen eleven winters. Dust had stayed by Flintboy's side light and dark, barely eating. Those twenty days had been the longest of her life . . . and his.

"Besides," Sparrow said. "I know that Briar regretted that decision. Every time I visited Paint Rock Village, she apologized again, and asked about you."

Dust lowered her eyes. "I don't care, I—"

"You don't care that she might be dead? That her son is in Walksalong Village, probably being tortured—"

She shouted, "I want the Paint Rock warrior gone!"

Sparrow slammed his bowl to the ground, and walked around the fire, stopping three hands from her. The delicate scent of pine needles clung to her long silver hair, and struck him like a blow to the stomach.

"Dust." His voice came out strained. "It is not simply that I wish to save his young life. I must find out what happened. In my Dream, I saw—"

"Dreams! I do not wish to hear another word about your Dreams! Try thinking of your clan. You used to know how to do that, before you were knocked in the head by that Spirit Helper!"

Sparrow's shoulder muscles went tight. When the strange little boy had first appeared in their lodge—the night Flintboy died—Sparrow had believed him real. The boy had roused Sparrow from a sound sleep by tapping Sparrow's forehead with his small fist, and whispering, *"Hurry, my shadow. Wake up. Grandfather Day Maker's children are hunting you."*

Sparrow clenched his fists. "I know my Dreams frighten you, Dust, so I will not burden you with their content—but do try to understand. Crowfire came looking for me. He may be the last living member of the Paint Rock Clan. The least I owe him is to do my best to tie his souls to his body." In a gesture of need she had seen a thousand times, he held his hands out to her, the palms up. "Give me a few more days. That is all I ask."

She glanced at his hands, and emotion flickered in her eyes. "Sparrow, what has happened to you? That wicked Spirit Helper—"

"Has done nothing!" He forced himself to stare up at the sparkling lodges of the Night Walkers. His throat had constricted, and he feared he might not be able to keep his voice calm. "He is not wicked, Dust. He is a child. Sometimes he's mischievous. He doesn't understand—"

"Do not tell me again, Sparrow. Please."

He walked forward until less than a handbreadth separated them, and looked down into her eyes. Blessed gods, how he longed to hold her.

"See me in here, Dust. I'm the same man you lived with and loved for thirty-five winters. I have not changed. If you would only try to—"

"Sparrow." She closed her eyes as if in pain. "Do not do this. My heart cannot stand it. I just . . . I want . . ."

She paused almost as if she longed to speak honestly with him, and Sparrow's blood rushed, preparing to do whatever he had to to help her step across the spun-silk bridge of pain that separated them. "Dust, what do you want? Please tell me. I'll do anything."

She seemed to be struggling with herself, deciding what she should and should not say.

Finally, she looked up. Their gazes held.

Her voice quavered when she said, "I want you to leave, Sparrow. I will give you seven nights. But no more. Either you go, or we go. Our people wish to leave now. I am taking advantage by asking them to stay at all."

Sparrow shoved his hands in the pockets of his elkhide jacket, and studied her tormented expression. "If you want me to go, Dust, I will."

He walked back to his stewpot. As he picked up his bowl, he said, "Now that we have that settled, why don't you sit for a time. I have a pot of tea brewed and more stew than I can possibly eat. We could talk. Perhaps—"

"No. Sparrow, I . . ." She turned to look down the hill at the gathering around her bonfire. "People are uneasy. If I don't return soon, they will mount a rescue party."

"I would never hurt you, Dust. They know that. And you know that."

She looked straight at him, and the golden fleck that rested just below the pupil of her left eye caught the light and held it like a tiny pool of water. "I no longer know what you will or will not do, Sparrow. Though I hope that's true."

Without another word, she headed down the trail toward the village.

Sparrow's eyes stayed on her until the darkness swallowed her, then he violently dumped the contents of his bowl back into the pot.

As he sank to the ground, he noticed, with irritation, that his arms shook.

# Nine

Little Wren huddled in her red and black striped blanket on the south side of the enormous plaza fire, watching the masked Dancers who pirouetted around the central fire, and absently listening to Matron Starflower tell the tale of White Kit's death. Her rusty voice had been speaking for over a hand of time, explaining every detail. Wren had paid attention through the part where Rumbler had plunged the knife into Kit's chest, then her interest had flown away like geese in winter. By now, she had heard the tale a hundred times. She watched the Masked Spirits.

They Danced in a circle around the fire. Their moccasins, covered with shell bells, stamped the earth, the rhythm simple, perfect. Wren could feel it rise through her legs and eddy all the way to the hairs on top of her head. Their pounded copper, shell, and stone eyes flickered in the firelight. Silent, they Danced round and round, their motion hypnotic.

Their presence sanctified the gathering, assuring that only the truth would be spoken.

The Spirit of Red-Dew-Eagle Danced by Wren, and she felt her blood tingle. His sacred mask was enormous, three times the size of a human face. Carved from walnut, and polished with sunflower oil, it gleamed blackly. The hideously twisted face had a long beak and large glistening shell eyes. The mouth curved up the right cheek so that the corner of the lips touched the corner of the eye. The Spirit leaned down and peered directly at Wren, and she instinctively slid backward, her heart pounding.

The Dew Eagles soared in the clouds beyond human sight. They collected pools of dew in the hollows between their shoulders, and when the Thunderbirds failed in their duty to water Grandmother Earth, the Dew Eagles tilted their wings and mist fell. They also snatched bad children in their talons and carried them off to be eaten by the Ice Monsters who lived in the far north.

Red-Dew-Eagle Danced on, and Wren let out a relieved breath, and looked at Rumbler.

He knelt at Uncle Blue Raven's side, inside the ring of Dancers, near the fire. A brightly painted elkhide draped his shoulders. Small and misshapen, he had chin-length black hair which framed his round face. He stared unblinking into the flames, obviously aware of the whispers demanding vengeance, and the fear in people's eyes. He had his bound hands propped in his lap, and twisted them anxiously. He looked scared.

Three freshly washed bodies lay atop buffalohides to Wren's left, next to Starflower, but Rumbler never looked at them. Offerings encircled the dead: stone knives, seed bead necklaces, precious seashells, and a variety of blankets and hides.

Elk Ivory sat cross-legged on the ground to Wren's right, her buffalohide coat darkly splotched with old bloodstains, her expression dour. She kept glancing sideways at Jumping Badger.

Jumping Badger stood at the edge of the firelight, his shoulder braced against a huge birch tree. Dressed in a hide shirt covered with bone beads, he looked like one of the sky gods come to earth. He'd left his long hair loose; it shone a deep black against the white bark.

All day long Jumping Badger had been parading around the village like an elder. Stealing the child and killing Lamedeer had improved Jumping Badger's reputation. Everyone who passed him bowed reverently. Women kept bringing him fresh cups of hot pine-needle tea to drink, or more venison stew to eat. He seemed to be enjoying the attention.

Beside Jumping Badger stood the ugly Trader, Cornhusk. He wore a smile, as if greatly entertained by this spectacle. From what Wren had heard, Cornhusk had better enjoy life all he could. Though Cornhusk had a wife in Grand Banks Village, there had been rumors going round that he'd violated the honor of a woman in the south, and the village chieftain had dispatched a war party to hunt Cornhusk down.

Warriors lounged on hides in front of Jumping Badger, telling jokes, and poking each other. Every now and then one of them would point to the bloody head on the staff planted to Jumping Badger's right, and whoop.

Wren hated it. Crows had pecked out the eyes. The black and gray hair hung in blood-clotted strands, and a strange expression creased the face. She wondered at that. What had the Paint Rock war leader been thinking in his last moments?

For some reason, the severed head made her think of the bloody little boy in the forest. Wren glanced around the council, afraid she might see him grinning at her over someone's shoulders. The boy's voice had chased her all the way home, his ghostly laughter echoing through her like a glacial wind. She kept dreaming about him, and had the uncomfortable feeling that this might be the beginning of a long and terrible trial.

Matron Starflower lifted her withered arms and Wren tried to pay attention again. Starflower's white hair fluttered in the cold night-scented breeze. She shouted, "The Dew Eagles stand as my witnesses that I have spoken truth this night!" The Dancers stopped as if frozen in time, some with feet lifted, others with arms up.

Starflower's frightened gaze lowered to the False Face Child. "This evil Spirit in a human child's body has killed three of our people, two of our greatest warriors, and our beloved White Kit. I cannot say what its fate should be. That decision will rest within each of your hearts. But I advise you to think wisely. The False Face Child does not even need to see or touch to kill. It was staked out beneath the Sunshine Boy when Mossybill and Skullcap perished." Murmurs swept the gathering. "How can any of us sleep at night with it living and breathing close by? I do not think I shall ever sleep again." She lifted a hand to the crowd, and closed her eyes. "I have spoken," she said. "Let others rise."

Red-Dew-Eagle led the masked Dancers away from the fire. They fell into line behind him, and shuffled to the outskirts of the gathering where they stood in the shadows, watching and listening.

Starflower sank wearily to the log that had been drawn up for her by the fire. Her eldest daughter, Yellow Leaf Blowing, draped a blanket around her frail old shoulders and said something soft. Starflower nodded and gratefully patted her daughter's hand.

Uncle Blue Raven stepped forward. He had a curious dignity about him. He stood tall and erect, his soft brown eyes calm. He waited until only the crackling of the flames filled the silence.

"I arrived in the council house after White Kit's death," he said in a deep ringing voice, "but I studied her wounds while her family prepared her for burial. I ask that each of you do the same before you cast your voice tonight. Though Rumbler, known as the False Face Child, did stab Kit, he did it out of a little boy's fear and desperation. The knife did not penetrate! It struck a rib! You may see this for yourselves. It struck a rib and the boy threw the knife down. That was how it happened." He made a helpless gesture. "I cannot say why Kit's souls fled. Perhaps out of fear. Perhaps Falling Woman simply decided to take Kit from her body. Kit had seen seventy winters. That is a long time for anyone."

Gasps and cries of disbelief mingled with the wailing of the bereaved. The crowd seemed to surge forward, closing in around Uncle Blue Raven like cougars scenting prey.

He shouted, "Hear me! You may each go into the council house and see the place where the deed was done. The amount of blood on the floor is not enough to fill a horn spoon. I give you my pledge!"

"And what of Mossybill and Skullcap?" someone shouted. "Did Falling Woman take them, too?"

Little Wren got on her knees to see who had spoken. Rides-the-Bear sat cross-legged, glaring at Uncle Blue Raven as if he wished to strike him. A muscular man of twenty winters, he had a thick square-jawed face and small, slanting eyes. The blue images of Falcon and Hawk painted his cape.

"Their deaths," Blue Raven replied, "trouble me deeply. They were friends to us all, but Starflower has already told you that Rumbler was across the village when they died. He could not have harmed them!"

"False Faces and sorcerers can send their souls flying! We all know this!" Mossybill's wife, Loon, shouted.

Wren craned her neck to see, but could only make out Loon's red cape.

"Come forward," Blue Raven called gently. "We all wish to hear your thoughts, Loon."

She pushed through the crowd and into the fire's orange halo. Her once-long beautiful hair had been hacked off in mourning. "This is foolishness, Blue Raven," she said. "Who has not heard the stories of this child's Powers?" Her swollen eyes searched the crowd. Nods went round. "They say it kills animals with a *word*. Perhaps that's what it did to my husband. He—he was foaming at the mouth, and . . ." Her voice went tight, and for a long while she could not speak. "And he died jerking and clawing at his own flesh!"

"I know, Loon," Blue Raven said softly, "but you must set your feelings aside and look at the facts."

"There are no wounds on my husband's body! Oh, some scratches, on his neck and arms, but those might have come from running through brush. I searched every part of him!" Her gaze fixed on the False Face Child, and she reflexively stepped backward. "I know only that

I have no husband, and my children have no father. I tell you this evil Spirit is more Powerful than Falling Woman! It murdered Mossybill. *I* am sure of it!''

Shouts of agreement rose, and Uncle Blue Raven's face tensed. He spread his hands in a pleading gesture. ''Please think about this, Loon. We must wait until we have all—''

''Wait?'' Loon shouted. ''For the False Face to kill another?''

''Please, Loon. If the boy were that Powerful, how do you imagine that we could attack his village? Why didn't he kill our warriors with a word the instant they arrived? Why is Jumping Badger standing over there next to that birch tree? Surely Rumbler saw him when he first entered Paint Rock Village. Why would the boy let Jumping Badger, of all people, live?''

Rumbler's head swiveled and his black gaze fixed on Jumping Badger, as if seeing the war leader for the first time.

Jumping Badger tried to stare the boy down, but couldn't. When he dropped his gaze, hisses eddied through the gathering.

Little Wren could feel it. Building. Fear clutched at her throat like an invisible hand. She huddled deeper into her blanket, and examined Rumbler. His intent gaze swept Jumping Badger from head to moccasins, as if memorizing every feature of the man who had murdered his people.

A chill tickled Wren's spine.

Frost-in-the-Willows leaned over. ''Stop fidgeting, girl. Do you wish to lie down in my lap?''

Her grandmother wore her white hair in a bun on top of her head, and the style highlighted the deep wrinkles that carved her brown face. Wren shook her head. ''No. I want to watch. I'm worried about Rumbler.''

Frost-in-the-Willows gave her an alarmed look. "Do you think it is a child to be pitied? It is a murdering Forest Spirit in disguise!"

"But . . ." Wren looked back at Rumbler. "He has a boy's eyes, Grandmother."

"You are not looking, girl. Like a dog fascinated by its own reflection in a pond, all you see is appearance. Look deeper. Find the fish swimming beneath the surface. That is the way to wisdom."

Wren toyed with the laces on her moccasins and wondered about the things Uncle Blue Raven had said. How *could* Jumping Badger have attacked Paint Rock Village if Rumbler possessed such great Power?

"Grandmother? Do you think the boy . . . the False Face . . . can fly? Starflower called him the Disowned and said he flew up to the roof after he killed White Kit. I know that some people say the Disowned is just an old man who lives far to the north, but if he's really a Spirit, I was wondering—"

"Shh! Blue Raven has a hand up. Try listening to your elders, not thinking a little girl's puny thoughts."

Wren closed her mouth, and puzzled over the Disowned comment. She had heard the story many times, about a young man who so desired his brother's wife that he murdered his brother to get her. The horrified woman killed herself in grief, and the young man, overcome with guilt, drowned himself. When his soul reached the Up-Above-World, the Night Walkers refused to let him enter. Wind Mother herself shoved him through a hole in the sky and sent him tumbling toward earth. The forsaken young man sprouted wings as he fell. He became a homeless Forest Spirit, fluttering from place to place, shunned by all other beings.

Could the Disowned be the same Forest Spirit that had

fathered Rumbler? Memory tugged. She had heard that somewhere. Maybe from Jumping Badger.

Uncle Blue Raven spoke to Loon. "For many winters, I fought at Mossybill's side. More than once, he saved my life." He paused, then added, "And more than once I saved his. I cannot believe he would have wished this spectacle. He risked his life to capture the False Face Child, and to bring him back to us safely. Do you think that Mossybill or Skullcap would have wanted to see us arguing over whether or not the child should live? Let us all speak directly. That is what we are discussing. Search your souls. The Walksalong Clan lost many precious members in this raid. Shall we spit upon their sacrifices? *They* believed that the False Face Child would bring us safety, and peace!"

"But all it has brought us is death!" Loon said, wringing her hands. "Let's kill it before we lose anyone else! The raid was a mistake! A terrible mistake! Let us admit it, and go on!"

Blue Raven threw up his arms when the clamor increased. "Wait! Quiet! Please!"

Elk Ivory stood up at the edge of the circle behind Blue Raven. She wore her shoulder-length hair tucked behind her ears. She shouted, "Listen to Blue Raven! This is not how we live our lives! Everyone has the right to speak, and we have the obligation to hear their words!"

Blue Raven turned and gave her a grateful look, but the din only grew worse.

Wren cupped her hands over her ears. The deer hair that stuck out around Rumbler's neck quivered and glittered in the firelight. He was shaking. The sight made Wren feel small and broken inside—like a featherless baby bird tumbling from a tree. He had seen his village burned, seen people killed before his eyes, and now this.

The people who had taken everything from him had decided it was a mistake.

*He must hate us.*

"Let us waste no more time!" Loon yelled. "I cast my voice for death! Who will join me?"

Usually these deliberations went on until midnight. The sudden question must have stunned people, because a hush fell. Whispers replaced the shouts.

Uncle Blue Raven said, "There are many others we need to hear, Loon. Where is Skullcap's wife? Where are the men who fought at his side during the battle? Perhaps they observed an injury that would not show up on the body. A hard blow to the liver? Or a—"

"Neither man received any blows." Jumping Badger's deep voice pierced the night.

All heads turned toward him, and a hush fell.

Blue Raven took a step toward Jumping Badger. "How do you know, cousin? Did you watch them every moment of the battle?"

"Do you dare to say that I would select injured men to carry out the sacred duty of bringing the False Face Child back to our village?"

"Cousin, in the heat of battle it is difficult to know—"

"They were not in the heat of battle! I ordered them to come with me to attack the child's house. Once I gave the child into their arms, they left!"

Uncle Blue Raven stood unmoving, but his expression said plainly that he did not believe this. "You did not use two of your best warriors in the fight? Anyone could have guarded the boy until the end of the battle."

Jumping Badger stepped away from the birch tree and lowered his fists to his sides. "I had no way of knowing how Powerful he was. Of course I assigned my best warriors! Do you challenge my words, cousin?"

"I do not. I simply wish to know—"

"Ask my men. They will tell you the same."

Wren's gaze went over the warriors. They sat like stones, waiting to see if Uncle Blue Raven would shame the victorious war leader by asking.

Blue Raven said nothing for a time, as if considering the matter. "What about after they left the battle, cousin? You cannot know what happened to Skullcap and Mossybill once they had run beyond your sight. Can you say for certain that they received no injuries on the journey home?"

"I say that if they did, the injuries came from the False Face Child!"

Rumbler stared at Jumping Badger with unblinking eyes.

"Do you wish this child dead?" Uncle Blue Raven asked. "You were the one who urged this raid against the advice of our elders. You were the one who said, 'We must have the child.' Will you now stand before us and concede your judgment was in error?"

Jumping Badger lifted his chin. "At the time, I believed the child would give us Power over our enemies, and keep our bellies from hunger. I see now that he will do none of these things. He is wicked beyond my imaginings."

Little Wren glanced at Rumbler. He was shaking worse, his whole cape glittering.

"Are you casting your voice, cousin?" Uncle Blue Raven asked. "Before you have heard all sides you would—"

"I would," Jumping Badger said, and swung around to point at the severed head on the staff. "Before Lamedeer died, he told me that old Silver Sparrow had come to Paint Rock Village to warn them we were going to attack and steal the False Face Child. He said that the False Face Child would be our deaths!"

Gasps eddied through the assembly. Silver Sparrow was greatly feared and respected. If he had said such a thing . . .

But Wren heard something strange beneath the general din. Jumping Badger's warriors whispered to each other, and shook their heads.

Wren's gaze went from face to face. They did not seem to agree with their leader's words. Would any dare to speak out against him? It would be a challenge to Jumping Badger's position as war leader, and would require a fight to the death. In mere instants, the whispering quieted, and the warriors sat with their heads down.

Jumping Badger continued. "My voice joins Loon's! I cast for death!"

"Death! Death! Death!" The cry rumbled through the warriors. They lifted their fists in a show of unity.

Uncle Blue Raven shouted, "It is too early to cast your voices! We have not heard from everyone!"

Jumping Badger tramped across the plaza, and one by one his warriors rose and followed. People watched until they ducked into their longhouses, then voices rose, shouting down those that disagreed. Shoving matches started, and men leaped to their feet to break up the fights. Women hustled children away from the fire.

Uncle Blue Raven yelled, *"Wait! Come back! We are not finished!"*

Wren got to her feet, cupped her hands to her mouth, and cried, "I cast my voice for life! Let the boy live! He does not deserve death!"

Rumbler swung around to look at her. Tears blurred his eyes.

"I wish him to live!" she cried. "Let the boy live!"

Rumbler tucked a shaking finger into his mouth and his eyes fixed on Wren, as if she were his only hope in the entire world.

At the top of her lungs, Wren shouted, *"Let him live!"*

Frost-in-the-Willows picked up her walking stick and swung it at Wren with all her might. Wren yipped, ducked the blow, and scampered backward. "Enough, child!"

"I have a right to cast my voice, Grandmother! I am part of this clan!"

Frost-in-the-Willow's toothless mouth pursed. "That may be, but you do not have to cast with such enthusiasm. Let us go. This council is over. The decision has been made."

"But Grandmother, I don't wish to go! I want to stay and find out what will happen!"

"Blue Raven plans to bring the boy back to our longhouse later, after he meets with Starflower. When she has decreed how the child will die, Blue Raven will come home. You can find out then."

"But—"

"Don't struggle against me, girl! I'll break your neck!"

Wren twisted free, and saw tears running down Rumbler's face. Without thinking, she took a step toward him.

Frost-in-the-Willows jerked Wren's arm painfully. "You are a weasel, girl! If you keep sticking your nose in the wrong places, someday it will get nipped off!"

Frost-in-the-Willows hauled Wren through the crowd. Wren had to duck repeatedly to keep from being struck by arguers' hands and elbows. The masked Dancers watched them pass, their copper, shell, and stone eyes glittering.

"Grandmother!" Wren cried as they neared the longhouse. "Let me go! I don't wish to go home!"

When Uncle Blue Raven lifted the door curtain, cold wind fanned the dying fire. Flames crackled, and sparks spun upward. Wren threw the hides off her head to look.

He stood holding Rumbler's hand. Two warriors flanked them, their eyes ablaze in the sudden firelight.

Blue Raven spoke to the warriors, his voice weary. "We all have our duties. Yours is to stand guard. Mine is to see that the boy is as comfortable as possible for the next seven nights. It will not be necessary for you to check upon him. I will do that. I wish him to sleep, and eat. Given what awaits him, he will need his strength."

Acorn said, "Very well, Elder. We will be here if you call out."

"Thank you."

Blue Raven let the curtain fall. He squeezed the False Face Child's hand, and whispered, "Come this way, Rumbler." He led the child to his own buffalo hides. "This will be your bed."

As though anxious to lie down, Rumbler trotted forward on his stubby legs and curled on his side, facing the wavering bed of coals. In the ruddy glow, his plump face shone.

Uncle Blue Raven spread two more hides over Rumbler. "You mustn't be afraid," he said. "I will be there with you. Do you understand?"

Rumbler closed his eyes.

Wren could see the frustration and sadness that lined Uncle Blue Raven's face. He bent and stroked Rumbler's tangled hair. "Lost Hill will not be easy for either of us, but I promise you, I will not leave you."

Wren sank to the floor. Lost Hill . . . She had only seen four Starvings, but the pitiful cries of the babies who'd been abandoned there haunted her souls.

Uncle Blue Raven walked three paces away to the pile of extra furs near Frost-in-the-Willows. Grandmother rested on her back, her wrinkled mouth open, sound asleep. Blue Raven spread two elk hides across the floor, and stretched out on top, then pulled another down and rolled up in it. In less than a quarter hand of time, his breathing dropped to the deep rhythms of sleep. He must have been exhausted.

Wren's gaze drifted around the longhouse. The soot-blackened vegetables tied to the rafters glowed silver in the starlight pouring through the smoke holes. Down at the far end of the house, Jumping Badger's family whispered. Someone laughed softly.

Lost Hill. Oh, gods.

During the winter, Wind Mother blasted it bare of snow. All the trees leaned southward, their ugly trunks twisted by constant storms. Though the hill had a beautiful view of Pipe Stem Lake, no one went there. Her mother had once told her that the cries of all those lost children lived in every blade of grass that sank roots into that forsaken earth. *People may not be able to hear the cries with their ears, Wren, but their souls hear them. The cries make a deep ache in the chest that won't go away until you walk far beyond Lost Hill.*

Wren turned to look at Rumbler. He was sucking his finger. The red gleam of the coals sparkled in his eyes. How alone he must feel.

Wren thought about it, then cautiously slid closer to him.

"Are you warm enough, Rumbler?" she whispered. "I would share one of my hides with you if you needed it." She pulled on the heavy moose hide and handed him a corner.

He did not move.

"If you become cold in the night, tell me. I'll help you."

Sobs puffed his chest. "I told you."

". . . What?"

"That your people were going to kill me."

His faint voice tugged at her heart.

"I'm sorry, Rumbler," she said, and quickly glanced around to make sure that no one else could hear. Blood had started to surge in her ears.

A trembling smile touched his lips. Hoarsely, he said, "I tried to fly to the Up-Above-World. Like you said."

Wren blinked in surprise. "Did you find your mother?"

"No, I—I couldn't get there. It was so dark, and cold. My Spirit wings wouldn't work. But I've been having dreams about her. I dreamed that she was here. Alive. She was trying very hard to find me, but she couldn't, and I had no voice to call out to her."

Wren smoothed the moose hide with her fingers. It felt soft and warm. "I used to dream of my mother, too. For six moons after she died, I had the same dream."

"What about?"

"I dreamed that the canoe had overturned and she'd been washed downstream. It had taken Mother moons to find her way home, but one day she walked into the village, and she hugged me so hard, Rumbler, I swear I couldn't breathe."

When loneliness filled her up inside, Wren still had that dream, and her pain eased.

A soft mournful sound came from Rumbler's throat.

Wren bit her lip.

After the deaths of her parents and brother, she had begged Blue Raven a hundred times to go and search the banks of the river again. He had, of course, and just knowing that they weren't there, dying or alone, had made it easier for Wren to sleep.

"Rumbler?" she whispered. "I'm going to go outside to look for your mother."

His mouth opened, as if he couldn't believe she'd said it. "You are?"

"Yes." She reached for her red cape and moccasins. "I can't be gone too long, but I'll try to search the area around the village."

"Tell her I'm here!"

"I will," she said . . . though she knew she wouldn't have to.

All day long, people had been laughing and repeating the stories told by Jumping Badger and his warriors. Briar had died quickly, clubbed to death by Jumping Badger himself, after Rumbler had been torn from her arms.

But none of that mattered.

Wren laced her cape and moccasins, and rose to her feet. "Rumbler, while I'm out, try to sleep. Even though you have seven days to rest and eat, you are going to need your strength to last until your mother comes for you. Lost Hill is a bad place. I'll wake you when I return."

Rumbler nodded, and tears flooded his eyes.

Wren tiptoed to the door curtain, and ducked beneath it.

Acorn and Buckeye whirled. Stone knives glinted in their hands. They looked like giants. Acorn was big enough, but Buckeye stood another three hands taller and twice as wide. Wren had to lean her head way back to see their faces.

"It's just me," she said.

"Little Wren! What are you doing out here?" Acorn scowled at her. "Get back to your hides." He gestured to the door with his knife.

"I'm full of night water, Acorn! I have to get rid of it or I'll never sleep!"

Buckeye made a gruff sound. "Let her go. But be back

soon, or I'll come looking for you myself. Understand?''

Buckeye said the words as though he meant he'd come looking for her to slit her throat.

''I'm not afraid of you,'' Wren said, and dashed across the plaza as fast as she could, out through the southern palisade gate.

Buckeye and Acorn chuckled.

Wren stopped and looked around. Huge birches towered over her. The lodges of the Night Walkers gleamed brilliantly tonight. Every tree and pebble cast a shadow. As the wind blew, splashes of silver danced through the forest, making the frost-coated leaves in the trail sparkle like strewn handfuls of quartz crystals.

Though she didn't expect an answer, Wren whispered, ''Briar-of-the-Lake? Are you out here?''

Trees creaked in the wind, and Wren strained to find words in them.

''Briar? I am Little Wren. If you . . .'' The hair at the nape of her neck crawled as if touched by an unseen hand. Wren glanced around, breathing hard. It hadn't occurred to her until now that . . .

''*Boy?*'' Her voice had gone tight. ''Boy, if you are out here, leave me alone! I'm here for Rumbler!''

She broke into a run, speeding around the trail that circled Walksalong Village. Every few paces, she called, ''Briar? Briar, are you here? Please answer!''

The night seemed to hiss and whisper around her, watching her through speckles of starlight. The faint howl of a wolf rode the gusting wind. It echoed across the hills like the distant roar of thunder. She ran harder.

''*Briar!*''

When she had finished the full circle, she bent over just outside the palisade gate, and braced her hands on her knees, gasping for air. Shadows seemed to coalesce around her, melting together, growing. Her eyes widened.

Something moved out there . . . something enormous . . . with hairy feet. She couldn't see it, but her souls started to tremble.

Wren leaped through the gate and rushed toward Acorn and Buckeye, her hair flying out behind her. Both warriors scowled as she skidded to a stop, breathing hard.

Acorn looked her over. "I thought you'd been eaten by a monster."

Wren squared her shoulders. "You think I'm such a child," she said, and darted between them into the long-house.

She tiptoed back to her hides, removed her cape, and started unlacing her moccasins.

Rumbler lifted his head, and gazed at her desperately. "Did you find her?"

"No, but I'm going to keep looking, Rumbler. While you are on Lost Hill, I'll go out into the forest every morning and night, and call to her. Don't worry, I . . ."

Rumbler pulled a buffalo hide over his head. The sounds he made reminded her of a hurt puppy.

They sounded like Trickster's cries the night he'd died.

She took off her moccasins and set them aside, then she crawled into her bedding.

"Rumbler?" she whispered.

When he didn't answer, she reached out, slipped her fingers beneath his buffalo hide and dug around until she found his hand. She squeezed it tightly. "I'm right here, Rumbler. Everything's going to be all right. I promise."

Rumbler gripped her hand as though he would never let go.

Jumping Badger moved through the longhouse with the silence of mist, clutching the fabric doll in both hands. He'd sewn it from basswood fabric, painted its eyes brown and lips red. A slit revealed the doll's empty stomach cavity.

Sleeping people snored and shifted as he passed. The four fires had burned down to gleaming beds of coals, and threw red light over the bark walls. The scent of burning cedar pervaded the chilly air.

Outside in the black cold, a ghost moaned. He could hear her scratching against the walls of the longhouse, trying to get in. To find him.

Jumping Badger's long black hair swayed as he knelt beside Little Wren. The bottom fringe of his knee-length shirt hissed over the hide-covered floor.

The girl had called out to Briar, led her here.

Little Wren lay on her back with her hides pulled up to her pointed chin. A wealth of hair haloed her pretty face. Her right arm stretched across the floor, her limp fingers holding the False Face Child's stubby left hand.

Jumping Badger bent down and whispered in her ear, *"I saw you outside in the forest."*

He rested the doll on the hide over her chest, and slipped his knife from his belt. Picking up a lock of her hair, he intimately brushed it over his cheek and lips. Then he kissed the hair, and blew on it, sending his soul down the shaft and into her body. His warm breath condensed into a white cloud.

Wren's eyelids twitched.

Jumping Badger cut the lock off, picked up the doll, and stuffed the hair into the stomach cavity. It made a dark glistening well.

Something thumped against the wall, and he lunged to his feet, panting like a hunted animal. Fists. Invisible fists striking the walls . . .

She wanted *him.*

Jumping Badger's gaze searched the dark corners as he walked back down the longhouse. When he reached the fire pit nearest his bedding, he threw the doll onto the coals.

Smoke fluttered up.

Little Wren gasped for breath.

Jumping Badger smiled as the doll's head burst into flame and the whole fire pit caught. The burst of light drenched the walls and ceiling.

Little Wren cried out, and sat bolt upright. Blue Raven threw off his bedding, lurched to his feet, and ran to Wren's side.

"Shh, Wren," he murmured. "You are safe. We are all well."

Wren blinked wide-eyed, her gaze searching the firelit darkness. "Oh, Uncle!" she whimpered and threw her arms around his neck. "I dreamed the longhouse was burning down around me!"

Blue Raven murmured something Jumping Badger couldn't hear, and kissed Wren's forehead.

The False Face Child rolled over and his gaze fixed on Jumping Badger. Black. Glittering.

Jumping Badger backed up to his hides. As he stretched out on top of them, he watched the False Face Child.

The boy lifted his chin and turned his face to the firelight, as if making certain Jumping Badger could see him. He smiled, his teeth glinting, then pursed his lips. The breath he blew at Jumping Badger came out in a sparkling stream.

Jumping Badger's belly cramped suddenly. He stifled his groan, crawled under his hides, and tugged them over his head.

# Ten

"Mother?" Planter called. "Mother, the Trader, Corn-husk, is here. He wishes to speak with you."

Dust Moon sighed. She'd plaited her long gray hair into a single braid, and let it fall over her left shoulder as she looked around her warm lodge. Three paces across, it had a low ceiling and hide-covered floor. A small fire burned in the middle of the lodge, throwing wavering light over the baskets that lined the floor to her right. Filled with four different kinds of corn, sunflower seeds, gourds, and nuts, they provided almost everything she needed. She hated the idea of going out into such a dreary morning. A beautiful buckskin dress lay on her lap, the quillwork almost finished. Blue and red chevrons covered the sleeves, and a yellow spiral coiled across the chest. It would be a gift for Planter, if she ever finished it. She'd been working on the dress since last summer.

Dust set the dress aside, pulled her deerhide cape over her shoulders, and rose to her feet.

As she ducked out of her lodge into the fog, she gave Planter a questioning look. A pretty woman of thirty-four winters, Planter carried her infant son bundled in her arms. Planter shrugged, letting Dust know she hadn't the slightest idea why Cornhusk had decided to visit them again so soon. A prestigious Trader, he rarely deigned to trade with the smaller villages.

"When I saw him coming, I built up the plaza fire,

and brought my pot of tea from my lodge. It's your mixture, Mother.''

"Thank you, Planter." Dust patted her daughter's hand. "He wished to see me? Not our clan patron?"

"He asked for you, Mother."

Fog ghosted through the village, revealing houses, then swallowing them again. The bare maple branches had been dripping since dawn, and pools of water filled every hollow in the plaza. Dust stepped around them as she headed for the central fire. No one else was out. The ten conical lodges of Earth Thunderer Village sat quiet and still.

"A good day to you, Cornhusk," Dust said and settled herself in her usual place on the log before the fire. The rich scent of hickory smoke hung in the air, but the crackling blaze did little to stave off the cold. The fog had rolled in so thickly that Dust could not even see Goose Down Lake to the south, or Sparrow's lodge up the hill to the north. "I'm surprised to see you here, Cornhusk. You were around only half a moon ago. I'm afraid we have nothing new to Trade. Especially not at your prices."

The ugly Trader grinned, showing rotted front teeth. "How are you, Matron?"

"I am well, Cornhusk. Please sit."

Cornhusk crouched across from her, tall and lanky, his hands extended to the flames. His small dark eyes kept flickering back and forth between Dust and Planter. His knee-length buffalo coat looked shabby. Patches of curly brown fur had fallen out, giving the coat a mottled appearance.

Planter sat down next to Dust, and rested her son in her lap. She resembled her father more than Dust, her round face owlish, with large eyes and Sparrow's beaked nose. She was the only child Dust had left. All Dust had to do was look into Planter's eyes and the tumultuous world seemed to settle down. She cherished her daughter's companionship.

"Please help yourself to the pot of tea, Cornhusk," Dust said, and pointed to the tripod at the edge of the blaze. Wooden cups nestled near. "It's my own mixture of rose hips, rose petals, and spruce needles."

"Thank you, Matron." He reached for a cup. As he dipped it into the pot, steam billowed up. "What a miserable day." He finished his first cup in four swallows, let out a satisfied belch, and dipped up another.

Dust Moon lifted a brow. Cornhusk had an irritating habit of eating and drinking everything in sight before he got around to conversation. She folded her arms beneath her cape and tried to smile.

Planter gave her a look that begged patience, and Dust sighed.

Silver strands had just started to invade Cornhusk's black braid. To hear him tell it, the gray had come from leading an adventurous life. He often regaled people with stories of the curious palace builders who lived far to the west, or the strange animals that crawled the swamps to the south. Somewhere in his journeys, his nose had been broken. It sat like a crooked thumb between his broad cheekbones. Wrinkles incised his forehead, but the rest of his oblong face remained smooth and brown.

Cornhusk smiled. "Yes, this is good tea, Matron."

"It soothes me." Dust reached for her own cup, and filled it. The fragrance of roses bathed her face. Resting the cup on her knee, she said, "What brings you here on this bleak day? If I were you, I would be holed up in some warm lodge somewhere, surveying my wealth."

"Oh, please, Matron." He held up a hand. "I am just a poor Trader." He chuckled and lowered his gaze to his tea. "But you are right. I should be far to the south by now. I am taking a grave risk being here.''

Dust's eyes sharpened. Whatever he was selling, his price had just gone up. ''Indeed. Why?''

''If the matrons of Walksalong Village were to find out that I'd been here, they would gladly plunge a stiletto into my heart.''

Dust had been fearing this, that Jumping Badger would hear of the Paint Rock warrior in their camp and come trotting in with a war party. Is that why Cornhusk had come? To warn her? Blast Sparrow and his wicked Spirit Helper!

Her stomach ached, but she asked calmly, ''Why would the Walksalong matrons care where you've been?''

Cornhusk finished his second cup of tea and gestured to the pot. ''May I have another? It's such a cold day.''

''As you please.''

''Gracious of you, Matron.'' He tipped the teapot up, and poured the last drop into his cup. ''Well, this is a long story. A very long—''

''Then get started, Cornhusk.''

He looked askance at her. ''Yes, well. You have heard, I'm sure, that Jumping Badger attacked Paint Rock Village?''

''Yes.''

A sad look creased his face. ''I'm sorry to tell you that he killed your friend Briar-of-the-Lake.''

Her chest tightened. She had loved Briar, more than she would admit to anyone, even herself. Though Paint Rock and Earth Thunderer villages moved several times a season, they had always been relatively close together. As a child, Briar had taken advantage of that, running the distance like a fleet-footed deer, to curl up in Dust's lap and confide her childish secrets. Then, after Rumbler's birth, Briar had come to live with Dust and Sparrow. The girl had needed a refuge from her frightened clan, and Dust had given her one. Those two winters had been happy ones in Dust's life. They had spent a great deal of time together, laughing and talking—and watching Rumbler. In many ways, she thought of him as her own son. His smile lived in her heart, alongside those of her other children.

They hadn't known until Rumbler started walking that something was different about him. His arms and legs didn't seem to be growing. Dust had tried feeding him every Power herb she knew, but it hadn't helped. When they'd finally realized he'd been touched by Falling Woman's hand, they'd both worked even harder, guiding and protecting him. Before he'd seen two winters, his Power had started to blossom. Everyone could feel it. When Rumbler tottled by, his round face alight, the hair on the backs of people's arms stood on end.

After Flintboy died, Dust's friendship with Briar fell apart. She had done so much for Briar, risked so much for her, and the one time Dust had truly required Briar's help, she had refused to come. Then, when Dust moved Sparrow's belongings out of her lodge, Briar came to see her to plead Sparrow's case, begging Dust to take him back. *He loves you so much,* Briar had said.

Dust frowned down into her teacup. The pale green liquid looked golden against the wood. The night that Flintboy died, Dust had needed Sparrow desperately. But Sparrow had risen from their robes, left their lodge, and disappeared into the darkness. He'd stayed gone for eighty-three days. She had grieved alone, her despair made worse by her worry over Sparrow. The night he returned, he'd danced about the village, spouting incomprehensible things about a Spirit Helper from the Up-Above-World, a god disguised as a little boy. The people in Earth Thunderer Village had watched his antics fearfully. Dust had not known what to think. Had Sparrow taken Flintboy's death harder than she'd thought? Some women who lost sons went mad. Perhaps that had happened to Sparrow? She'd coddled him. She'd listened to him. She'd pleaded, and shouted, and begged Sparrow to come to his senses, to take their lives and clan business seriously, again. But he'd patiently explained that he couldn't. His Spirit Helper had shown him another path. *From now on, Dust, Power will often need me more than you do.*

Dust sipped her tea. For two winters those words had been eating her from the inside out.

Briar had maintained that if Dust would just get to know Sparrow's Spirit Helper, she might like him. She remembered her own response: *"Have you been bitten by a foaming-mouth dog?"*

"How did Briar die?" Dust asked.

"You don't want to hear. Trust me. You know Jumping Badger. He's a monster."

"I *do* want to hear, or I would not have asked."

"Very well, but remember that you can't always believe things Jumping Badger says. The man is a notorious liar. Be that as it may, he claims that while his warriors raced through Paint Rock Village, killing and setting fires, he took two men to Briar's house. He found her inside, clutching the dwarf boy to her breast. She begged him not to hurt the False Face Child. Offered him anything if he would just let the boy live. But Jumping Badger tore the boy from her arms, threw the child like a sack of nuts to his warriors, and ordered them out of the house." Cornhusk smiled grimly. "Then Jumping Badger forced Briar down. He raped her while the whole of Paint Rock Village was burning around them! Can you believe that? Jumping Badger astounds even me!" Cornhusk's eyes had dilated, as if the story excited him.

"Then," he said, and casually waved a hand, "he clubbed her to death."

Dust clutched her cup more tightly. "How do you know that last part? If there were no warriors to witness the act—"

"Jumping Badger told me! I swear, the story comes straight from his own lips." He ran a finger around the rim of his cup. "Of course, I had to pay him to hear it, but it was worth it."

Worth it. Of course. A slow anger built beneath Dust's heart. Cornhusk had not canoed across the lake for six days, then run for another day across land, to tell her about Briar. All this was a prelude to the real news he carried. He was giving her a glimpse of the information before he tried to sell it to her.

"And what of the boy? What did Jumping Badger do with Rumbler?"

Cornhusk smiled like a cat at a mousehole. "I will tell you. Truly. That's why I came. But I wish to ask a small favor first."

"Indeed."

Cornhusk's smile faded. "It is very valuable information, Matron. Especially to you."

"To me? Why?"

Cornhusk made a gesture of self-reproach. "Forgive me, but I thought you might wish to save the boy? I had heard that you eared for him."

Images of Rumbler's bright eyes flitted through her souls. "Blessed gods, you mean they plan to kill him?"

"Oh, yes. I stayed at Walksalong Village until I heard the verdict, then I ran straight to you."

"Why would they steal him and then—"

Cornhusk lifted a hand as though to calm her down. "It seems that the Paint Rock war leader, Lamedeer, told Jumping Badger something terrifying before he died."

"What?"

"First—"

"Yes! Yes! Name your 'small' favor."

Cornhusk seemed to be examining the wood grain in his cup. He hesitated, then said, "This is a difficult matter for me to discuss. Let me put it this way. A young woman at one of the villages in the south tempted me beyond my powers to resist and I—"

"Bedded her."

"Yes, but it wasn't my fault, you see. I tried to explain this to her husband, but he—"

"Wants you dead, because the Flicker Clans cut people apart for adultery."

"Er—well—yes. I think her husband kills two or three men a moon. This woman, she is insatiable. Not to mention *very* beautiful."

"How many war parties are searching for you?"

"Three, I think." Cornhusk shrugged. "Not that I'm scared. I'm too cunning for them to find me, but I do need a tiny little—"

"Will you please get to it!"

Cornhusk set the cup back near the teapot, and wiped his hands on his mangy buffalo coat. "Silver Sparrow's Powers are renowned far and wide, Matron. You may not think much of him personally, but his speeches about the gods have become famous. People repeat fragments of them wherever I go. Truly, his reputation has grown faster than any holy man I have ever heard of. Just mentioning his name in the south causes gasps and scurrying." Cornhusk looked up.

"And you are hoping that Sparrow will . . . ?"

Cornhusk's nose wrinkled, as if what he was about to ask was such a trifle. "Curse my enemies for me?"

Dust leaped to her feet and shouted, *"Are you crazy!"* Planter's infant son shrieked and Planter clutched him to her chest. "If the Flicker Clans ever found out, they would slaughter Earth Thunderer Village!"

He said, "They might, but once you have heard the rest of the story, Matron, I think you will consider that to be the least of your worries."

Dust felt weak. She forced herself to sit down again. "Go on."

Cornhusk laced his fingers around one knee. "I'm not certain how much of this is true. Jumping Badger told me one thing and his warriors told me another. But Jumping Badger's story is this: He says that Lamedeer told him that your husband—"

"*Former* husband."

"Yes. Sorry. Anyway, he said that Silver Sparrow went to Paint Rock Village fourteen nights ago to warn Lamedeer that Jumping Badger was going to attack and steal the False Face Child. He also . . ." He blinked and straightened when he saw Dust sag. "Matron? Matron? Are you well?"

"Mother?" Planter said in concern.

So that's why Sparrow had gone to Paint Rock Village. She wondered if everyone but her knew. She glanced at Planter and found her daughter staring at her from beneath her lashes. Hallowed Spirits, he had Dreamed Briar's death and not even told her? She clenched her fists.

"I'm fine. Continue."

"Do you need a cup of tea?" He reached for the empty pot. "No, well, perhaps a—"

"Tell your story!"

"So," he rushed to add, "Lamedeer said that the False Face Child would be the death of the Walksalong Clan, and . . ." Cornhusk lifted a finger to emphasize his next words. "Then Lamedeer said that Silver Sparrow had cursed Jumping Badger. Sparrow supposedly prophesied that Jumping Badger's Power would drain away until he was like a camp dog, kicked by everyone.''

It sounded just like something Sparrow would have said. Blast him! ''What does this have to do with saving Rumbler?''

As Grandfather Day Maker warmed the world, the mist shredded, blowing through camp in gossamer veils. Dust could just see the faintest outline of Sparrow's rounded lodge on top of the hill. The wet bark shone.

Cornhusk propped his elbows on his knees. ''I spoke to several of Jumping Badger's warriors. On the run home, they said he acted like a fool. He insisted upon walking in the rear of the war party. Imagine! A war leader in the back! It's disgraceful. They also said he would never let his fireboard out of his sight. He stopped carrying it in his pack. When he wasn't using it to start fires, he tied it around his throat. He—''

''This is all fascinating, Cornhusk, but I don't see why—''

''He's afraid of the dark, Matron!'' Cornhusk laughed out loud. ''Don't you see? He thinks he's lost his Power. The great war leader of the Walksalong Clan is terrified that your hus—former husband's—curse is killing his souls!''

If what he said were true, then coming to her was indeed dangerous. Traders had to be very careful what stories they carried from village to village, or they wound up dead.

Dust studied his ugly face. ''And?''

''Jumping Badger wants to make a deal with you!''

Planter shifted uneasily and, when Dust turned to her, Planter subtly shook her head. Dust knew what it meant, *Don't trust him.*

Dust glanced up the hill again. Sparrow stood outside his lodge, his waist-length white hair shining, his broad shoulders accented by the cut of the elkhide jacket she had made for him. Remnants of old love, and new hurt, mixed painfully in her chest. She had trusted him with her life, and the lives of their children . . . and he had shattered that trust. Gods, she wished he had not. Or that she could forgive him. But too much anger and pain still breathed in her souls. She glared at Cornhusk.

"What is this 'deal' he is offering?"

"Oh, that's the best part. The Walksalong matrons granted the boy seven nights of life, then condemned the False Face Child to be placed on Lost Hill. That's the hill where they abandon babies during Starvings. If the weather is not too severe, the boy will probably last six or seven nights. Maybe even eight if there is snow for him to eat. You know how strong children are. Jumping Badger wants to help you free the child before he dies." Cornhusk rubbed his hands together as if in delight. "What do you say?"

"To what? You've told me almost nothing! How does he plan to free the child, and what does he wish in return?"

Sparrow knelt and began arranging kindling in his fire pit, but she could feel him watching her. She concentrated on Cornhusk.

"Oh," Cornhusk said, and made a negligent gesture. "Jumping Badger's plan is simple. The Walksalongs have a specific ritual for Vigils. The Vigil Keeper is not allowed to leave Lost Hill until the child is dead, but no one else can come to visit the hill, either, except for the person designated to bring the Keeper food and drink twice a day."

"Then Rumbler will be out there alone with this Vigil Keeper?"

"Yes, and if you and Silver Sparrow come to Walksalong Village, Jumping Badger says he will kill the man keeping Vigil! After that, you may take the boy and run. If you agree to this, I will meet you at the base of Lost Hill, on the lakeshore, and then take you to Jumping Badger.

"What does he wish in return?"

"Another favor." Cornhusk drew his thumb and index finger together to show her how tiny. "A very small one, Matron. He wants Sparrow to remove the curse! Sparrow has to show up himself, of course, so that Jumping Badger can *feel* the curse being removed, but isn't this simple?" Cornhusk clapped in childlike delight. "Sparrow curses my enemies, then he removes the curse from Jumping Badger, and you can have the Power child!"

If Rumbler lived long enough. If the matrons had granted him seven nights of life, then he was staked on Lost Hill right now, shivering in the icy cold, braving the winds that raged around Pipe Stem Lake. . . . And it would take them at least seven days to get to him.

Dust stood, and braced her knees. "Stay here," she said. "I will talk with Sparrow. Planter, please see that our guest is fed while I am gone."

"Yes, Mother."

As she started up the hill, sunlight pierced the mist and shot golden lances around her. Where they struck, the wet ground glistened. She skirted the puddles, but it did little good. Within moments her soaked moccasins clung to her feet.

Sparrow threw a piece of wood on his fire, and walked to the edge of the hilltop to watch her approach. One of his bushy white brows quirked.

He cupped a hand to his mouth and yelled, "No, he isn't dead, Dust! And I won't rush him along!"

Dust climbed the hill, threw him a disgruntled look as she walked past him, and stopped in front of his fire to warm her hands. Through the lodge door, she could see

the Paint Rock warrior, lying on his side, one arm flopped
out before him. He looked very young. Fifteen or sixteen
winters. She must know him, but she couldn't place his
face, or name. He'd probably recently been given a man's
name, which explained why she'd never heard it, but she
wished she knew his lineage. Every member of the Turtle
Nation was related somehow. He might be her uncle's
brother's son, or something. Upon meeting a stranger in
the forest, a person always began the conversation by
asking the stranger's clan. Lineage provided a basis for
friendship.

Sparrow edged around the fire pit to curiously peer at
Dust. His round face and hooked nose shone with mist.
He arched his brows expectantly. "What?"

"Sit down, Sparrow. I have news."

Sparrow eased onto his stump across the fire, watching
her. It took less than one hundred heartbeats for her to
get to the part about the curse he'd supposedly placed on
Jumping Badger. She stopped, folded her arms, and
glared at him. Beads of fog glittered on her long gray
braid, and pearled the shoulders of her deerhide cape.
Behind her, the smoke from the village coiled across the
sky like a lazy blue-gray serpent. Four young boys had
risen and, laughing, trotted down to the lake to fill water
gourds.

Sparrow raised his hands, as if to defend himself.
"First of all, I did not curse Jumping Badger. Any problems he's having are his own fault. I don't know why
Lamedeer said that. I assume he was desperate and
wanted to throw a scare into Jumping Badger. If the story
had caused Jumping Badger to hesitate, even for a mo-

ment, it would have given Lamedeer more time to save the lives of his people. It would also have weakened Jumping Badger's position with his warriors. Who wants to go raiding with a cursed man?''

Dust still glared.

''Secondly.'' He made an airy gesture. ''I didn't tell you about the Dream, because every time I mention my Spirit Helper you turn into a wild snarling beast, and I didn't want to see it.''

''Most of your Dreams are ridiculous, Sparrow, but if I'd known about that one, I would have rallied our warriors, and sent them to help defend Paint Rock Village.''

''You would?'' he asked in surprise. ''I thought you didn't believe my Dreams?''

Her eyes narrowed menacingly. ''Do you recall that night you came running down the hill to tell me to order our warriors to make a thousand arrows? You said an enormous flock of crows was going to gobble up our entire nut harvest, and that if I didn't—''

''Half of that Dream came true, Dust! The flock of crows blackened the whole sky! How was I supposed to know they'd come to eat the beetles who were devastating the trees?''

''It was your Dream. That's how.''

Sheepishly, he answered, ''Well, I was a new Dreamer then. I hadn't figured out how to interpret the images. I—''

''Anyway,'' she interrupted, deliberately ending the lengthy explanation he'd planned. ''Every time I believe you, and you're wrong, people laugh at me behind my back. That happened quite often two winters ago. My reputation couldn't take much more.''

''*Your* reputation?''

''Of course I view your 'Dreams' warily. But I wish you'd told me your Dream about Briar.''

Sparrow bowed his head. "I wish I had, too. But you must know, Dust, that the addition of our fifteen warriors would have made no difference. Even if we'd called out every healthy person, we could have mustered no more than twenty-five or thirty people. Jumping Badger's forces number over one hundred. He—"

"I know that." She tucked her arms beneath her cape, and shifted uncomfortably. After several moments, she said, "Let me tell you the rest."

"There's more?"

"Yes, and it's probably a trap. Jumping Badger is offering a trade. He promises to kill the Vigil Keeper and deliver Rumbler to us, if you will just remove your curse. But you and I have to go to Walksalong Village so that he can feel you remove it, or he'll let Rumbler die."

"*Go* to Walksalong Village?" he shouted. "Those people hate us, Dust! If we dance into their plaza, we're going to have enough holes in our bodies to winnow seeds. I hardly think—"

"Cornhusk is going to go ahead of us, Sparrow. He'll speak with Jumping Badger and arrange a safe meeting place for you to remove your nonexistent curse, then we'll go to Lost Hill together, Jumping Badger will kill the Vigil Keeper, and you, and I, and Rumbler, will run like rats from a pack of starving wolves."

"This sounds like suicide, Dust."

"Are you coming or not?"

Sparrow looked into the fire while he considered this insanity. Hickory smoke rose from the flames in perfect coils, smelling sweet, warming his face. Jumping Badger couldn't be trusted. His own warriors said he'd gone mad. Which meant that no one could predict what he might do. Cornhusk and Jumping Badger had created a nice, reasonable plan—for them.

Sparrow looked up. Should he tell Dust now, or after they'd met with Jumping Badger?

Dust examined his thoughtful expression, read it perfectly, and said, "Blast you, you'd better tell me."

"Well, I was just thinking. If I remove the curse before we have Rumbler in our hands, Jumping Badger has no reason to keep his part of the bargain. Does he? Did I miss something?"

Dust's face slackened. "Great gods, I didn't think—"

"I did, and I'm not removing my curse until after the Vigil Keeper is dead and you and Rumbler are far away."

"But Sparrow, that will leave you alone in hostile country, with—"

"Well, there is another way." He searched her face, judging her mood. The probability that he'd die had softened her expression a little. "I'm going alone. I—"

"No.

"Dust, I—"

"No!"

"Dust, there is no need for you to be there. I can go, get Rumbler, pretend I'm removing the curse, and come home."

She shook her head, and her long braid shimmered. "Rumbler may need me. I'm a Healer. You're just a Dreamer."

Sparrow tilted his head to show his admiration. "What an accomplishment, Dust. I never imagined anyone could make the word 'Dreamer' sound so trivial."

"I'm going."

Perhaps a little too jauntily, Sparrow said, "Oh, come now, Dust. You're just being arrogant. Do you really think I could have lived with you for thirty-five winters and learned nothing about Healing plants?"

"Why, yes," she said.

He ignored her answer. "Do you recall the time that Planter was climbing the tree and fell out on her head? You were off at a nearby village. Didn't I put moss poultices on Planter's wounds and boil willow to cure her headache?"

"Ah. An expert."

"There is *no* reason for you to go!"

Dust brushed at a speck of ash on the front of her cape, then studied the sky for a time. When she looked back at him, he might have been gazing at a face carved on a post. "I'll be ready to leave in one finger of time. I was thinking of giving in and asking Planter to care for the Paint Rock warrior. Is that acceptable to you?"

"I swear, Dust." Once she'd made up her mind, it took a bolt of lightning in the brain to change it. "This is very dangerous. I wish you would—"

"Yes, or no?"

Sparrow kicked at one of the hearthstones. "Planter is almost as good a Healer as you are. I would be grateful if she would care for Crowfire."

"How soon can you be ready?"

"I just need to pack a few things. Some food, another shirt, maybe—"

"Make it less than a finger of time. If we run all the way we'll get close to the canoe landing tonight. Meet me at my lodge."

In their clan it was customary for young, or poor, warriors to show unquestioning loyalty to their war leader's orders by lifting and shaking both fists. Sparrow did it automatically, just as he had in his early days as a warrior.

Dust's brows lowered, as if she didn't particularly appreciate the gesture. She turned to go, but didn't.

"What about Cornhusk?" she said with her back to him.

He gazed at the bottom of the hill where Planter and the Trader sat. Cornhusk had a bowl in one hand, and was shoveling food into his mouth with the other. "Tell Cornhusk that I won't curse his enemies, but I will give him a charm to protect him."

"That should be good enough."

Dust turned slightly to meet his eyes. "I know this is dangerous, Sparrow. I also know you don't have to do this. I am grateful for your help."

As if she knew her tender words would kindle his heart, and she couldn't bear to see it on his face, she hurried down the hill.

Sparrow studied her back, her shoulders already squared for the perilous trial ahead, and a smile of respect came to his lips.

He ducked into his lodge and grabbed his pack.

# Eleven

Wren wandered the longhouse, using her chert knife to pry up stone flakes that had been trampled into the dirt near the doorway, and to pick at the bark peeling from the sapling frame. Often, she lifted the leather door hanging and peered out at the blustery afternoon. All day long, Wind Mother had been acting like an enraged bear, slapping tree branches, scratching the ground, kicking twigs and gravel into Walksalong Village. Even the Cloud Giants looked angry. Black and brooding, they tumbled over each other, racing across the sky.

Wren dawdled, studying the poles that framed the door. Since the False Face Child might die today, her grandmother had ordered Wren to dress in new finely tailored pants, and a knee-length shirt. White spirals decorated the blue fabric. When the boy died, Uncle Blue Raven would come into the village and ask everyone to gather for the final ceremony where they boiled the boy's body and stripped it clean of flesh. Usually, the dead child's bones were buried beneath the floor of the longhouse. That way, if he chose to, his soul could enter a woman's womb and be reborn. But Wren didn't know what her clan would do with Rumbler's bones. They hated him so much they might throw his bones to the village dogs.

She hacked at one of the doorway poles, and her grandmother snapped, "For the sake of the Ancestors, Wren, come and sit down! You've got Bogbean jumping at her own wheezes!"

The two old women had been spinning dog hair since midday and several long sticks lay beside them, wrapped with different colors of the yarn. Frost-in-the-Willows looked especially tall and weedy next to Bogbean's girth. Even during Starving times Bogbean remained corpulent. It always astounded Wren.

"I don't want to sit down, Grandmother," Wren protested. "I'm too nervous."

"About what?"

Bogbean put a hand on Frost-in-the-Willow's arm. "She's worried about the False Face Child. When Blue Raven took the boy out to Lost Hill, Wren begged him to let her go along."

Frost-in-the-Willows arched her thin white brows. "It is against tradition and you know it, Little Wren. You will see your uncle, and the boy, at suppertime when you take Blue Raven his meal."

"But I—"

"Don't talk. Listen." Her grandmother pointed a stern finger. "No one may go to the hill, except you. You must honor the obligations that go along with that privilege. You go, you deliver food, and you return home. That is how it's done."

Wren turned her gray chert knife in her hands. "I wish Rumbler didn't have to—"

"Starflower determined his fate. It is done. Stop thinking about it."

More gently, Bogbean said, "Grandfather Day Maker makes no promises that we will see all the days we wish to, Wren. We must live the best we can, and be happy that our lives are no worse than they are."

Frost-in-the-Willows made a half disgusted, half amused sound. "Don't you realize, Wren, that the False Face Child is lucky? If Blue Raven hadn't begged Starflower for leniency, the boy would be out in the plaza this instant with a fire under his feet. Be thankful."

In a small voice, she said, "I am. Thankful."

"Besides," her grandmother added, "people usually get what they deserve."

Wren slowly lowered her knife. The smiling faces of her mother and father, and little Skybow, appeared on her souls. Then Trickster trotted happily into the picture, his white tail wagging. Without warning, tears rolled down her cheeks. She looked dumbly at her grandmother.

"What's wrong with you?" her grandmother asked. "You look like a hurt animal!"

"D-did my family deserve to die?" Wren demanded to know. "Did Trickster? He never did anything wrong! He was a good dog, and a good friend to me. I—"

"No one wishes to hear your babbling!"

How many times had adults told her they didn't want

to hear what she had to say? As though her thoughts could not possibly matter.

Wren tucked her knife back into her belt sheath, grabbed her white fox-fur cape from the pegs near the entry, and ducked outside into the gale. Long black hair whipped around her slender face, tangling with her eyelashes.

"Oh, let her go," she heard her grandmother say. "She is such a troublesome child. She always has been. I remember right after—"

In the empty plaza, the village fire pit had blown clean of ashes. Long streaks of gray created a starburst around the rocks. She ran past it to the northern palisade gate. Lost Hill sat at the bottom of the trail. As long as she did not set foot on the hill, she would not be violating any rules. She glanced up at the afternoon rays slanting across the forest. She had at least two hands of light left, and the gods knew, no one in Walksalong Village was going to miss her. At least not until the time came for her to carry Uncle Blue Raven's food to him at dusk. She would be home long before that.

Pinecones and twigs scattered the trail. Wren leaped them as she ran.

Where the trail veered around the toppled maple, Wren bent over to peer into the gaping hole left by the roots. Water had leeched from the ground and soaked the pebbles in the bottom of the hole. They resembled polished jewels.

Wren reached down, and plucked a red stone from the side of the hole. One of the sacred colors, red meant life. Red stones also frequently hid the quivering body of the bad twin, Red Flint. She held it to her ear, didn't hear it breathing, and put it in her cape pocket, then she started running again.

With each gust of wind, shadows and sunlight swayed

across her path. She sprinted past the bare oaks at the foot of the trail, and out onto the beach. Waves dashed the shore, throwing spray two body lengths high. As the droplets fell, they sparkled like the rainbow. Wren watched them for a few moments, then glanced to her left at the grove of trees where she had seen the bloody boy. Though it had happened eight nights ago, it seemed like eight heartbeats. Her pulse raced as she searched the tangled deadfall, and brush. *". . . You will come with me. Power has decided."* In the daylight she wasn't so scared, but when she had to come down here to deliver Uncle Blue Raven's food at dusk . . . she prayed she didn't wet her new pants.

She glanced at Lost Hill.

Uncle Blue Raven sat near the top with an elkhide around his shoulders. His bow and arrows lay beside him, and he had a small fire going. About fifty hands down the hillside from the fire, Rumbler lay. His small misshapen body had been stretched out and his hands and feet bound, then staked down.

He rested about two hundred hands from Wren, but she could see him clearly. He wore only moccasins and his black shirt. The shell ornaments sewn across his chest winked when the wind blew them. The cold must be eating at his bones, but he looked so still, so brave.

An eagle spiraled over the hill, and Wren wondered if it was really an ordinary bird or a Thunderbird in disguise. The personal Spirit Helpers of Grandmother Earth, Thunderbirds possessed great Power. They gave Grandmother Earth drink when she thirsted, cleansed her when she needed refreshing, and kept her fruitful. They also stoked fires in their skyforges and threw flaming arrows at the forests to burn away underbrush and create lush green meadows. From early spring to late fall, the Thunderbirds diligently tended to the needs of Grandmother Earth, then, in winter, they played. Often that play included changing themselves into eagles.

Wren's brows pinched. The eagle's circles tightened. He picked up speed. When he neared the top of Lost Hill, a whirlwind of dirt and old leaves churned up beneath him. The funnel twisted into the sky like a dirty serpent. It stormed across the slope, blasted Uncle Blue Raven, then corkscrewed its way down the hill. Just before striking Rumbler, the funnel vanished. All the old leaves it had been holding aloft came fluttering down.

Wren's jaw slackened as they landed around Rumbler, covering him like a thick brown blanket.

"Did you call out to the Spirits for help, Rumbler?" she whispered. "Is that why . . ."

He lifted his head.

Wren straightened in surprise. She hadn't expected him to hear her. The breeze must have been just right to carry her voice to him. She glanced at her uncle to make sure he wasn't watching, then gave Rumbler a quick wave.

Rumbler looked at her for as long as he could, his mouth moving, then he sank to the ground.

Defeat filled Wren. She tried to memorize every line in his face, the way his stubby arms and legs lay, even the glimmers on his black shirt. If a person had to die, it seemed to her that the people responsible should at least have to watch it happen. Perhaps if everyone in Walksalong Village were required to sit Vigils, fewer people would be condemned.

Wren had to force herself to swallow before she could breathe.

She stayed at the bottom of Lost Hill, watching, until the light began to fade, and she knew she had to go home.

Silver Sparrow added branches to the morning fire. Frost coated the grass, and outlined the trail like fresh snow. His breath misted as he leaned over the soot-coated pot hanging from the tripod at the edge of the coals. The tea smelled tangy. Made of dried crabapples and hardened chunks of maple sap, it had a deliciously tart flavor. He'd been up for about a hand of time, getting the fire going, boiling water for tea, setting out gourd cups, and rolling his hides. His pack sat an arm's length to his left. Dust slept on the other side of the fire, her beautiful face serene. Beyond her, a long forested ridge curved down to the shore of Leafing Lake. The treetops gleamed in the faint gray of dawn. The brightest lodges of the Night Walkers twinkled above the indigo water.

Sparrow sank back upon his deerhide, and watched the winking dance of the sparks as they climbed through the winter-bare oak branches into the dark sky. Yesterday had been a very long day. From early morning, until almost dark, they had run, walked, and run some more, until they'd reached the three canoes that Earth Thunderer Clan always left hidden in the brush along the lakeshore. He could feel every one of his fifty-three winters in his joints.

Sparrow rotated his shoulders. "Blessed ancestors," he whispered. "I hurt all over."

He reached for one of the cups, and dipped it full of hot tea. When he started to drink, his reflection stared back, his beaked nose, bushy white eyebrows, and blunt chin clear. His white braid draped his left shoulder. As he tilted his head to examine the wrinkles around his eyes, Dust spoke.

"You look ancient." She still lay rolled in her blankets.

"I look wise."

"You've started to believe that drivel people say about you, Sparrow."

He grinned. "Why don't you rise so we can be on our way."

She propped herself on one elbow and long silver hair tumbled over her shoulders. "Blessed gods, it was a cold night. My bones ache."

"I fear we shall see more cold nights before this is through, Dust."

She yawned. "Where do you think Cornhusk is?"

"I don't know. Probably half a day ahead of us. He canoes the lakes, and runs the trails, constantly. You and I are lucky if we can run for a finger of time before we sprawl face first into the dirt."

Dust gave him a faintly amused look, and threw off her blanket. Like him, she'd slept in her clothes. She extended one long brown leg, and massaged her calf muscles. Her groan affirmed his opinion about their aging bodies.

"Hurts, eh?"

"No worse than the rest of me." She got to her feet and walked to the fire. The creases in her leather cape would fall out as they traveled, but right now they resembled a thick web. Dust knelt, and reached for her pack which lay at the edge of the hearthstones. Drawing out a wooden comb, she began running it through her hair. The long waves from yesterday's braid picked up the fire's gleam and seemed to flicker and spark.

Sparrow had missed this morning ritual more than he'd realized. Seeing it again brought him a pleasurable anguish. When they'd been married, every night before retiring he'd combed her hair for her. Beneath his hands, that lustrous wealth had gone from deepest black to pure gray, and he'd cherished the changes in each strand.

"We should reach Walksalong Village in six days, shouldn't we?" she asked.

"Yes. If we push ourselves to the limit of our elderly endurances. We should make it on the evening of the day between the new moon and the full moon."

"But's that's good, isn't it? We'll be able to pick up Rumbler and escape under the cover of darkness. We'll be home by the full moon."

Sparrow swirled his tea. "I hope so."

Her comb halted. "What does that mean? You didn't Dream something, did you?"

"No. I just have this knot in my belly. I'm worried that Jumping Badger might do something completely unexpected."

"You mean like surround us with fifty warriors?"

He nodded. "Yes."

She started combing her hair again. "Well, then you'll have to deliver one of your famed speeches."

"Famed? My speeches?"

"Cornhusk says so."

He sipped his tea. "In Jumping Badger's case, I doubt any of my speeches, famed or not, will have an effect. I barely know him, Dust. I met him once, ten winters ago when we were still Trading with the Bear Nation. He wasn't even war leader then. He was a surly boy. I was in Walksalong Village to speak with their Headman, Blue Raven. His mother, Frost-in-the-Willows, was there, and Jumping Badger strutted through the longhouse."

"Well, he's afraid of you. That's enough."

Sparrow gulped the rest of his tea, and poured the dregs on the fire. Steam exploded as drops of water bounced across the logs. "Just in case it isn't, maybe I'd better start thinking up speeches."

Dust tugged her hair over her right shoulder and began plaiting it into a thick braid. "What are we eating?"

"I thought we'd pull one of those food bags out of your pack."

"You've always been lazy, Sparrow. You haven't started anything? Nothing at all?"

"I started the tea."

Sparrow reached for a cup, dipped it full, and handed it to her.

Dust set it on the ground, and finished her braid. After she'd tied it with a cord, she tucked her comb into her pack, and drew out two birch-bark bags, one painted blue, the other red. "Here," she said as she tossed him the blue bag. "Since it's too late to start anything hot, this will have to do."

Sparrow unlaced the bag and drew out a thick slice of beaver jerky. "What's in the red bag?"

"Corn cakes." She pulled one out and took a bite.

He eyed it longingly. "With roasted hickory nuts?"

She nodded, closed the bag and tucked it back into her pack.

Sparrow ripped off a piece of tough jerky and chewed. And chewed.

They ate in silence.

Wind Mother ambled through the valley, rustling the trees and grass, and swinging the pot on the creaking tripod.

Dust shivered. "Great panther, it's cold."

Sparrow rose to his feet, picked up the deerhide he'd been sitting on, and walked around the fire. "Yes, and Rumbler is staked out in this, with no cape or blanket." He handed her the hide. "We should—"

"Keep the hide, Sparrow. You need it as badly as I do."

He roughly draped it over her shoulders. "Don't tell

me what I need. I know far better than you, and always have.''

He walked back to his side of the fire, and tucked his cup into his pack. The sky had begun to gray. ''Dawn Woman is waking,'' he said. ''We should get to our canoe.''

Though she wore her fox cape and wolfhide mittens, the cold wind sucked the warmth from Wren's body. In the dim blue-gray light, the snowflakes appeared to come out of nowhere, pirouetting down silently onto the Sunshine Boy's naked branches, and Wren's upturned face. Snow glistened on her eyelashes.

She knelt beside Trickster's grave. ''I don't know what to do, Trickster. A nightmare woke me. I was cold with sweat and crying. I—I was back at the river, where my parents' canoe washed up, and I knew that Mother was dead, and all my strength with her.'' Snow began to fill the grave again. She brushed it away. ''I was alone, and I didn't know which trail led back to Walksalong Village. But I could hear you barking, Trickster, far away, and I tried to follow your voice. I knew that if I could find you, I would be safe.''

She wiped her nose with her mitten, and let out a halting breath. The snow swirled down like feathers plucked from the Night Walker's lodges. Four hands blanketed the meadow. It looked bright and luminous in the pale morning glow.

''I forgot to bring you a toy today, Trickster. I'm sorry. Tomorrow I—I'll bring your blanket. I've been sleeping with it around my feet at night. But I think you need it more than I do.''

Wren gazed down with blurry eyes. "Do you remember Rumbler? He was staked down"—she turned and pointed to the spot twenty hands away—"right there. Remember how he cried?"

Wren tucked her hands beneath her fox-fur cape and shivered. "I'm afraid that he . . ."

Movement caught her eye. A hundred hands away, down near the trail, something dark passed between the tree trunks. She held her breath, listening, watching. Probably a deer.

She brushed Trickster's grave clean again. "Rumbler's in real trouble," she whispered. "I'm afraid he's dying. I know it's the will of our people, Trickster, but he hasn't done anything to deserve death. I think that Mossybill, Skullcap, and White Kit just died. It happens. People die for no reason. My parents and Skybow did." More softly, she added, "And you did."

She shivered, and whispered, "I've been thinking terrible thoughts, Trickster. I want to do things that I know are wrong. Things that will get me into a lot of trouble. I've seen twelve sun circles. I should know my place and my duties to my clan. But I—"

Wren jerked to her left again. As dawn neared, light grew in the shadowed places, and she could make out what appeared to be two men. Both tall. They stood in the trees just off the trail. One had his arm braced against a tree. They stood very close together, as if speaking confidentially.

Wren whispered, "I love you, Trickster. I'll be back. I promise."

Rising to her feet, she crept into the brush that bordered the meadow, and worked her way toward the men, ducking under branches, sidestepping deadfall, until she could see them more clearly.

Cornhusk faced her. His rotted front teeth gleamed

when he smiled. "I canoed like a warrior," he said. "They're old. It will take them longer, but they should be here tomorrow night, or perhaps the morning after."

The man standing with his back to Wren dropped his hand from the tree and clenched it into a fist. "I have the meeting place picked out." *Jumping Badger!* "First, Sparrow will remove his curse. Then I'll kill them both. After that, I'll steal the False Face Child and sell him to the Flicker chieftains. They pay handsomely for such prizes. They cut dwarfs apart slowly, eating the flesh as they go, to gain the dwarf's Spirit Power."

Cornhusk straightened. "What purpose will killing two old people—"

Jumping Badger took a threatening step toward the Trader. "Four nights ago, I had a Power Dream. In it, I saw Silver Sparrow's army of ghosts. They swooped down upon me from the clouds, and slithered up from holes in the ground." Jumping Badger leaned closer to Cornhusk, and Wren could see his dark eyes glimmer as he said, "They're hunting me, Trader. I have to stop them. If even one member of Silver Sparrow's clan survives, I will die. That is my Dream."

"Well, that's very interesting, Jumping Badger, but I don't want any part of this!"

Jumping Badger thumped Cornhusk's chest with a hard fist. "Then only your wife will be able to recognize the pieces of you I leave behind."

Cornhusk said, "I'm home so rarely, I doubt even she would recognize them, but I—"

"And don't try to run off before I'm finished with you." Jumping Badger's voice went low. "Understand?"

Cornhusk jerked a nod. "I do. Yes."

"Good."

Jumping Badger stalked away through the forest, leaving Cornhusk alone. The Trader wiped his brow on the sleeve of his buffalo coat, vented an exasperated, "Crazy!," and bent down to watch Jumping Badger through the weave of branches. When Jumping Badger had walked out of sight, Cornhusk slowly followed.

Wren eased down to the snow.

"Oh, Spirits. I don't have much time."

# Twelve

Blue Raven glimpsed Wren coming down the trail from the hilltop, a bag of food slung over her shoulder. She waved, and Blue Raven smiled. Her white fox-fur cape hung about her like a shimmering mantle. She'd pulled up the hood as a shield against the wind, but a few locks of her long black hair had escaped and danced about her pretty face.

From fifty hands down the hillside below him, Blue Raven could hear a thin cry rise and fall. The sound clawed at him, deep, like a talon buried in his souls.

He sank back against the aged oak trunk. Snow drifted out of the twilight sky in a leisurely fashion, swaying and spinning before alighting on Lost Hill. Though a Cloud Giant hovered above him, most of the sky remained clear. The feathered lodges of the Night Walkers had just begun to appear, popping into existence out over the vast blueness of Pipe Stem Lake.

Blessed gods, he wasn't sure how much longer he could take this.

Snow had covered everything except Rumbler's head. His disembodied face stared unblinking at Blue Raven, the black eyes alive with fear. Over the past six nights, his cries had grown shrill. Blue Raven didn't understand it. By now Rumbler should barely have the strength to draw breath.

Blue Raven blinked and forced himself to break eye contact with Rumbler. When he looked into the boy's eyes, fire ran along his bones, crept into his shaking muscles, and became a raging inferno in his heart. The intensity of the pain left him shaking.

He fumbled with his mittens. He kept going over the stories his mother had told him, things she'd heard from old Silver Sparrow himself, about how Rumbler's father, the evil Forest Spirit, used to whisper to him in his robes at night, and how the Night Walkers obeyed the boy's commands. Anyone who had ever dared to harm the boy had died hideously—or so people said.

Blue Raven frowned, wondering.

A silver sheen glimmered across the surface of Pipe Stem Lake. People fished on the shore. The catch must have been poor, or by now they'd be back in the village cooking supper. Blue Raven tried to imagine himself at home, wrapped in hides before a blazing fire, talking with Frost-in-the-Willows, telling her the Vigil was over, and they could all sleep again. He wished . . .

Two small fists, tethered to a stake by a short rope, broke through the blanket of snow, fingers open, reaching.

*"Lamedeer!"* Rumbler shrieked. He rolled over, and tugged against his ropes, sobbing breathlessly.

Since Rumbler had seen Lamedeer's severed head on the post in the village plaza, Blue Raven assumed he called to Lamedeer's ghost. That, or the cold and hunger had taken the boy's senses.

"Blessed Spirits," Blue Raven whispered. "Why is this taking so long? It's winter. The marrow of his bones should be frozen by now."

Wind blasted the hillside, and Blue Raven turned his head. When he looked again, a white blanket of snow covered Rumbler. Smooth and unbroken, the boy might have never been.

As Blue Raven watched, a huge gray owl leaped from the grove of trees at the crest of the hill, and soared down toward Rumbler. The bird circled, flapped once, then gently alighted on Rumbler's chest.

As if the sight had cut Blue Raven's souls from his body, he seemed to float high above the earth, no longer cold, or buffeted by the gale. Graying strands of hair danced before his eyes, but he barely saw them.

The owl flapped its wings, and snow blew from Rumbler's face and chest. Then the big bird hopped down and perched on the stake which pinned Rumbler's feet. He *hoo-hoo*'d once, then silently soared up and away through the falling snow.

Blue Raven whispered, "Stop being a fool. Owls are predators. Scavengers. That's all. The bird probably thought Rumbler was dead and hoped to find a meal. It must have been surprised when it discovered the boy was alive. It . . ."

From deep in his souls, his grandfather's ancient voice rasped, *You have seen thirteen winters, grandson. It's time you learned the strange ways of the gods. You must stand your first Vigil. Watch the child. Protect it from hungry animals. Let no one touch the baby until it is dead. That is your duty as Vigil Keeper. Curious things may happen. Often they do. Each is a test. The gods will be watching you. You mustn't let them turn you from your duty.*

Blue Raven remembered running all the way to Lost

Hill clutching that forsaken baby to his chest. A wan patchwork of sunlight had flashed through the naked hickory and oak limbs, and he had to squint to keep from colliding with trees. The child had gurgled and cried. Though the little boy had only beheld four mornings, the threads of his heart had been like iron. It had taken forty-two hands of time for that baby to die—and Blue Raven's souls to wither to dust. But nothing strange had happened. Nothing he could recall, he—

Wren startled him, kneeling at his side. "Good evening, Uncle."

Blue Raven sucked in a breath. "Wren. Hello."

She carefully unslung her pack. "I brought you slices of roasted goose and a bowl of cornmeal mush." She drew out two covered wooden bowls and placed them in front of him, along with a horn spoon. The mush still steamed. "Are you well?"

"Well enough, Wren. Thank you for coming. Now go home. Tell your grandmother that the child still lives."

Her large dark eyes strayed down the hill, and agony lined her face. "Would you like me to collect wood for you first, Uncle? It won't take me very long."

Blue Raven reached out and squeezed her arm. She had made the same offer for the past six nights, and her bravery always swelled his heart. "If you wish to, it would be a great help. But it is not necessary, Wren. I can collect wood later."

"I wish to, Uncle."

Wren dashed up the hill toward the stunted grove of elms and oaks that whiskered the top. Against the deep blue of evening, the trees resembled skeletal arms. The Cloud Giant had traveled out over the lake, leaving the clean sky spotted with the Night Walker's feathered lodges.

Wren's white cape blended so completely with the

snow that she looked ghostly as she moved among the dark trunks, cracking off dead limbs and placing them in the crook of her left arm.

Rumbler screamed suddenly, and Wren spun around so fast her load tumbled into the snow.

Blue Raven shuddered.

As Wren bent to pick up the wood, her ravaged expression tore his heart.

Where did she find the courage? For many moons she had been living with death. This must be harder on her than any of them imagined. He wished that Frost-in-the-Willows had chosen someone else to bring him food, but his mother probably considered this just punishment for the abandoned water bags.

Wren made her way down the hill as swiftly as she could, slipping on ice, and dumped her load onto his woodpile. She fed branches to the fire. Flames leaped and swayed, blinding him to the night.

"Thank you, Wren." Blue Raven put a mitten on her cheek. Her lean angular face had flushed from the cold, and she was breathing hard. "These past few nights have been hard for you. You have made me very proud."

"I don't know how you do this, Uncle."

He let his hand fall to his lap. "I do it because I must."

In a sudden move, she threw her arms around his neck, and hugged him. Her voice came out strained. "I wish you could come home."

"I will," he whispered, kissing her hair. "Perhaps tomorrow. Don't worry about me."

She nodded against his neck. "Try to rest, Uncle. You look so tired."

Vigil Keepers could nap for brief periods, but never really sleep. With Rumbler's cries, even his naps had been tortured. He must look as exhausted as he felt. He stroked Wren's back. "Tell your grandmother I hope to see her soon."

Wren picked up her pack and slung it over her shoulder. "Good night, Uncle. I love you."

"Be attentive on your way home, Wren. You haven't much light left."

She nodded. "I will. I'll see you at dawn." She sprinted up the hill for the trail.

Blue Raven watched her disappear over the crest, then he picked up a piece of roasted goose and ate it, savoring the rich flavor. A soft orange gleam had begun to warm the sky to the south, rising from the freshly lit supper fires in Walksalong Village.

He concentrated on it, willing himself home.

Dusk fell in smoky veils across the lake, draining the colors from the water.

Wren hid behind a boulder, her back pressed against the cold stone, watching people climb the hill from the lake. At her feet lay the bulging pack, bow, and quiver of arrows she'd hidden earlier in the day. She didn't expect to need them, not tonight, but . . . but she might. . . .

Four old men led the procession, laughing softly, telling stories about the day's fishing. To the west, across the face of Lost Hill, remnants of sunlight gilded the bellies of the Cloud Giants, turning them a deep dark blue.

Old Bogbean and Loon trudged up the trail next. Wren couldn't see their faces, but she knew their voices.

"You don't have to tell me!" Bogbean whispered. "I sleep at his end of the longhouse. All night long, I have to listen to him whispering to that rotting head. It singes my backbone!''

"What does he say?" Loon asked.

"Mostly he makes threats. Can you imagine? Threatening a dead man?"

"Many of the men in my longhouse fear he's lost his souls. They say that unless he has fifty warriors around him, he shrieks when a finch chirps."

"He's always been odd. When he was a child, he used to knock out his playmates' teeth and carry them in his pocket, to gain power over their souls. Keeping this rotting head is probably the same . . ."

Their voices faded as they climbed higher up the hill.

Wren stood, barely breathing. The wavering gleam from Uncle Blue Raven's fire had turned the shadows slippery and liquid. More people followed Bogbean and Loon, speaking quietly. It took forever for all of them to pass.

When the last one had climbed to the top of the hill, Wren leaned from behind the boulder, and looked around. She'd seen the bloody boy down here, and the darker it got, the more her fear increased. But she *had* to do this.

She ran down the trail toward the lake.

Uncle Blue Raven's fire flared as he tossed another piece of wood onto the blaze. He yawned, and stretched out on his side, pillowing his head on his arm. His eyes fell closed almost immediately.

But Wren waited. Even if he woke, the flames should blind him to her movements, but she dared not take chances.

Wren laced her hood tightly beneath her chin, and started sliding across the snow. She could feel every hair on the inside of her wolfhide mittens. Like tiny fangs, they nipped at her fingers.

A hundred hands away, Rumbler lay on his back, gazing up at the Cloud Giants who hunted the darkening heavens. Their gleaming bodies billowed, changing shape, as they stalked the owls and other night birds.

Pipe Stem Lake had turned into a sea of winking silver eyes. Waves splashed the beach. Wren slid closer to Rumbler. When she got to within twenty hands, she whispered, "Rumbler?"

He lifted his head. "Wren?"

"Shh!"

Her white fox-fur cape made her almost invisible, but she glanced at her sleeping uncle, then back at the trail, before slithering toward Rumbler. "I'm sorry it took me so long, Rumbler. There were people fishing on the lake. I had to make sure no one saw me." She opened her cape and drew out her pack.

The aroma of meat seemed to strike Rumbler like a physical blow. He trembled all over. "What did you b-bring me?"

Wren lifted out a thin slice of roasted goose and Rumbler opened his mouth. She fed him three slices, then rummaged in her pack for a skin bag. "Here," she said as she tipped one corner to Rumbler's lips, "this is snowberry leaf tea. It was hot when I left the longhouse."

Rumbler drank the sweet liquid with his eyes closed. The faintest trace of warmth clung to the tea, and it steamed in the frigid air.

Chunks of ice dotted his chin-length hair. The snow must have melted on his head earlier in the day, and the water frozen as night deepened. His beautiful round face had gone hollow and clay-colored. His cheekbones stuck out like a corpse's.

For a moment, her souls refused to see.

"Rumbler? Are you all right?" she asked as she tucked the empty bag beneath her cape.

Tears blurred his eyes, but he did not seem to have the strength to blink them away.

"All of my echoes have died," he said. "All of them. My mother's heartbeat, Grandmother Tail's laughter, even S-Stonecoat's bark, they are all gone. Wren, I—I have to catch a bird. Will you help me catch a bird?"

She studied his face. He couldn't keep his eyes still, they kept sliding and jerking back, trying to stay on her. "I'll help you, Rumbler."

Wren spread one side of her fox cape over him, and hugged him against her. He shivered harder, his body twitching and jerking.

"Rumbler," she said. "I've been looking for your mother. Every day, just as I promised. Either she hasn't come, or she won't show herself to me, but I haven't given up. I—"

Rumbler's mouth opened to the stars and night, and he cried, but no sounds came out.

"Maybe your mother's echo is just so faint you can't hear it over the wind, Rumbler. You know how loud Wind Mother's been for the past quarter moon. All she does is howl through the forests."

He tugged at his ropes.

Wren pulled off her right mitten, looked at his bound hands where they lay above his head, and grasped hold of them. They felt swollen and icy cold.

"Rumbler?" Wren said, fear edging her voice. "Your hands. Are they—"

"I can't f-feel them."

Wren sat up, and swiftly massaged his stubby fingers. "How about now?"

He shook his head.

Wren held his hand more tightly. She'd seen people with frostbite. The frozen fingers turned black and had to be cut off to save the rest of the hand. Sometimes the Shadow Spirits started feeding on the dead flesh, and the person lost his arm.

"Wren, I need to . . . to . . ." He went quiet, as if he couldn't remember what he'd been about to say. After several instants, he repeated, "Wren, I have to catch a bird. Will you help me catch a bird?"

"Yes, I will, Rumbler," she choked out.

He smiled. "You are my friend."

The struggle drained from Rumbler's eyes, and his head lolled to the side.

"Oh, Rumbler—"

"Look," he said, barely audible. "Do you see him?"

Wren forced her neck around.

Starlight had turned the snow a pale blue. She searched every drift and cornice, then the dark tree line and sparkling shore. The snow crept and spun. "Who, Rumbler?"

"He's been coming to me every night. Singing. He—he Sings to me."

The frozen ground beneath Wren's feet melted to quicksand. Her knees went wobbly. "Who? Who does?"

Rumbler's eyelids drooped, then flared, as if he wanted to keep looking at her, but couldn't. "He wants me to go now, Wren. I have to go . . . with him."

Wren frantically looked around again. "Who, Rumbler? Who is he? Is it the—the bloody little boy?"

He closed his eyes and his muscles relaxed.

"Rumbler?" Panic fired her blood. "Rumbler, you're not dying, are you?"

Wren put her hand on his chest to check his breathing. She couldn't feel anything! She gripped him by the shirt-front and rolled him to his side. He flopped over like a string doll.

"Rumbler, no!" She tugged hard at his bound hands, then scrambled around to pull on his feet.

. . . Something broke inside her.

Wren jerked her knife from her belt and sawed through his ropes as fast as she could.

# Thirteen

The pops and hisses of the fire woke Blue Raven. His tired body felt like lead. For a time, he granted himself the luxury of watching the firelight flicker across the backs of his eyelids. When he'd been young, and sitting Vigils, he'd tried to find messages in those dancing orange shapes. Tonight the images looked angry. He could make out warriors waging a fierce battle, and giant winged beasts sailing across flaming skies. . . .

The fire hissed again. Blue Raven opened his eyes to see heavy snow falling. He looked toward the hilltop, then down at the lake, but he could see neither. They had been engulfed by the deluge of flakes. The snow fell straight down, hissing as it died in his fire.

It took him over a hundred heartbeats to find his bow and quiver beneath the snow, then he sat up, and gazed down the hill.

An unbroken blanket of white covered Rumbler. The boy had stopped crying.

"Please, Falling Woman, let this Vigil be over."

Blue Raven rose to his feet, slung his bow and quiver over his shoulder, and started down the hill. As he trudged through the knee-deep snow, he felt as if he might be the only creature alive in the world.

The scents of winter taunted his nose, frozen mud and fragrant pine needles.

He stopped at the place he remembered staking Rumbler down, but found nothing. Thinking he'd misjudged the distance, he slogged farther down the hill. In the firelight, it was like moving through a glittering ocean of gold dust.

Blue Raven looked around and frowned, searching for any sign of a body buried beneath the snow. He started uphill again.

Halfway to his camp, he cut a strange dip, the barest of undulations in the snow, and knelt to examine it. About four hands wide, the dip ran straight down the hill for as far as he could . . .

He lurched to his feet, and stumbled down the snowy slope, following the drag marks.

Rumbler must have been too weak to walk, so the kidnapper had wrapped the boy in a hide or blanket and dragged him across the snow. But why hadn't he simply carried the boy? Rumbler's little body should have posed no problem for a man or even a woman—

A sharp pain lanced his chest. "Blessed ancestors."

The pain grew fiery. Blue Raven bent over, gasping for breath. It took thirty heartbeats before the stabs calmed to a dull rhythmic ache. The entire time, he whispered, "Oh, Wren, Wren. Do you know what you've done? It's been nearly forty winters since a girl was Outcast from the clan, but the matrons will have no choice. You've left them, and me, no way out.''

Blue Raven's heart continued to pound, each beat like a hammer swung against his chest wall, but he forced himself to straighten up. How long had the snow been falling this heavily? They might not be that far ahead of him. If he could find them before dawn and bring them back, Wren would be safe. He would tell no one, and swear her to secrecy. Oh, she would feel his wrath! He'd have her scraping the flesh off fresh hides for the rest of her life.

He called, ''Wren? *Wren!*''

He bounded ahead, kicking up a white haze. At the current rate of snowfall, the trail would be gone in less than half a hand of time. Each moment that passed, his hope of finding them diminished.

The trail led to the water's edge, headed west, and vanished.

Blue Raven trotted a short distance westward, then turned back and headed east. As the storm rushed overhead, a few of the Cloud Giants stretched themselves too thin, and dim starlight touched the lake. The reflection wavered over the beach. Blue Raven picked up the trail and ran. Wren had tried to drag Rumbler between the water and the snow, figuring the waves would obscure her trail, but she'd had to dodge the incoming waves. Every now and then, drag marks scalloped the snow.

She appeared to be heading due north, toward Leafing Lake.

The pain ate at his ribs, forcing him to slow to a stagger. He *had* to find Wren.

''Walk!'' he ordered himself. ''Keep walking. Wren! Wren, where are you?''

*In the dream, I touch my nose to the cold green surface of the pond, trying to fathom who this stranger is that stares back at me.*

*I remember the first night I returned home after my Spirit journey.*

*I told you everything. Gave you the broken pieces of my heart and souls, prayed you could show me how to fit them together again.*

*As you always had.*

*You looked at me as if you hadn't heard.*

*Sitting there before the fire in your plain doeskin dress, I could see you growing dark, growing dark everywhere at once.*

*And I managed to be farther away from you inside myself than anywhere else I've ever been.*

*Love is pain.*

*I know this.*

*I just can't get used to it after the lifetime of joy we shared.*

*I tilt my head to the side, examining my reflection, the deep wrinkles that line my cheeks and forehead.*

*What happened to the man you loved?*

*I keep thinking he must be in here somewhere.*

*I've begun to fear that you're the only one who can find him.*

*And you don't want to.*

*Gods, Dust, I . . . I'm lost.*

*Without your eyes looking at me inside, I don't know who I am.*

*I don't know who anyone . . .*

\*   \*   \*

"Sparrow?" Dust Moon called, and rolled over in her blankets to face him.

He lay on the other side of the fire pit, his forehead and bushy eyebrows showing above his elkhide. Before going to sleep last night, they'd built a crude structure by leaning deadfall limbs against a rock outcrop, then covering them with brush. Through the open ends of the structure, Dust could see how much snow had fallen. She sat up. "Sparrow?"

"Mmph."

"Sparrow, there are several hands of snow on the ground!"

Groggily, he asked, "Where are the Night Walkers' lodges?"

"It's snowing, you fool. I can't see anything more than ten hands away."

She crawled to the small triangular opening on her left, and scooped away enough to stick her head out, gauging the dim light that filtered through the storm clouds. "All I see is snow."

"Dust, I'm exhausted. I feel like I've slept for about four hands of time. Let's rest a little longer." He huddled into his bedding.

"I'm not sleeping, and neither are you. The drifts on the trail are probably head-high. Even if we get to our canoe immediately, we're not going to reach Walksalong Village before late afternoon." She crawled back, and started rolling up her blankets. "Sparrow? Get up. Now!"

He blinked his eyes open.

"Imagine how Rumbler must be feeling," she said as

she tied her blankets with a basswood cord. "That should wake you up."

"I have been," he said in a quiet voice. "I Dreamed about him all night long. Strange, haunting Dreams. My Spirit Helper was there beside him, speaking with Rumbler, but I couldn't hear what they were saying."

At the mention of his Spirit Helper pain lanced her heart, bringing back memories of Flintboy's death and the terrible days of wrenching loneliness that had followed. A curious low roaring filled her ears, as if she held shells to them, and her throat ached with the urge to weep or strike something. For two winters she had been fighting to overcome the sting of his abandonment, but had failed.

"Well, I hope you're not relying on your Spirit Helper to get Rumbler out of this," she said bitterly, "because if you are—"

"He's a teacher, Dust, not a savior."

A cold breeze blew through their shelter, tousling Sparrow's long white hair and sprinkling his round face with snow. Dust watched glittering flakes alight on his beaked nose.

"If he's a teacher, why don't you ask him to teach you something valuable? Like how to fly. Or maybe how to wave your hands and make irksome things, like snowdrifts, disappear."

Sparrow rolled over. "Do you really think you'd be here, Dust, if I knew how to do that?"

She tied her rolled blankets to her pack, rose to her feet, and kicked him as hard as she could. "I said get up."

Sparrow winced. "You know, I've been a great many places, and known a lot of women. I've visited spirit worlds in the sky, worlds beneath the earth, even worlds that ride the backs of Cloud Giants. But all of the women

I met in those worlds were kind and compassionate."

Dust nodded. "That's because they were dead, and if you don't rise in the next ten heartbeats, you'll be seeing a lot more of them."

She pulled her hood up, and bulled through the drift that blocked the open end of the shelter. Snow lay hip-deep on the ground, and mounded on the brush and dead-fall. It frosted the dark limbs of the trees. "Oh, gods, this is worse than I thought."

Flakes plummeted down around her. *Rumbler can't survive in this. He can't!*

She had held thirteen children in her arms while they died—held them and rocked them, and sung to them with her heart bursting in her chest. Not Rumbler, too. She couldn't let him die!

She ducked back inside the shelter, and crawled to the fire pit. They'd purposely built up a thick layer of coals last night, then, after supper, they'd rolled the circle of hearthstones into the middle of the pit. The hot stones had heated the shelter through most of the night and, she hoped, they had also insulated the coals beneath.

Dust used a branch to push the stones to the edges of the pit again, re-creating the ring, then she stirred the ashbed. A few hot coals glimmered to life. Dust carefully isolated them in the middle, then started cracking her branch into smaller pieces of wood. As she arranged the twigs over the coals, she blew on them gently. The coals flared. Finally, flames crackled through the tinder. Dust added larger pieces of wood. The teapot, still half full, hung from the tripod to her right. She arranged the legs of the tripod so that the pot hung just at the edge of the flames.

"I'm going to cook mush, Sparrow. It's fast. The tea should be warm soon."

Sparrow crawled from beneath his warm hide, and

started for the opposite end of the shelter, but Dust's voice stopped him.

"Wait."

He turned. "What for?"

She picked up his pack and rummaged around for a pot. Cone-shaped, with a soot-coated bottom, it made a bulge against the leather. She tossed it to him. "Fill that with snow while you're at it."

Sparrow left, using the pot to shovel snow out of the way. After a few moments, he returned, panic in his eyes. He knelt beside Dust, scooped two handfuls of snow from the cook pot into the teapot, and said, "This is the worst storm I've seen in winters."

"What else happened in your Dream, Sparrow?" She took the cook pot from his hands, and worked the pot down into the coals. The remaining snow instantly started to melt. "Was Rumbler all right?"

"No. He was barely alive."

Dust pulled two bags from her own pack. As she rested them on the hearthstones, her arm shook. She said, "I love that little boy, Sparrow. We have to get there."

"We're trying, Dust. But, I swear . . ." He gestured to the snow.

"Yes, I know. It seems as if every Spirit in the forest is working against us, doesn't it?"

She opened the birchbark bags, dropped several chunks of hardened maple sap into the cook pot, then added a handful of dried blueberries. She used a stick from the woodpile to stir the mixture. When it started to boil, she would add acorn meal.

Sparrow tucked his hands into the pockets of his jacket. Firelight shadowed his wrinkles. "I don't always understand the ways of Spirits, Dust. But I do know that sometimes events that seem unfortunate are really very good from another person's point of view. Perhaps this storm benefits Rumbler in some way. I admit I don't see how, but I haven't given up hope. You mustn't, either.''

The tender concern in his voice touched her. She folded her arms beneath her cape and held them like a shield over her heart. "I haven't given up. I'm braver than that.''

He smiled, and the lines around his eyes crinkled. "Oh, yes. I know. Do you recall the Summer Dances forty-three winters ago? I was ten and as scrawny as a drowned chipmunk. Twitter, the bully, had knocked me down and was sitting on top of me, spitting in my face. You sneaked up behind him, whacked him in the head with a rock, and when he fell sideways, you said, 'Sparrow's half your size, Twitter. If you ever hurt him again, I'm going to poison your food.' ''

Despite herself, she smiled. "He knew I meant it, too. My mother was a great Healer. The first lessons she taught me were about poisonous plants and their uses.''

Sparrow tilted his head. "You'd seen seven winters, Dust. Twitter was *four* times your size. I couldn't believe how brave you were.''

They looked at each other for a long moment. Between them lay a lifetime of shared joys and sorrows. Once, not so long ago, only the sorrows had hurt. Now the joys did, too.

The cook pot boiled over, sending froth cascading onto the coals, and Dust leaped for the bag of acorn meal. She dumped half of it into the pot, then stirred it with her stick. "This will be done very soon.''

He reached for his pack, drew out cups and bowls, and set them on the ground, then searched for their horn spoons. As he tucked them into the bowls, he said, "I think the tea is warm. I'll fill our cups.''

Sparrow dipped her gourd cup full, and set it near her

feet. "You know," he said, taking the chance, "Planter's house sits next to yours."

"Did you think I was unaware of that?"

He toyed with his cup. "Planter told me that you often call out to me in your sleep. I know it probably doesn't matter to you, but I wish I were there, Dust. To hold you. I really do."

Planter's small betrayal hurt, but not nearly as much as the look in Sparrow's eyes.

Dust swallowed the lump in her throat, and said, "Hand me your bowl, Sparrow. The mush is ready."

Wren brushed snow from her eyelashes, and bent to examine Rumbler. He lay inside her fox-fur cape, his head sticking out through the neck hole. His round face looked as pale as the whirling flakes. He still couldn't focus his eyes; they kept darting about, the lids falling closed, then jerking wide. He'd been mumbling incoherently, speaking to people Wren couldn't see.

"R-Rumbler?" she said, her teeth chattering. "Are you all right?"

"Little Wren?" he called, as if he couldn't see her. "Wren?"

"I'm . . . h-here. Right here, Rumbler."

She twined her fists into the fox-fur collar, and stumbled forward another three steps, dragging Rumbler along the shore of Pipe Stem Lake. Snow danced around them like white wraiths. The muscles in her shoulders and legs ached so badly that she kept wobbling off the shore and into the deep drifts that had blown against the base of the hill.

She staggered out, and went on. She had to, or Rumbler would die, and . . . and, now, she might die, too. As soon as Uncle Blue Raven discovered what she'd done, he would go to the village matrons, and they would authorize a search party.

Hot tears burned Wren's eyes.

How could two children outrun fifty warriors?

*. . . Oh, gods, what have I done?*

She could feel the Sunshine Boy watching from the darkness, grinning, waiting for the right moment to sneak inside her or Rumbler. Every wave that washed the shore, and breath of wind that stirred the trees, whispered to Wren, *Hurry! Hurry!*

She threw all of her strength into pulling the cape forward a few more paces, then stopped, and braced her shaking legs. Sobs ate at her chest. She bowed her head and let herself cry. The tears tasted warm and salty. Soon, it would be morning, and warriors would be crawling through the forests.

Jumping Badger *would* find them. It might take him a day, but eventually somebody would stumble onto their trail, and then they . . .

Wren's head snapped up. She blinked, and her blood throbbed. "Yes," she whispered. "Yes, Spirits, of course! If we can make it."

She leaned forward, weaving drunkenly as she tugged Rumbler off the sandy shore and into a snowy meadow. Her aching arms burned, but she kept going, slogging through the drifts.

Across the meadow, at the place where the Dancing Man River emptied into Pipe Stem Lake, lay the canoe landing used by the Traders.

# Fourteen

Cornhusk lay in Frost-in-the-Willows' longhouse, wide awake, listening to Jumping Badger whisper to Lamedeer's rotting head. It gave Cornhusk a bellyache. How could anyone sleep with that grisly war trophy staring at them? Jumping Badger had set the head on a short staff, six hands tall, and leaned it in the corner near his bedding. Cornhusk lay twenty hands away, by the door, and still found the stench overpowering. He could not understand why Frost-in-the-Willows allowed Jumping Badger to keep it inside. Staked in the plaza it would stand as a reminder of their victory, but inside the longhouse it was just a putrefying head. The eyes had sunken into the skull, becoming hard and dull, and the hair had started to slip. Every time Jumping Badger moved the staff, long graying black clumps fell to the floor.

"You think I can't hear you," Jumping Badger whispered, his nose less than a handbreadth from the rotting head. He knelt, his hands braced on the walls on either side of the head, staring into the decaying eye sockets. "But I can. Everything you say to the dwarf child echoes in my head a hundred times. I know exactly what you're planning. You and that accursed Briar."

Old Bogbean, who lay to Cornhusk's left, tossed to her side and covered her head with her blankets. Several other people muttered.

Jumping Badger did not seem to notice. His gaze stayed locked with Lamedeer's.

"Don't try it!" Jumping Badger hissed. "I will find him. Do you hear me? He'll never be able to hide!"

One elderly man rose, picked up his hides, and walked halfway down the longhouse before spreading them out again. In the reddish glow of the coals, Cornhusk could see the old man shake his head as he lay down.

"Don't you laugh at me! Don't you laugh!"

A little boy burst into tears, crying, "Mother? Mother, hold me!"

"Shh. Shh, it's all right," the mother said and gathered the boy in her arms.

Bogbean threw back her blankets, sat up, and blurted, "Jumping Badger!" Her fat face had a crimson sheen. "You are frightening the children. Go to sleep!"

Jumping Badger turned and his stony gaze darted over his sleepless relatives. Slowly, as if reluctant to, he sank to his bedding again, and pulled a black-and-white striped blanket over his body.

Sighs of relief eddied through the longhouse. A few people muttered, then silence fell.

Cornhusk studied Jumping Badger through one eye, waiting to see if the crazy War Leader had truly ended his heated debate with the severed head. When he heard no more, Cornhusk closed his eyes, and exhaled hard.

Ever since Jumping Badger had told him he planned to kill Silver Sparrow and Dust Moon, Cornhusk hadn't been sleeping well. He ought to warn them. He knew that. He just hadn't figured out how to save their lives and his own at the same time. Jumping Badger had been watching Cornhusk like a bobcat eying a mouse. He couldn't go into the forest to relieve himself without seeing Jumping Badger's eyes glinting through the weave of branches. The man obviously feared that Cornhusk's conscience might foil his plans.

It posed a strange dilemma for Cornhusk. Until the past few nights, he'd prided himself on not having a conscience. He was a practical man, used to bending with the prevailing wind, and making few, if any, moral judgments about people or their curious customs. Above all, he made it a rule never to interfere with warriors or murderers. Oh, he spread rumors now and then, to enliven conversation, but nothing that might get him killed.

Until now.

He'd willingly carried Jumping Badger's message to Earth Thunderer Village. He'd convinced Dust Moon that if she and Silver Sparrow came to Walksalong Village, she could save the False Face Child. So, if Jumping Badger killed them and sold the child to the Flicker Clans for their bizarre rituals, Cornhusk could expect a greatly shortened life span. Dust Moon's daughter, Planter, had heard the whole story. She would certainly hire assassins to hunt Cornhusk down. He would flee, of course, but someday the story would reach the ears of someone who'd cared for Silver Sparrow or Dust Moon, and Cornhusk would be wakened in the night by the sound of his own throat being slit.

The problem nagged at Cornhusk. He turned it in his mind, trying to see it from different angles. He couldn't decide which he preferred, to be killed by Dust Moon's relatives, or to take his chances that Jumping Badger, being a warrior, might die before he had the opportunity to carry out his threats.

He had one other option. He could head west as fast as his well-muscled legs would carry him, and try to avoid all the possible consequences of his foolish actions.

But he didn't particularly like that one. Trading in this country had proven not only pleasant, but extremely lucrative. He didn't wish to leave. He had a stash of riches that . . .

The whisper of moccasins brought Cornhusk fully awake. He shifted in his warm cocoon of hides, and raised himself on an elbow to hear better. Long hair fell down his naked back. Two people approached the long-house, their steps placed with great care, but faintly crunching the snow outside. Strange, the dogs hadn't made a sound.

He turned to survey the hundred-hand length of the longhouse. Dim light trickled through the four smoke holes in the roof and picked out the hide-wrapped bodies of the inhabitants. Old man Buckheel continued to snore like a mad cougar, and Little Twine, his four-winters-old granddaughter, fidgeted in her sleep. She lay to Jumping Badger's left, one arm over her eyes, her fingers opening and closing as though reaching out for someone. She had been whimpering earlier, the sound barely audible.

The moccasins neared, and their owners began whispering.

Cornhusk's eyes widened when he saw Jumping Badger silently reach for his bow and quiver of arrows. The war leader slipped from beneath his deerhides, and secreted himself in the corner, beside the rotting head.

Cornhusk looked at the door. The leather curtain swayed, revealing glimpses of black trees and falling snow.

He slid an arrow from his own quiver and nocked it in his bow. The smooth willow felt icy.

Jumping Badger glared at Lamedeer, whispering, "Is this part of the ghost army Silver Sparrow is gathering to kill me for what I did to Briar? Hmm? Answer me! They can't hurt me. Not so long as I'm near a fire after nightfall. You told me this yourself, I . . ."

The moccasins halted just beyond the door curtain and the voices grew louder.

"Tell me again how you came to know about this?" Matron Starflower's voice carried.

"I couldn't sleep. I went out to Lost Hill to see if my husband's murderer was dead yet—and I couldn't find Blue Raven."

"You are certain he was there earlier?"

"Yes," the woman answered. "I was down at the lake fishing when Little Wren took Blue Raven his meal. I saw her deliver the food, then gather wood for Blue Raven's fire. I waited for Wren to return. I wanted to ask her about the False Face Child. But she never came back."

"Well, let's find out what her family knows."

The door curtain drew back and in the square of silver light Matron Starflower stood beside Loon. Glittering white hair fringed the rim of Starflower's hood, but only darkness filled the interior. Loon's hair had been hacked off in mourning, but her shell earrings flashed as she ducked beneath the curtain.

When Starflower spied Jumping Badger, she jerked, and her eyes flared.

"What are you doing hiding there, War Leader?" She pointed at him with her long walking stick. "Come out of the shadows so I can see you! We may have a calamity to deal with."

Jumping Badger stepped forward. He towered over her, twice her height. "What's happened?"

"Loon woke me from a sound sleep to tell me that your cousin Blue Raven is gone."

"Gone? Where? Why!"

"That is what I came to find out. I must see Frost-in-the-Willows."

Jumping Badger called, "Frost-in-the-Willows? Matron Starflower would speak with you!''

At the opposite end of the longhouse, a form rose, and sleepily answered, ''Starflower? What's wrong?''

The longhouse suddenly came alive with dim bodies, sitting, standing, rolling over to watch.

Starflower pushed her hood back and quietly walked down the longhouse. Jumping Badger followed, his bow in his hand.

Starflower stopped at the foot of Frost-in-the-Willows' bedding. ''Where is your son?''

''You know very well where Blue Raven is. He's on Lost Hill.''

''No. He is not. Where is your granddaughter?''

''As for Wren, I do not know. She was supposed to return after delivering her uncle's food, but she didn't.''

''And you did not send anyone out to hunt for her?''

''Why should I? Wren often wanders off alone. You know that, Starflower. She always returns, though she takes her own good time in doing so.'' Frost-in-the-Willows pulled her blanket up beneath her chin. ''Deliver your message plainly, Starflower. Are you accusing my son of something?''

''Blue Raven and Little Wren are gone, and so is the False Face Child.''

Jumping Badger gasped and took a step toward Starflower. ''The boy is gone?''

''He is.''

Frost-in-the-Willows waved a hand. ''Well, perhaps the boy finally died, and Blue Raven and Wren took its body down to wash it in the lake before bringing it back to the village. That is customary. Have you searched the shoreline?''

''Not yet. But we will,'' Starflower answered. ''I wanted to speak with you first. Is that the only explanation you can think of?''

"Yes, of course! I haven't seen Blue Raven in six days, and Wren is as unpredictable as Wind Mother! But if they are both gone, they are probably together."

Bows clattered against arrows as warriors reached for their weapons, preparing for whatever came next. The flurry of activity set the infants in the house to wailing.

Starflower leaned against her walking stick. In the reddish gleam, her long hooked nose jutted from her wrinkled face like an eagle's beak, and her gray hair resembled matted spiderwebs. "My first thought was that your son and granddaughter had released the False Face Child and run off with him."

Jumping Badger edged closer, peering down at Frost-in-the-Willows with glowing eyes. "Is this possible?"

"It's ridiculous!" Frost-in-the-Willows said. "Blue Raven is Headman. He knows the price for such an act. Why would he throw away his life, and Wren's future, for the False Face Child?"

Jumping Badger's voice came out low: "Because he's a traitor. Lamedeer told me. I didn't wish to believe, but now . . ." He swung around to point at the grisly head in the corner, and every eye in the longhouse followed his arm. "It must be true. My cousin is in league with the ghosts. He heard the prophecy that the False Face Child would be the death of the Walksalong Clan, and released the boy anyway. Matron, we must leave at first light! We have to find that boy before it's too late!"

Frost-in-the-Willows angrily threw off her hides and reached for her moccasins. "Blue Raven has done everything in his Power to guide and protect the Walksalong Clan, Jumping Badger. *You* are the one who talked the matrons into stealing the boy. If we should question anyone's loyalty, it's yours."

Cornhusk saw several people around him nod.

"But I am still here, old woman," Jumping Badger answered. "Your son is not."

"We do not know that yet," Starflower said, lifting a hand to end the argument. "Prepare a search party, War Leader. I want the three of them found by dawn. If necessary, you may kill the boy, but I want the other two alive." She turned back to Frost-in-the-Willows. "This may be a long night. We have many things to discuss."

Frost-in-the-Willows put on her cape and rose to her feet. "I will build up my fire, and put on a pot of tea."

Jumping Badger stood rigid as a granite pillar.

Starflower's eyes narrowed. "What's the matter with you, War Leader? I gave you an order!"

He wet his lips. "I heard, Matron, but I . . . you didn't really mean you want me to form a search party now? Tonight?"

"I just said so, didn't I? Start on the shore of Pipe Stem Lake, but be ready to follow their tracks wherever they might lead you."

Jumping Badger didn't move.

Cornhusk could swear the war leader's knees had started shaking.

"Tracks?" Jumping Badger said, his voice shrill. "In the darkness? We'll never be able to find anything tonight! We may as well wait until morning when we can see what we are doing."

Starflower walked closer to him, her head tipped back. "I said *now*, War Leader. I won't tell you again. By morning their trail will certainly be gone. Tonight you might spot something. Make torches. Have your men carry them as they search."

"Torches," Jumping Badger said through a relieved breath. "Of course. Yes, Matron. I will run to the other houses to notify the warriors there."

"Take the best, War Leader, but no more than twenty.

And leave Pumpkin Blossom's house alone. In the morning, I will tell Springwater that, while you are away, he is war leader and responsible for protecting the village. But you may select warriors from any other house you wish.''

Jumping Badger went back to his bedding and began stuffing things into his pack. When he'd finished, he put on his thick beaverhide coat, slung his bow and quiver over his left shoulder, and reached for Lamedeer's head. Lifting it high in the smoky air, he shouted, ''I wish all seven warriors in this house to meet me in the plaza in one finger of time!''

Groans rose as men threw off their blankets and reached for weapons.

Jumping Badger did not glance at Cornhusk as he ducked through the doorway.

Cornhusk sank into his bedding, waiting.

Frost-in-the-Willows and Starflower added wood to the fire at the far end of the longhouse and sat down to talk. He could hear their quiet voices, but couldn't make out any of the words. Loon stood behind Starflower, arms folded, her short hair shining in the firelight.

The seven warriors filed past him and ducked out the doorway.

The remaining people rolled into their bedding again, and conversations gradually died.

Cornhusk silently gathered his hides, tied them to his pack, and slipped out into the snow.

# Fifteen

Golden rays of light shot across the cloud-strewn sky, and the sudden reflection off the snow blinded Blue Raven. He stumbled to a stop.

Wren's trail ran up the hillside in front of him, shallow, and wind-blown. She weighed so little, she'd been able to walk on top of the drifts, dragging Rumbler behind her. Her tracks barely dented the snow, but they were there. Blue Raven's trail, by comparison, resembled a swath cut by a desperate moose. Every step he took, he sank into the hip-deep drifts and had to fight his way out.

Dancing Man River lay to his left. He propped his hands on his hips and granted himself a moment of rest. A luminous halo of mist rose above the tumbling water, and colors twinkled through the haze.

Blue Raven's gaze followed Wren's trail. She seemed to be heading for the Traders' canoe landing up above the falls.

Blue Raven hurried. In less than two hundred paces, the trail vanished in a meadow. Dancing Man River ran wide and blue in front of him.

Blue Raven labored on, paralleling Wren's tracks for as long he could see them, then trying to guess the logical course she would have taken . . . *straight across the meadow, into the towering trees, and onto the beaten path along the shore. Everyone walks the Dancing Man*

*River Trail. It's a major route between villages.*

He had to force his way through a thorny bramble of sumac and raspberries to reach the path. Obviously Wren would not have crossed here, but he expected to find her tracks up ahead. Deer had trampled the snow, packing the trail. Drifts blew across it in places, but the walking would be much easier. Blue Raven headed north.

Light slanted through the naked trees, throwing a wavering golden patchwork across the snow. Here, beside the river, the smell of damp earth rose powerfully.

Wren might have been determined when she'd cut Rumbler loose, but exhaustion must be setting in now. Exhaustion and the realization of what she'd done, the terrible judgment she'd used. She'd probably rehearsed the fate of every girl in Walksalong who'd ever done anything wrong. Some had been Outcast, a few had been killed. Their faces and names fluttered through Blue Raven's souls: Running Doe, Meadow Leaf, poor little Caprock. Wren must be more lonely and desperate than she'd ever been in her life.

Blue Raven kicked his way through a drift, praying she would have the good sense to turn around . . . and . . . he heard a voice.

He held his breath and scanned the shadowy forest. It had been faint, but clear. Sweet, joyous laughter. As if a child hid in the forest, watching his progress with amusement. Blue Raven searched the brush and tree limbs. In his hurry, his eyes almost passed over the Traders' canoe landing. "Oh, Wren, no. Tell me you didn't."

He ran toward the place where the Traders always pulled their canoes up on shore.

He saw it. Wren's trail came out of the forest, and onto the landing.

"Oh, for the sake of the ancestors! *Wren?*" he shouted, and whirled around. "Wren!"

Four canoes lay beached on the gravel.

But there had been five at dawn. He could see her moccasin prints, and the scratched gravel where she'd pushed the boat into the water.

Blue Raven closed his eyes. He had to think. He could continue his pursuit, or return to the village, and ask the matrons to authorize a search party. Twenty warriors could certainly find her more quickly than he could. But he knew Wren. She would hide from them, using all the skills he'd taught her. Which meant things would go much worse for her when they finally dragged her back to Walksalong Village.

But if Blue Raven found her first, he might be able to convince Wren to return of her own free will. Such an act would appeal to the matrons' aging hearts.

He prayed.

A slim red canoe sat on the far right, a paddle lying inside. Blue Raven shoved it into the water.

Sparrow led the way, wading into the snow, packing it down with his moccasins. His legs had been shaking since noon, when they'd dragged their canoe ashore and hidden it in a pile of brush.

"Not much farther, Dust."

Panting, she answered, "That's what . . . you said . . . a hand of time ago."

"That was just to keep you going. I'm telling you the truth this time."

Her feet crunched snow. He forced his own legs to keep climbing.

The pines along the route drooped mournfully beneath the weight of snow; several limbs had broken off, others touched the ground. Every time the cold breeze blew, they squealed and groaned.

Sparrow crested a windblown hilltop, and spread his legs to keep his knees from buckling. Below him, the blue waters of the Dancing Man River emptied into the deep green expanse of Pipe Stem Lake. Walksalong Village sat on the opposite shore, its tall palisade a rough oval around the six longhouses. A fire blazed in the middle of the plaza. Sparrow sucked in a breath and stepped behind the trunk of an old oak. From this distance, only the keenest eyes would spot them through the intervening tangle of trees, but he didn't wish to risk it. There had to be sixty or seventy people standing around that fire. Maybe more.

Dust came up beside Sparrow, breathing hard. She cautiously peered around the trunk at the village, and Wind Mother buffeted her fur-lined hood. "That's a large fire for this time of day."

"Yes. It is."

She gave Sparrow a sidelong look. "If that were my village, I'd say the people looked nervous."

Sparrow couldn't see them very clearly, but several people waved their arms. A few paced back and forth. Four old white-haired women sat together on the north side of the fire. "It looks like a village council meeting."

Dust wet her chapped lips. "What do you think has happened? Did they discover Jumping Badger's treachery? Are they organizing a war party to hunt for us?"

Sparrow lifted a shoulder. All day long as they'd battled the snow, Dust had talked about Rumbler, about how she knew he was alive, because she could feel him in her heart.

Gently, he said, "It's more likely, Dust, that Rumbler is dead, and they're preparing the Death Feast."

She shook her head violently. "He's alive, Sparrow! I . . . I can feel him."

He reached out to touch her cheek, but stopped. His hand hovered over her shoulder a long moment before he closed his fist on air, and tucked it back into the pocket of his elkhide jacket. "Well, there's only one way to find out." He gestured to the trail. "Shall we?"

Dust walked ahead, wading into the snow. Her legs shook so badly she had trouble keeping her balance as she broke trail. After ten paces she stopped. She turned halfway around to look at him, and he could see the struggle in her eyes. "I'm sorry, Sparrow. I—"

"No, I'm sorry." He put a hand on her shoulder, and eased around her. "I should be leading the way."

"You've been leading all day," she said in an agonized voice. "I know you're tired, too."

"I can manage for another hand of time. Besides, we're almost there." He pointed. "Do you see the tallest hill north of Walksalong Village? The one with the trees on top?"

Her head wobbled in a nod. "Yes."

"That's Lost Hill. We're supposed to meet Cornhusk at the base of the hill on the shore of Pipe Stem Lake." He shielded his eyes and studied the position of Grandfather Day Maker. The sun stood just above the trees behind them. "I'd say we have about another two hands of time before nightfall, and another hand of time after that before it's dark enough that we can chance approaching Lost Hill." He lowered his hand. "It's not just that I'm exhausted. I really think we should stop for a while."

When she opened her mouth to object, he added, "We don't want anyone to see us, Dust. If we sit down long enough to drink something, and rest our legs, the sun will sink a little lower, and the shadows cast by the trees will help to hide us. Then we'll make our way to the canoe landing. Cornhusk said he'd leave a boat on this shore for us. We can't even think of going near it until it's dark.''

Dust searched his eyes, as if to make certain he'd told her the truth, that they really could afford to stop, then she nodded. ''All right, Sparrow. But only for a finger of time.''

''Agreed.''

Sparrow inspected the trees that lined the trail to his right, the humps of snow-covered brush, boulders, and weaves of deadfall. ''There's a fallen log over there, Dust. Why don't you stay here until I've beaten down a path.''

''Gladly.''

He stepped off the trail and bulled his way up the slope. When he finally reached the fallen log, he brushed the snow off, then waved to Dust. ''There's a wonderful view of the lake from up here.''

She started up the trail, and Sparrow unslung his pack, removed his quiver and bow from his shoulder, and sank down on the log. His aching legs throbbed. ''Hallowed Spirits,'' he groaned, ''I needed this.''

''I can't wait to join you.''

Wan sunlight fell through the branches, and sprinkled Dust's body with bits of gold. Her face had flushed, and her eyes had a dull look, as though she had just enough strength to take one more step.

When she got close enough, she grabbed onto a low-hanging limb, and eased down onto the fallen log beside Sparrow.

''Are you all right?'' he asked.

She stretched her back muscles, and winced. ''Just weary.''

''Me, too.''

Sparrow untied his water bag from his belt and handed it to her. "Drink deep."

Dust pulled open the knot, tipped the bag up, and tried to hold it steady while she drank, but water spilled over her chin and down the front of her cape. She managed five gulps before she had to lower the bag. As she handed it back, she said, "I think we should eat a corn cake, too. It will give us back some of our strength."

"You're going to grant me a corn cake?"

"Just one."

He smiled.

While Dust searched her pack for the right birch-bark bag, Sparrow drank, relishing the feel of the cold water going down his throat.

A wispy flock of Cloud Giants sailed overhead, their bellies shining a rich yellow. Against the blue sky, they resembled tongues of flame. Sparrow reknotted the laces on the gut bag and rested it between them. When he exhaled, his breath frosted. The storm might have broken, but as the afternoon fled, the cold deepened. By the time they met with Jumping Badger, the world would be a frozen monster.

He gazed down at Walksalong Village. "It's odd, isn't it? Once, many winters ago, the Bear Nation and the Turtle Nation were one. Now we barely speak."

"Well, it's their fault," Dust said as she handed him two corn cakes. They'd been fried on both sides and he could see the toasted hickory nuts that speckled them. His mouth watered. "They raid us constantly. What do they expect?"

He bit into his cake and chewed slowly, relishing each bite. It tasted sweetly delicious. "It's more than the hostilities, Dust. We've all grown in different directions. They even bury their dead differently than we do."

"Yes, I've heard." Around a mouthful of corn cake, she said, "They're savages."

"Are they? We bury our people in individual graves, placing a few precious items around them that they will need in the afterlife. The Bears strip the flesh from their loved ones' bones, mix the bones with those of their ancestors, then bury them, and their possessions, in a mass communal pit. They think that mixing the bones assures people will be together in the afterlife." He took another bite, chewed and swallowed. Whirlwinds of snow bobbed over the hills. "I don't know that their way is any worse than ours, Dust. We're both trying to make certain our people are happy."

She finished her first cake, brushed the crumbs from her hands, and bit into a second. "Well, perhaps, but I still—"

A twig cracked in the forest.

Neither one of them moved.

Then Dust subtly shifted. She murmured, "Behind you, Sparrow. See him?"

He followed her gaze, and saw the man creeping through the trees. Sparrow calmly picked up his bow, eased an arrow from his quiver and nocked it. "Who is he? Can you tell?"

"No, I . . ." Her eyes narrowed. "Wait. It may be Cornhusk."

The bald patches of hair on his buffalo coat looked dark in comparison to the glistening fur. Sparrow cupped a hand to his mouth, and called, "Cornhusk?"

The man hurried forward, slogging through the snow. Stringy hair framed his broken nose and rotted front teeth. "Yes! It's me. Don't shoot!"

"What are you doing here?" Dust asked. "I thought we were supposed to meet you at the bottom of Lost Hill?"

"Yes, Matron. You were." Cornhusk stopped, and bent forward to catch his breath. "But Jumping Badger plans on killing you the instant you appear there."

Dust's expression turned deadly.

"I swear I didn't know!" Cornhusk blurted.

"What's happened?" she asked. "Tell us quickly."

Cornhusk came forward like a man walking through poisonous vines. His small dark eyes darted from Sparrow to Dust and back again. "The False Face Child is gone. He—"

"*Gone?*" Tears filled her eyes. "You mean he—"

"Oh, no, he's not dead! I mean I don't think he's dead. He might be, but—"

"For the sake of the ancestors, get to the point!"

"Yes. Certainly." Cornhusk held up his hands and nodded. "This is what happened. In the middle of the night, Matron Starflower and a woman named Loon came into the longhouse where I was sleeping. They said that Blue Raven, the Vigil Keeper—"

"The Headman of Walksalong Village was assigned as Vigil Keeper?" Sparrow asked.

"Yes. But Blue Raven and the False Face Child are gone. Starflower suspects Blue Raven of treason, of actually cutting the child loose and taking him away. The whole village has gone insane! You won't believe the things they're saying down there!"

Dust asked, "What are they saying?"

Cornhusk slowly lowered his hands, as if still worried they might shoot him. "The matrons are discussing how they should kill Blue Raven after they catch him. Burn him alive. Stake him out in the snow. Cut him apart and feed him to the dogs. They aren't even certain yet that he released the boy! They're rushing things, if you ask me. And that poor little girl, I can't imagine—"

"What girl?"

"Oh. Uh—Blue Raven's niece. Her name is Little Wren. She was to take Blue Raven food and drink twice a day while he kept Vigil. She's missing, too, and the matrons have decreed that if she was involved in the crime she should pay with her life. Blessed ancestors, the girl has seen twelve winters!"

"They would kill a little girl?" Dust said, her voice going rough. "Why?"

"Because of the curse, Matron." Cornhusk edged closer. "Remember? Lamedeer said that the False Face Child would be the death of the Walksalong Clan. As the matrons see it, by saving the boy, Blue Raven and Little Wren have condemned their entire clan."

Dust bowed her head and shook it. "Didn't I tell you, Sparrow? They're savages."

Cornhusk glanced at Sparrow. "You must leave. Now. The child is gone. There's nothing here for you."

Dust fingered the hem of her cape, and Sparrow could see the thoughts churning behind her eyes. "Why would Blue Raven save Rumbler?"

Cornhusk flapped his arms like a demented goose. "I don't know! None of this makes any sense."

"Where would he take him?"

"Well, I should think, Matron, that if he cared enough to save the child, he would take him any place the boy wanted to go!"

Dust nodded. "Yes. I suppose he would."

Cornhusk glanced over his shoulder. "Now please go. I don't want to be responsible for your mutilations. Jumping Badger—"

"Where is Jumping Badger?" Sparrow asked suddenly, his gaze searching the blowing snow.

"Gone. Matron Starflower ordered him to hunt down Blue Raven. He formed a search party and left last night. He hasn't returned yet." Cornhusk shifted his weight to his left foot. "Frankly, I hope he never comes back! All night long he whispered to Lamedeer's rotting head. Saying crazy things about ghost armies, and how you, Sparrow, were in league with the ghosts, trying to kill him."

Sparrow slipped his arrow back into his quiver and slung his bow over his shoulder. "Tell me *exactly* what Jumping Badger said."

"Well, many things. He told Lamedeer that he could hear everything Lamedeer said to the dwarf child, that it echoed in his head." Cornhusk smirked in disgust. "Then he said something like, 'I know exactly what you're planning. You and that accursed Silver Sparrow.' He also said that as long as he was near a fire after nightfall nothing could hurt him. I tell you, he's lost his wits. His souls are flitting around like bats."

Sparrow said, "How many warriors did he take with him?"

"Twenty. He also took Lamedeer's severed head."

Dust whispered, "How curious."

"Oh, no, that part makes perfect sense. Trust me. Nobody else is going to talk to Jumping Badger." Cornhusk backed up a step. "Now, I must leave before Jumping Badger returns. Please tell no one you saw me. Do you understand? No one!"

Dust rose to her feet and faced him. "We'll do as you ask, Cornhusk, but I must say, I don't understand why you risked coming to warn us. There was no profit in it. What made you do such a thing?"

He grinned, showing his rotted teeth. "I got you into this. I had to get you out."

"That's very noble, but—"

"No, Matron, not noble. Practical." He glanced at Sparrow. "Your former husband has quite a reputation. If he died and someone thought it was my fault, I wouldn't have long to live."

Sparrow smiled. "Especially not if I cursed you myself before I died."

Cornhusk's grin vanished. "Er—that was another reason."

"Well, whatever your reasons," Dust said, "we thank you."

"Happy to have served you well, Matron." As he hurried into the forest, down the trail he'd cut earlier, he called, "Don't forget, Silver Sparrow! After Jumping Badger finds Blue Raven, he'll be coming for you! He still thinks you cursed him!"

Sparrow cupped a hand to his mouth, and replied, "If you see him, tell Jumping Badger I'll be waiting for him. *With* my army of ghosts!"

Cornhusk stumbled, and almost slammed into a tree before he caught himself. He smiled uneasily, lifted a hand, and disappeared into the shadows.

Dust squinted at him. Snow had melted on her long gray braid, and it sparkled with water drops. "Why did you say that?"

Sparrow reached for his water bag. As he tied it back onto his belt, he said, "Just what do you think I do to get my reputation? Turn myself into birds? Lope around in the bodies of big cats?"

She stared at him.

Sparrow slung his pack over his left shoulder. "Pack up, Dust. I know where Rumbler's headed. We might be able to—"

"How do you know?"

Sparrow grabbed the corn cakes bag and thrust it at her. "I'm an old man, Dust. Hope is all I have."

Rumbler lay on his back in the bow of the canoe, snuggled warmly in Little Wren's white fox-fur cape. Wind Mother liked the cape; she kept gently stroking the fur, making it shimmer like frost at dawn. Rumbler touched it with his puffy fingers. He didn't know why Little Wren had given it to him. This cape was warmer than the deerhide one she wore. Or why she had dragged him off Lost Hill. Her people had wanted him to die. Did they wish her to die now, too?

Rumbler frowned at his right hand. His thumb and the first finger looked the same, but the tips of his second and third fingers had started to swell and turn dark purple. Two knuckles on his little finger had gone black. Every finger on his left hand had a swollen tip.

Wren sat on her knees in the rear of the canoe, paddling hard. Sweat beaded her brow. For four days, they had been going very fast, shooting along the shore like an arrow. Wren's oar stroked the water on the left side of the boat, then the right. A long silver V spread out around them. Wren's braid hung over her right shoulder. She had a face like a wood carving. Brown and cut sharply, the eyes big, like a flying squirrel's.

But her soul was a wolf's.

Sometimes the she-wolf looked out at Rumbler, and the air suddenly tasted like running over hills with the wind in his mouth, and the tang of freedom on his tongue. When that happened the whole world had the flavor of polished copper, bright and sour.

He had never known anyone with a wolf's soul.

Rumbler let out a deep breath, and turned his head to the right, watching the wooded shore pass by. Tall beech and maple trees stretched their arms toward Grandfather Day Maker, offering their morning prayers. So far today, he'd seen four deer drinking from the lake.

Wind Mother ruffled Rumbler's hair, Singing to him,

her voice soft and pretty, trying to get Rumbler to go to sleep.

He yawned, and looked at Wren.

She shifted her oar to the other side of the canoe, and smiled at Rumbler.

The spaces in his heart where his blood lived swelled and ached. His throat went tight.

He swallowed, and smiled back.

# Sixteen

Little Wren's shadow moved over the shelter wall as she duckwalked to the fire pit, and checked the soup pot hanging from the tripod over the low flames. The scent of smoked turkey and onions filled her nostrils.

"It's not boiling yet, Rumbler, but it won't be long now."

He sat leaning against the massive trunk of an oak tree, wrapped in her foxhide cape. His chin-length black hair clung to his cheeks, framing his beautiful round face. He gazed at her through unwavering black eyes. He'd been looking at her like that since she'd first tied her cape around him, and dragged him off Lost Hill. He couldn't walk. She hadn't had any choice. Besides, she'd been plenty warm. She'd packed her deerhide cape earlier, thinking that Rumbler would need it. She'd ended up wearing it instead.

He couldn't seem to stop shivering. It worried Wren. She'd seen people die from being out in the cold for too long. Even though people found them and brought them back to the longhouse, they'd gone to sleep and never awakened. Rumbler seemed to be getting stronger, though. He could lift his own teacup now. He could only hold it for a few instants before he had to set it down, but when she'd first handed him a cup, his fingers hadn't worked at all. The wooden cup sat on the ground beside him.

"Do you need more tea?" Wren asked.

"No, I . . ." He looked into his cup. "I still have some."

Wren's pack rested near the woodpile, to the left of the fire pit. She dragged it over, found her wooden spoon, and stirred the soup. She'd packed enough food for five or six nights. After that, they would have to hunt.

She didn't know what they would do or where they would go. But she knew she couldn't go home.

Once, many winters ago, a girl named Caprock had taken one of the sacred masks from the council house, and run off with it. Wren had only seen four winters at the time, but she'd heard that Caprock had planned to sell the mask to a holy woman in a Bear-Turtle village. The war leader before Jumping Badger had hunted her down and dragged her back, screaming, to Walksalong Village.

Matron Starflower had ordered her to be burned alive.

Stealing a False Face Child was much worse than stealing a sacred mask.

Wren peered absently at the soup. It had started to bubble.

She laid down her spoon, and pulled a bag of cornmeal from her pack. After she'd added a handful to the soup, to thicken it, she folded the top over, and tied it again. They didn't have enough to allow even a few grains to leak out.

"Just a little longer, Rumbler," she said and sank down cross-legged beside the fire.

Their tiny shelter had warmed up. Wren just hoped the heat wasn't melting the snow that mounded the deadfall, and hid it from view. She'd deliberately built a small fire—had considered not building one at all, but Rumbler had desperately needed warmth.

Grandmother Earth had made the shelter for them. Over the tree's long life, limbs had died and piled up around the trunk. Then grape vines had grown over and through the pile, creating a sheltered hollow about two body lengths wide. The animals had discovered it first. Wren had been looking for a windbreak when she'd spooked a deer bedded down in this place. She'd dragged up a few more poles to close the opening to her left, then pried a hole in the roof to allow the smoke from their fire to escape, but the interior had already been carved out perfectly, the sharp twigs broken by the animals, the ground hard-packed.

Wren removed two wooden bowls from her pack, along with the other spoon, and set them in front of her.

She ladled both bowls full, then went to lean beside Rumbler against the oak trunk. The bark felt cold through her cape. She set her own bowl down, and held Rumbler's out to him.

"Can you take this, Rumbler?"

He reached for it, hooked his thumbs over the rim and curled his injured fingers beneath the base. The bowl shook, the spoon inside clicking against the wood. He carefully lowered it to his lap.

Wren studied the bowl and his bowed head. "Do you need help, Rumbler?"

He didn't answer.

Wren got on her knees beside him, lifted the bowl,

filled the spoon and blew on it, then held it to his lips. "Be careful. It's hot."

Rumbler ate the first mouthful, and Wren dipped a second.

As he chewed it, he said, "This is good."

He ate two more spoonfuls.

She smiled. "My mother taught me to make it. In the autumn she always added things like sunflower seeds, walnuts, gooseberries, and currants. She taught me lots of things."

Rumbler watched Wren with shining black eyes. On occasion, like now, she had the feeling that he could see right through her skin and muscles to her souls. It made her backbone tingle.

"My mother taught me things, too," he said.

"She was a Healer, wasn't she? I heard that from someone."

Rumbler nodded, and ate another mouthful. "She's a great Healer. Did you know that if you boil the thick inner bark of hoary willow roots, it will cure a cough?"

Wren frowned. "No, I didn't. We use cedarberry tea for coughs."

"The juice of marsh willow dripped into the nostrils cures headaches," he added, "and if you put hemlock berries in cold water with maple sap, then leave it for a week, it makes a good beer. You can also use the beer to wash wounds. They heal faster."

"What about burns?" She fed him another spoonful. "My people have never figured out the right plant for that."

"We cook poplar buds with bear grease. It works as a salve on burns, cuts, or other injuries." Rumbler let out a long breath. "I think that's all I can eat, Wren. Thank you, I . . . I don't feel very well."

She set the half-empty bowl down, and searched his

round face. "Maybe you should try to sleep, Rumbler. You'll feel better once you've gotten a good warm night's rest."

Obediently, he lay down. Wren tucked the edges of her fox-fur cape around his stubby legs, then sat back and picked up her own bowl. As she ate, Rumbler watched her, his eyelids growing heavier.

The thick soup tasted delicious, and it soothed her, reminding her of happy nights around the fire with her parents, brother, and Trickster. Without even thinking, she looked at the spot beneath her cape where Trickster's rawhide toy hung from her belt. Though she hadn't seen him, or heard him barking, she felt certain that Trickster's ghost stood guard close by. She'd heard steps behind her, crunching the snow, as she'd hauled Rumbler up the hill toward Dancing Man River, and to the—

Rumbler murmured, "I had a dog, too, named Stone-coat."

Wren lowered her spoon to her bowl. "How did you know I was thinking about Trickster?"

"My dog followed us after the warriors captured me. Stonecoat fought for me. He jumped on the big man. But the warriors killed him and ate him."

Wren numbly stared into her bowl, barely seeing the chunks of turkey, and onions. Her people often ate dogs; if they were properly fed the meat had a sweet taste. But if someone had killed Trickster and eaten him before her eyes, it would have broken her heart.

She set her bowl on the floor. "I'm sorry, Rumbler. For everything that's happened to you." She shook her head. "I'm sorry for your hands, too."

He blinked tiredly at his fingers. The top joints of his first three fingers had swollen. His little fingers resembled bloated black slugs. Rumbler tried to wiggle them, and winced.

In a small voice, he said, "Wren?"

"Yes, Rumbler."

His black eyes devoured her souls. "Why did you help me?"

She shrugged and studied the crisscrossing poles that formed the roof. Vines as thick as her arms wove through the tangle. Taller animals, like the deer, must rub on them. The smooth shiny wood reflected the firelight. "You needed me to, Rumbler," she answered.

"But your people will kill you for it, won't they?"

"I don't know. But I couldn't leave you out there. It was as if I had to save you, or—or I was going to die myself."

She used the back of her hand to wipe away the tears that blurred her eyes. "My cousin Jumping Badger should never have stolen you. It was wrong."

Rumbler tilted his head and his eyes went vacant. He whispered, "After the warriors took me away into the forest, he did terrible things."

"What kinds of things?"

"He ordered his war party to rape the women and little girls, and to cut open the bellies of pregnant women. They drew the babies from the wombs. One of them, one . . . he . . ." Rumbler swallowed repeatedly as if fighting nausea.

"Rumbler?"

"He—he was a boy baby. He cried when the warriors lifted him from his mother's belly. The warrior took him, and—and bashed his brains out on a rock."

Rumbler had started breathing hard, as if seeing it all again.

Wren frowned. "But I thought . . . didn't you say that the warriors carried you out of the village at the beginning of the battle?"

"Yes."

"How could you know what they did afterward?"

Rumbler bowed his head. "I saw it."

"Did they carry you up on a hill where you could look back?"

"My eyes . . . they fly sometimes, Wren. I see things in faraway places."

Wren bit her lip. Dwarfs had strange Powers. She'd heard stories about them all her life. But she'd never heard of a dwarf with winged eyes. A thought occurred to her.

"Can you see my uncle?"

"Are you worried about him?"

"He might get in trouble."

"Because you helped me?"

"Yes."

Rumbler closed his eyes and tipped his head back. The blue veins in his temples pulsed.

Quietly, she gathered their bowls and cups and duck-walked to the fire where she emptied them back into their respective pots. She scowled at the dirty dishes, hating the idea of going out into the snow to wash them. *I'll do it in the morning. I'll rub them clean with snow. That will be good enough.* She set them near the fire, and crawled around the pit for her own blankets, which lay near the woodpile.

Before spreading them out, Wren glanced at Rumbler. He hadn't moved. She unrolled her blankets. The woodpile rested an arm's length away. As she lay down, she pulled a stick from the pile, and placed it on the coals. Flames licked up, crackling and spitting sparks.

"Rumbler?" she whispered. "Are you all right?"

In a soft voice, he answered, "Oh, yes, Wren. Everything's going to be all right."

Dust Moon nearly leaped out of her skin when she heard the wind. "What the . . ."

She sat up in her blankets. It had snowed on and off throughout the night, but now a deep blue sky arced overhead, filled with the glistening lodges of the Night Walkers. She rubbed her eyes, and tried to steady her breathing. The roar had wakened her from frightening dreams about clouds and shadows. Rumbler's beautiful round face had peeked out at her more than once.

The deep-throated growl grew louder.

"Sparrow, do you hear that?"

They'd camped in a meadow on the southern shore of Leafing Lake, where the snow had been blown clean away. Tall wind-sculpted drifts scalloped the edges of the meadow, and ringed the grove of pines on the hilltop behind them.

Sparrow lay rolled in his hides to her right. When he lifted his head, his beaked nose gleamed silver.

"What, Dust?"

"Are you deaf? Don't you hear it?"

Sparrow brushed his white hair behind his ears, and cocked his head first one way, then another, listening to the frigid night. His breath condensed into a white cloud before him. "Hear what?"

Dust Moon's mouth gaped. "That eerie howling as if Grandmother Earth is being torn apart by a pack of wolves! You really don't hear it? I can feel the roar in my souls!"

Sparrow slowly turned to face her. His bushy brows drew together. "In your souls?"

"Yes! It's like an earthquake coming. You know how you can hear the quake before it strikes?"

"Yes, I do." He shoved his hides away, and sat up. "I have the feeling, though, that you may be the only one who hears this roar."

"What are you talking about?"

Sparrow's eyes went over the pines, and the snow that packed the forest, then drifted to the lake. It resembled an endless glimmering sea. Silver ribbons of waves rolled onto the shore. "Souls have a language of their own, Dust. Yours may be trying to tell you something."

"I'm sure it is. It's trying to tell me that old age has finally grabbed you by the foot, and you're going deaf. You *must* hear that!"

"No, I don't, and I wish you . . . wouldn't . . ." Sparrow blinked as if to clear his vision. "What in the name of the ancestors is that?" He pointed to the northeastern horizon.

Dust turned.

Out across the lake, a black wall of clouds rose over the water. As she watched, it rolled closer, the leading edge tumbling, blotting the stars as it came.

"Get up, Dust. Move. Hurry! Run for the trees."

Sparrow grabbed his bedding, snatched his pack, and dashed up the slippery meadow for the pines.

Dust bent over to gather her blankets, but her eyes stayed on the storm. "What is that?"

"A storm!" he shouted, and violently waved an arm at her. "Come on!"

Cloud Giants sailed in from every part of the sky, huge giants, wispy giants, they all rushed to join the storm. As their bodies melded with the black wall, it billowed higher into the night sky.

"Blessed Grandfather Day Maker," she whispered in awe. "It's alive."

By the time Dust had dragged her blankets into her arms, and slung her pack over her shoulder, the storm had swallowed half the sky.

"Come on, Dust!" Sparrow called from the hilltop. "It's coming fast!"

She ran up the icy meadow toward the snowdrifts that ringed the pines, but before she made the trees, the wind struck her like the fist of the gods, slamming her sideways, knocking her off her feet and ripping her blankets from her arms. She tried to grab for them, but they whipped away, flying upward as if they'd sprouted wings.

*"Dust!"*

Sparrow ran for her, grabbed her, and pulled her to her feet.

"Hold on to me!" he yelled. "Don't let go!"

Sparrow guided Dust into the lee of a large granite boulder, and forced her to crouch down behind it. The rock blocked some of the wind, but the storm ripped off a blizzard of pinecones and needles from the branches behind them and hurled them down.

Dust yipped sharply when a piece of gravel struck her cheek and drew blood.

"Get down!" Sparrow shoved her down flat, and covered her with his own body.

White hair streamed over his shoulders like the ghostly arms of a dancer. Through the veil, she glimpsed pine boughs lashing into each other as snow blasted from the sky.

Jumping Badger walked around Lamedeer's head, his steps light. The firebow that draped his neck patted softly against his long beaverhide coat. He'd planted the staff, upon which the head rode, in the middle of Blue Raven's trail. The traitor had pulled his canoe up on shore and camped here last night. The head stood as a reminder to anyone who doubted his abilities that he had sniffed out his cousin's trail. Not that it had been difficult. Blue Raven had made no attempt to disguise the deep swaths his body had cut. Jumping Badger couldn't decide why. Many winters ago, Blue Raven had been a renowned warrior. If he'd stolen the boy and meant to escape, why would he leave such an easy trail?

He kicked snow at Lamedeer's head. "Eh?" he whispered. "You would cover your trail. So would I. Why didn't he?"

A prickling started beneath Jumping Badger's heart. He had learned to recognize Lamedeer's ghostly laughter. He couldn't hear it with his ears, but his body could. It was like being tickled with a bear's claw, sharp, irritating.

He walked around Lamedeer again. Over the past hand of time, he'd worn a circular path in the snow.

Shadows danced across the snowdrifts as his warriors lifted their heads to watch him. They sat fifty hands away, huddled around the nightly fire. They moved uneasily, lifting a shoulder, toying with a piece of wood, shaking their heads. They spoke in hoarse whispers.

Behind them, at the edge of the fire's halo, a dark shape floated through the trees. Burned. She had been burned blacker than the darkness, her body consumed. But not her eyes.

They lived. Bright and shining.

Those eyes peered at him from behind a tree trunk.

"Go away!" Jumping Badger shouted. "You can't hurt me! I'm more powerful than you are! If you don't leave me alone, I will cut your son into little pieces when I find him!"

The eyes died. The forest stilled.

Jumping Badger studied Lamedeer. The dead war leader's face had changed. Most of his hair had fallen out, leaving huge bald spots on the crown and left side of his head. The few graying black locks that remained hung in filthy strands over the right eye. The other eye had sunken into the socket and formed a hard yellow crust, but Jumping Badger could *feel* it gazing at him—like a deer watching him through thick brush.

"You are strangely silent tonight," Jumping Badger noted. "Have you given up trying to drive me mad with the echoes?"

When Lamedeer said nothing, Jumping Badger leaned down and shouted in his face, *"Talk to me!"*

Frightened murmurs rose from his warriors.

Jumping Badger whirled. "Be quiet! I can't hear anything with your noise!"

Elk Ivory stood up. She said something to Acorn, then broke from the group and walked toward Jumping Badger. Tall and muscular, she had shoulder-length black hair and striking brown eyes: when she looked at a man, he felt as if he'd been bludgeoned. She wore a heavy buffalo-hide coat, the curly fur turned inside to rest against her skin. Painted green hawks and falcons decorated the lower half of her coat. At thirty-eight winters, she was the oldest warrior in Walksalong Village. She had made a reputation for herself in her seventeenth winter when she'd killed the war leader of an enemy village in his own plaza. Jumping Badger remembered her triumphant homecoming. The warriors who'd fought at her side had carried her into the plaza on their shoulders. She had never married. Perhaps warring was the best use of her dried-up womb.

Jumping Badger smiled grimly as she approached. He'd grown up hearing the stories about her undying love for Blue Raven, about how it had driven her to become a warrior, so that she might fight at her lover's side. In the end, her sacrifice hadn't mattered. Blue Raven had rejected her. The reasons were a little vague.

"A pleasant evening to you, War Leader," Elk Ivory said. She glanced distastefully at Lamedeer's head.

"What do you want?"

"To speak with you."

"Then do so."

"The other warriors have asked me—"

"They are banding against me! The traitors!" he bellowed, and noted the reactions around the fire. Shoulders tensed. Grumbles went round.

"I did not say that, Jumping Badger." Elk Ivory looked him straight in the eyes, and he had trouble holding that intense gaze.

"Then say what you mean. I have more important things to consider tonight than you."

Jumping Badger's chest prickled again, and rage fired his blood. He swung around to Lamedeer. "Don't laugh at me! Why are you laughing?"

*"Because you are such a fool."*

Jumping Badger's souls went cold. A gust of wind shook the staff, and the decaying mouth opened slightly.

Fear stiffened his backbone.

Elk Ivory placed a hand on Jumping Badger's shoulder, and he jumped. She gently forced him to turn around and face her. "Are you well, War Leader?"

"Just deliver your message, old woman!"

"Your warriors are wondering why we are continuing to follow Blue Raven's trail when it is apparent that neither the False Face Child, nor Little Wren, is accompanying Blue Raven."

Jumping Badger straightened. "I don't know where the loathsome girl is. She probably ran off and got eaten by a cougar. Who cares? As for the False Face Child, what makes you think he would be walking? Are all of my warriors feebleminded? Did it never occur to you that after nights of lying in the cold and snow the boy would be incapable of walking? Blue Raven is, of course, carrying him up from the canoe, and back down to it!''

Elk Ivory tucked her fists into her coat pockets. Firelight flickered through her black hair. ''May I suggest something else?''

''No, I don't care to—''

''Just listen. When we made it to Lost Hill, Blue Raven's fire had gone cold. Dishes and blankets lay where he'd been sitting. Not the sort of things a man planning on running away would leave.''

''If you have something to say, say it!''

Her brown eyes turned stony. ''Tomorrow afternoon, at the latest, we will catch up with Blue Raven. None of us believe that he stole the boy. It seems clear that Little Wren is the culprit. She must have released the False Face Child while Blue Raven slept, and been long gone by the time he awoke. That's why we've only seen Blue Raven's footprints. He discovered her crime and decided to try and track her down before anyone else discovered what she'd done.''

''That's ridiculous! Why would he—''

''He loves that little girl. I know him, Jumping Badger. Blue Raven's sense of honor and duty to his family is powerful. He's hunting for her, hoping to bring her back and beg the matrons for mercy. It's his way. That's also why he's not bothering to disguise his trail. He has nothing to hide.''

He sputtered, ''B-but—''

''*You imbecile. You've been following the wrong trail. Now you'll never find the False Face Child, and he'll kill you. Just as I said. I'm so glad you brought me along. I want to be there to see it happen!"*

Jumping Badger shrieked like a madman and threw himself on the head. He tore the staff from the ground, and swung it with all of his strength, flinging it and the head out into the dark forest.

His warriors lurched to their feet and grabbed for weapons. Acorn ran forward. He stopped just behind Elk Ivory, breathing hard, his rough-hewn face shining with sweat.

"What is it?" Acorn asked. "What's happened?"

Elk Ivory subtly used her chin to point to the severed head that blackened the snow forty hands distant.

Acorn glanced at it, swallowed hard, and nodded as if in sudden understanding. "Well. If you need me . . . just . . . just call."

"I will, Acorn," Elk Ivory said. "Return to your tea. All is well."

Acorn gave Jumping Badger a weak smile. "Good evening to you, War Leader."

"Get away from me!"

Acorn backed up, then headed for the fire. When he arrived, he was barraged with whispered questions. Acorn knelt before the fire and shushed them.

Elk Ivory stood tall and calm. Observing.

Jumping Badger spread his hands. "I don't know why he does that to me," he said. "I think he's trying to drive me mad."

"Who? Acorn?"

"Lamedeer!" he shouted. "You have no idea what it's like to have one ghost talking ceaselessly in your head, while another prowls the darkness waiting to get her hands around your throat. At least tonight the echoes are silent. They are always worse at night, right after I climb into my bedding. Like a hundred hearts pounding at once, they—''

''Jumping Badger?'' Elk Ivory's voice had gone low and concerned. ''The Midwinter Dance is two moons away. Perhaps you should ask permission to participate in the ceremony. If you ask Sky Holder for his blessings, he might rid you—''

''You think I'm a cursed man, don't you?'' He knew the very thought terrified his warriors. ''Don't you see what's happening here? I'm not cursed!'' He gestured to the head lying in the snow. ''One of Lamedeer's souls still lives in his head! I've received a great gift, Elk Ivory. The gods have given me the ability to speak with that soul, to learn from it.''

Her eyes bored into him. ''I think you need to see a Healer, Jumping Badger. People often do. It is not something to be ashamed of. All living things fall sick. A Healer will blow ashes upon your body to cleanse you of the evil that's come to live in your souls.''

''There's no evil in my souls, old woman! My Power grows daily. You're just too blind to see it.'' He glowered at her, then cupped a hand to his mouth and shouted at his warriors, ''And so are you! You're all as blind as moles!''

His Power had drained away to nothingness, and he knew it, but he couldn't let them know it. It enraged him to think that that despicable old lunatic, Silver Sparrow, might be waiting outside Walksalong Village right now, and Jumping Badger had no way of reaching him to force him to remove his curse. If he could only . . .

''*The prophecy will come true,*'' Lamedeer's deep voice hissed from the shadows. ''*You will wind up treated worse than a mangy cur. I have seen it, your own relatives kicking you, and spitting upon you.*'' More laughter. ''*It's a glorious sight.*''

Jumping Badger scrambled through the deep snow, screaming, "You don't know that! How could you? It won't happen!"

His warriors rose to their feet, and stood nervously before the fire.

Jumping Badger pulled the head from the snow, and shoved his nose less than a handbreadth from the dead war leader's. "I'll kill anyone who tries to treat me that way. Do you hear? Anyone!" In a low, threatening voice, he added, "Even you, Lamedeer. Don't forget, I hold your soul in my hands. If you don't do as I say, I'll never let you rest. I'll . . ."

His warriors' voices rose, and Jumping Badger spun around.

The sound of branches cracking came from the forest. The voices around the fire halted. Several warriors rose and sneaked to the north end of the camp, searching for the intruder.

Snowflakes started to fall. A wall of indigo clouds rolled overhead, gobbling up the lodges of the Night Walkers. Jumping Badger frowned.

"Oh, not another storm," Elk Ivory said. "I hate—"

"It's not a storm," Jumping Badger whispered as his eyes opened wide. The black shape in the forest had grown. She stood leaning over the trees, two hundred hands tall! Her charred hair waved against the starry sky. "It's *her*! She's coming for me!"

A shrill keening began, angry, forlorn, as if the Forest Spirits were fleeing for their lives.

Jumping Badger rose to his feet. *"Run!"* he screamed. *"Everyone run!"*

The leading edge of the storm exploded around him, blasting bedrolls and packs, roaring like a wildfire. Warriors ran in every direction, screaming and shouting. The wind ripped Lamedeer's head from Jumping Badger's arms, and sent it sailing away.

Jumping Badger dove for a tree, wrapped his arms around the trunk, and shrieked at the top of his lungs.

He could hear Elk Ivory yelling, *"Forget your packs! Find cover. Crawl under the nearest log!"*

The storm raged for less than a finger of time, but when it passed, and Jumping Badger managed to dig his way out, he could not believe he still lived. He shouted, "Light a fire! Someone, hurry! Buckeye, I order you to light a fire!"

The lodges of the Night Walkers threw a pale silver light over the clearing where their fire had been. The hulking warrior Buckeye ran to the place where the pit had been and frantically began scooping snow away, trying to find it.

Every trace of their camp, every vestige of their lives, had been swept away.

Warriors began to emerge from the forest, brushing snow from their hair, cursing as they hunted the deep drifts for belongings.

"I found hot embers, War Leader!" Buckeye shouted. "A moment and I will have a fire going!"

"Hurry!" Jumping Badger screamed. *"Hurry!"*

His whole body shook as he watched Buckeye run to crack dead branches from a tree, and run back to toss them upon the red eyes of coals. Buckeye bent over and blew into the pit. Smoke curled up, followed by a few pathetic flames.

In the fire-spawned shadows, Jumping Badger could see her. Looming tall and black, her arms whipping back and forth, silently railing at him, cursing him.

As Buckeye piled more wood on the fire, she receded into the darkness, waiting.

Jumping Badger expelled a breath and tried to control his shaking.

Fifty hands away, Jumping Badger saw the staff sticking up through the snow. He trudged to it and pulled Lamedeer's head free.

The rotting mouth had curled into a broad smile.

"Did you think a little wind would scare me? You old fool, I—"

"You had better be scared," Elk Ivory said as she stood up from behind a tangle of brush, her pack in her hands. She gave Jumping Badger a hard look. "We've just lost our packs, bedding, and supplies. If we don't find them, we can't go on."

# Seventeen

Wren woke again long before dawn. She threw a branch on the fire and yawned. She had been feeding the flames throughout the night, to keep Rumbler warm, and he seemed to have slept well. He lay curled in her white foxhide cape, his round face mottled with firelight. His chest rose and fell in the slow rhythms of deep sleep.

Wren rose and set last night's turkey and cornmeal soup at the edge of the flames to warm, then hung the teapot from the tripod, and pulled out their cups. When she saw the dirty bowls, she muttered under her breath. Her mother had always told her never to leave unpleasant tasks for morning, that they became more onerous by the light of day. Wren hated the thought of braving the cold to clean them, but her bladder was about to burst anyway.

As quietly as she could, she gathered the dishes, and duckwalked to the mound of snow that blocked the entry. Using her bowl, she scooped away until a blindingly beautiful night sky met her eyes.

Wren tucked the dishes in her cape pockets, and crawled out on her hands and knees. Starlight glistened through the forest, blazing from the snow-covered branches and twigs. In the midst of a tall maple, silver owl eyes blinked at her.

The stillness of the predawn world awed her. Not a breath of wind stirred the trees. The elegant, swirling lines of the drifts looked as if they'd been sculpted by the gentle hands of Earth Spirits.

She walked away from the shelter and emptied her bladder. Cold nipped at her bare skin. She pulled up her pants and tucked her hands in her cape pockets. As she followed her own footsteps back, she used snow to scrub their bowls clean. Somewhere to the south, a fox yipped, then broke into a bark-and-howl serenade that echoed across the rolling hills.

Wren inhaled a deep breath of the cold air, and listened, hoping the call would soothe her fears.

She'd been trying not to think about what she'd done, but the awful truth kept shouting at her.

She looked eastward. Some of the old people would be rising by now, Walksalong Village coming to life. This was Wren's favorite time of day. If she were there, she'd be snuggled under her warm hides, listening to the hushed voices that filled the longhouse, sniffing the wafting aroma of breakfast being cooked.

She murmured, "I'll never be there again."

It hadn't occurred to her when she'd cut Rumbler loose that the price she'd pay for saving him would be losing everything that mattered to her.

The emptiness in her chest expanded. She would do the same thing again. She knew she would, but . . .

Wren tucked the clean dishes back into her cape pockets.

Perhaps, in a few winters, she would hire a runner to go to Uncle Blue Raven, asking his advice. She knew the matrons would never let her come home, but she wanted to see her uncle again. Surely they would allow that. Even if they didn't, maybe he could sneak away to meet her.

Wren stared blindly at the starlit snow. Her footsteps were wells of shadow . . . like her heart. Where would she go now? What would she do? And what of Rumbler? She'd rescued him. He was her responsibility. She had to make certain he was all right before she could even think of her own future. But his village was gone, his clan dead. Neither of them had relatives they could turn to. No, that wasn't true. *She* had no one to turn to. Rumbler might.

Wren crawled back into the shelter and saw that Rumbler had wakened. He sat on the fox-fur cape before the fire, a pot of tea boiling. His cheeks had a rosy hue, and his eyes seemed brighter.

"Are you feeling better, Rumbler?"

"Yes. I found tea in your pack, Wren. I hope that was all right."

"Yes. Thank you for making it." She took their cups and bowls from her pockets and set them by the fire, then sat cross-legged across from Rumbler, and filled the cups. The tangy fragrance of fir needles bathed her face. "Smells good."

Rumbler sipped his tea, and smiled. He'd been wearing that same black shirt with the shell ornaments for almost a moon. Wrinkled and filthy, it hurt to look at.

"I brought one of my shirts for you, Rumbler," she

lied—she'd actually brought it for herself. "I hope it fits."

Wren set her teacup down and dragged her pack over. When she pulled out the pale blue shirt embroidered with whelk shells and columella beads, his mouth dropped open.

"For me? You brought that for me?"

Wren handed it to him. "You need it."

Rumbler carefully propped his cup on one of the hearthstones and reached for it. As he ran his frostbitten fingers over the fine fabric, made from the soft inner bark of the basswood tree, pain lined his face. He whispered, "I've never had such a beautiful shirt. Thank you, Wren."

"Why don't you put it on? It's been in my pack by the fire all night. It should be warm. Tomorrow we'll wash your black one so you'll have an extra to wear."

Rumbler awkwardly slipped his dirty shirt over his head. Wren stared at him. His short arms only reached to his hips, and they bowed outward from his body. His neck also seemed longer than a normal person's neck. He put on the pale blue shirt. The whelk shells flashed in the firelight. He smoothed it down with his hands, then smelled the sleeve. "It smells like flowers," he said.

"My grandmother makes me wash our clothes in rose hips," she explained. "She says it helps to keep away bugs."

The sleeves hung almost to his knees. Wren leaned over and rolled them up for him.

Rumbler smiled, then his expression changed. He slowly lowered his arms. "You'll never see her again, will you? Or any of the rest of your family?"

"If Jumping Badger catches us, I'll see them, but not for long. I imagine they'll kill us pretty quick."

Rumbler lightly touched one of the whelk shells on the

sleeve. He seemed to be contemplating the shape and texture. "You gave up everything for me, didn't you, Wren?"

"I still have my life, Rumbler. And so do you." She sipped her tea, and concentrated on the tart flavor. She didn't want to let him see her cry. That would just make him feel bad, and he'd already suffered enough at the hands of her clan. "Do you think the soup is warm? I'm hungry."

Rumbler watched her as she leaned over the soup pot. The look in his eyes was not that of a child, but an ancient old man who'd seen too much of life. Despair lived in those dark depths. Very softly, he said, "I'm sorry, Wren."

"You didn't do anything wrong, Rumbler. Don't be sorry."

Wren picked up a horn spoon and stirred the soup. It had thickened overnight. "This is more like mush than soup, Rumbler, but it's hot."

"I like mush." Rumbler smoothed his hands over his knees. "My mother and I ate mostly seeds and roots."

"Didn't you have meat in your village?"

"We had meat."

Wren frowned. "Then why didn't you have any to eat?"

Rumbler smiled faintly. "I asked my mother that once. We were eating corn gruel for supper, and I saw that my cousins in the next lodge were roasting venison and wild ducks, and I remembered that a man had paid my mother that very morning with a duck and a haunch of venison. I wanted that meat so badly it made me angry. I said to my mother, 'People are always bringing you meat to pay for your Healings. Why can't we ever eat it?' " He tilted his head as if remembering fondly, but with pain.

"What did she say?"

"She said, 'Would you deny your cousins the meat so that you might have it?' I said, 'I like meat, Mother. Couldn't I have it just now and then?' Without another word, my mother rose to her feet, took my bowl of corn gruel, and walked to my cousin's lodge. She gave my bowl to my youngest cousin, Lynx, who was three winters old. In exchange, she took away Lynx's steaming bowl of duck. My little cousin's eyes filled with tears, but she did not say a word. She just started eating my corn gruel. My mother walked back and handed me Lynx's bowl of duck, then sat down again, and started eating her corn gruel.

"I looked at the duck, then at my little cousin, and I went over and returned her bowl. Lynx smiled so joyfully, I cried. When I came back to my mother's fire, she said, 'So. What made you happier, my son? Having a bowl of duck? Or giving the bowl of duck away?' "

Rumbler's eyes shone. "I like mush."

Wren thought about the story as she ladled his bowl full. "When you are stronger, I would like to hear more stories about your mother. I think I would have liked her." She handed the steaming bowl to Rumbler.

"You will like her," he said and set it in his lap, waiting for her to fill her own bowl. When she had, Rumbler started eating like a boy who feared he'd never get another meal. He shoveled soup into his mouth as fast as he could.

Wren ate slowly, enjoying each bite. The flavor of the onions had suffused the cornmeal, and tasted deliciously spicy. Not only that, during the Moon of Frozen Leaves, turkeys scattered at the first sign of a hunter. They might not get any more of this succulent meat until spring.

A branch in the fire burned through and snapped, making the flames leap and sputter. The sudden light threw Rumbler's shadow on the back wall like a Dancing ghost.

Wren tried not to see. It reminded her of the first moment she'd seen him, hanging from the ceiling like a deadly black spider, his eyes alight. He seemed different now. Innocent and vulnerable. How could a boy change this much in such a short time?

"Do you want more, Rumbler? You didn't eat very much last night, and you're going to need your strength."

He handed her his bowl. "Divide it between us. You will need strength, too, and we may not have a chance to eat again until nightfall."

She ladled half of the remaining soup into her bowl and half into his. But when she handed his bowl back, she said, "Actually, I brought along a bag of elk jerky. So if we grow hungry along the way, we can eat some of that."

Rumbler smiled. "You are so smart, Wren."

To hide her embarrassment, she took another bite of soup, and shrugged. "My uncle Blue Raven taught me how to pack for long trips. He used to be a great warrior. My people tell many stories of his courage." Her heart ached. "During one battle, twenty winters ago, he saw that a young warrior was about to be shot. Uncle Blue Raven threw himself in front of the youth. The arrow pierced my uncle's shoulder, but he killed the enemy warrior anyway. On cold nights, that old wound still bothers him." She filled her mouth with soup to drive back her sudden tears.

Rumbler's bowl trembled in his hands. He lowered it to rest on his knee. "He is brave. I liked him."

Wren swallowed. After thirty heartbeats, she could manage a smile. She said, "I will miss him."

They finished their meals in silence, not looking at each other.

As the fire burned lower, the leaping shadows retreated

to the dark corners, and a soft crimson glow filled the shelter.

Rumbler softly asked, "Did you say goodbye to Trickster?"

Before Wren realized what was happening, sobs wracked her chest. She choked out, "I told him I—I was going to do something that would get me into a lot of trouble."

Rumbler looked at her with his whole heart in his eyes. "Did Trickster answer?"

Wren wiped her runny nose, trying to remember the exact moment. She hadn't heard him bark, or whine, but ... "No," she answered, "but I think he wagged his tail."

Rumbler smiled.

Wren felt better. Talking about Trickster gave her strength. "Rumbler? Where are we going to go? I've been worrying about that. I was hoping that maybe you had relatives in one of the nearby Turtle villages."

"Yes, but I ... I have to go home first, Wren."

"Home?" she asked in confusion. "You mean to Paint Rock Village? But Rumbler, I heard Jumping Badger himself say that he'd burned it to the ground. There's nothing left. Why would you—"

"There's something ... someone ... I have to search for."

She knew who he must mean. "I—I'll help you look, Rumbler."

He frowned at his swollen fingers. He would lose the tips of the first three fingers on each hand, and two knuckles from each little finger. As if wishing to speak of something else, he said, "You are going to have to help me cut off these fingers, Wren. I can feel the Shadow Spirits creeping into my hands."

"I will, Rumbler. You tell me when."

He fought to blink back his tears. His eyes sparkled. "Will you help me catch a bird, Wren?"

His voice sounded even more desperate to speak of something else.

Wren reached up to the tangled branches in the roof, and began pulling off strips of bark. "I'll weave these strips into a net right now, Rumbler. There won't be any birds until Grandfather Day Maker rises, but we can find the place to set up our trap."

Dawn's pale purple gleam dyed the tops of the tallest trees, but most of the shore remained cloaked in slate-colored shadows. High above Blue Raven only the brightest of the Night Walkers' lodges twinkled. The rest had succumbed to the waking of Dawn Woman.

Blue Raven studied the shore as he paddled by. Yesterday, in the middle of the day, he'd seen a trail leading from the water to the tree line, but it had been so faint, it might have been made by anything, deer, wolves, or people. He'd paddled on by . . . but the image had nagged him, keeping him awake. He'd risen around midnight, gotten into his canoe, and started paddling back toward this stretch of beach, hoping to take a closer look.

After six days in a canoe, eating only what he could collect from the forest when he stopped at night, Blue Raven paddled like an old man. The way it tugged at his shoulder muscles, the oar might have been made from granite, instead of wood.

He had seen no signs of a pursuing war party. But they were there. They had to be. He knew the souls of the Walksalong matrons.

He'd found only one of Wren's camps, the one she'd

made on the first night of her journey. It had been snowing. When she'd packed the canoe in the morning, she hadn't covered her trail from the shore to the water. Perhaps she'd been frightened, and rushing. Or maybe she'd thought the snow would fill in her footprints. Whatever the reasons for her carelessness then, from that point onward she had covered her trail like a wounded warrior who knew he was being followed.

Blue Raven's brows lowered. A strip of deeper shadows ran straight up from the lake to the rocky shore. He dipped his paddle into the calm green water, and slowed. He couldn't be sure from this distance, but the shadow looked like a trail. . . . Not the one he'd seen yesterday. This was much clearer. More recently made.

As he neared the trail, he noticed a glint of white in the brush at the edge at the water. He steered closer. The painted bow of a canoe, almost hidden, peeked from the tangle of vines. The trail led up to it, then veered away, into the forest.

Blue Raven's heart pounded. He paddled hard for the shore, leaping out in knee-deep water. He dragged the canoe up onto the sand, and went to study the tracks.

The trail *had* been made by people.

Two people.

# Eighteen

The nagging pain in his arm woke Sparrow. He opened his eyes, and saw that Dust lay curled against him, her head pillowed on his arm. Despite the pain, he didn't move. He would give almost anything to awaken with her in his arms every morning. He inhaled the delicate scent that clung to her hair, and slowly let the breath out. It floated away in a white cloud.

After her blankets had blown away, she'd been forced to choose between freezing to death or sharing his elk-hide. To his irritation, it had taken her over a finger of time, and a good deal of pacing back and forth, to decide. When she'd finally crawled under the hide, she'd ordered him not to touch her, and vowed she wouldn't touch him.

Sparrow smiled. Dawn Woman's pearlescent gleam fell through the trees, dappling Dust's beautiful face with lavender light. Sometime during the long cold night, her body had won the battle with her pride and she'd snuggled as closely to him as she could.

He silently reached out and touched the long silver hair that spread over his arm. The softness consoled him.

Groggily, Dust whispered, "Stop that."

He roughly pulled his arm from beneath her head, and it thumped the ground. "You're the one who decided we were friends again. I woke up with you glued to my side tighter than pine pitch."

Dust opened her eyes. "That's because you slipped

your arms around me in the middle of the night, and pulled me against you, Sparrow. I was just too tired to resist."

Momentarily stunned, Sparrow didn't know what to say. A thousand times in the past two winters he'd dreamed of doing exactly that. So . . . he probably had.

"Well," he said as he shoved out from under the hide and stood up. "Forgive me. My arms didn't know any better. After thirty-five winters, they thought that was where they were supposed to be."

His moccasins squealed on the snow as he plodded away from camp, and into a thick grove of maples. As he emptied his night water, he saw Dust sit up. Her hair swung around her like a moonlit mantle.

Something about the morning light. He couldn't take his eyes from her. She rolled their hides, then stood up and, like a cat stretching in the sun, lifted her arms over her head while she arched her back. Dressed in plain knee-length moccasins, a doehide dress, and buckskin cape, she did not look like a powerful clan matron. She looked delicate and young, reminding him of the weedy girl he'd started to love in his fourteenth winter. He'd had to wait twenty moons before he could even ask her father if he could court her. But it had been worth it. He'd been forced to admire her from afar, like now, and it did something to a man's souls, transforming ordinary yearning into a hallowed sensation.

Even now, after all the children she had borne him, he looked at her and felt reverence.

Dust rummaged in her pack, drew out cooking pots, bowls, and horn spoons, then stood and walked behind a boulder.

Sparrow started breaking off the dead lower branches of the maples. He moved from tree to tree until he could carry no more, then returned to the camp, dropped his wood near the rolled hides, and picked up his bowl. He began to scoop a hole in the snow. Just as he finished, Grandfather Day Maker crested the eastern horizon. Brilliant daggers of light shot across the sky, lancing the drifting Cloud Giants, and spilling yellow across the rolling hills. The snow glimmered, and sparkled.

Sparrow stopped to enjoy the moment.

Crows cawed in the distance, their voices joyful, as if greeting Grandfather Day Maker.

"You think he's going to Paint Rock, don't you?" Dust asked as she walked from behind the boulder.

"Yes," Sparrow said.

He started cracking twigs from the branches he'd collected and dropped them into the hole.

"But why, Sparrow? There's nothing there for him."

"Wouldn't you go home, Dust?" He reached for his pack, and drew out his fireboard, his drill, and the small wooden box of charred fabric. He carefully arranged the blackened threads atop the twigs, and moved his fireboard into position over the tinder. "Even if you'd been told that your village was gone, and everyone you loved was dead, wouldn't hope drive you back?"

She sat on the rolled hides and leaned forward. "Perhaps, but I know the horrors of life. I've spent fifty winters learning to see them without seeing them. He's seen nine winters. His eyes only know how to see."

Sparrow fumbled with his fireboard and drill. "I'm afraid for him, too, Dust."

She shoved her hands into her pockets and heaved a breath. "All of his life he's been protected. People have treated him like a rare and precious trade pot. During the Paint Rock battle, the pot was dropped. I fear he'll shatter if he has to stand over the dead bodies of his family."

"Dust . . ." Sparrow propped his fireboard on the

ground. "He may have already shattered. He's been through a terrible ordeal."

"Let's just try to reach him as soon as we can, Sparrow. If his souls are—not right—maybe I can help him."

"We're trying, Dust."

Sparrow got down on his right knee, and placed his left foot on the fireboard to hold it in place. He inserted his drill, a stick about as long as his arm, into a prepared hole in the flat fireboard. Ordinarily it took about ten heartbeats to get a spark, but on very cold days it always seemed to take longer. He vigorously spun the drill between his palms. After thirty heartbeats the friction of the hardwood drill against the soft fireboard produced smoke. Sparrow pressed down harder, and spun the drill as fast as he could. Finally red sparks glowed to life in the drill hole. He laid his drill aside and carefully dumped the sparks into the nest of charred fabric. As he blew on them, the charred threads began to burn, and fell into the bed of twigs, igniting the bark. A tiny flame licked up, then the twigs caught, and fire danced to life. Sparrow pulled larger sticks from the woodpile, and gradually added them until he had a decent blaze going.

Dust extended her hands to the flames. "Sparrow? Do you think . . . I mean . . . Rumbler must be hoping that Briar is alive."

"I'm sure he is."

"If what we've heard is true, he's going to go home and find her . . . you know what Cornhusk said about how she . . . she was clubbed. The wolves and hawks may have been at her." Dust shook her head, unable to finish the sentence. "I'm afraid of what Rumbler might do, Sparrow."

"I know what I'd do." A bed of coals had formed in the fire pit. Sparrow used a stick to pull some of them to the side, then packed snow into the teapot and set it on the coals to heat. "If I came home and found your body lying in a burned heap of timbers, I'd go mad, Dust. Completely mad. I would use every vestige of Power I could pull from the earth and sky to punish those who'd hurt you."

At the emotion in his voice, her extended hands turned to fists. "I'd feel the same way if I found Planter or . . . or my grandchildren murdered."

Sparrow smiled sadly at the list, but said, "Yes, I know you would."

"Rumbler is Powerful, Sparrow. What if he does something foolish?"

"Like call out to the Up-Above-World for huge rocks to rain from the skies? Well, the Walksalong Clan will be pummeled to mush. But I doubt that will happen. Power lives in Rumbler's body, true, but he can't control it yet. At least, I don't think he can."

"We'd better hope he can't." Her dark eyes narrowed. "If the Walksalongs become mush, we'll be looking at a long war with the Bear Nation."

Wind Mother whipped through the forest, jostling the trees and battering the snowdrifts. A glimmering white haze spun through their camp. Sparrow bowed his head to fend off the onslaught, while Dust quickly pulled up her hood. The forest sighed and moaned before going quiet again.

When Sparrow looked up, his mouth open to say something else, his heart stopped.

A man stood next to the boulder behind Dust. Tall, with long graying black hair, and an oval face, an elkhide wrapped his shoulders.

Sparrow froze.

Dust's hand slipped beneath her cape for the stiletto on her belt.

From behind her the man saw no movement. He cautiously stepped closer.

Sparrow did not look at Dust as he rose to his feet, but he knew she was watching his every breath, studying his movements to judge the threat.

Sparrow called, "It has been a long while, Blue Raven."

Dust's breathing quickened as she pulled her stiletto onto her lap, and slowly turned toward the Headman of Walksalong Village.

Blue Raven scanned both of their faces, then spread his arms. "I left my bow behind the boulder. I am unarmed. I came to talk. Please." He glanced at Dust. "You are Dust Moon? Matron of Earth Thunderer Clan?"

Dust nodded.

Blue Raven took another step toward them.

"I have heard many people speak of your courage and kindness." Blue Raven inclined his head to show his respect. "I hope you will extend some of that kindness to me this day. I give you my pledge that I do not come in anger."

"Then why are you here?" Sparrow asked.

"I overheard you talking—"

"You mean you were spying on us!" Dust said.

"Well, Matron"—Blue Raven smiled wanly—"a man does not simply march into the camp of Silver Sparrow. Perhaps in the old days when he was a renowned Trader, but not now. For three moons' walk, people cower at the mention of your husband's name—"

"*Former* husband."

Blue Raven seemed taken aback by that. He glanced at Sparrow, and continued. "Many people whisper that Silver Sparrow is no longer human, that he sails through the forests at night in the body of an owl, or bat. I thought it wise to watch your camp for a time before I stepped from my hiding place.''

Sparrow said, "What do you want?"

Blue Raven cautiously said, "The two of you are searching for the children, and I am searching for the children.'' The lines on his forehead deepened. "Together we have more of a chance of finding them, and we must find them soon, or I fear—''

"You mean . . ." Dust lurched to her feet. "Rumbler isn't with you?"

Blue Raven shook his head. "With me? No, of course not.''

"Didn't you cut him loose?"

*"Me?"* Blue Raven cried. "I had nothing to do with it! My niece, a girl of twelve winters, was responsible. She must have felt pity for him. When I was asleep, she—''

"Ah." Sparrow nodded, suddenly seeing how the pieces of the story fit. "Well, Blue Raven, many things have happened that you are not aware of. Please sit down. Share our fire." He gestured to the crackling flames.

"I do not wish to sit. I—''

"You may stand if you wish, but the truth is not easy to tell or, I imagine, to hear." Sparrow exhaled a frosty breath.

Blue Raven glanced back and forth between them, fear growing in his brown eyes. "Then, please, tell me quickly.''

Sparrow crouched and scooped more coals around the teapot. "Jumping Badger and twenty warriors are on your trail. Starflower ordered them to hunt you down because she thinks you saved Rumbler.''

"But that's foolish! Why would I—''

"We don't know the why of it. But they think you betrayed them." Sparrow rephrased the story Cornhusk had told them: "Lamedeer supposedly said that I said the False Face Child would be the death of the Walksalong Clan. Correct?"

Blue Raven nodded. "Yes. Did you—"

"No, I didn't, but that's another story. Your people think you have doomed them by saving the boy. They have labeled you a traitor."

Dust added, "And your niece, Little Wren, as well. They have condemned her to death."

Judging by Blue Raven's expression they had just confirmed his worst fears. "Oh, gods. This is much worse than I ever . . ." He shook his head. "Yes, much worse. I—I need to think. There must be a path through this insanity. A way to repair the damage. I just . . . I must find it."

Sparrow frowned at the fire. "Well, we all have our problems, Blue Raven. Ours is to find Rumbler before Jumping Badger does. I don't suppose you have any notion of where he and his war party might be, do you? So we can avoid them?"

"I don't," Blue Raven answered. "In fact, since I made no attempt to disguise my trail, I should already be dead. The storms may have delayed them, but they will not have stopped them. Not if what you say is true. Jumping Badger is honor bound to find me."

"And your niece, don't forget," Dust added coldly. "Among the Turtle Nation, we would never condemn a child to death. You Bear Nation people must be monsters to—"

"Matron." Blue Raven looked Dust straight in the eyes, and lowered his hands to his sides. "Please. I did not make this decision, and I have never cast my voice to condemn a child. I love my niece very much. No matter what I have to do to save her, I will."

Dust's eyes locked with Blue Raven's. "Even if it

means going against the orders of your clan matrons?''

Blue Raven hesitated. As Headman he could never admit to such a thing. ''I think the Walksalong matrons are . . . confused. Misinformed. Once they understand the facts, I'm certain they will see reason.'' But he exhaled unsteadily, and put a hand on his belly, as if to still its churning.

''Despite the confidence of your words, Blue Raven,'' Dust said, ''you do not appear certain. Though I pray you are right.''

Blue Raven smiled. ''I value your prayers, Matron. Please keep praying.''

Sparrow pointed to the pack beside Dust. ''Dust, I'm hungry, could you hand me—''

''The food bags,'' she finished, and reached for them. ''I think Blue Raven could use something in his stomach, too.''

# Nineteen

Blue Raven sat cross-legged on the snow between Silver Sparrow and his former wife. While Sparrow went about fixing cornmeal gruel for breakfast, Matron Dust Moon tried to appear casual, plaiting her silver hair into a thick braid, but her gaze never left Blue Raven, and he felt it like an icy dagger in his chest.

The pink echoes of sunrise danced through the Cloud Giants, giving a rainbow shimmer to parts of the morning sky.

Blue Raven sipped the cup of tea they had offered, and said, "This is excellent."

"Thank you," Dust Moon replied. "It's my own mixture."

"Do you purposely dry the rose petals, or let them dry naturally on the plant?"

"I pick them fresh and dry them near a fire. The flavors keep longer."

Silver Sparrow added dried blueberries to the bubbling cook pot and stirred it with a horn spoon. "She first blended that tea thirty-three winters ago. It was autumn, the Moon of Blazing Leaves, and Dust had been out with our oldest son picking berries at a hunting camp north of here called Cranberry Bog. She started gathering a little of this and some of that, and when she brewed it that night for supper, we all thought it delicious. She's made it ever since." Sparrow smiled fondly, but not at Dust Moon, at the cook pot.

Pain briefly lit the matron's eyes, but just as quickly vanished. Silver Sparrow glanced up at her, and clenched his jaw.

Blue Raven did not know much about women, but he knew something about men. Silver Sparrow still loved Dust Moon.

Sparrow got to his feet. "Dust, while this finishes cooking, I think I will go and look for some of our things that blew away in the storm last night." He turned to Blue Raven and his eyes narrowed. "Just as a precaution, let me tell you that Dust Moon carries a stiletto and a knife, and knows how to use them. I taught her. In addition, I will always be in sight of camp. My eyes will rarely be off you, Blue Raven. Understand?"

"Yes. I do."

Silver Sparrow walked toward the trees to Blue Raven's left.

Blue Raven waited until he'd passed beyond hearing range, then said, "He treats you as a wife, Matron, not a former wife."

She continued braiding her hair. "Well, he's been doing it for most of his life. He can't help it."

"How long were you joined?"

"Thirty-five winters."

Blue Raven propped his elbows on his drawn-up knees. Dust Moon watched him, the wrinkles in her forehead deepening. As the light shifted, the boulder behind her glittered and sparkled. "Divorcing must have been difficult after so long. I, myself, have never been married, but I've heard divorced people say they felt as if they had lost a part of themselves."

The coldness in her eyes thawed a little. She pulled a cord from her pack and tied it around the end of her braid. "Why did you never marry?"

Blue Raven found himself riveted by those dark confident eyes. Despite her age, she was a beautiful woman. Her thick silver braid draped her right shoulder, and most of the lines in her face bespoke a lifetime of laughter.

"The woman I wanted did not want me, and I did not want the woman who did want me. It's simple, really, I just—"

"Why didn't you want her?"

"Well"—he shrugged—"she was a warrior. A very brave one, and I—"

"Couldn't bear the rivalry?"

"No, no," he said too quickly, and stopped, wondering about that. In truth, Elk Ivory had always been a better warrior than he and, at one time, it had bothered him. He might have had more brute strength when it came to bare-handed fighting, but her skill with bow and knife . . .

"I see you had to think about your answer," Dust

Moon said and lifted an elegant gray brow. "That's good."

Blue Raven suddenly felt trapped, and wondered how he'd gotten here. It didn't happen often. Usually his experience at debating carried conversations. "Well, the real truth is that women are like Cloud Giants to me. Untouchable. Mysterious."

A gust of wind tousled her hood, buffeting it around her oval face. She clasped it closed at the throat. "That much is obvious. If you understood women at all, you wouldn't be here."

"What? Excuse me?" Blue Raven shook his head. "I don't understand."

Dust Moon tossed a branch into the fire and lifted her teacup again. After a long drink she said, "Why didn't you suspect that your niece might wish to rescue Rumbler? You should have. Didn't she give you hints before it happened?"

Blue Raven straightened. "Hints?"

"Yes, of course. Children think they're very clever, but they're really guileless. When they're upset or desperate, they ask too many questions about the wrong things, or get in fights to make you pay attention to them, and once they have your attention they try very hard to pour out their troubles to you. Unfortunately, adults rarely listen. We are all too busy with our own 'very important' concerns to listen to a child."

Blue Raven stared at her, remembering Wren's tormented expression six days ago, that last night on Lost Hill. "I knew the Vigil was hard for Wren. After the deaths of her parents and brother, she—"

"How long ago did they die?"

"Eight moons."

Dust Moon's face twisted in sympathy. "Go on. After the deaths of her family . . . ?"

"Well"—he waved a hand—"she seemed obsessed with saving things. Any baby bird that blew out of a nest wound up in our longhouse eating worms that Wren ground herself. And last summer she walked the shore of Leafing Lake each morning, collecting and carrying beached fish or stranded clams back to the water. She—"

"She didn't just give you hints, Blue Raven. She told you plainly that she couldn't bear to see anything else die." Dust Moon shook her head, as if disgusted by Blue Raven's blindness. "The poor girl. Losing her parents and brother must have wounded her far more deeply than you suspected."

"I suspected she hurt a great deal, Matron, but perhaps you are right." Blue Raven set his empty teacup in the snow. When Earth Thunderer Clan selected this woman as their matron, it showed great wisdom. She was as insightful as she was ruthless. "I'm afraid I know even less about children than women. I—"

"But how can that be?" Dust Moon interrupted. "You've never been a woman, but you were certainly a child. Don't you recall how you felt in your twelfth winter? Don't you remember the things you did to get attention?"

Blue Raven used the toe of his moccasin to push around his teacup. He did, of course. He'd been a wild animal, tearing through the longhouses, brandishing his child's bow. His mother had made sure he'd quit that by breaking his bow and tossing it into the fire. He said, "My father spent much of his time warring, and my mother . . . well, I'm sure she cared about me, but—"

"But not enough." She nodded. Wind teased loose strands of her gray hair and blew them around her dark eyes. "No wonder you became a Headman rather than marrying. Leading people is much easier than being an equal, isn't it? Looking down is far more comfortable than eye to eye. Eye to eye forces you to care, and you don't really know how to do that, do you?''

Defensive, he said, ''Well, you too are a leader. You should know.''

''Yes. That's why I asked.''

''Matron,'' Blue Raven said in a pained voice, ''are your questions always so . . . piercing? Talking with you is very much like being repeatedly stabbed.''

From behind him, Blue Raven heard Silver Sparrow laugh. It was a closed-mouth, almost choking sound, as if he'd been trying to quell the urge. Dust Moon lifted her head and scowled as the aging Dreamer walked into camp. His elkhide coat, decorated with tiny red spirals and dark green trees, bore a light coating of snow. It must have blown down from the trees.

''What are you laughing at?'' Dust Moon demanded to know.

Silver Sparrow crouched before the cook pot. ''The tone in Blue Raven's voice. I've heard it so often in my own, it sounded like an echo. Who's hungry?''

Blue Raven didn't know whether or not he dared smile. Silver Sparrow casually lifted a spoon and stirred the steaming pot, while Dust Moon looked on as if she longed to order his hands and feet bound, while she piled wood around his feet herself.

Blue Raven hadn't really eaten since he'd left Lost Hill, six days ago. He'd been so worried about Wren, he'd barely noticed his gnawing hunger. Now, just the thought of food turned him desperate. ''I didn't bring anything with me, and I—''

''Where are my blankets?'' Dust Moon said with an edge to her voice as she scanned Sparrow's empty hands. ''Did you look for them?''

Silver Sparrow stirred the gruel. ''I looked. I didn't find.''

''Not even one of them?''

''Not even a piece of one of them, Dust. Given the force of that wind last night, I suspect every shred is floating in Green Spider Lake by now.'' Silver Sparrow tasted the gruel, nodded approvingly, and held out his free hand. ''Would you pass me the bowls, Dust? This is done.''

Dust Moon picked them up, and slapped the bowls into his palm with such force that Sparrow's hand dipped into the flames.

The Dreamer concentrated on keeping his expression bland, but the odor of scorched hair filled the camp. ''Thank you so much, Dust,'' he said, and turned to Blue Raven. ''Do you have a bowl in your pack? We only brought two.''

''I'm afraid I don't even have a pack,'' he said. ''I left hastily. May I use this cup?'' He lifted it.

''That's fine.'' Sparrow took the cup.

As Sparrow filled the cup and bowls and handed them around the fire, the scent of steaming blueberries rose. Blue Raven used his fingers as a spoon. The mixed sweetness of cornmeal and berries affected him like a lover's touch. The more he ate, the more calm and content he became.

When he'd finished, Blue Raven scooped his cup in the snow to clean it, and said, ''I overheard you say that you thought the children might be heading for Paint Rock Village. It has been many winters since I've traveled this trail. With the snow, how long do you think it will take us to get there?''

''Us?'' Dust asked. ''We're not traveling with you!''

''Matron, please, it will better for everyone if we co-operate with each other. I—''

''Give me one good reason why we shouldn't kill you, and leave you here to rot?''

Blue Raven steepled his fingers in front of his mouth, and thoughtfully answered. "Because, Matron, I am the only one who might be able to talk the Walksalong elders into allowing Little Wren to live. You seemed worried about my niece earlier. You said that anyone who would condemn a child to death must be a soulless monster. If you kill me, you will also be killing Wren. If you do not help me, you may, inadvertently, be responsible for her death. You don't wish to see her dead, do you?"

Dust's jaw moved beneath the thin veneer of skin. "No. No, I don't."

Silver Sparrow rested his spoon in his bowl. "If we push ourselves, and don't see any new storms, we might make it to Paint Rock by the day after tomorrow."

Dust Moon gave Sparrow an anxious look. "The children have been traveling a day longer than we have. Do you think we really have a chance of cutting them off before they arrive?"

"It's possible, Dust, but I—"

Blue Raven said, "Rumbler was not well, Matron. I don't imagine the children *can* move very fast. When they left Lost Hill, Wren was dragging the False Face Child on a blanket, or hide. She dragged him all the way to the canoe she stole."

Pity lit Dust Moon's eyes.

Blue Raven handed his clean cup to Silver Sparrow, and got to his feet.

"If you will allow me, I left my bow and quiver behind the boulder. I would like to—"

"Not yet," Sparrow said. "Before any of us touch our weapons, let's establish the details of our new alliance. First, if Jumping Badger and his war party appear, I expect you to attack them, not us. If I even think you might do otherwise"—he pointed a finger—"I'll kill you, Blue Raven."

Blue Raven said, "I'm not sure I can shoot at my own relatives, Silver Sparrow, even if they are shooting at me. But I pledge that I will not aim my bow at you or your . . . at Matron Dust Moon."

"Or at Rumbler, if we find him," Dust Moon added. Sunlight flickered in her suspicious eyes.

"Or at Rumbler," Blue Raven agreed. "My only goal right now is to find my niece before anyone else from my clan does. I don't know what we will do after that, but, together, Wren and I will figure out something."

Sparrow nodded. "Go ahead and get your bow." Then he picked up his own bow.

Blue Raven walked around the boulder.

Sunlight glimmered and twinkled over the snowy forest. The loud melodious calls of cardinals rang out, whistling *cheer, cheer, cheer!* followed by a swift *woight, woight, woight, woight.*

The net in her hands, and a coil of cord looped over her wrist, Wren led the way down the trail. Last night's windstorm had cracked branches from the trees, and madly strewn them across the snow. Rumbler trotted behind Wren, trying to keep pace with her while dodging the obstacles in his path.

"There it is," Wren said, and pointed to the small clearing sixty hands away. Pine siskins covered the ground, feeding on seeds that had blown from the thick winter grasses. "This will be perfect."

She'd dragged Rumbler up the trail last night past this place. It had been filled with birds then, too. Rosebushes bordered the clearing on the south side, straight ahead of them.

Rumbler's white fox-fur cape swung around him as he swaggered to catch up. An ache built under her heart. He looked so small, and feeble. A search party surely followed them. How would they ever outrun it? And, worse, they were wasting daylight. This instant they should be racing up the trail as fast as they could, not netting birds.

Rumbler stopped at her side, breathing hard, and peered at the clearing. "Where do you wish to set the trap?"

"Near the roses. That way we can hide behind the bushes. Come on."

As Wren and Rumbler entered the clearing the siskins burst into flight, their yellow backs flashing as they winged up and circled through the trees. They returned to perch in the branches a short distance away.

Wren knelt, and Rumbler dropped to his knees at her side. She placed the loop of cord, and net, on the snow. The net stretched about six hands across. Loosely woven with different-sized strips of bark, no one would call it pretty, but it would do the job. Her mother's voice seeped through a door in Wren's souls, saying, *That, my sweet daughter, is an embarrassment. A wolf could leap through those holes.* A fleeting smile turned her lips. Wren searched the ground for two branches about the length of her arm. She planted them in the snow and hooked two corners of the net to the tops of the branches, then she stretched the net out behind the sticks and piled snow over the bottom of the net to keep it in place. When she'd finished, the trap looked like a lean-to structure.

"Here," Rumbler said. From his cape pocket he drew out a few morsels of corn bread, and handed them to Wren. His blackening fingers shook.

Gently, Wren took them, and scattered the morsels beneath the net. "Rumbler? Why don't you go and sit down behind the bushes. I'll be right there."

"All right, Wren."

He rose on wobbly legs, and the hazy sunlight shafting through the trees striped his beautiful round face. As he passed Wren, he put out a small hand and patted her arm, then continued on toward the bushes.

Wren tied both ends of the cord to the two sticks holding up the net, and grasped the remaining cord in what seemed to be the middle. Loops unfurled behind her as she made her way to the rosebushes.

Rumbler whispered, "Are we ready?"

"Almost." Wren drew up the slack in the cord and ducked down. "Now we are. Be quiet, Rumbler."

Rumbler nodded, and stretched out on his belly in the snow. His eyes shone as blackly as the deepest forest shadows.

Wren took a breath.

The spicy scent of rose hips taunted her nose. The animals had eaten off the tips of the bushes, and the rose hips on the outside, but inside, shielded by thorns, the seeds had been untouched. She could see them speckling the briar's interior, and longed to put on her mittens and gather a handful, but she remained still and silent.

The siskins hopped from branch to branch over their heads, singing and chirping. A few cocked their heads to eye the trap.

"Wren?" Rumbler whispered. "What's happening? Are—"

*"Shh!"*

He bit his lip.

Two siskins fluttered down near the trap, and began pecking at the snow.

Wren tightened her hold on the cord.

The rest of the flock leaped from the trees, and swooped down, alighting in a rustle of wings.

Rumbler twisted his head at a funny angle, and Wren

realized he'd found a gap in the bushes where he could watch the trap.

One of the siskins hopped closer. The bird pecked around at the base of the sticks, examining the net, its head tilting first to the left, then to the right. It seemed to sense something amiss, but couldn't quite figure it out. The siskin ate for a while longer, glancing at the cornbread crumbs, then stopped and took another long careful look at the net. Finally, he hopped underneath it, and tasted a crumb. Then he began gobbling as fast as he could.

The other birds noticed. In a flurry of wings and chirps, five more siskins fluttered beneath the net.

Wren could hear Rumbler's shallow breathing. He turned his head and looked at her.

With lightning quickness, Wren jerked the sticks from beneath the net, and it collapsed on three birds. The others skittered from beneath the net's edges and soared up and away, and the whole flock burst into flight.

"Come on!" Wren yelled. She leaped to her feet and ran for the net.

The trapped birds struggled beneath the weave, pecking at the net and each other. Wren used both hands to slide the net beneath the birds and scoop them up, turning the net into a bag. The birds shrilled as she twisted the weave to secure it. "Look, Rumbler! We did it. Whichever ones you aren't going to need, we'll have for supper tonight."

"We can't eat them, Wren."

Rumbler sat in the snow beside her and held out his wounded hands for the net.

Wren gave it to him, but said, "Not even one of them? What would that hurt? There isn't much meat on a siskin but it would add flavor to gruel."

He shook his head. "I need to ask one of these birds

to help me, Wren. I can't eat his relatives.''

As he untwisted the net and slipped his hand in with the birds, one of the siskins screamed. Rumbler's fingers tightened around the bird's body, and he drew it out, then released the other two birds. The freed siskins shot away like arrows.

Wren sat in the snow beside him, watching. "What now?"

Rumbler pulled the bird to his chest, and relief crossed his face. "I'm the one who has to do it, Wren."

"Do what?"

He tenderly stroked the siskin's head with his thumb, and murmured, "You're safe. Don't be afraid. Shh. Shh."

Wren frowned.

Rumbler lifted the bird to his forehead and closed his eyes. His lips moved soundlessly, as if speaking to the bird. The siskin chirped, then struggled against his hands, and Rumbler suddenly opened them, freeing the bird. It circled the clearing, then flew straight up.

Wren shielded her eyes to watch. The black spot grew smaller and smaller until the bird vanished into the gleaming golden bellies of the Cloud Giants that crowded the blue sky.

Then she lowered her hand, and looked at Rumbler. Tears filled his eyes.

"What did you say to the bird, Rumbler?"

He whispered, "I asked the siskin if he would fly to the Up-Above-World and look for my mother. If she's there, then I . . . I don't . . .''

Wren slipped her arm around his narrow shoulders, and he buried his face against her deerhide cape. "Then you don't have to go home?"

He nodded.

*And you won't have to see her body. You can remem-*

*ber her as she was before my clan killed her.*

Wren said, "Rumbler, I've been thinking that maybe we should leave our canoe hidden here, and go the rest of the way on foot."

"In case they're following us?"

She nodded and hugged him. "Yes. The bird will find us on the trail, won't he? If he has a message from your mother?"

Rumbler wiped his nose. "Yes. And we need to go. I know we are in danger."

She helped him up, and started for the trail, but his feet didn't crunch the snow behind her. Wren turned.

Rumbler stood at the edge of the clearing with his face tipped up, and all the hope in the world shining in his eyes.

She shifted, waiting.

Then said, "It's a long way to the Up-Above-World, Rumbler. It may take the siskin a while. Give him the time he needs."

Rumbler bowed his head. Tears dripped onto his moccasins. After several heartbeats, he nodded, and followed in her footsteps.

Early morning sunlight glittered from the still water of Leafing Lake, and flashed on the paddles of the Walks-along warriors.

Elk Ivory knelt in the rear of the canoe, timing her strokes to Acorn's, who sat in the front. Muscles bulged beneath the shoulders of Acorn's tan shirt as he dipped his paddle and pulled. Sweat drenched his collar, dotted the ridge of hair on the top of his skull, and created a sheen over the shaved sides of his head.

They had been driving hard, canoeing until well after dark, and rising long before dawn, tracing Blue Raven's path along the shore.

Tracking him had been like following a three-winters-old toddler. Elk Ivory's belly churned every time they found one of his campsites.

As they headed for the western tip of Leafing Lake, the nine other war canoes caught up with them, cutting chevrons in the glassy water. Their bow waves rocked Elk Ivory's boat. Jumping Badger's canoe brought up the rear. He sat in the prow with the severed head propped before him, while Rides-the-Bear did the work of paddling. An eerie silence possessed their war leader. For the past three nights, he'd said nothing to any of them—though he'd whispered constantly with the rotting head of Lamedeer.

She had heard of such things, of men losing their souls, but she'd never—

*"Look!"* Buckeye shouted from the canoe that had overtaken them. A canoe lay beached on the sand up ahead.

"Come on, Acorn. Let's see if we can't beat them there," she said.

Acorn nodded, got on his knees, and lengthened his powerful stroke. The canoe darted forward.

Cornhusk waved his arms to the children who sat behind the elders at the farthest reaches of the firelight. The long-house stirred as people watched Cornhusk. "Come closer, little ones. This is a story for you, too."

Three little girls edged forward and snuggled into their parents' or grandparents' laps. The girl to Cornhusk's right had long braids that dragged the floor. She tucked her finger in her mouth and leaned back against her grandmother's chest. The grandmother, Matron Oriole-Soaring-Down, propped her chin on top of the little girl's head. Short gray hair fell around her cadaverous old face.

Cornhusk surveyed his audience. He'd arrived in Winged Dace Village about three hands of time ago, and done some Trading; then Oriole-Soaring-Down had invited him to her longhouse. If everything went well here, he'd be Trading all night. After hearing this tale, people would be throwing precious valuables at him and asking almost nothing in return.

"Well?" Oriole-Soaring-Down said. "You promised to tell us about Walksalong Village. We have heard much gossip, but I doubt the truth of it. Please enlighten us."

Cornhusk narrowed his small dark eyes, and hissed, "Listen. Listen, well. This is a tale of great sorrow and woe."

Bright blue, red, and yellow fabrics shone as people leaned forward to hear better. Beadwork shimmered. Shell earrings danced.

Utter silence descended. Just as he'd intended.

Cornhusk looked into the eyes of those sitting closest to him. "I was there. I left only after the village was ravaged by a deadly windstorm. This is not gossip. It is truth. Terrible truth. It is a tale of a Headman's betrayal and cowardice. A tale of a little girl's evil hatred for her clan. I tell you truly, thousands of winters from now legends will be Sung about the Spirits that roamed Walksalong Village during the Winter of Crying Rocks. They will Sing of the wicked False Face Child, and the courageous war leader who captured him, Jumping Badger. They will Sing of the hideous deaths of those who dared to touch the boy. *I was there.* I saw Mossybill and Skullcap writhing and screaming in agony."

He paused and scanned the faces around him. No one seemed to be breathing. Even the little girl with the long braids had gone as still as a corpse.

Yes, it would be a profitable night, indeed.

"I saw poor old White Kit's body covered in blood. The—"

"Kit is dead?" Oriole-Soaring-Down croaked. Her wrinkles deepened. "Is this true? I had heard this, but did not believe. Are you certain?"

Cornhusk nodded slowly for effect. "The False Face Child stabbed her with her own knife, Matron, and then"—he swooped a hand toward the firelit ceiling, and every eye jerked upward—"the boy flew to the rafters of the Walksalong council house like a bird. I heard this from Matron Starflower's own lips."

Oriole-Soaring-Down's mouth tightened in pain. "I will miss Kit. She was a good and kind woman. A fine leader. Go on, Cornhusk. Tell us more about the evil girl and the False Face Child."

He lowered his voice again, forcing people to bend toward him. "After he stabbed Kit, the wicked boy flapped around the ceiling, shrieking like an enraged eagle. He dove at Starflower and tried to pluck her old eyes out so she could not look upon his face. . . ."

Moans and gasps filled the house, and Cornhusk held up his hands for silence. In a ringing voice, he said, "You know the stories! The boy's father is an evil Forest Spirit cast out of the Up-Above-World, and condemned to walk the earth forever! I tell you truly, the boy is even more Powerful than his father. The animals come to the boy's call, and with a single hand he can pull the Cloud Giants down from the skies!"

People shifted and whispered. Their voices began to rise.

*This is not gossip, I tell you! It is truth. Listen. Listen to me . . . !*

# Twenty

Wren pushed a low-hanging pine bough aside and stepped into a blinding pool of afternoon sunlight. Her long black braid gleamed. They had been walking in silence all day, scooping snow when they grew thirsty, nibbling at the elk jerky when their stomachs squealed. Wren kept her steps short, hoping that Rumbler could keep up, but as the day dwindled, he fell farther and farther behind. Wren turned, and saw him about twenty body lengths back. He'd been shaking since midday, but he refused to stop. While she waited for him, she basked in the warm sunlight and examined the trail ahead.

It wound sinuously around boulders taller than Wren. Deer and elk frequented this trail for snow lay like a sodden dirty blanket over hundreds of water-filled hoofprints. It would be hard going. Already her muddy pants clung to her skin like granite. Shielding her eyes, she squinted up at Grandfather Day Maker. Three hands of light remained before night.

A branch cracked, and Wren spun to see Rumbler stumble into a fallen log. A tuft of white fox fur torn from her cape perched like a tiny headdress on the branch he'd broken.

"Rumbler? Are you all right?"

He tucked his hands beneath his arms, and sank into the filthy snow. As he rocked back and forth, he said, "I'm f-freezing."

Wren ran back to him, her soaked moccasins squishing in the muddy trail. His beautiful round face had gone as pale as a magpie's belly, and his black eyes glittered.

"Rumbler?" She pulled off her mittens and felt his face. "Rumbler, you're fevered! When did this start? I didn't notice—"

"It's—it's m-my hands," he said, and winced when he drew them from beneath his arms.

Wren knelt in the snow before him and took his right hand in hers, carefully inspecting it. His thumb and first finger looked all right, but the blackened tips of his second and third fingers had swollen to three times their normal size, and would have to come off. She feared she would have to take two joints from his little finger. His left hand was worse. He would lose the tips of each finger, and two from his little finger.

"I can't b-bend them," he said. "They hurt badly when I woke this morning. They've grown worse."

"That's because they've thawed." She gently placed his hand in his lap. Fear gnawed at her. She'd brought along all the tools she would need, but the thought of cutting off human fingers frightened her. She'd severed many animal joints, the legs of water fowl, deer, bear, and a number of smaller animals like rabbits and squirrels, but they'd been dead. What if she couldn't cut on living flesh? What if she could, and the bleeding wouldn't stop?

"Rumbler, do you think I should—I mean, I think maybe it's time."

"Yes. Please hurry, Little Wren." He bravely set his jaw.

Wren surveyed the forest. To her right, a small sunny clearing nestled in the middle of four sassafras trees. The shriveled fruits clinging to the branches had a purplish sheen. Wren said, "That spot over there looks dry, Rumbler. Let's camp beneath those trees."

Rumbler tried to rise, but his shaking legs wouldn't hold him. Wren gripped his left arm and helped him up, then guided him into the sun-drenched clearing. The roots of the trees had grown together beneath the soil, pushing it up into a hillock higher than the surrounding forest floor, so the snow here had melted and drained away first. Wren lowered Rumbler to the ground at the base of the largest tree. He leaned back, and closed his eyes.

As she slid her pack from her shoulders, and dropped it beside him, Wren said, "I'm going to collect wood, Rumbler. I'll be fast, I promise."

"Th-thank you . . . Wren."

She went to the closest sassafras tree and cracked off all the old deadwood that littered the lower part of the trunk, then trotted back and dumped it in a pile near her pack. Rumbler had his eyes closed and his lower lip clamped between his teeth.

"I'm hurrying," Wren said. She opened her pack and pulled out her fireboard and drill. "After my mother severed frozen fingers, she stanched the flow of blood with hot coals."

He started rocking again, back and forth, back and forth. Perspiration beaded his nose. "Just . . . hurry."

When flames leaped through the sassafras branches, spitting and sparking, Wren opened her pack, and removed a coil of basswood cord, a sharp white chert blade as long as her palm and two finger-widths across, and a fire-hardened bowl.

"Could you put on some s-snow to melt, too, Wren? I need water."

"Of course."

Wren drew out the soot-coated teapot and tripod and set them up at the edge of the flames. Picking up the bowl, she ran to the nearest snowbank, packed it full, and returned. She scooped the snow from the bowl into the pot, and sat back to prepare herself for what came next. More than anything else, she remembered the gouts of blood as her mother severed fingers.

She glanced into the pot. The melting snow sizzled. "Rumbler, do you just want a drink, or does the water have to be hot? Did you want tea?"

"I—I just need water." He sat forward and struggled to remove the large copper gorget he wore around his neck. The engraved image of a gnarled uprooted tree shimmered in the sun. Beneath the gorget, a leather Power bag hung. Shaking, Rumbler handed the necklace to Wren.

"Here, Wren. Please. Open my Power bag."

Wren took the magnificent necklace, slid the copper gorget aside, and loosened the laces on the bag. Inside, three smaller painted bags nestled in a clump, one red, one green, and one blue. The green one had another uprooted tree painted on it in white.

"What are these, Rumbler?"

He sucked in a shuddering breath and through the exhalation said, "Pull out the r-red one, please."

Wren did. "What now?"

"Place a pinch of the mixture in a cup of water, and . . . and stir it."

Wren pulled a cup from her pack, poured it full of melted snow water and set it on the ground beside her. As she unlaced the red bag, an explosion of fragrance assaulted her nose, bittersweet, like withered fruits. She lifted the bag and peered inside. The contents had been finely ground. "What is this, Rumbler?"

"Papaw s-seeds." He gestured weakly to the cup. "I must drink it. Before we begin."

Wren took a pinch of the powder and put it in the cup. "Is that enough, Rumbler?"

He nodded. "S-stir it well."

Wren pulled a twig from the woodpile and blended the tea until the liquid turned a pale green-brown, then she handed it to Rumbler. He tried to take it, but his shaking hands wouldn't grab hold. Wren pulled the cup back, walked to his side and knelt. As she held the cup to his lips, she said, "This smells awful, Rumbler. Does it taste bad?"

He finished the tea in five swallows and made a face. "Yes, but the seeds numb the b-body, and free the souls." He leaned back against the sassafras trunk again, and stared down at his hands. "This will take . . . a while, Wren. Before I'm ready."

"That's all right. It will give me a chance to get ready, too."

Wren pulled a branch from the woodpile and stoked the fire. Garlands of sparks winked and flitted up through the lances of sunlight. When she had more coals, she would scoop them aside into a pile. In the meantime, she needed a flat stone.

Wren walked away. Rocks thrust up everywhere, but most were frozen to the ground. She kicked at a stone about the right size, but it didn't budge, so Wren headed on. The trail had been churned up by hooves. She might find a loose rock there.

As Grandfather Day Maker sank lower in the sky, the shadows reached eastward like long sharp talons. High above, a hawk drifted against the blue sky, her wings blazing in the sun.

Wren tried to stay on top of the snow that lined the trail, but her moccasins kept slipping into the mud, sucking with each step. By the time she reached the first boulder her calf muscles ached. She braced a hand on the tall rock, and rested a moment. Orange lichen splotched the surface. Wren traced the beautiful patterns with her fingers. Over her shoulder, she glanced back at Rumbler. He stared off into the recesses of the forest . . . but he seemed all right.

Chunks of stone lay around the base of the boulder. In the summer, water seeped into cracks in the rock. When it froze, it often split the stone and cracked off spalls. She toed the mushy snow with her moccasins, but didn't see any flat spalls. Then, as she stepped around the boulder, she placed her hand in a new spot and the stone grated beneath her palm. Wren tugged the spall from the boulder and studied it. About the size of four of her hands put together, it would work, she thought. Clutching it to her chest, she made her way back toward their camp.

As she entered the sassafras grove, she called, "Rumbler? How are you?"

"Ready. I—I'm ready, Wren."

He turned, and she could see that his pupils had dilated to fill his eyes like glowing suns. The sight stopped her dead in her tracks. He'd given her that same look in the council house fourteen days ago. She forced a swallow down her tight throat. Had he eaten ground papaw seeds that day? To ease the pain of the rope cuts?

Wren gathered her courage and started forward again. She sat cross-legged next to the fire and placed the granite spall on the ground between them.

Rumbler leaned forward to put his left hand on the flat surface. The blackened fingertips looked grotesque against the sparkling gray and white background. "I'm ready, Wren," he repeated.

She reached for her white chert blade and the fire-hardened wooden bowl. "How long will the numbness last, Rumbler?"

"Two hands of time."

Wren sucked in a breath. Before she began, she reached beneath her deerhide cape and patted the chewed strip of rawhide hanging from her belt. *Help me to do this right, Trickster. I'm really afraid.*

Her hand wavered when she picked up the sharp blade.

"It's all right, Wren," Rumbler said and spread his fingers as wide as he could. "You can do it. You have to."

She put her left hand over the top of Rumbler's, to hold it still, and had started to lower the blade, when the goshawk that had been circling high above sailed down, and silently alighted on one of the sassafras branches over Rumbler's head. Wren blinked, startled.

A white weasel stood up on its hind legs to her right, its dark eyes glinting as it watched them. Then a flock of over a hundred finches swooped into the trees, and burst into song. Their clear trilling notes lilted through the forest.

Rumbler leaned his head back, and gazed up at them.

Wren whispered, "They're certainly curious today," but the beautiful songs eased some of her dread.

Rumbler smiled. "My father sent them."

"To make sure I don't hurt you?"

"No," Rumbler said. "To give you their Power. Can't you feel it? It's like sugar maple sap in my veins."

Wren *did* feel something, but she wasn't sure it was Power. It felt more like terror. She itched all over. "I'm going to start, Rumbler, all right?"

"Yes."

Wren clamped her jaw to keep her teeth from chattering, and got on her knees. She lowered the blade to the second joint of his little finger, and swiftly started sawing, heedless of the blood that gushed and flowed down over the granite. When the bone grated beneath her blade, she sliced around it, severing the tendons and ligaments, then pressed down hard to cut through the middle of the joint. The fingertip popped loose and rolled across the spall. Trembling, Wren set it on the ground, and quickly began work on the next finger. When she had finished the left hand, Wren threw her blade down and grabbed a stick. She scooped hot coals from the fire into the wooden bowl, set it on the granite spall, and lifted Rumbler's left hand, preparing to plunge the bleeding fingers into the bowl. But hesitated. Tears came to her eyes. *Oh, Trickster, please . . .*

"Rumbler, I . . . I can't . . ."

He pulled his hand from hers and, like a butterfly landing on a flower, lowered his fingertips to the coals.

"That's long enough!" she cried when she could smell the meat cooking. Wren jerked his left hand from the bowl. The scent of burned flesh filled the air.

Rumbler placed his right hand on the stone and spread his fingers.

Wren hurried, sawing, slicing, and moving on as rapidly as she could.

When the last digit came off, she took his right hand, and swiftly touched each fingertip to the coals, just long enough to stop the blood, then she let go and collapsed in a heap.

Smoke billowed from the charring bowl. Wren didn't have the strength to pour the coals back into the fire pit. She lay on her side in the dirt, panting, and listening to the cacophony of birdsong. Finches fluttered through the branches, hopping lower as if to get a good look at Rumbler. They cocked their heads first one way and then another. Blood had spattered the white fox-fur cape he wore, and speckled his round face.

Rumbler wiggled the stubs of his fingers. His expression was one of curiosity as he bent forward to examine the black bloody joints that lay on and around the spall.

Suddenly, he lifted his head. His gaze fixed on nothing.

Wren sat up. "Rumbler? What—"

"My eyes . . . they . . . they're flying, Wren. Flying far away."

Wren folded her arms beneath her cape and hunched forward to halt her shivers. "Where are they? What do you see?"

His mouth opened, but he didn't answer for a time. His black eyes widened until they seemed to fill half his face. He murmured, "We can't follow the regular trails any longer, Wren. That's where people will be looking for us. There . . . there is a new way. The animals are making it for us."

"Will we . . ."

Rumbler's eyes closed and he crumpled onto his side.

Wren gasped and scrambled toward him, but his chest rose and fell in a steady rhythm. She sank to her knees. "Blessed ancestors, Rumbler," she whispered. "I thought you were dead."

Wren touched his damp hair gently. She had come to care for him very much in the last half moon—almost like a brother.

The finches burst from the trees and sailed up and away, winging eastward.

Cautiously, she looked for the weasel and the hawk. She didn't see the hawk anywhere, but tiny paw prints marked the path the weasel had taken through the patchy snow west of the grove.

Wren stared at them. Had Rumbler's father, the wicked Forest Spirit, truly sent the animals, or had they just been drawn by the smell of a human camp? Finches and jays often flocked to people, hoping for handouts. And the weasel and hawk . . . well, they were predators. Perhaps the smell of Rumbler's rotting fingers, or the food in her pack, had lured them.

Wren picked up her bowl. One of the coals had burned through the bottom, leaving a smoking hole. She grimaced and tossed the bowl into the fire. Her cup would be good enough. She could eat and drink from it.

Flames licked around the edges of the bowl, and shot through the hole, then the whole thing blazed.

Wren looked at Rumbler again, at his mangled hands. A trickle of blood oozed from the third finger on his right hand. It would probably stop by itself. He'd lost the top joint of every finger on his left hand, and two joints from his little finger. On his right hand, he'd lost the top joints of every finger except his first. He must have kept it tucked beneath his thumb to protect it.

Wren shook her head, surprised that she'd been able to do it at all.

As she stooped over and started picking up the blood-soaked fingertips, a shudder went through her. They felt oddly inhuman, cold and bloated. But she held them tightly. Letting blood was a holy act. It fed Grandmother Earth, and the creatures she loved. Women, especially, were responsible for blood. Each moon they saved their bleeding cloths, wrung them out, and carried the blood to the fields, where they poured it upon the ground. The Sacred Sisters, corn, beans, and pumpkins, used this blood to nourish their children, which resulted in strong and plentiful crops for the people. Wren's mother had told her that everything worked in circles. Circles within circles. *"That's what life is all about, my daughter."*

Wren solemnly carried the severed joints to the edge of the sassafras grove and dug a hole in the dry forest duff. As she placed the offerings in the hole, she thought about her mother. She would have been proud of Wren today.

The thought made her smile.

Wren pushed soil over the joints and sat quietly for a time. Sunlight dappled the ground around her, shining on old leaves and twigs. She thought about the family she had lost. About her clan, and Uncle Blue Raven. He must be frantic by now. Both about her disappearance, and the possibility that Jumping Badger would find her and drag her back to Walksalong Village.

Wren looked up and as her gaze drifted through the unfamiliar forest, and the unknown hills in the distance, she longed so for home that she thought she would die of the longing.

Weakly, she lay down, and pillowed her cheek on the soft fragrant earth. Memories dove at her, clawing and pecking. She couldn't stop them. She'd been holding them back for days, and now they were wild to get at her.

She lay still, her face in the dirt, the sunlight streaming down around her, remembering people who were dead, and warm longhouses she would never see again, feeling her heart being torn to pieces inside her chest.

When at last she sat up, she found Rumbler staring at her.

He lay curled on his side, his black eyes glistening with firelight.

"I'll be your family, Wren," he said softly. "I promise."

Skybow's face appeared on her souls, and desperation spread through Wren. Like the waves that eddied outward from a rock thrown into a pond, it ran along her bones, and lapped at her fingers and toes, and the top of her head.

"I'm just scared, Rumbler," she replied and brushed dirt from her cheek.

"I won't let anyone hurt you, Wren, so long as I am alive."

She gave him a wan smile, and got to her feet. "How do you feel? Are your eyes still flying?"

He shook his head. "No, they're back. Let me show you the trail I saw. Sometimes, after the Spirit of the papaw seeds leaves my body, I forget things."

Wren trotted to his side.

Rumbler used his one good finger to draw in the dirt. "It starts just up ahead by a lightning-struck spruce. There's a scooped-out place where a wolf likes to sleep . . ."

Jumping Badger lay in his blankets by the fire, the wood-pile an arm's length away. He constantly added branches to keep the flames going throughout the night. It meant he could never allow himself to fall into a deep sleep, and that fact had begun to show. The black circles beneath his eyes had turned to bruises, and his hands shook constantly.

He had planted the staff with Lamedeer's head in a snowdrift, thirty hands away. Firelight flickered over the sunken yellow eyes and sagging flesh. Almost all of the hair had fallen out. Not even the man's closest relatives would recognize him now.

*Soon, yours won't recognize you, either.* The hideous voice seeped from the head. *You hear them out there, don't you? Soon. They will fall upon you like fanged lightning beasts.*

Jumping Badger tugged his blankets up to his chin. The darkness beyond the halo of light whispered and chittered, the ghosts watching from the shadows. They had been coming in for days, one at a time, joining Briar, waiting for Silver Sparrow's command to attack.

*Yes, you see them.*

"Shut up, you fool," Jumping Badger hissed at Lamedeer. "Don't you ever sleep?"

He wished he knew of a fresh burial somewhere close. He would stop the ghosts. An old witch named Prancing Tree had taught him. Jumping Badger had followed him for the first time in his eighth winter. The skinny grayhaired old man had left Walksalong and sneaked off into the night. Jumping Badger had tracked him by moonlight. First, the old man had traveled as a cat, the tracks soft, clawless. Then he'd trotted as a dog; the claw marks had deeply cut the soft earth. He'd found the old man in a burial ground three hands of time later, sitting alone before a boiling pot. A hideous grin had twisted his toothless face. As Jumping Badger crept closer, he'd seen the bones lying around the pot, and the holes in the ground. The pot cooked the flesh of children who'd been dug from their graves.

Lamedeer laughed, and Jumping Badger shouted, "I wish we were at Paint Rock Village! There are plenty of little corpses there. I would eat their hearts before your eyes, and make stilettos from their bones to kill you!"

Several of the nearby blanket-wrapped warriors flopped to their other sides, or covered their heads. Jumping Badger's eyes sought out Elk Ivory, and he found her, just as he did every night, watching him from across the fire. Her dark eyes gleamed.

"Don't you sleep, either, old woman? Stop staring at me!" His voice had progressively risen until the last word came out a shout.

Acorn got to his feet, and sleepily stumbled out into the forest, getting as far away as he could without actually leaving the safety of the camp. Apparently he found someone else out there, for Acorn's whispers carried on the cold night wind: "I don't know . . . crazy . . ." he said.

The other warrior responded, but Jumping Badger couldn't make out the words.

He rolled to his back and gazed up at the feathered lodges of the Night Walkers. With the fire so close, he could see only the brightest of the lodges. They glowed like eiderdown in the sunlight.

Strange, but on nights like this, he often thought about his former wife, Hollow Hill. He touched the ridge of scar tissue that puckered on his throat. She had been the first to learn that he could speak with ghosts. All he had to do was acquire a clump of hair or a tooth, and he could control the living person. The hair acted like a doorway to the person's souls. Jumping Badger could open it and go inside where the souls lay naked and vulnerable, then do anything he wished. He had risen to the position of war leader only because he'd wounded the souls of the other men who had challenged him. After he'd been inside them, their blood had gone as weak as an old woman's. One of them had run in the face of battle. That had ruined his chances. Another had accidentally shot a member of his own war party. No one trusted him any longer.

Hollow Hill had discovered the truth. She'd always been nosy, which is why he'd been forced to beat her so often. She'd asked too many questions, and pouted when he gave her no answers. One evening, right after old Prancing Tree had been burned alive for witchcraft, Jumping Badger had gone down to bathe in the river. He'd left his Power bag necklace by the side of their bedding. Against all the sacred rules of her clan, she had searched it, seeing the fingernail clippings, different-colored strands of hair, teeth, and bits of dried flesh.

When he'd returned, she'd demanded to know what he did with such gruesome things.

*She called you a witch.*

"I shouldn't have gone to sleep that night, I—"

*Especially after you'd split her mouth with your fists, and blacked both her eyes.*

"Nothing more than she deserved. Can you imagine a woman daring to touch a man's Power bag? I should have killed her."

*You are a witch.*

"I take Power where I find it. That's all."

A dragging noise came from the forest to his right. Twigs cracked. He turned. The noise heaved itself to the edge of the firelight, and stopped, but a bitter cold seeped from its body, and spread across the camp. Jumping Badger threw another branch onto the flames, and pulled his blankets around his throat, shivering.

*What is it? Do you see it?*

"I never see them clearly," he whispered. "They are shadows dancing at the edges of the light, or flaming eyes. But I hear them and smell them. The ghost last night was a stinking mess. It reeked of garbage middens."

*Soon, you are going to have to give me new eyes. How do you expect me to see the future when I can't even see you?*

"And how shall I do that? Do you expect me to carve out some living person's eyes and put them in your skull?"

More warriors rose from around the fire and tramped into the forest. Jumping Badger scowled after them, then returned his attention to Lamedeer.

"Whose eyes would you like? Eh? Elk Ivory's, perhaps? She is a nosy old woman I would be glad to be rid of. She is almost as ruthless as Hollow Hill."

He tossed to his side to look at her.

Elk Ivory's eyes had narrowed, and sweat beaded her broad flat nose. She'd tucked her shoulder-length black hair behind her ears.

"Ha!" Jumping Badger laughed. "Are you afraid of me, old woman? You should be."

He reached up and grasped his Power bag, where he kept bits of each of his warriors. For the most part, he had collected single strands of hair, but he also had threads of fabric soaked with her menstrual blood. He had scavenged them many winters ago, when he first thought she might prove a threat to his rising authority.

Jumping Badger caressed his Power bag. "Take care, old woman," he said and grinned at her. "You do not wish to anger me."

Softly, she replied, "It's not your anger that frightens me, Jumping Badger."

# Twenty-One

Sugar maples dotted the way, their dark brown trunks blending with the lengthening evening shadows. High overhead, the branches created a sable weave against the dusk sky.

The thick white hair flowing down Sparrow's back had turned an unearthly shade of blue. Dust Moon kept her eye on it. Sparrow had insisted they walk in single file, Blue Raven first, himself second, and Dust Moon last. While she understood his good intentions, it meant that all day she'd been forced to trudge through the deep mud churned up by their moccasins. Her legs ached, but she refused to admit her weakness in front of the Walksalong Headman. Not only that, she knew that they had to press onward, or the children would surely beat them to the ruins of Paint Rock Village.

Her moccasins suddenly slipped, and she had to flail her arms to keep from toppling. She stopped and took a breath. Mud oozed up around her feet. The warm sunlight had melted most of the snow, though white patches glistened in the dark recesses of the forest.

She'd spent most of the day watching Blue Raven. Slightly taller than Sparrow, his graying black hair framed an oval face with brown eyes. The elk hide over his shoulders swayed as he walked, revealing the knife tied to his belt. A bow and quiver hung over his shoulder.

She started walking again, her arms out for balance, placing her moccasins with care.

She'd been chewing on the things he'd told them about Rumbler and Little Wren. While she understood his need to find his niece before Jumping Badger did, the rest of his plan remained hazy. He'd said that together he and Wren would "figure out something," but that made no sense. A girl in the Bear Nation had no life outside her clan. Yet, the Walksalong matrons had condemned the girl to death. If he took Wren home, she would surely be killed. No clan matron could afford to rescind such a judgment. It would weaken her authority. That is . . . unless the matrons were given a very important reason for changing their decree. Blue Raven had to offer something in return for Wren's life. Something that would mollify the matrons, and lessen the force of Wren's crime.

The "something" seemed clear.

*He has to take Rumbler back.*

If she stood in Blue Raven's moccasins, that's what

she would do: find the children, take them home, and offer both to the matrons as an appeasement—while pleading for Wren's life. She might suggest to the matrons that, as part of Wren's punishment, the girl be forced to sit Vigil over the boy while he died, or she might even recommend that Wren be ordered to kill Rumbler. That was the, only truly equitable resolution. Wren had saved him, and risked her clan by doing so. If she killed him, and thereby saved her clan, the matrons might spare her life.

The trail took a sudden steep drop, heading into the narrow valley below. To her right stood a tan cliff fifty hands high. As it curved around the south side of the meadow, the cliff sloped ever downward, until it vanished into thick golden grass. Snow encircled the bases of the boulders that scattered the valley. To the north, evergreen trees mixed with leafless maples. Almost hidden by the shadows at the edge of the trees, a herd of deer grazed.

Dust Moon lifted a brow at Blue Raven. Walking into their camp had just muddied the waters for him. Obviously Dust Moon and Sparrow would not allow Blue Raven to take Rumbler. Did the man think he could kill them both, grab the children, and run?

Dust Moon sighed in relief when she stepped from the slippery trail onto grass.

Blue Raven halted and put his hands on his hips. As he surveyed the land, he said, "I had forgotten how beautiful this country is."

"You've been here before?" Sparrow asked, and filled his lungs with the scents of wet grass and moss.

"Yes, many winters ago. On a raid."

Dust Moon kicked at the stone in the grass. "How many of my people did you kill?"

Blue Raven peered at her over his shoulder. His soft

brown eyes tightened. "I killed a few, Matron."

"You can't remember how many?"

". . . Two."

He said the word softly, plainly.

Dust Moon said, "Well, at least there was no pride in your voice. But there was no regret in it, either."

Against the blue gleam of evening his oval face looked softer, almost feminine. "I cannot regret following the orders of my clan elders, Matron. I did my duty to my people. Would you have your warriors feel shame for defending their people?"

"How did you feel when your matrons selected you to be the Vigil Keeper for Rumbler?" Dust Moon asked. "Were you defending your people?"

Blue Raven lowered his gaze. Wind tousled his graying black hair around his face. "They did not select me, Matron. I asked for the duty."

"You *asked* to watch a child die?"

"Yes. The boy was afraid. I promised him I would not leave him."

He had soft vulnerable eyes, filled with a sadness that compelled trust.

Dust Moon quietly ground her teeth. *Blessed gods, this man may be more dangerous than any warrior I have ever known.*

Sparrow unslung his pack, and said, "Well, I think it's time to make camp. It's getting dark, and we are all tired."

Blue Raven pulled his gaze from Dust's stony expression, and said, "I'm ready to rest. If you trust me to be out of your sight for a finger of time, I would be happy to collect wood for the fire."

Sparrow said, "I don't trust you to be out of my sight at all, but it would be helpful if you collected wood in my sight. Stay at the edge of the meadow."

"As you wish." Blue Raven walked toward the trees on the north side of the meadow.

Dust watched him go, a curious sensation in her belly. *Like looking at the back of a snake's head. You're never sure when it might turn and strike.*

"He's interesting, isn't he?" Sparrow said as he crouched and opened the laces on his pack. He drew out his fireboard and drill, and gave Dust Moon a half-smile. "It's hard not to respect him."

She said nothing, and Sparrow's shaggy gray brows drew down over his hooked nose. He lowered his gaze to his pack, pulling out pots, bowls, cups, and spoons. "What's wrong, Dust?"

She shook her head, dismissing the question.

"I've never known you to hold your tongue on my account, Dust. What's the matter? Is it something I've done?"

She scowled down at him. "You always think everything's your fault, Sparrow. Why is that? Some long-buried guilt? What have you done that I don't know about?"

He hesitated, said, "Well, hopefully quite a few things. It would be unnerving if you knew me as well as I know me." He added, "You have the food bags, Dust."

"I assume that means you would like them." She slipped out of her pack and handed it to him. He took it, loosened the laces, and removed the cornmeal bag. "We'll have to hunt tomorrow."

"A succulent turkey or fat duck would be welcome."

"Start praying now, then. This time of season, Turkey Above is very stingy with her children."

As he stood, the golden fur on the collar of his elk-hide jacket caught the pale twilight glow, and shimmered like a net of fallen stars. Sparrow shoved his hands into his pockets and grimaced at Blue Raven. "He's changed over the winters since I last saw him."

"How so?"

"He's calmer, more self-possessed. Thoughtful."

"Hmm." Dust Moon bent over to start gathering grass for fire-starter. The blades squealed as she ripped them up. "He used to be anxious, insecure, and thoughtless?"

Sparrow answered simply, "He used to be young."

"You were younger then yourself. How could you tell?"

"I was never as young as Blue Raven, Dust. A wife and children change a man's perspective, make him—".

"Age him, you mean."

"Well . . . yes. Can such a man be trusted?"

Dust Moon pulled up one last handful of grass, stacked it atop the others, and rubbed her fingers on her cape. Arms piled high with wood, the Walksalong Headman had started back across the meadow. The lodges of the Night Walkers brightened the sky over his head.

Dust said, "I have been turning that question all day."

Starlight gilded the curve of his hooked nose as he lifted his head. "Indeed?"

"Yes. If I wore his moccasins, I would feel trapped, Sparrow. He must take Rumbler back to Walksalong Village. As an offering to save his niece."

Sparrow's cheeks flushed. As dusk changed to night, his white hair took on the color of a mourning dove's wings. "Ancestors Above. I can't believe I didn't see that. Of course he has to take Rumbler back. Thank the Spirits you are here." Sparrow spontaneously reached for her hand.

Neither of them said anything. They twined fingers for a few instants, then Sparrow seemed to realize what he'd done, and let go.

Dust's fingers tingled. It was the first time in almost

two winters that they had touched without fear or anxiety, without demands, touched each other merely as old and trusted friends.

"Sparrow, I—"

"No, Dust." He lifted a hand. "For the sake of the gods, don't say anything. I can't stand a lance in my heart."

"I wasn't going to—"

"Of course you were. You were about to say, 'See, Sparrow, we can be allies, just not mates,' and I don't care to hear those words again."

With injured dignity, she said, "I wish you wouldn't pretend you can track my souls."

"You mean that isn't what you were going to say?"

"No, it isn't," she lied. More than anything else, she missed his friendship, the nights of whispering secrets snuggled together, of laughing as they watched the firelight on the ceiling. But she couldn't risk her heart again. Not even if she wanted to. If she trusted him enough to share her heart and body with him, and then he shattered that trust by answering his Spirit Helper's call when her world was shredding . . .

"Well," Sparrow said. "I'm listening."

Wind Mother had been tearing at Dust's long silver braid all afternoon, tangling its loosened strands. She smoothed them with her fingers. "I was wondering how he plans on killing us."

Sparrow propped his hands on his hips. "Now there's something to make a man's supper go down easier."

"He seems to need us for the moment, and I'm not certain why."

Sparrow lowered his voice. Blue Raven stood about eighty hands away. "Because he fears Rumbler's Powers. With us along, he thinks he'll be safe."

"Or maybe he's waiting for his cousin's help. I suspect Jumping Badger would gladly exchange the children for you, Sparrow.''

His bushy gray brows plunged down over his hooked nose. ''I'm not so . . .''

Blue Raven walked into camp, dumped his load of wood on the ground, and opened his elk-hide wrap to show a dead rabbit hung from his belt. Blood drained down its head. As he untied it, he said, ''You have shared so much with me. I offer you something in return. This rabbit leaped from behind a tree, and stopped less than sixty hands away. I took him with a single arrow through the neck.''

Sparrow gave him a much friendlier smile than Dust would have thought possible. ''You must have been listening to my stomach. It's been screaming for meat for days.''

Dust Moon held out a hand to Blue Raven. ''Let me clean it while you break those branches into shorter lengths.''

Blue Raven handed her the rabbit.

Their hands briefly touched in the transfer, and Dust Moon pulled away as if bitten. Blue Raven noticed, but didn't seem offended. In fact, he stepped back and smiled as if apologizing for touching her.

''I—I'll get started on the wood,'' he said.

''And I'll fix the fire,'' Sparrow added. He glanced at Blue Raven, then Dust Moon, and when he'd satisfied himself that she was in no danger, he picked up a flat rock from the ground and began scooping a hole. He piled the dirt into a rough circle around the fire pit, to protect their fire from the wind, and the rest of the meadow from their fire.

Blue Raven broke a branch over his knee, and the crack echoed in the stillness. ''How much farther to Paint Rock? We should arrive tomorrow, shouldn't we?''

Sparrow filled the hole with the dry grass Dust Moon had plucked, and set his fireboard beside it. "Probably tomorrow night. If it's as warm tomorrow as it was today, we'll be struggling through knee-deep mud. It won't be easy."

Blue Raven broke another branch, and tossed it onto his growing pile. "It's unfortunate that there isn't another trail, one less traveled by game. By the time we leave in the morning, this one will be a quagmire of deer and elk hoofprints."

"Something to look forward to," Dust Moon said with a groan.

Sparrow smiled, and began spinning his drill in his fireboard. "It's just for a few more hands of time, Dust."

"I realize that, Sparrow, but it will feel like forever."

The color of the cliffs had gone from tan to a glowing silvery blue. She let her souls absorb the beauty for a few instants, then gingerly knelt in the grass and laid the rabbit before her. Every muscle in her body ached. She rotated her right shoulder and winced.

"Long day, wasn't it?" Sparrow asked, concern in his eyes.

The hoarse sound of the drill spinning in the fireboard combined with the cracking of wood and hooting of owls to create a familiar evening serenade.

"I'll be fine once I've eaten."

She drew her chert knife from her belt, and sawed off the rabbit's head. The small body had cooled enough that the fleas who'd called it home were scrambling for their lives, crawling out of the fur by the dozens, hopping onto her skirt and over her hands. She stood the rabbit on its haunches and began peeling the fur back from the neck and shoulders. When she reached the front legs, she pulled each up and out of the hide, then rolled the skin down the back and belly to the hind legs. After she'd worked the hide over the rump, she pulled the hind legs free. Beautiful pink meat lay on the grass before her. She took the inside-out hide and straightened it. Later tonight, she would use her knife to scrape off the bits of tissue that clung to the skin, then she would set it near the fire to dry and smoke. It would make a warm pair of mittens for Rumbler.

His round face appeared on her souls and smiled at her, but she knew he must be terrified, fleeing for his life with a stranger from an enemy clan. What would he be thinking tonight? She ached to see him.

Dust Moon set the hide aside, and picked up her knife again. She cut a shallow hole just beneath the rabbit's ribs, then slit the animal open to the pelvis, and pulled out the viscera. The rich scent of warm blood filled the air. Her stomach growled.

Sparrow looked up from his fire drill. "Smells good, doesn't it?"

As she sifted through the viscera, picking out the kidneys and liver, she said, "Much better than cornmeal gruel and dried meat." She placed the internal organs on the hide, then reached inside the rabbit's chest cavity for the heart and lungs.

Flames crackled in the fire pit, and a wavering orange halo lit the camp.

"Blue Raven?" Sparrow looked up. The Headman stood stiffly, his arms folded. "Throw me a few pieces of that wood."

Blue Raven gathered an armload and brought it to Sparrow's side. "I broke them into small-enough lengths that they should fit in the hole," he said.

Sparrow pulled several branches out and laid them over the burning grass in crisscrossing patterns. "Perfect," he said. "Thank you."

Dust carried the rabbit, and organs, into the light.

She examined the lungs first. A variety of diseases showed up there, spotting the lungs with white or black, but these appeared clean. Next she looked at the liver. Worms often invaded the organ, creating ugly yellowish cysts and ruining the meat, but it was clean, too. She threw the lungs away, and dropped the liver into the cook pot, followed by the heart and kidneys.

"How should we cook the rabbit?" she asked. "Roasted over the fire, or boiled in a stew?"

Blue Raven spread his hands. The gray in his long hair sparkled in the firelight. "Your pleasure, Matron. I will be happy either way."

Sparrow said, "I would love a good greasy leg of roasted rabbit."

"Yes, I know you would, Sparrow, but it will go further if we add it to a stew. What we don't eat tonight, we can warm for breakfast."

Sparrow's mouth quirked. "If you knew how you were going to cook it, why did you ask me?"

"I'm a polite person."

Sparrow laid his fireboard and drill aside, and leaned toward her. "When did this start?"

Blue Raven laughed, then, as if embarrassed, he tried to choke it back, which made it worse.

Sparrow grinned.

Dust Moon smiled, too. "I may eat this rabbit by myself."

"Uh, forgive me, Matron," Blue Raven said.

Dust Moon stuffed the rabbit in the cook pot and handed it to him. "Here. Cut this up while I prepare the rest of the stew." As she cleaned the blood from her hands on the dry grass, she said, "Sparrow, I gave you the food bags earlier. Give them back."

"Oh, I forgot. Here. Catch." He tossed her the cornmeal bag, then the onions, dried slices of pumpkin, and a bag of sunflower seeds. "Is there anything else you want?"

"Yes. My pack. I don't trust you with it."

Sparrow handed it around the fire. "The corn cakes are gone, Dust. I'm no longer a threat."

Blue Raven looked up. "I hope I am not responsible for that. I ate two on the trail today."

"No," Dust Moon said with a shake of her head, and her voice changed, growing more menacing. "The things you are responsible for are far graver, Walksalong Headman."

Blue Raven saw her expression, and his smile faded. He cut off the rabbit's right hind leg and began stripping the meat from it, letting the muscles drop into the cook pot. "What things, Matron? Perhaps if we discuss your accusations, we can come to some—"

"I doubt it. You and your people are beyond my understanding." Dust Moon tossed her long gray braid over her shoulder, then drew up her knees and wrapped her arms around them. As darkness covered the forest, the temperature plummeted. She could already see her breath.

Blue Raven finished the last rabbit leg, added it to the stewpot, and set the stripped bones aside.

"Hand me the pot."

"Yes, of course." Blue Raven gave it to her, and said, "I realize there are many differences between our peoples, Matron, but we are all the children of Falling Woman. We agree upon that. Let us begin there."

Dust lifted a brow. *A peacemaker. Beware, old woman.*

She dumped the rest of the onions and pumpkins into the pot, then added half the remaining sunflower seeds, and thrust the pot at Sparrow. "Make yourself useful. Pour some water into this, and into the teapot, and hang them on their tripods over the flames."

Sparrow lifted both fists and shook them, then grabbed for the pot before she could do anything dangerous with it. He untied his water bag from his belt, and began filling the pot, but he didn't quite succeed in smothering his smile.

She glowered at him, but spoke to Blue Raven. "Very well. We'll begin there, Headman. How could you steal one of Falling Woman's chosen people, a Power child— and a relative of your ours, since we are all descended from Falling Woman—and then decide to kill him?"

Blue Raven pulled his elk hide more securely over his shoulders. Two owls serenaded each other across the valley, their calls lilting on the cold breeze. He solemnly responded, "Matron, three people in my village died after the arrival of the False Face Child."

Dust didn't respond. She contemplated the tight line of the man's jaw. "What happened to them?"

"Truly? I do not know." Blue Raven picked up a stick from the woodpile and tapped it on the ground. "Rumbler said he'd killed them, but I—"

"How?"

"Let the man finish, Dust," Sparrow said, and lounged back on his elbows. White hair spread around his shoulders like a luminous cape.

She repeated, *"How?"*

Blue Raven said, "I don't think the boy did it, Matron. The first to die, Matron White Kit, had seen almost seventy winters. The other two, both warriors, had just returned home from battle."

"So White Kit may have died from old age," she said, "and you think the other two died from injuries they took while murdering Rumbler's family?"

He laid his stick across his knees and frowned at it. "I thought it possible. Unfortunately, only one other person in the village agreed with me."

Dust's heart twinged. "Little Wren?"

He nodded. "At the village council meeting, when everyone else was shouting for death, she cast her voice for life."

"Of course she did," Dust said softly.

A frigid gust of wind blasted their camp, and Blue Raven pulled his elk hide up over his head, holding it closed beneath his chin. Firelight danced through the brown and golden hairs framing his face. "I pleaded with the matrons for leniency, but by that time terror had swallowed their senses; my words might have never been."

"Your niece is a brave girl, Blue Raven," Sparrow said and stirred the cook pot. The aromas of rabbit and pumpkin circled their heads. "I pray your people don't kill her for it."

Blue Raven clenched the stick. "They will have to kill me first, Silver Sparrow."

"As I understand it, Headman,"—the lines around Dust Moon's eyes crinkled as she smiled—"that's precisely what your relatives have in mind."

Elk Ivory twirled an oak twig in her fingers, watching Acorn stride up the trail toward her. Scattered triangles of light shone on his drawn face. They had dragged their war canoes ashore at the place where Blue Raven's tracks joined the two strangers. That had been two days ago. They hadn't moved since.

Acorn crouched beside her, his burly shoulders massive beneath his bear-hide cape. He'd just come from a bath in the lake, and the bristly ridge of hair that ran down the middle of his skull gleamed wetly. He whispered, "What's he doing?"

"I can't say, but he's been at it since dawn."

About ten body lengths away, Jumping Badger sat in the highest branches of an oak tree. Strips of wood had been fluttering down for two days, creating a pale golden pile around the oak's trunk.

Acorn nervously scanned the forest. "Where's the head?"

"In his lap."

"Has he been talking to it?"

"That's who he was shouting at a short time ago. Didn't you hear him?" When Acorn shook his head, Elk Ivory added, "I'm surprised. I assumed our relatives back in Walksalong Village could hear him."

Wind Mother whipped through the forest and blew Elk Ivory's shoulder-length black hair around her brown eyes. She squinted, and tightened her hold on the collar of her buffalo coat, keeping the wind out. The green paintings of Falcon and Goshawk that adorned the lower half of her coat waffled, almost seeming to fly.

She surveyed Acorn's troubled face, and asked, "What's wrong?"

He propped his forearms on his knees. "Something happened. I was down bathing, and many warriors approached me demanding to know what we are doing here. They think one of us should tell the war leader that we ought to be going. We sat here all day yesterday while Jumping Badger perched in that tree. If we do not catch Blue Raven soon, we may never find him."

Elk Ivory scratched her broad flat nose. As Grandfather Day Maker climbed higher into the bright blue sky, light lanced through the branches, striking Acorn in the face and causing him to squint.

"Then I think the 'one of us' should be you, Acorn. I tried speaking with Jumping Badger night before last. He doesn't like me."

"But you are much braver than I am. Everybody says so."

"Do they?"

"Oh, yes. The whole clan knows it." Acorn nodded humbly, plucked a blade of dry grass from the ground and put it in his mouth. He chewed the blade while he diligently avoided her eyes.

Elk Ivory said, "Then, how fortunate you are to have this opportunity to build your reputation. People will be singing of your valor for many winters."

The blade of grass stopped wiggling. He removed it and glanced at her. "Well, truthfully, I am not that upset about being a coward. It has its advantages. Life, for one."

"Jumping Badger won't kill you."

"He's as crazy as a wingless bat!" He shook his grass stem at her. "How can you be so sure?"

She looked up at the oak tree. Jumping Badger lifted the wood he'd been carving, and put it up to his eyes, gazing at her through the eyeholes.

"Blessed Spirits," she breathed. "It's a mask. He's been making a *mask*."

Acorn's head swiveled around so fast he almost lost his balance. "He can't do that! He's never been cleansed!"

Elk Ivory stood. "Nevertheless, he's done it."

Acorn rose beside her, his mouth open.

Few warriors ever made a mask. The cleansing process, called the Water Purification ritual, required that a warrior renounce killing, and cast all of his or her weapons into a river. After that, the warrior had to sit in the river for three days and three nights. Running water removed the taint of death gained in warfare. If an uncleansed warrior carved a mask, the taint would seep into the heart of the mask and bring disease and death to his people.

Hostile voices filled the camp as, one by one, people saw what Jumping Badger had done, and began to coalesce around the central fire.

Elk Ivory rose and strode for Jumping Badger. Acorn headed for the fire, crying, "Be calm! Wait!"

As she neared the maple, Jumping Badger climbed down the tree to meet her, the mask tucked beneath his arm. He sneered at his warriors, then laughed in Elk Ivory's face, saying, "I have given Lamedeer new eyes! He was complaining because the yellow crust of decay had blinded him. He sees much better now, old woman."

Jumping Badger propped the staff on the ground, then tied the mask over the rotting face. It was a crude thing, carved to resemble a crow's head with a long beak. Lamedeer's sunken eyes showed through the holes. "Lamedeer has seen Blue Raven's trail. Come. We must go." He turned to walk away, and Elk Ivory grabbed his arm, stopping him.

"You have risked the lives of your people by making this mask. How could you—"

"Leave me be, old woman!" He roughly shook off her hand. His handsome young face twisted. "I am working to save our people! That is our goal, and that is what I have—"

"Then why would you make a mask that you know will bring death?"

Jumping Badger leaned closer to her, his eyes boring into Elk Ivory's. "Get out of my way. I must find and kill the evil boy before he kills us."

"And Blue Raven and Little Wren?"

Jumping Badger thumped the staff on the ground. "They are traitors, Elk Ivory, but I do not plan to kill them. The matrons told me to bring them back to Walksalong Village for judgment. That is my plan."

Jumping Badger stalked toward the crowd around the fire. Warriors backed away. Acorn clenched his fists at his sides and stood his ground, but Elk Ivory could see that he'd started swallowing convulsively.

The hushed conversations died.

"War Leader," Acorn greeted, "it is good to—to see you. We have been concerned about you."

Jumping Badger glared at Acorn. "Get ready. All of you! We are leaving immediately. I know where my cousin is going!"

Jumping Badger turned on his heel and, before anyone could mutter another word, let out a shrill war cry, and loped northward, calling, "Follow me!"

"Wait! Aren't we taking the canoes?" Acorn shouted.

"They are on foot!" Jumping Badger yelled. "Lamedeer has seen it!"

Alarmed warriors reluctantly took up their packs and headed after their war leader, casting worried glances at Elk Ivory.

Acorn walked up beside her. "What do you think about this?"

"I do not know."

Acorn ran his hand over his bristly ridge of hair, as if to relieve his tension. "Well, perhaps we should try to ignore it. Our task is to obey the matrons' orders to find Blue Raven, Little Wren, and the False Face Child."

She considered a long time before saying, "Yes, obeying is not so easy when it means you must follow a man who's been dead for nearly a moon."

Acorn's lips turned up, but the resulting grimace could hardly be called a smile. "Where do *you* think Blue Raven is headed?"

"I think he's following Wren. So the better question is, where is Wren headed?"

A gust of wind flowed across the tan meadow grasses and made the trees moan. "Where, indeed? Wren has never been west of Going Wolf Village. She doesn't know this country. That means she must be following whatever routes the False Face Child tells her to."

"If so, we have much to fear, Acorn. A boy from the Turtle Nation will know far more trails than we do."

"Yes. His people move constantly during the spring and summer moons."

Elk Ivory added, "He may even know trails no one else does. When I had seen nine winters, I used to climb sheer cliff faces to get where I wanted to go."

"And wrestled any cougars that tried to stop you, I'd wager."

"Why would I wrestle when I carried a bow, fool?"

He grinned. "I should have known. A skilled bows-woman at nine winters."

"Not particularly skilled, but arrogant enough to make up for it. I always had faith that I could—" She stopped suddenly.

"What's the matter?"

"Perhaps that's the answer."

"What? Childish arrogance?"

"Arrogance and faith." Elk Ivory walked around the fire pit to her pack. As she slipped the strap over her shoulder, she said, "The only way we are ever going to find them is if we learn to think like children again, Acorn."

She broke into a trot, following the war party. Acorn's steps pounded behind her.

# Twenty-Two

Cornhusk bit off a juicy chunk of venison and chewed it. Fat dripped down his chin onto his mangy buffalo coat. He rubbed it in, then gripped the roasted piece of venison in both hands, and grinned at his hosts. They had seated him on a pile of buffalo and elk robes, placed heaping bowls of squash, beans, and walnut bread before him, and kept refilling his cup with soured-corn drink. The stuff tasted vile, but had a powerful Spirit. After only two cups, he'd started smiling at *old* women!

"I have always had the highest esteem for the people here in Silent Crow Village. Your hospitality is unmatched," he said around another mouthful of venison. He took a swig of corn drink and wiped his mouth on his sleeve. "How do you make this drink? It's marvelous."

Spotted Frog, the clan patron, belched and smiled. A corpulent man with a bloated face and elaborately braided black hair, he had only two teeth left in his mouth—both in the front on the bottom. Firelight flickered over the sloping roof of the conical house, and shone from Spotted Frog's greasy cheeks. He wore a magnificent silver pendant cut in the shape of a wolf. Eight people crammed the house around them, quietly waiting for the formalities to end. More people crouched just outside the doorway, cooking supper over the plaza fire, carrying on their own conversations. Cornhusk's arrival always sparked a village gathering.

"It's a secret method," Spotted Frog explained. "No other clan knows it. First, we take the cobs, weight them down, and sink them into Bayberry Pond. The Water Spirits there are very strong. They creep into the kernels and eat away at the insides. And we all know what happens after we eat. When the kernels have filled with enough slime, we pull them up, scrape the cobs, and mix the mush with maple sap and water. Then we leave the sour-corn pot near the fire to warm. In five or six days, it is ready to drink." Spotted Frog lifted his cup and guzzled several swallows. "Yes. Very tasty. I'm gratified you like it."

Cornhusk peered down into his cup. His small dark eyes peered back. He didn't see any slime clinging to the sides of the cup. "I am . . . honored," he said, "that you would reveal your secret method to me, Spotted Frog. I vow never to tell anyone."

Cornhusk picked up his venison leg again. A beautiful young woman knelt at his side and refilled his cup from a pitcher. He bit into the smoky meat. *Think smoke, not slime. Smoke.*

Spotted Frog tossed his gnawed bone into the fire and picked up his pipe bag. The blue, yellow, and white porcupine quillwork glimmered in the light. Whelk shells hung from the fringe, clicking pleasantly. Spotted Frog removed a clay pipe, and beaded tobacco bag. As he tamped the tobacco into the bowl, he said, "We have heard strange rumors about Walksalong Village. Have you been there recently?"

Cornhusk took one last bite from his venison bone and lowered the remains to his bowl. "Yes. I was there ten days ago."

"Are things as bad as the rumors say?"

"Terrible. But what have you heard?"

Spotted Frog stuck a twig into the fire and lit his pipe with it. As he puffed, blue tendrils of smoke curled upward toward the soot-blackened ceiling. "A runner from Sleeping Mist told us that Jumping Badger had attacked their village, killed half the inhabitants, then run south and slaughtered Paint Rock Village. The runner also said that Jumping Badger had stolen the False Face Child. Is it so?"

Cornhusk wiped his hands on the front of his buffalo coat. "Yes. True. All of it."

Spotted Frog took another puff, then handed the pipe to Cornhusk. "Is it true, as well, that as soon as the False Face Child reached Walksalong Village people starting falling dead like flies after a hard frost?"

"Well." Cornhusk shook his head in disdain. "That is an exaggeration. Three people died. Not at all like flies after a frost."

Two old women to Cornhusk's right elbowed each other and hissed, as if congratulating each other on being right.

"The Sleeping Mist runner said that the False Face Child stabbed one of the clan matrons, and that the two warriors who'd brought the boy into the village spat up their insides, and died screaming like clubbed dogs."

Cornhusk sucked on the pipe and held the rich smoke in his lungs before slowly letting it out. "Fairly accurate. But I was there, Spotted Frog. I *saw*. The warriors foamed at the mouth first, thrashing about like gutted fish, shrieking and wailing." He shrugged. "Then they spat up their insides and died."

Hushed murmuring broke out, and quickly grew to a din. Spotted Frog held up a fist to quiet the people. The conversations languished into silence.

The patron rubbed his triple chin. "Then it was worse than we have heard."

Cornhusk handed the pipe back, and prepared to deliver the speech he'd been practicing—the one they all expected him to give. That was, after all, why the villagers had crowded in and around the house. After he'd delivered his speech at Winged Dace Village, the people had showered him with riches. Since Silent Crow was a Turtle Nation village, he'd have to change some of the details, reverse the roles of heroes and villains, and add a few tidbits from Turtle Nation legends, but he had no doubt these people would respond in a similarly generous fashion.

He sat forward and lowered his voice to a bare whisper. "I tell you truly, Spotted Frog, thousands of winters from now legends will be Sung about the Spirits that roamed Walksalong Village during the Winter of Crying Rocks. They will Sing of how the clan matrons condemned the False Face Child to death, and how one courageous girl named Little Wren, and a brave Headman named Blue Raven, cut the boy loose and ran away with him. Of how they tricked the wicked madman, Jumping Badger—"

"The boy is free? He's a-alive?" Spotted Frog spluttered. "We had heard he was dead!"

Cornhusk shook his head slowly. "No, he's with Blue Raven and Little Wren, running for his life from a search party of over two hundred warriors."

"Two hundred! I didn't know the Walksalong Clan had so many warriors!"

"Oh, yes." Cornhusk waved a negligent hand. "Perhaps even three hundred. But naturally the matrons would not allow Jumping Badger tŏ take them all. That would have left their village defenseless."

In a small anguished voice, Spotted Frog asked,

"Blessed Spirits, how can Blue Raven and the children hope to escape?"

"They won't escape," Cornhusk prophesied. "At least, it seems unlikely, since Jumping Badger is being guided by the Spirit of Lamedeer himself."

Gasps rang out, and a chorus of shouted questions.

*"Great gods, why? . . . Lamedeer was one of us! He wouldn't . . . Oh, it cannot be! I don't . . ."*

Over the chaos, Spotted Frog shouted, "Lamedeer was my cousin's son. He would never betray the False Face Child!"

"Not while he was alive, no," Cornhusk yelled back, and waited until the excited villagers went quiet again. "But Jumping Badger is Powerful. He cut off Lamedeer's head, and called out to the most worthless, evil Forest Spirits in the land. No one knows how he did it, but Jumping Badger managed to convince the soul inside Lamedeer's rotting skull to do his bidding. They talk constantly."

Spotted Frog blanched. He set his pipe on one of the hearthstones, and hunched forward. "You mean Lamedeer speaks with Jumping Badger? That he actually hears my dead cousin's voice?"

"Speaks to him? Lamedeer shouts at Jumping Badger! I stayed in old Frost-in-the-Willow's longhouse for several nights, and the things I heard quivered my souls. Jumping Badger never slept. Whispers and moans came from his bedding. Sometimes he leaped to his feet, grabbed the staff where Lamedeer's head perches, and shook it with all his might. Shook it until I thought the severed head would fall to pieces. But it didn't. Lamedeer's jaws just fell open in a hideous mockery of laughter. I swear. I saw it!"

Spotted Frog nervously twisted his bloated hands. Firelight shadowed the deep wrinkles that made up his triple chin. "What happened then?"

You could have heard a straw hit the floor. Wide eyes filled the house and crowded the doorway.

"Jumping Badger went mad. He screamed and threatened the dead war leader. He—"

"But . . . what threat could matter to a dead man?"

Cornhusk took another sip of his slime drink, and propped the cup on his knee. "Jumping Badger said 'Don't forget, Lamedeer, I hold your soul in my hands. If you do not do as I say, I'll never let you rest.'"

Gasps of fear eddied through the house. Outside, feet scuffed the ground. Cornhusk smiled to himself. No greater threat could be uttered. If a Turtle Nation warrior's body was not properly cared for, washed and massaged with oil, then buried in its lone grave, the soul would wander the earth forever, angry and alone. It would wreak vengeance on its clanspeople, bringing them diseases, accidents, and famines.

Spotted Frog's elderly wife, Pup Woman, knelt by his side. Plump, with short gray hair, she had bulging black eyes that seemed to stick out as far as her buck teeth. Pup Woman cupped a hand to Spotted Frog's ear. As she whispered, Cornhusk lowered his eyes. Not so much out of deference as fear. Pup Woman had been known to call upon sorcerers to poison her husband's enemies, or to enter their dreams and carry off their souls. Smart men did not tempt such a woman.

Cornhusk swirled the liquid in his cup. Strange. The more of this slime a man drank, the better it tasted. And the better he felt. An almost giddy sensation possessed him. He would have to watch what he said. He wouldn't want to get the heroes and villains of his story mixed up. Accidentally saying, as he had at the Bear Nation village last night, "The Blessed Jumping Badger led his courageous warriors in a desperate search for the traitors, and the evil False Face Child,'' could get him flayed and roasted.

He swallowed more slime.

Pup Woman stood, and Spotted Frog lifted his hands to gain the attention of the people.

He called, ''Pup Woman has given me wise counsel. She asks how we can sit here, warm and comfortable, when there are two heroic children, and a desperate man, out alone in the forest, fleeing hundreds of vicious warriors. We must help them!''

A clamor rose as people began talking at once.

''Our ancestors would expect no less!'' Pup Woman shouted.

Over a dozen heads nodded that Cornhusk could see. This wasn't going at all as he'd planned.

''But, wait!'' Cornhusk said. ''How can your tiny village hope to stand against Jumping Badger and his war party? How many warriors does the Silent Crow Clan boast? Fifteen?''

''Twenty. Maybe.'' Spotted Frog looked up at Pup Woman. ''Is Big Red Foot well yet? He had a nasty—''

''Spotted Frog! Listen to yourself. You are speaking of twenty warriors if you pull the sick from their blankets. Your clan is no match for a Walksalong war party!''

''Not alone,'' Pup Woman said and squared her shoulders. ''But if we send out runners asking for help—''

''From where?'' Cornhusk shouted, overcome with dread. If this pathetic village got slaughtered, the blame would be on his head, and enough people already wanted him dead. ''Who is brave enough to offer warriors when Jumping Badger might attack them next? Eh? Think about this. Paint Rock is gone. They *can't* offer anyone. Sleeping Mist has been decimated. They *won't* offer anyone. Earth Thunderer—''

"That's it!" Spotted Frog waved his hands wildly. "We'll send for old Silver Sparrow! We know he's a demented fool, but people in the Bear Nation fear him. We'll get him to curse Jumping Badger, maybe all of Walksalong Village. That should throw terror into—"

"Oh, please!" Cornhusk groaned and dropped his head in his hands. "This is howling at the moon, Spotted Frog. Save your strength for your own people. There is no telling who Jumping Badger wishes to hurt after he captures Blue Raven and the children. What if you are next?"

Pup Woman's eyes narrowed and Cornhusk felt his spine prickle.

"Er, Matron," he said, "forgive my impudence. I did not mean to sound as if I were casting my voice against your proposal. I have no such right, and I know it. I ask only that you consider this carefully. I enjoy coming here. I would hate to see Silent Crow Village turned into a pile of cinders and rotting corpses. You know as well as I that if Jumping Badger were to get news of what you said this night, he would fly here faster than a shooting star and"—he threw up his hands—"your people would be charred corpses!"

"The brave do not fear death," Spotted Frog said, and reached for Pup Woman's hand. He brought it down to his flushed cheek. "We will risk our lives gladly to save the heroes. If we do not, who will?"

Cornhusk slumped over his cup. The fumes from the sour-corn drink made his eyes water. Through tears, he said, "Well, if you are determined to do this thing, at least let me tell you the rest of the story."

"There's more?"

He nodded glumly. "Yes. Much more. You see, it was I who saved the lives of Silver Sparrow and Matron Dust Moon." When he heard the words that came out of his mouth, panic surged through him. Why on earth had he said that!

Spotted Frog clutched Pup Woman's hand more tightly. "Go on. How did it happen?"

Cornhusk morosely tipped up his cup and drained it dry. Well, this was a Turtle Nation village, perhaps it would not get back to a Bear Nation village. "They came to Walksalong to rescue the False Face Child, but Blue Raven and Little Wren had already run off with the boy, and Jumping Badger was out looking for them. At great risk to myself, I sneaked away and ran up the trail to warn Silver Sparrow and Matron Dust Moon that they should flee before anyone from Walksalong Village saw them, or they would surely be killed. Silver Sparrow exploded in anger!" Cornhusk lifted his fists and swung them around his head. "I ran back to Walksalong Village, but soon thereafter, the storm struck. It blasted Walksalong Village and all that surrounded it. Trees ripped from the ground and flew about like cloth dolls. The longhouses burst wide open and the bark coverings flew to pieces. Roof poles somersaulted across the plaza."

"Did anyone survive?" Spotted Frog asked in a tremulous voice. "Or were they all destroyed?"

Cornhusk whispered, "Not a longhouse stood. Most of the elders were killed. Children dashed about the ruins screaming for parents, aunts, and uncles. I have never seen anything so terrifying, Spotted Frog. Matron Starflower was cut in half by flying debris. Bogbean and old Beadfern died when their longhouses collapsed. I know that the Turtle Nation does not believe in Silver Sparrow's Powers, but what else could have caused such devastation?" He shook his head. "You would have believed. If you had been there. If you had seen what I saw. You would have believed that Silver Sparrow is capable of destroying the whole world!''

''Wren?'' Rumbler called. ''The trail ends up here. Be careful!''

''I will.'' Her voice echoed as she braced her back against the steeply tilted slab of granite and slid along it. The narrow trail, no more than two hands wide, ran just at the base of the granite cliff. Below, a badly eroded talus slope of crumbling rock angled downward to a small green pond. Mist curled over the pond. Grandfather Day Maker remained hidden, but crimson spikes of light shot over the horizon and turned the mist a soft rosy hue.

Wren concentrated on her feet. Cougar prints marked the sand in front of her toes. Big ones, twice the size of Wren's palm. They had been following animal trails, as Rumbler had foreseen, but the way had turned out to be much more difficult than they'd expected. Jagged piles of stones often blocked the path, forcing them to squeeze through cracks, and scramble over talus. Wren had torn out the knees of her pants scrambling on all fours across the last slope. Blood stained the blue hide, and crusted her lower legs.

As she edged closer to what appeared to be a precipice, she saw Rumbler on a ledge about fifty hands below, looking down. Half her height, from up here he appeared tiny, his arms and legs stubs protruding from his trunk. Chin-length black hair blew about his round face. She had torn off the hem of his old black shirt, washed it in water steeped with pine needles, and wrapped his hands with it. She'd slipped her wolf-hide mittens over the bandages to protect them. The mittens swallowed his arms all the way to his elbows.

"Wren? I thought this was the trail, but . . ." His voice faded in and out with the wind as she slid closer. "I don't . . . think . . ."

Wren shouted, "But we followed the tracks you saw in your Dream! You told me that first we'd find the place a wolf had slept, and that if we stayed on his paw prints, he would lead us to a moose, then we would spook a deer, and her hoofprints would lead us to a cougar's trail. We've done everything you said we should."

"The cougar's trail ends . . . Wren. At this ledge." He gestured to the prints in the sand where he stood. "In my Dream, the cougar took us home."

Jumbled boulders filled the space between Wren and Rumbler. She sank her fingers between the rocks, and lowered herself a step at a time, feeling the way with her toes.

When she had climbed down onto the ledge beside Rumbler, he flapped his arms helplessly. "I'm sorry, Wren. I may have gotten us lost."

Spruces and oak trees splotched the hillsides. It upset her that Rumbler's Dream might have been mistaken. She had heard of it happening to other Dreamers, when their Spirit Helpers tricked them, or deliberately made the Dream so difficult the Dreamer couldn't possibly understand it. But Rumbler? In all the stories Jumping Badger had told, Rumbler had never once been wrong.

She said, "The cougar's tracks were on both paths at that last fork in the trail. Remember? Maybe we should have gone to the left, not the right."

"Maybe, but . . . I thought this was the way."

"Should we go back? It won't take long."

He tucked the mittens gingerly beneath his arms. She

had checked his fingers over breakfast, and found them healing, but the pain must be bad.

Rumbler stared at the precipice. The sheer granite wall fell seventy hands straight down. The cougar must have growled in dismay when she got here. Then what? What did she do after that? She didn't go back the way she'd come. There were no prints headed the other direction.

Wren closed her eyes, and tried to put her souls into a cougar's body, to imagine what she would have done, where she might have jumped or—

"Wren? The bird hasn't come back. Why do you think he hasn't?"

She opened her eyes. Rumbler stood facing the east, his back to her, but she could see the slump in his young shoulders.

"*Yet*, Rumbler. The siskin hasn't come back *yet*. Siskins are very small, and it's a long way. Give him more time."

But she'd been worrying, too. If the bird had flown to the Up-Above-World and couldn't find Rumbler's mother, then it meant one of two things: Either Briar still lived, or her soul had not been able to find its way to the afterlife. The second possibility was probably eating Rumbler alive. Homeless ghosts wandered the forests crying for loved ones, miserably eating the dregs from empty village cook pots. Wren had overheard old Starflower talking about this two winters ago. She'd said that such ghosts rarely knew they were dead. They knew only that they had to find their families. Some ghosts— especially those that had died a long way from home— never found their families, and were condemned to run forever, calling the names of people who had long since traveled to the Up-Above-World. Other ghosts found their families, but the living could not hear them, and this drove the ghosts into madness. After moons of shouting into their husband's or mother's face, the ghost would begin causing disasters to try and gain the living's attention. Homeless ghosts often ended up harming those they most loved.

Wren smoothed her moccasin over one of the cougar prints. "Rumbler? Are you afraid?"

He looked at his mittens. "I want to go home, Wren. I want to go home and crawl under my hides in my mother's lodge, and sleep until she wakes me for supper."

Wren nodded.

Sometimes she dreamed that she'd just awakened, and could hear her mother moving around the longhouse, whispering to her father and little Skybow. The smell of breakfast filled the air. Trickster lay on her feet, his body warming her toes, and she didn't want to move, or breathe, because she knew the dream would fade.

She put a hand on Rumbler's shoulder. "Stop worrying, Rumbler. It doesn't do any good. Besides, I'm thirsty, aren't you?"

"Yes."

Wren sat down and swung her feet over the edge. "Sit beside me, Rumbler."

Rumbler sat down, but his gaze rested on the horizon. "I'm s-sorry, Wren. I don't know what happened."

As dawn approached, the sky gleamed like polished amethyst.

Wren untied the water bag from her belt, and took a long drink, then handed it to Rumbler. He clasped it between the palms of his mittens, and drank.

"Do you think your Spirit Helper is tricking you? To teach you a lesson? I've heard that happens to Dreamers."

Rumbler lowered the bag to his lap, and blinked at the fine braided leather ties. "My mother used to say that 'a person who finds a Spirit Helper will never have peace, and a person who loses a Spirit Helper will never have purpose.' I don't know what the second part means, but I understand the first part. My souls are twisted up today, like a ball of twine tossed around by children. I don't think my Helper is tricking me, but . . . he might be."

"Your Dreams don't have to be right all the time, Rumbler. Not for me anyway."

He peered at the jumbled gray rocks piled in the ravine far below.

"What is it, Rumbler?"

"I've been wrong before, Wren." His face contorted as he fought not to cry.

". . . When?"

"The day of the battle. I had a vision." He closed his mouth slowly and swallowed. "I—I told the elders there would be no attack. I told them Paint Rock Village was safe."

Wren took the water bag back, and gulped two more swallows. "Is that why you didn't blast Jumping Badger when you first saw him?"

"No, I . . . something happens, Wren, when I'm really scared. I—I can't move or think. I can't even scream. My body feels like a punky log."

Shame reddened his cheeks, and he fiddled with his hands, rubbing dirt from his cape, brushing at the ledge.

"It wasn't your fault, Rumbler. Your Spirit Helper told you Paint Rock was safe. How were you supposed to know it wasn't?"

Rumbler used his mitten to wipe his nose. "He wasn't my Helper, but he was a very Powerful Spirit."

Some bad Spirits were renowned for tricking shamans, but they showed up in known forms. "Did the Spirit come to you as an old woman with a long crooked walking stick?"

"No. It wasn't Falling Woman."

"A wolf with human arms and legs?"

"I would recognize Sky Holder, Wren. This Spirit came to me as a boy. A little boy with glowing yellow eyes."

"A . . . boy." Wren clutched the water bag harder. "Did he have cuts all over him? Was he covered with blood?"

Rumbler jerked around to look at her. "Do you know him? Was he your Spirit Helper, Wren?"

She could see the thoughts building behind his black eyes, like thunderheads in the north fit to blast the world to dust. If the Bloody Boy were Wren's Spirit Helper, and he had deliberately tricked Rumbler so that Jumping Badger could attack and slaughter Paint Rock Village, then perhaps Wren could not be trusted, either.

"I don't have a Spirit Helper, Rumbler," she answered. "I've never even been on a vision quest. My grandmother says I'm too young."

Rumbler inclined his head slightly, gazing at her through one eye. "Then how do you know about the boy?"

"Well." She gestured with the water bag. "He came to me the night before the council where you were condemned. I was down by Pipe Stem Lake, filling water bags, and I heard laughter. I turned and there he was." Remembering sent a shiver up her spine.

"Did he speak?"

"Oh, yes," she said with an exaggerated nod. "But I didn't understand anything he said. He asked me if I knew why ghosts built houses."

"Ghosts don't live in houses, Wren. Not on earth. They live in feathered lodges in the Up-Above-World, but—"

"That's what I told him, but the Bloody Boy told me

they built houses because they were afraid of us. He said the ghosts knew they didn't have enough lightning arrows. Then he told me that our world was about to end, and I had to see the houses for myself—''

"Did he tell you where they were?" Rumbler drew a spiral in the dirt with his mitten.

She shook her head. "No, but he asked me to come with him, and told me he couldn't do it by himself."

"Do what?"

"Warn people." She pulled the laces on the water bag tight and retied it to her belt. "I told him the only place I was going was home. Then he really scared me, Rumbler. He told me he was sorry, but he couldn't stop it now. He said, 'You will come with me. Power has chosen.' "

Rumbler's gaze darted around, touching on rocks and trees, and paw prints. After a short interval, he said, "The ways of Spirits are strange."

"You don't understand it, either?"

"No."

Wren crossed her feet at the ankles and swung them while she thought, wondering about Spirits, and if she was on the journey the Bloody Boy had told her about and just didn't know it. She didn't like that idea.

"Rumbler, I've been thinking about what we'll do when this is all over. How do you feel about maybe becoming Traders? You and me together. We could see strange new lands. I heard a Trader tell once of a western people who build mountains and put their houses on top. And he said that even farther west they make stone houses, one on top of the other, until they have palaces many stories high that climb into the heavens." Wren turned and found Rumbler looking up at her with so much hope and love in his eyes that it almost hurt to look at. "Wouldn't that be fun, Rumbler? We could be Traders."

He smiled. "I would like that, Wren."

She put an arm over his narrow shoulders. "Traders must have powerful Spirit Helpers, though. You already have one, but I'm going to need one, too. Uncle Blue Raven always promised that he would take me on a vision quest. But he never had the time."

"I—I can take you, Wren! I have been many times." Rumbler slid closer to her on the ledge, and put a mitten on her hand. "It's very hard, but I will help you."

She grinned. "Thanks, Rumbler. What's it like having a Spirit Helper? You have had one since your fourth or fifth winter, haven't you?"

Rumbler tipped his head back to look at the billowing Cloud Giants. They tumbled and played as they rushed westward. He kept his eyes on them a long time, and Wren wondered if maybe he wasn't talking to his Helper right now. She squinted at the big gold cloud that hovered above them. The longer Rumbler gazed at it, the more it seemed to glow.

Rumbler said, "Sometimes having a Spirit Helper hurts, Wren. It feels like a stiletto in your heart, twisting. But then there are times when you feel good about it."

Her grin drooped. "Maybe I don't have to have one after all."

Rumbler bit his lip, as if embarrassed. "Some people have pleasing Spirit Helpers, Wren. Their Helpers show them where to gather the best roots, and nuts, or maybe the best places to fish. Maybe you will get one of those."

"Is yours mean because he's so Powerful? Because you are the son of a Forest Spirit?"

Rumbler kicked his feet in time with hers. "I think so."

Wren wiped her sand-coated hand on her torn pant leg. "Have you ever seen him? Your father?"

"Oh, yes," Rumbler said and nodded. "When I was very small he used to come to me at night, to sing me to sleep. His voice sounded like death."

Her scalp stung. *"Death?"*

"Well, yes, I mean, like the sound Grandmother Earth would make if all the trees, and birds, and animals died. If Wind Mother was gone, and the rivers dried up, and people disappeared."

"That sounds like silence to me, Rumbler."

He nodded. "Yes. Loud silence. I used to clamp my hands over my ears when my father sang, so it wouldn't hurt so much."

She frowned at Grandfather Day Maker. As he ascended through the Cloud Giants, bright sunlight flooded the forest. The mist suspended above the pond shredded into long yellow filaments, and began to vanish.

"You know something, Rumbler?"

"What?" He squinted up at her.

"Sometimes I don't understand a word you say."

He gently patted her arm with his mitten. "You just need to get to know me better. You are not as scared of me now, as you were, are you?"

"No. Have you been trying not to be scary?"

"Oh, yes, very hard."

Wren smiled. "I'm not afraid any longer, Rumbler. There are moments when you still worry me . . . but . . . I . . ."

In the rapidly changing light, Wren thought she saw something, down the talus slope to her left—a line of shadows dotted the crumbling rock. She got on her knees, and shielded her eyes. Little piles of stones cast the shadows.

"Rumbler," she said, and pointed. "There's the cougar's trail! Do you see it? The weight of his paws pushed up the stones. The trail is right there. It's been there all along!''

Rumbler lurched to his feet. ''Where? I don't see it.''

''Maybe you're not tall enough. But it's there! Right over there. I promise!''

His white cape swung around him as he scrambled across the treacherous slope looking for the piles of stones. When Rumbler reached the trail, he stood up, shouting, ''Wren! Look! Do you see those big oaks to the north? That's Paint Rock Village!''

Wren followed his mittened hand. Twenty or more ancient oaks formed a half-moon in the forest, their bare branches stretching high above the normal canopy. Against the gleaming dawn sky they resembled blackened skeletal arms, hundreds of them, reaching out, trying to touch . . . something.

Rumbler trotted along the cougar's trail, his moccasins slipping on the talus, calling, ''Come on, Wren!''

# Twenty-Three

Dark blue Cloud Giants gathered overhead, pulling spindly veils of snow behind them. Against the golden sheen of sunrise, the veils shimmered and wavered as though dancing over the hills on their own feet.

Elk Ivory stopped to watch them. The cold morning air carried the earthy fragrances of wet bark and spruce needles. She breathed them in, enjoying the moment's rest. Feet pounded behind her, accompanied by heavy breathing and curses as the remainder of the war party navigated the mud.

Acorn came up beside her, and wiped the sweat from his brow. The ridge of hair down the middle of his shaved skull sparkled in the sunlight. He'd removed his bear-hide cape, rolled it up, and tied it over the top of his pack. Sweat stained the arms and chest of his red shirt.

He panted, "Why are we . . . stopping?"

"I was waiting for you to catch up."

He gave her an incredulous look. Murmurs broke out behind them as warriors came through the mud, stopped, and began asking questions.

"Are the tracks the same?" Acorn asked as he crouched in the mud to examine them.

"Yes," she answered.

Despite the river of meltwater around their feet, the tracks couldn't be mistaken. Three people had walked here last night. Two men and a woman. One of the men was Blue Raven. The size and shape of his feet had been etched on her souls during the days when they had warred together. She would know them anywhere. But she had no idea who the other two people might be. The woman's tracks did not belong to Little Wren, and not a single track had been left by a boy.

"I wonder who they are?" Acorn said as he rose to his feet. "Accomplices? From the Turtle Nation?"

Elk Ivory rubbed her fingers over the smooth wood of her bow, slung over her right shoulder. "I do not want to believe it," she said, "but it is possible."

Acorn propped his hands on his hips and let out a deep breath. "It does seem that things have changed, Elk Ivory. Perhaps Blue Raven *was* carrying the boy all along, heading for a planned meeting where he would deliver the boy to his Turtle relatives.''

"If so, where are they headed now?"

He lifted his hands. "A safe village. Perhaps Sleeping Mist. They hate us. They would certainly harbor a Walks-along traitor.'' Acorn shifted uncomfortably. "It must have occurred to you by now that they may be paying him. I do not know how they might have arranged such a thing, though I have considered that the culprit might be that ugly Trader, Cornhusk, but however they managed it—"

"If they managed it."

"Yes—if," he granted with a wave of his hand. "I imagine they would have offered great wealth to the man who rescued their Powerful False Face Child."

Her gut knotted. If Blue Raven had done these things, she truly did not know him. She gazed at the tracks. He had a distinctive crease in the bottom of his right moccasin; it zigzagged across the middle of his foot.

"You must admit," Acorn said softly, for her ears alone, "it seems that Jumping Badger was right. We have not seen one track that we could definitely say belonged to either a little boy, or a girl."

"All that means is that Blue Raven has not caught up with them yet."

"But he 'caught up' with two other people. He walked into their camp, and sat before their fire. As if he knew them."

Elk Ivory thought about that as she studied the trail. The moccasins they were tracking had churned up the mud all the way down to the meadow in the valley below. Was that smoke? Rising from the edge of the meadow? It might be mist curling up. She kept her eyes on it. "He did not walk into their camp without hesitation, though.

You saw the tracks. He stood behind the boulder for some time before he showed himself.''

"True. So maybe he did not know them, and needed to make sure the people fit the descriptions he'd been given. The result is the same. He met them, joined them, and is traveling deeper into Turtle Nation country with them. It appears that he has—''

Shouts rang out behind them. They both turned in unison and tried to peer through the jostling warriors.

"What is this?" Acorn said. "A runner?''

"Where?''

Elk Ivory stepped closer to him, trying to see over the bobbing heads.

Acorn pointed. "There. Is that Springwater?''

A chill prickled Elk Ivory's spine. "Yes, I think so. But the matrons selected him as war leader for the village while we were gone. What is he doing here?''

"I do not know, but my stomach doesn't like this.''

"Nor does mine. Let us hear his tale.''

Elk Ivory shouldered through the crowd, and Acorn pushed along in her wake.

When they broke through, they saw Springwater talking with Jumping Badger. The tall youth stood bent over, his hands on his knees, trying to catch his breath, but he kept glancing at the crude mask that covered the severed head. Jumping Badger held the staff stiffly at his side, as if it were a badge of his authority. Springwater seemed to sense its malevolence. His soot-smudged face twisted every time he looked at it. Filthy torn clothing hung from Springwater's lean frame. Though he had seen only twenty winters, he resembled an old man this morning. Wrinkles cut lines across his forehead and at the corners of his brown eyes. His long black braid had not been combed out in days. It hung over his shoulder in a tangled mat.

Springwater panted, "Frost-in-the-Willows . . . has been elected as the new . . . head matron. She lived only through the grace of the ancestors. The house fell d-down around her . . . but did not crush her. No one could believe it when she . . . she came crawling out of the rubble."

Jumping Badger spotted Elk Ivory and his eyes glowed with deadly intent. "Tell it again. So everyone can hear."

Springwater nodded, and sucked in a breath. As he straightened to his feet, he called, "I have been running for three days and nights to reach you! I have not slept. I have not eaten. I—I had to find you!"

"What's happened?" Elk Ivory strode closer.

"Our village . . ." Springwater spread his shaking legs and braced his knees. "It has been destroyed. We—"

*"War?"*

"No." He shook his head. "A storm. Wind Mother struck without warning. The forest exploded. Whole trees toppled onto the longhouses. The poles of the palisade were ripped up and flung about like war lances. People running through the plaza were impaled. Others died from smashed skulls, and severed limbs. When the longhouses collapsed, they fell in upon the fire pits. The dry wood and bark burst into flames. The screams . . . the screams were terrible. You cannot imagine. The screams, and roaring flames, and Wind Mother's howling! Those of us who remained unhurt ran into the infernos to pull people out, but half of our relatives died."

Springwater paused to take a breath, and glanced around at his relatives. No one moved, but every face asked the same question.

Springwater made a calming gesture with his hands. "I have brought news of each of your families, truly, but I must sit and eat first. Please. I can barely stand."

"Acorn," Elk Ivory said, "help Springwater, then build a fire, put on some food, and tea. We will resume our search once we know the fates of those we love."

"Yes, I'm going." Acorn hurried to Springwater's side and helped him off the trail toward a fallen log.

Warriors rushed after them, whispering hoarsely.

Jumping Badger turned and his gaze pinned Elk Ivory. "What do you think now, old woman? Hmm? Did I not tell you that the False Face Child was wicked beyond our imaginings? That he would be our deaths?" He lifted the staff with the masked head and thumped it on the ground. There was no hair left to fall out, but hideous green fluid leaked from the punctured brain and oozed down the staff. "Do not forget, it was your former lover who loosed this pestilence on us all." He leaned closer to her and hissed, "When I find him, he will pay with his life."

He started to turn and she said, "I do not think that is wise."

Jumping Badger stiffened. "Your thoughts do not concern me!"

"If Blue Raven's mother is now head matron, she may not wish you to kill her only son. Or do you value your own life so little?"

Jumping Badger's jaw went hard. Morning sunlight slanted through the trees and streaked his handsome face and cape. "My duty—"

"Your duty, War Leader, is to follow orders. And *I* will make certain you do. Besides"—she tilted her head toward Springwater—"I suspect that the matron's messenger carries new orders for us. Shouldn't you ask? Perhaps we have been ordered home. If things are as bad as Springwater says, then our village has never been more vulnerable than it is now. Our enemies may be mounting war parties. Anyone who ever wished to attack us must know that now is the time."

Elk Ivory turned and headed for the fallen log where Springwater sat surrounded by murmuring warriors.

Jumping Badger shoved past her, almost knocking Elk Ivory off her feet, and strode ahead into the warriors' circle like an avenging god. He halted before the exhausted Springwater, and propped his staff in front of him.

Springwater looked up, but his eyes only grazed Jumping Badger before settling on the crow's-face mask that covered Lamedeer's rotting head. The crudely carved beak jutted out at an odd angle. Through the holes sunken yellow eyes looked back. Springwater's nostrils flared at the stench, and he sat back on his log, trying to get as far away as possible without rising and leaving. "Did you have a question, War Leader?"

"Yes. Before you begin the tales of families," Jumping Badger said in a loud voice, and lifted a hand to get everyone's attention. Acorn, who stood twenty hands away, near the fire pit, straightened. "Tell us the wishes of Matron Frost-in-the-Willows. Has she ordered us home?"

Springwater shook his head. "No. Oh, no, War Leader, she said you must continue your pursuit. She wishes you to find Blue Raven, Little Wren, and the False Face Child, no matter the cost. She fears that if the boy lives our clan may be completely destroyed."

Jumping Badger pushed his beaver-hide cape aside, and placed a hand on his hip. "And what did she say we should do when we find the traitors?"

Springwater blinked, as if sensing some undercurrent he didn't understand. He glanced at Elk Ivory and she nodded to him, telling him it was all right to say it straightly.

Springwater answered, "She said that she wishes the boy dead, and that you, War Leader, should use your own best judgment as to the fates of the other two.''

A smile twisted Jumping Badger's lips. ''Already our new head matron shows wisdom.''

Springwater hastily added, ''Though, of course, she said she wishes you to bring them home to face their clan, if possible.''

''Of course, if possible, but—''

Elk Ivory interrupted, ''I'm sure Matron Frost-in-the-Willows was distraught, and meant to repeat Starflower's orders that we *must* bring Blue Raven and Little Wren home alive. Grief confuses people. Matron Frost-in-the-Willows surely did not intend to give us permission to kill her only son and granddaughter. Doesn't that make sense, Springwater?''

The tall youth frowned. ''Well, yes, but I repeated her words exactly, Elk Ivory, as was my duty. Beyond that, I cannot say what she might have meant.''

''It is impudent to interpret orders, old woman,'' Jumping Badger said. ''I am sure that after the destruction of our village the new head matron realized what danger we might be facing, and meant exactly what she said.''

Elk Ivory glanced at Acorn, who stood by the fire pit with his fireboard and drill in hand. Flames had just begun to crackle through the tinder, throwing a flickering light over his face and burly shoulders. Acorn shook his head, and turned away.

Elk Ivory lowered her eyes.

*Yes, you are right, my friend. We cannot move yet. The other warriors would not support us yet. But soon.*

''What about my wife?'' young Soaring Falcon called, unable to wait any longer. ''Is she alive? And my two children?''

Springwater nodded, and held up a hand. ''Yes. Yes, your family is safe. They were down fishing at Pipe Stem

Lake when the wind struck. They huddled behind—"

"And what of my family—"

"No, I wish to be next! What of my mother and father, are they—"

"Please!" Jumping Badger shouted. "One at a time! Cottonwood, you first."

Elk Ivory turned and walked away. She had no husband or children. Her parents had died many winters before. The fates of her cousins and aunts and uncles could wait.

She tramped down the trail toward the meadow where, earlier, she thought she'd seen a wisp of smoke.

A shrill cry rang out behind her, then the sound of a man sobbing. She did not turn. Tonight, and for many days and nights to come, she would be listening to the stories, and comforting the grieving.

But now she needed to scout what appeared more and more to be a camp.

Elk Ivory stepped into the grassy meadow and walked directly to the smoldering fire pit.

Two coals remained in the bed of white ash, glowing red when the wind gusted. The bones of a rabbit lay on the hearthstones.

The man and woman had slept together, their bodies pressing down the grass in distinctive patterns. Blue Raven had slept fifty hands away, his back to a large boulder, perhaps as a shield from the wind, or because he wished to be out of the firelight in case his pursuers burst into the camp in the middle of the night. Or because he didn't fully trust his new partners.

She lifted her eyes and studied the tracks that cut a swath across the grass to the north.

"Springwater has just given you another two or three hands of time, my old friend," she murmured. "Use them wisely."

# Twenty-Four

Rumbler stumbled down the muddy slope in front of Wren, running home as fast as his short legs would carry him. He'd been falling a lot, and his moccasins and the lower half of his white fur cape bore a thick coating of mud. Old leaves stuck in his short black hair.

Wren followed more slowly, her hand on her bow. She'd thrown her cape back over her shoulders to expose her quiver, and the cool afternoon breeze flapped her long hair. Mud crusted her pants, and speckled her knee-length shirt. The white spirals decorating the blue fabric looked dingy from the long days on the trail.

As they neared Paint Rock Village, the acrid scents of smoke and decay grew stronger.

They had seen no signs that anyone had traveled this trail before them, but Wren kept looking, expecting to see eyes peering at her from behind brush. Whether they would be ghostly eyes, or the eyes of living, breathing warriors, she did not know, but she and Rumbler had been very lucky so far, and she feared it couldn't last.

She scanned the forest. Ancient sycamores lined the way. Their branches laced together over her head, filtering the wan sunlight, and throwing a golden patchwork over the slope. Squirrels leaped through the trees, chattering and barking.

When Wren noticed that Rumbler had vanished, she hurried after him, slogging through the sucking mud. At the bottom of the slope, she gasped, and suddenly back-pedaled, her legs trying to run despite what her eyes told her.

"He's d-dead. He's dead!" Her mouth had to say it twice, before her eyes believed it.

She slipped and fell into the muddy trail, staring wide-eyed at the man slumped against the sycamore trunk. A Walksalong arrow pierced his chest, pinioning him to the tree, and an ax had bashed a gaping hole in his skull. Most of the flesh had been pecked from his head, and chewed from his arms and legs. His belly had been ripped out.

From her right, Rumbler's soft voice said, "His name was Calling Hawk."

Their gazes held, hers wide with fear, his anguished.

"He was my mother's uncle's son." Rumbler turned and walked away.

Wren got to her feet and shook off some of the clinging mud, then followed Rumbler into the ruins of what had once been Paint Rock Village. A large flock of crows burst into flight, cawing as they circled over the trees.

The destroyed village stunned her.

At the edge of the huge oaks to her left, eight piles of charred rubble marked the locations of lodges. Burned bodies lay rigid in the middle of each, their arms and legs twisted at impossible angles, mouths gaping in silent cries.

Sacred masks dotted the plaza, as if they'd been carried out by fleeing people, and dropped when the people fell. Red-Dew-Eagle rested twenty hands away, his twisted face toward her, his long beak and shell eyes coated with dirt. His glare built a fire in Wren's belly.

She turned away.

Bodies lay everywhere. The stories Jumping Badger and his warriors had told about their great victory suddenly came into focus. All of the women and girls lay on their backs, their distended legs spread. The animals had torn their bloated stomachs out, and chewed most of the flesh from their bones. To her right, murdered babies sprawled, some on their faces, others on their backs—as if the wolves had dragged them around like toys.

Wren's heart slammed a dull staccato against her ribs.

The men and boys had been mutilated, their genitals cut off, and stuffed in their mouths. She could see them locked behind half-open teeth. The bodies must have gone rigid before the animals found them, and the wolves hadn't been able to chew off the lower jaw yet.

Rumbler started walking, his steps painfully slow and quiet.

Wren forced her legs to follow.

"This was Red Pipe," he whispered and pointed to the old man who lay facedown in the dirt. A beautiful buffalo cape with blue and yellow porcupine quills sewn around the collar covered his back. "He was our clan patron."

Rumbler took three more steps. After a deep breath, he pointed to a little girl, and said, "This is my cousin Lynx. Remember? I told you about her?" His voice went hoarse, and tears filled his eyes. "The story about the duck and the . . . the corn gruel?"

"I remember."

Wolf tracks covered the ground around the girl's gnawed body.

Wren lifted her eyes to the forest. Dark forms moved through the shadows. Their arrival must have interrupted the wolves' feast, but the pack would return as soon as darkness fell—and Rumbler and Wren had better be gone, or they might be eaten, too. A few wolves could be bluffed, even by children, but a large pack would not easily yield such a wealth of meat.

"That was my mother's lodge." Rumbler lifted his chin toward one of the charred rubble piles across from the main plaza fire. In a voice almost too low to hear, he asked, "Do you see her, Wren?"

Wren's gaze darted over the chaos of blackened poles, and bark walls. "No. I don't see anyone in the house, Rumbler. You didn't see her in the plaza?"

He shook his head.

"Could she have been in one of the other houses?"

A tiny flicker of hope had entered his eyes, and she could see it building to a blaze of certainty. "When your people attacked, we were both in our house. That is the last place I saw her. If she isn't there, and she isn't—"

"What about when your eyes were flying, Rumbler? After Mossybill and Skullcap captured you. Did you see your mother then?"

He wet his lips. "No. I didn't see her in the village at all. Wren? Do you think . . . maybe . . . ?"

She walked forward and put a hand on his back. "Maybe, but I think we should keep looking for a while. Do you remember what she was wearing? That way I could help you look."

Rumbler gestured awkwardly with his mittens. "The only thing that wouldn't—wouldn't have been eaten or burned, was a silver gorget, about this big." He drew a circle in the middle of his mitten to indicate the gorget was about as big as his palm. "An upside-down tree is etched into the silver."

"And she has a green tree tattooed on her forehead, isn't that right?"

He nodded, and whispered, "Thank you, Wren. For helping me."

"Why don't you go that way, toward the lodges, and I'll search the far side of the plaza."

"All right."

Rumbler walked for the remains of his own lodge, and began searching the wreckage. Just before Wren turned away, she saw him pick up something, clutch it to his chest, and then tuck it into his cape pocket.

On the opposite side of the plaza bodies scattered the outskirts of the village—mostly those of children. Arrows stuck out of their backs. Two little boys had died with their arms around each other, as though they'd had just enough time to see that the other lay close, and reached out. Not even the wolves had been able to tear them apart.

Sickness welled in her throat.

Jumping Badger had said . . . he'd said that they had struck Briar's house first, and stolen Rumbler. Why did they have to keep killing? Why shoot little children who were running away? What harm could the children have done?

A breath of wind blew through the valley and stirred a patch of hair on one of the babies' heads. Wren could suddenly feel it between her fingers, soft and fine—

Her stomach rose into her throat; she hit the ground on her knees, retching violently. Her bow landed five hands away. Her eyes blurred as another spasm shook her. The smell of rotting bodies and burned lodges seemed to grow more powerful with every breath she took. She retched until her belly ached and her nose ran.

Then she sat up.

Rage, like a poison, seeped through her body. It swelled her head and chest, made her skin tingle—and bestowed a bizarre clarity on her thoughts. The faces of every warrior who had been here flashed across her souls, and she hated each one. Hated them with a passion she would never have imagined she could feel. If they had stood before her now, she would have gladly killed them.

*But they are my relatives. How can I wish them dead?*

*Elk Ivory taught me how to make arrow points. Black-tailed Wolf taught Skybow how to cast a lance. Think, Wren! They could not have done this. Elk Ivory would never shoot a child of four winters in the back. Black-tailed Wolf would never cut open a woman's womb and bash the baby's brains out. It must have been . . . a few warriors. Jumping Badger's chosen. They must have done this.*

Wren nodded to herself, and groped for her bow.

As Grandfather Day Maker dipped toward the western horizon, eerie shadows were born among the ruins. Charred twisted arms that earlier had reached for nothing suddenly stretched toward Wren, dozens of them, edging closer and closer. Her fingers tightened on her bow. Did the souls that lurked near those grotesque bodies know she belonged to the Walksalong Clan? Could they smell it in her blood?

A small terrible cry pierced the quiet.

Wren spun around, calling, "Rumbler?"

He had climbed into the forest behind the burned lodges, and lay curled on his side near a pile of scorched debris.

*"Rumbler?"*

She ran across the plaza, veering around the gnawed corpses, and climbed the hillside to him.

As soon as she knelt, she could see that it wasn't a pile of debris, but a body. The burning roof must have collapsed on top of her. Melted hair matted the right side of her head, but wolves had ripped away the scalp on the left side, revealing the skull. Wren could see the places she'd been struck in the head with a war club. Dents and cracks covered the bone.

Rumbler touched the silver gorget at her neck, then drew his hand back, shucked off his mitten, and tucked his one good finger in his mouth.

Wren sank to the ground behind him.

Blessed gods, Briar-of-the-Lake had been alive after the battle. Alive and determined to get away. Fragments of burned clothing marked her path from the lodge to the hillside. It didn't seem possible. In her condition, to crawl out from under a burning heap, and drag herself this far up the hill . . .

"She told me s-she would come for me," Rumbler said. "That was the last thing she said."

Wren braced her bow over her knees. "She tried, Rumbler. She tried very hard."

The afternoon air had gone still. A whisper of wind, the distant chirp of a squirrel, roared in her ears.

Silent tears shook Rumbler.

Wren put a hand on his arm and squeezed. Briar could be here, right this instant, screaming at Rumbler, trying to hold him and speak with him, and he couldn't hear her.

For a time, Wren studied the wolves prowling the forest. Now and then she caught the glint of a yellow eye, or a lolling tongue. She thought she could count five.

"Someday, Rumbler, when we are great Traders, I promise you that we will hire the most Powerful shaman in the world to find her soul and carry it to the Up-Above-World. She won't have to stay here forever."

Rumbler rolled over, his round face wet with tears, and reached for Wren. She set her bow aside, stretched out beside him in the old leaves, and hugged him close while he cried.

Wren had never seen her mother's body. As she gazed upon the burned, chewed corpse, she did not know which was kinder, seeing and knowing, or not seeing and suffering the terrible hope that someone you loved still lived.

A big black wolf came to the edge of the trees, no

more than fifty hands away, and lifted its muzzle to sniff the air. Baring its teeth, it took a step down the hill, and let out a low growl.

Wren whispered, "We have to go, Rumbler. We have to go now."

As Grandmother Moon rose through the branches, a seashell opalescence spread across the deep blue sky, and flooded the forest, lighting the path at Dust Moon's feet. She heaved a sigh of relief. She could still see the children's footprints descending the trail toward Paint Rock Village.

They had come down several hands of time ago, before the trail froze, their feet slipping and sliding in the mud.

Dust Moon sighed. She had desperately wanted to be here when Rumbler arrived, to cushion the blow of seeing the devastation and the faces of so many dead relatives. The failure hurt.

She trotted to catch up with Sparrow.

"Well, they beat us here," she said.

Sparrow's bushy brows lowered. In the moonglow his long white hair blazed. "They had a day's head start on us, Dust. Let's just hope that they haven't been here and gone."

"Gone?" she said, surprised. "Where would they go?"

"I haven't the slightest idea. But we need to find them tonight."

Dust Moon frowned. The Headman strode down the trail in front of them, his graying black hair and the elk hide over his broad shoulders shimmering.

Dust quietly asked, "Why? Did he say something?"

''No. But he has to make his move soon. With or without us, he can find the children now. Even if they didn't camp near Paint Rock, they're leaving a clear trail, and they can't be more than three or four hands of time ahead of us. Maybe less, because Rumbler certainly wandered the ruins for a while.''

Dust Moon looked at Blue Raven and her eyes narrowed. The stench of battle and death rode the night wind, growing stronger as they neared Paint Rock Village. It seemed to be drawing him down the hill. His pace had picked up to a near run.

''What do you recommend we do to protect ourselves?'' she asked.

''I recommend that we keep a close watch on him.''

''What else can we do that we haven't been doing? I sleep half the night, you sleep the other half. We're both exhausted. Shall we tie him up?''

Giant sycamores arched over the trail above them, their branches rustling and creaking with the wind. In the barred and broken moonlight, they appeared to converse with each other, swaying close, then pulling back, making extravagant gestures with their leafless arms.

''I don't think Blue Raven would allow it, Dust. After all, he's being hunted by his own people.''

Dust Moon stumbled in a deep frozen track. Sparrow grabbed her arm to keep her from falling, and she staggered against him. They stood there in the trail, looking into each other's moon-silvered eyes, and Dust could feel his chest rising and falling, and smell the sweat and wood smoke that clung to his elk-hide coat. The familiarity had a curious effect on her, on the one hand salving her wounded heart, on the other making her long to run away. The longer she stood there, pressed against him, the more strength flowed into her veins. His touch had always done that to her. Steadied. Comforted. It hurt to be reminded.

"Are you all right?" he asked.

"Yes." Dust pulled away. "I just needed a short rest."

"It's no wonder. We pushed hard today. Your stamina on this journey has surprised me, Dust."

To avoid the softness in his eyes, she looked down the trail. "So much for our vigilance. Blue Raven is gone."

"He's in the village. I saw him just a few moments ago." He pointed. "Through the gap between those oaks."

"I haven't heard any voices. Do you think that means—"

"The children aren't there. Probably."

Her heart sank.

Sparrow turned and continued on down the trail. Dust trotted along behind him, trying to dodge the holes and roots in the trail.

When they walked out into the plaza, Sparrow stopped dead.

Dust put a hand to her mouth.

Moonlight gleamed from over a dozen wolves, feeding upon the bodies. They snarled and barked as the three humans appeared. Several of the wolves tried to eat faster, ripping bones from the chewed bodies, before loping away. They stood at the edge of the forest with their ears up, waiting to see what happened next.

Blue Raven drew his bow, and ran into the midst of the plaza, shouting, "Go on! Get out of here!"

The wolves scattered into the shadows, but their eyes shone like daggers of flame.

Blue Raven walked the line of burned lodges, his bow clutched in his hands.

Dust Moon called, "Rumbler? Rumbler, are you here?"

"No," Blue Raven answered. "But they were. Their tracks lead up the hill behind this burned lodge, then they come down and head almost due east, toward the shore of Leafing Lake." He pointed with his bow.

Dust hurried past Sparrow and Blue Raven, veered around the charred remains of the lodge, and climbed the hill to see what the children had found. Moonlight outlined the places where they had lain in the mud, and threw a dusty radiance over the—the corpse.

The face had been burned beyond recognition, the hair melted, or torn from the battered skull. The clothing . . .

From the depths of her memory, Cornhusk's voice hissed:

*She begged him not to hurt the False Face Child. Offered him anything if he would just let the boy live. But Jumping Badger tore the boy from her arms, threw the child like a sack of nuts to his warriors, and ordered them out of the house. Then Jumping Badger forced Briar down. He raped her while the whole of Paint Rock Village was burning around them! Can you believe that? Jumping Badger astounds even me! Then he clubbed her to death.*

Dust reached for the silver gorget and tipped it to the light. The upside-down tree flashed.

Her heart thundered as images of Briar danced through her souls . . . Briar as a little girl curled in Dust's lap, laughing . . . Briar in agony as she gave birth to Rumbler . . . Briar when she had lived with them, working, talking, asking Dust's advice about Rumbler's upbringing . . . Briar pleading with Dust to take Sparrow back, to forgive him, *He loves you so much.*

For an instant she could not move.

Then, in a sudden wash of realization, her hand closed around the pendant, and a sob rose in her throat.

Without a word, Sparrow knelt beside Dust and gathered her into his arms.

"Oh, Sparrow, it's—"

"I know," he whispered, and stroked her hair. "I'm sorry, Dust."

She clung to him, shaking, and her eyes traced the path Briar had taken from the burning lodge. "She must have been on fire when she—"

"It doesn't matter now, Dust," he murmured in her ear, and kissed her hair. "What you and I must do is to help her son. That's what she would wish. Rumbler is not here. We must find him."

Dust tightened her arms around his waist, holding him until she could say, "Help me bury her?"

"Of course."

He slipped out of his pack and drew out two bowls, handing one to Dust.

It didn't take long. The mud on the hillside, filled with rocks, went down six hands before it turned to frozen dirt. They scooped out a grave large enough for her body, then gently tugged Briar into the hole.

The charred corpse rested on its back, staring up at them pleadingly, the fingers out as if reaching.

"Sparrow?" Dust said. "You know the sacred Songs, can you—"

"Yes," he answered, and tenderly touched her moist cheek.

He rose to his feet and lifted his arms to the Spirits who lived in the Up-Above-World. His deep voice rang through the forest:

> *Sky Holder, great Sky Holder, come walking,*
> *Come walking,*
> *Lift Briar's soul in the great Dance,*

*Blow ashes on her body,*
*Sky Holder, come walking,*
   *Come walking,*
*Teach her how to fly,*
   *Sky Holder, come walking from the sky.*
*Teach her how to fly away with you.*

Sparrow knelt beside Dust, and together they scooped the mud and rocks back over Briar.

When they'd finished Dust wiped her face with her sleeve. "Thank you, Sparrow. I—I'm ready to go now. If we—"

"Forgive me," Blue Raven interrupted, "but you don't mean you wish to travel at night?"

"Yes, she does," Sparrow said and helped Dust Moon to her feet. He kept his arm around her waist, as much for comfort, she knew, as to support her. "With this moonlight, every acorn casts a shadow. If we're careful, we should be able to track them."

Dust separated herself from Sparrow and started following the children's trail down the hill and across the plaza to the east.

Sparrow called, "Dust, wait." Then he turned to Blue Raven. "Are you coming?"

Blue Raven heaved a tired sigh, and threw up his hands. "Of course I am." He plodded forward, adding, "I'm sure you wish me to take the lead so you can watch me, correct?"

"Yes," Sparrow replied.

Blue Raven strode past Dust and down the hill. Here, at the edge of the plaza, and across the meadow beyond, the trail could not be mistaken. It cut a black swath through the moonlit dirt and grass.

Sparrow grasped Dust's arm, pulling her close, whispering, "Keep your bow at hand. Now, in the darkness, is the best time to stumble, spin around unsteadily, and plunge your stiletto into someone's belly. I plan on being prepared, but I may not have time to respond. You must. I want you to stay a good four paces behind me.''

She pulled an arrow from her quiver, nocked it, and held the bow aimed at the ground. ''Go on. I'll be ready. Just remember to drop when I say drop.''

He grinned and the moonlight gleamed over his teeth and hooked nose. ''Like one of the meteorite people. Don't worry, I—''

*''Look!''* Blue Raven called.

Dust and Sparrow turned. In the moonlight, they saw Blue Raven's arm shoot out.

On the hillside, perhaps a hand of time away, a tiny orange gleam lit the darkness.

Elk Ivory lifted a hand, and the war party halted behind her. From this hilltop she could see the entire valley below. Moonlight gleamed over the surrounding hills, and frosted the bare tree limbs.

Hushed murmuring broke out behind her.

She clenched a fist for silence.

The resinous smells of tree sap and decaying bark floated on the cold night wind.

Jumping Badger pushed up beside her, his grisly staff in his right hand. The crow's-head mask glowed eerily in the pewter light. ''What is it, old woman? Why did you stop when we are so close?''

She looked at him, at his long black braid, and the scar across his throat. His beaver-hide coat bore shreds of old leaves and pine needles.

''I thought I heard a shout.''

Jumping Badger's eyes slitted. "A man's shout? A child's? A woman's?"

She shook her head. "I'm not sure. I think it was a man's voice."

"Your former lover?"

"I couldn't tell whose voice it was, War Leader. I am not even certain it was a human shout . . . but I thought it was."

"Then we must be cautious. We do not wish to frighten our prey."

He turned to the war party and softly ordered, "Most of you have been here before. Fan out. Surround the village just as we did before. It should take two or three hands of time to work the surround, which means it will be dark when we close in. Do not let your arrows fly until you hear my call—whistled like a nighthawk— *peent, peent.* You may kill the evil False Face Child on sight, but save the others for me."

Jumping Badger trotted ahead. The warriors followed him down the hill. When he gestured half of the war party circled around the north, while the other half took the southern trail with Jumping Badger.

Acorn stopped beside Elk Ivory. "Personally, I hope we find the village empty so we can camp and eat. I'm starving. Which trail are you taking?"

She massaged her forehead a moment. "Do you truly believe that any living human being would make camp in a destroyed village?"

"You mean you don't think Blue Raven would."

"Would you?"

He considered the question. "No. At least not a village destroyed by my people. I'd be afraid the ghosts would rise up from the corpses and tear my souls from my body."

"So would I."

Acorn scratched his neck. "So. Where would you make camp?"

Elk Ivory scanned the shimmering grayness of hill and valley. To the north, a dark shroud of clouds billowed into the star-strewn sky, and she could smell snow in the wind. By morning, the land would be a trackless expanse of pure white. "You have hunted elk, Acorn. Where do they bed down?"

He shrugged. "When I have seen them, which isn't often, it is always high on the hillside. They choose a point overlooking the main trails where they can keep watch. They seem to know when they're being hunted."

"Most intelligent animals sense the hunter's presence." She propped her hands on her hips. Patches of snow lingered on the northern slopes. They blazed like white fire tonight. "I am not going to join the surround. I think I will scout the hilltops."

Acorn briskly ruffled the ridge of hair on his head, a sign of irritation. "Jumping Badger will accuse you of disobeying his orders. When we get home, the matrons—"

"*If* we get home, I will worry about it then." She gestured toward the easternmost hilltop. "In the meantime, I will be there. Searching."

"Very well," he said through a sigh. "When the excitement is over around the village, I will come looking for you."

"Don't bother," she answered. "I will find you." And she stepped off the well-worn trail into the grass, heading across the moonlit meadow.

# Twenty-Five

Wren finished washing their bowls out with snow, and headed back for the shelter. They'd made it by leaning fallen saplings around a large boulder. The front of the boulder had been scooped out by winters of rain and wind, leaving a lip of overhanging stone on top. It made for a perfect campsite. They had laid poles on three sides of the boulder, which meant they had to move some to the side when they wanted to come in or go out. Eight hands high, the shelter stretched fifteen hands long and about eight wide. An adult would have a hard time fitting in, but it had turned out to be perfect for two children.

She clutched the clean dishes to the front of her dark blue shirt, moved the shelter poles aside, and crawled in. The firelit warmth struck her painfully. Rumbler sat in the middle of the shelter before the low flames, his back against the boulder. He looked sad and lost. Wren moved the poles back into place, sealing the warmth in.

Firelight flickered over Rumbler's short black hair, and downcast face. Once they'd built up the flames, the shelter had warmed quickly. Rumbler's fox-fur cape and his mittens rested in the corner to his left. The pale blue shirt he wore, decorated with whelk and columella shell beads, looked fresh down to his hips, but then it bore a coating of dried mud.

Wren stowed the clean dishes in her pack and slumped

against the boulder beside him. He hadn't said a word through supper.

"Rumbler? Let me check your hands. The spruce-needle tea is steaming. I think we should clean them."

Pus had soaked two of the black strips of cloth that wrapped his fingers, and it worried her. She'd been washing out the cloths in spruce-needle tea every night and drying them before the fire so they would be fresh in the morning, but the Shadow Spirits had entered the wounded fingers anyway.

Rumbler studied the bandages, then held them out to her.

Wren reached for her folded deer-hide cape and gently laid his hands on top of it. "This won't take long, Rumbler, then you can go to sleep. I know you must be very tired. After I found out . . . I—I slept all the time."

He concentrated on his hands. "Mossybill . . . he ruined them. Just like Marmot's hands. They'll never work right again."

"I know, Rumbler." She carefully unwrapped the fingers, and laid the strips of cloth aside. "But at least they look better." The cauterized flesh had shrunken around the protruding bones and, in most cases, healed well. But the stubs of his two little fingers remained red and swollen.

When Wren lifted the right little finger to get a better look at it, Rumbler flinched.

"I'm sorry," she said, and turned it gently. "The Shadow Spirits have made a whole village in here, Rumbler. I wish I had listened more carefully when old Bogbean gave her Teachings on Healing plants, then I would know what to—"

"Licorice," Rumbler whispered.

"What?"

He looked up, and she could see the hollow ache that

sparkled in his eyes. "The leaves or ground roots of the licorice plant will kill Shadow Spirits."

Wren cocked her head. "Do you have any? In your Power bag, maybe?"

Rumbler shook his head. "No, I just carry the Great Three Spirits."

Wren sat back and eased her finger down on top of her folded cape. "I've never heard of them. What are they?"

Puzzled reluctance crossed his round face. "I'm not supposed to say," he murmured. "Among my people only the chosen are taught about the Great Three."

"Like in a Healing Society? Do you have to go through a ritual before you can learn about them?"

Rumbler nodded. "Yes, and it's very scary." He lifted his hands and scrunched them so they resembled talons, then made a hideous face. "Monsters come from the underworlds and drag you down into the darkness at the center of Grandmother Earth's belly. If you don't get eaten by the strange creatures that live there, then you get to learn about plant Spirits."

Sparks popped in the fire, and whirled upward toward the smoke hole. Wren said, "My grandfather used to see monsters in the underworld. What sorts of monsters did you see? Can you tell me, or is that secret, too?"

"I can tell you. We talk about Spirit journeys all the time," he said in a low voice, "so people can understand their strange ways better."

Wren leaned back against the boulder and crossed her legs at the ankles. "My grandfather once saw gigantic bats, the size of bears, in the underworld. He said they swooped down on galloping buffalo and sucked blood from their necks. A big flock of those bats chased him from the underworld, diving and squealing at him the whole way. I heard that story for the first time in my third winter, and it scared the liver out of me. That night,

I pulled my blanket around my neck so tightly I almost suffocated. Did you ever see those bats?''

''No,'' Rumbler said with wide eyes. ''But I've seen snakes with wings, and trees with human legs. Everything down there is either trying to trample you or bite you. The worst monsters are all teeth. They slide around on their chins with their fangs bared.'' He demonstrated, thrusting his jaw forward and gnashing his teeth.

Wren lowered her brows. ''I always thought I might want to be a Healer, but maybe not.''

Rumbler looked at his hands, then at her. ''You would be a great Healer, Wren. Look what you did for my fingers. Most of them are almost well.''

She smiled shyly at the praise. ''I've always liked Healing people. That's why I would like to know what the Great Three are, in case I need them to save someone's life in the future. But I don't want to go against your society's Teachings. That wouldn't be right.''

''I'll tell you,'' Rumbler said softly, and lowered his gaze to his hands. ''Because you want to be a Healer. And—and because I want to tell you.''

Wren could see in his face that he thought it might be a small way of repaying her for taking care of him. His smile brushed her souls like pure white feathers. ''I won't tell anyone, Rumbler. I promise.''

He nodded, and took a breath. ''The Great Three are papaw seeds, yew needles, and the leaves of mountain laurel.''

''What do the Spirits cure?''

Rumbler slid closer to her, and the wavering firelight threw his shadow over the boulder like a prancing Earth Spirit. ''These are dangerous Spirits, Wren. If you don't treat them with respect, they will kill you.''

''I promise not to touch them, Rumbler. I just want to know what they do.''

Rumbler wet his chapped lips, and whispered, "You can touch them if you want to. I know you wouldn't use the plants for bad things, Wren." After a brief hesitation, he continued. "You already know about the Papaw Spirit, that the seeds ease pain. But the leaves are also good in poultices. You can apply the poultice to an abscess and it will start going down immediately." His gaze darted around the firelit shelter while he thought. "The Yew Spirit cures fevers, and pain in the joints. It also helps to expel afterbirth. The last is the Mountain Laurel Spirit. She is also the most Powerful of all, Wren. I knew a man once who was out gathering the leaves and accidentally got some of the honey from the flowers on his fingers. He must have touched his mouth before he washed his hands. He made it back to the village, but he died horribly."

The serious look on Rumbler's face fascinated Wren. At times like this he stirred a sensation of awe in her chest—and a little fear. The deep dark wells of his eyes had gone black and shiny.

Wren wondered if maybe Mossybill and Skullcap had met the Mountain Laurel Spirit. She said, "Why would you carry a plant like that, Rumbler?"

"Because mountain laurel cures as well as kills. Tiny amounts dissolved in water will ease heart pain, and jaundice. If you mix the leaves with a lot of water to make a wash, it will kill lice and ticks. But if you ever touch the mountain laurel, Wren, you have to wash your hands quickly. The tiniest bit rubbed in your eyes, or mouth, will make you very sick."

Wren dipped a cup of spruce tea from the pot at the edge of the fire, and set it on the floor. As she swished one of the soiled black strips into the steaming liquid, she said, "If it can kill lice, maybe the same kind of wash would also kill Shadow Spirits. I don't mean that

I wish to try it on your fingers, but sometime I would like to see if it works.'' At the look of fear on his face, she added, ''Don't worry, I'll try it on me first.''

His fear grew to horror. He murmured, ''But . . . you are all I have.''

Wren smiled sadly as she squeezed out the cloth. ''Yes, we're both alone now, aren't we? Our families—''

''We have each other.''

Wren nodded. ''Yes, we do. Thank the Spirits for that.'' She reached for his hand. As she washed around the swollen little finger, she said, ''I've never had a friend like you, Rumbler. I mean a real friend. Other than Trickster. The children in my village didn't like me very much.''

''Why?''

Wren lightly pressed on the flesh around the bone, and pus oozed out. She cleaned it away, rinsed the cloth again, and continued with her poking and prodding. Rumbler squinted against the pain.

''I don't know,'' she answered. ''Dark Wind and Vine, two girls my age, said my mother's death had stunted my growth, and that I didn't know how to act like a girl.'' Strange that those words still hurt. She could feel them like daggers in her stomach. ''They said that's why no one liked me.''

Wren dipped her cloth again and wrung it out, wondering what Dark Wind and Vine would be doing tonight. Sitting around the supper fire with their families, laughing, and teasing each other? Maybe speculating on what had happened to Wren and the False Face Child. She tried to shove the images away before they took hold, but they crept inside her on spider feet. She saw her grandmother smile, and heard old Bogbean chuckle, and every thread in her souls longed to be there with them.

"I think you act like a girl," Rumbler said. "Except a lot braver. Braver than most boys, too."

Wren smiled. "I'm brave, but you're braver than me, Rumbler. I don't think I could have let somebody cut off my fingers."

He brought his newly cleaned little finger close and grimaced at it, while Wren worked on the other little finger. "I knew you wouldn't hurt me, Wren."

"Then you had more faith in me than I did, Rumbler. I wasn't sure I—"

"You saved my life. You gave me your food, and your cape and—and this beautiful shirt." He touched the pale blue sleeve, adding, "You couldn't hurt anything, Wren. Not on purpose."

Wren pretended to concentrate on draining the Shadow Spirits from his finger. That way she wouldn't have to admit to wanting to break Dark Wind's nose, or tell him about the time she'd knocked out Leaping Elk's front teeth. He'd deserved it, the little bully. He'd been tormenting Trickster, stabbing at him with a sharp stick. At Trickster's yelp, Wren had run into the plaza to find Trickster's front shoulder bleeding.

Wren looked at the knuckles of her right hand. It had taken almost a moon for them to heal. Which was half the time it had taken Leaping Elk to grow new teeth.

She dipped her cloth once more, wrung it out, and spread it over the hearthstones to dry. As warmth seeped into the cloth, the tangy fragrance of spruce needles filled the shelter.

"Why don't you roll up in the fox-fur cape and try to sleep, Rumbler. I'll finish putting away the food bags."

Rumbler yawned, and reached for the white cape. As he slipped it over his head, he said, "Wren? I—I've been thinking about something."

"What, Rumbler?" She got on her knees, reached for

the blue food bag, and tucked it into her pack.

"Do you remember me talking about my father?"

"Yes."

"I've been thinking that maybe we should go and try to find him."

Wren had just picked up a yellow bag. Instead of putting it in her pack, she lowered it to her lap, and turned to peer at Rumbler.

He gazed at her from beneath long lashes, his lower lip clamped between his teeth, as though afraid of what she might answer.

Calmly, Wren said, "Do you know where he lives?"

"I think so. Once, when I was very little, I heard my mother whispering to my grandmother about it. She said that after my father discovered she was heavy with child, he decided to go far away, to the Picture Rocks in the north."

Wren sank to the floor. "Aren't the Picture Rocks the place where all the Faces of the Forest gather for grisly ceremonials? They eat baby's hearts, and decorate themselves with human bones?"

Rumbler nodded. "Yes. But they won't be doing those things now, Wren. They hold their ceremonials in the spring and autumn."

She blinked. "They do?"

He nodded.

"Rumbler, I didn't think anybody knew when they held their ceremonials."

"The Faces don't want people disturbing their rituals. That's why they keep them secret. But some people know about them."

"Rumbler, I—"

"I won't let them eat you, Wren. They know me. They'll listen to me."

She tucked the yellow bag into her pack, and tried to

force nonchalance into her voice. "I'll go with you wherever you want me to, Rumbler, but we should think more about this. Tomorrow, when we're rested, we'll—"

*"Wren? Little Wren?"*

The voice froze her blood.

Rumbler whirled to his left, peering breathlessly at the southern end of the shelter. "Wren? Who—"

"It's my uncle. Rumbler, they've found us! Oh, gods. You have to get out! Hurry! Get out of here!"

Wren grabbed her bow and quiver, then suddenly jumped for the pile of dirt she'd dug from the fire pit. She scooped it over the fire, dousing the light.

In the sudden darkness, she heard Rumbler scramble toward her on his hands and knees. He breathed the words in her face: "Wren, where should I go? What should I do?"

"I don't . . . I . . ." She'd started shaking, and had to clench her fists to get a hold on her nerves. "Rumbler, here, take my bow and quiver." She shoved them into his hands. "Do you remember that trail that leads over the hill and down toward Leafing Lake?"

"Yes."

"If I can, I'll meet you down on the lakeshore tomorrow morning. Do you understand? Run! If you get killed then everything I've done was for nothing. I want you to live. I'll try to find you tomorrow."

"But Wren, I . . ." Tears constricted his voice.

Wren found his shoulders, hugged him, and said, "Wait until I've stepped out the opposite end of the shelter before you go."

She spread the wall poles as quietly as she could. Moonlight streamed in, shining on Rumbler's terrified face, and the bow and quiver in his hands. "As soon as I'm gone, you crawl out through here. Shinny up through that crevice in the rocks. No one should be able to see you. Understand?''

''Yes.''

She crawled for the other end of the shelter and moved the poles aside. ''Ready?'' she whispered.

Rumbler whispered, ''I love you, Wren. Goodbye.''

Wren gave him a confident nod, then lurched through the opening and madly dashed down the hill, hoping to lead the hunters on a good chase before they caught her.

*''Wren? Wren, it's Uncle Blue Raven! Wait! Stop!''*

She leaped a fallen log and ran headlong for the deer trail she'd seen as they'd climbed the hill at sunset. In the moonlight, the trail gleamed like a slithering white snake. When she hit it, she ran flat out, her legs pumping for all she was worth.

Feet pounded after her.

''Wren, for the sake of your ancestors, stop! I've come to help you!''

Wren ran harder, her lungs panting.

The trail rose steeply, then plunged down through a fragrant grove of spruces. Thick roots laddered the trail. Wren leaped the first two, but the third jutted up sharply. She tripped over it, and toppled face first into the frozen dirt. She scrambled to her feet, and started to run again, but someone tackled her from behind, bringing her down hard.

''No!'' she shouted. ''Let me go! Let go!''

''Wren, it's me! Stop fighting!''

He forced her onto her back, and she gazed up at her uncle's face. His soft brown eyes tightened when he looked at her.

''Oh, Uncle.'' The choking sobs caught her off guard.

Blue Raven picked her up and hugged her against his chest. ''Blessed gods, I've missed you, Wren.''

# Twenty-Six

"Uncle?" Wren said as she pushed back and searched his face with blurry eyes. "My heart soars to see you, but why are you here?"

Blue Raven gently brushed her tangled hair behind her ears. "You mean why is there no war party with me?"

She nodded. "I thought that once you had figured out what I'd done, you would call a village council meeting and Starflower would order a war party to hunt Rumbler and me down."

"She did," Blue Raven said. He released his hold on her, and sank to the ground. "At least that's what I've heard, and I believe it. I'm sure that when Starflower discovered both of us missing, as well as the False Face Child, she went a little mad. I would have if I'd been her. I think I might have even sent word to neighboring—"

"What do you mean, she discovered *both* of us missing?"

He ran a hand through his hair. Patches of moonlit snow mottled the forest behind him. Wren's gaze scanned each one, looking for movement, expecting to see warriors streaming out of the shadows.

Blue Raven said, "I woke and found Rumbler gone, then I saw the drag marks where you had hauled him off Lost Hill, and I thought that if I could find you before morning, and bring you and Rumbler back, maybe no one would ever find out what you'd done."

Wren sat cross-legged in the trail in front of him, her head bowed. The white spirals on her blue shirt shone in the moonlight. "But you didn't find me by morning." She looked up. "What happened then?"

"I got to the Traders' canoe landing, and had to make a decision."

"You came after me?"

He stroked her hair and smiled, but it was a sad smile. "I couldn't let you face this alone, Wren."

Wren looked away. In the valley below, the ruins of Paint Rock Village lay quiet. She could imagine the horrors glowing in the moonlight.

"I didn't do anything wrong, Uncle," she insisted. "We did. Our clan did. We should never have stolen Rumbler."

"I agree, you know I do. But there is more to it, now." He stretched his back as if it hurt. "You and I—and Rumbler—need to think this whole thing through. Where is the False Face Child?"

Wren twined her hands tightly in her lap.

"Wren?" Uncle Blue Raven tipped her chin up so he could look into her eyes. "I want you to listen carefully. I have heard . . . things . . . and I suspect they are true."

"What things?"

"I have heard that you and I are both under death sentences."

"But why you, Uncle? Why—"

He held up a hand. "Think, Wren. It was snowing heavily the night we left. But you and Rumbler left perhaps two hands of time before I did. What our clan found in the morning were my tracks leading away from Lost Hill. What would you assume?"

"That—that you had taken the boy?"

"Of course. To make matters worse, anyone following

me will have seen that I met with two people, and will certainly assume that I must have planned—''

''But Uncle! We can run away!'' She clutched weakly at the elk hide tied over his shoulders. ''We don't have to go back to Walksalong Village!''

Blue Raven smiled, and lightly touched her forehead. ''Your life is there, Wren. With your nation, and your clan. Don't you want to go home?''

Her belly knotted. She smoothed her hands on the soft elk fur, and let the warm fires and laughter of the long-houses drift through her souls. ''It's all I've dreamed about, Uncle, but I don't think I will ever be able to.''

''Well, I think there is a way.''

Fearfully, she asked, ''What?''

He clasped one of her hands. ''I can explain my way out of this. I was just following you. But you have no excuse. You are guilty of the crime you are accused of. The only way to convince the matrons to reverse their order . . .''

Hazy forms emerged from the darkness, and tramped up the trail toward them. Blue Raven heard them and said, ''Ah. Finally.''

The man had waist-length white hair with an owlish face and beaked nose. His mud-spattered pants and coat almost blended with the shadows. The woman wore a hooded cape, but within the hood Wren could see a wrinkled face and thick gray braid.

''Great gods,'' the man said, ''your niece can run.''

''You'd run, too,'' the woman panted, ''if you thought a war party was after you.''

Wren looked at the two strangers. They were not of the Bear Nation. Their clothes bore Turtle Clan markings. To her uncle, she whispered, ''Who are they?''

Blue Raven held a hand out to the woman, and said, ''This is Matron Dust Moon from Earth Thunderer Village, and this is Silver Sparrow. I know you've heard of him. They have come to take Rumbler home with them."

Wren glanced back and forth between her uncle and the Turtle people. That's what he'd meant when he talked about meeting with two people. Confusion ate at her souls. Only moments ago, she had thought her uncle was going to tell her that they had to take Rumbler back to Walksalong Village, but now she didn't know what he'd meant.

Tears burned her eyes. "You mean Rumbler has a home to go to?"

Matron Dust Moon walked forward and knelt beside Blue Raven. She pushed back her hood, revealing glittering gray hair, and said, "Because of your courage, he does, Little Wren. Where is Rumbler?"

Wren wiped her nose with the back of her hand. Was this trickery? Uncle Blue Raven said a Walksalong war party pursued them, but he sat here in the company of two Turtle Nation people! How did such a thing come to be?

She studied the strangers, and her confusion increased. She'd never heard of Matron Dust Moon, but people told frightening tales about Silver Sparrow. She could hear Jumping Badger's voice the night of the council meeting saying, *"Before Lamedeer died, he told me that old Silver Sparrow had come to Paint Rock Village to warn them we were going to attack and steal the False Face Child. He said that the False Face Child would be our deaths!"* She'd heard other things about Silver Sparrow, too, and didn't like the idea of Rumbler going home with a man who loped around at night in the body of a badger.

Wren eyed him severely.

Silver Sparrow glanced over his shoulder to see if she

might be scowling at somebody else, then his bushy gray brows lifted. "What's the matter?"

"I've never heard Rumbler mention you."

"I imagine he's had more pressing things to talk about."

Wren tipped her head suspiciously. "I think he would have mentioned knowing a Powerful Dreamer like you."

Silver Sparrow made a helpless gesture. "Well, I'm flattered that you think so, but people in the Turtle Nation aren't nearly as impressed with my Dreaming skills as your people are, Little Wren. I—"

"We talked a lot about people we loved. I didn't hear your name."

Silver Sparrow squinted at her. "You've known me for less than one hundred heartbeats, and already you're sure I'm a liar?"

Dust Moon groaned. "Yes, of course she is, Sparrow! You have that effect on women. Let me handle this."

He kicked at one of the roots in the trail. "Please."

Dust Moon leaned toward Wren with an intensity that frightened her. Wren instinctively pulled back, and Dust Moon sighed. "Forgive me, Wren, I'm just worried sick about Rumbler. You see, I brought him into the world with my own hands, and he and his mother lived with Sparrow and me for the first two years of Rumbler's life. He is like a son to us. We love him very much. Please. Where is he?"

Bewildered and distrustful, Wren didn't say anything. She just clamped her lip between her teeth to stave off the tears that swelled her throat. If these really were people who loved Rumbler, she should tell them, and quickly, so they could stop him before he'd climbed the hill and made it down to the lakeshore. But . . .

Dust Moon studied Wren's expression, then touched her hands tenderly, and backed away. "Let's give Little

Wren some time," she advised. "I imagine this has been a terrible day for her, too. I don't know about everyone else, but I could use a hot cup of tea and some supper. Sparrow, why don't you and I gather wood. Blue Raven and Little Wren will want privacy."

She rose to her feet, and headed up the hillside into the trees. Silver Sparrow gave Wren a brief glance, then followed Dust Moon. As they climbed higher, their moonlit faces bobbed through the forest like bodiless ghosts.

Wren peered at her uncle from the corner of her eyes. "Are you going to let them take Rumbler?"

Blue Raven's brows lowered, an expression she had seen a hundred times. She knew what it meant. "I thought we would let Rumbler make that decision."

"R-Rumbler?"

Blue Raven seemed to be considering his next words with great care. He spoke softly. "I did not know Rumbler for long, but in the time that I knew him, I judged him to be a boy of uncommon valor and integrity. You know him much better than I. Is that how you see him?"

"Oh, yes, Uncle. I could tell you stories of things he has faced on this journey, and you would see his valor."

Blue Raven nodded. Wren waited for him to say more, to finish what he'd—

"Wren, I believe that when Rumbler hears that you have been condemned to death, and that the only way to save you is for him to return to Walksalong Village and give himself up, he will—"

"*No!*" She lunged to her feet, her breast heaving. "No, Uncle, please, you can't ask him to—to . . . he— he's so frail, and he loves me, and trusts me. I *won't* let you!"

"Wren. Please. Sit down." Blue Raven held out a hand to her.

Wren stepped away from it.

He drew up his knees, leaned forward and braced his elbows on them. Long graying black hair fell over his shoulders. "Wren, I can't watch you die. Imagine—"

*"Imagine how it will make all of us feel,"* a woman's voice said from the shadows.

Blue Raven slowly spread his arms, and got to his feet. "Who—"

"Keep your hands away from your bow."

His bow remained slung over his shoulder. "Elk Ivory."

Wren watched the woman emerge from behind the trunk of a sycamore, her bow nocked and at the ready. Tall and muscular, she moved like mist, her steps silent as she descended the trail. The green birds painted on her buffalo coat shone black in the moonlight.

"I should have known you'd be the one to find me," Blue Raven said.

Wren turned to run.

"Don't!" Elk Ivory ordered. "I do not wish to kill a girl, but I will, Little Wren, if you do not sit down this moment."

Blue Raven said, "Sit down, Wren. Do as she says. Elk Ivory is not here to hurt us."

Wren dropped in the trail, her heart pounding sickeningly. She did not see any other warriors, but she knew they must be close.

Uncle Blue Raven walked toward Elk Ivory. "Where is my cousin? I expected—"

"That's far enough, old friend," Elk Ivory ordered. "Stop right there. Where is the False Face Child? And the other two people you've been traveling with?"

Blue Raven hesitated, then waved a hand, as if buying time. Finally, he answered, "I turned the boy over to them, and we parted ways."

Wren looked at her uncle as if his souls had flown.

Elk Ivory squinted. "Don't lie to me, Blue Raven. I just arrived, but I heard a little of your conversation. Wren is the one who cut the False Face Child loose. You said you'd just been following her, that she was 'guilty of the crime.'"

Wren saw the muscles in her uncle's back knot and bulge through his shirt.

"Elk Ivory, you know me better than almost anyone." Her uncle's voice had gone soft, intimate. "I ask that you hear my story, and repeat it exactly as I tell it."

Elk Ivory's bow lowered slightly. "You know I will."

"Yes." Blue Raven nodded. "I do." He inhaled and let the breath out in a rush. "I tell you straightly that *I* cut the boy loose. Wren found the boy and me gone from Lost Hill and followed us. I did not even know she was behind me until yesterday." He paused, then added, "I am the one to blame. The only one."

"Uncle," Wren said and rose on trembling knees. "That's not—"

"Hush, Wren! Do not say a word. Do you understand me?"

Wren glanced at Elk Ivory, then nodded.

Elk Ivory again asked, "And who were the two people you were traveling with?"

"Relatives of the boy's."

"They paid you?"

Blue Raven blinked, and both Wren and Elk Ivory could tell it was the first time he'd even thought of such a thing.

"Yes, they paid me."

Elk Ivory's mouth puckered. "You were right about one thing, Blue Raven: I know you. Well enough to know when you are lying."

Blue Raven bowed his head and shook it. "I have told

you the truth. I cut the boy loose. I sold the boy to his relatives. What more do you need to know?''

"I—"

*"Nothing,"* Jumping Badger said as he eased out of the forest, followed by ten warriors.

Elk Ivory gaped in surprise.

Jumping Badger had his bow aimed at her, and for a moment Wren thought he might shoot. Black greasy hair clung to his cheeks. The warriors behind him whispered, as if uncertain what they should do next.

Jumping Badger said, "I knew you would do something like this, old woman."

Elk Ivory straightened, and glared. "Like what? Find the people we were hunting?''

"I saw you cutting across the meadow after you left Acorn, and I asked myself why you would disobey my orders. I came up with only one reason: to go locate your former lover, to warn him, so that he could—"

"You fool! If I had come to warn Blue Raven, would I have my bow leveled at his chest?''

The warriors behind Jumping Badger fanned out, surrounding them.

Jumping Badger took three steps closer, his bow aimed at Elk Ivory's face. The fine fletching on his arrow caught the light and shimmered. "It would be much easier to believe you if you had killed Blue Raven the instant he confessed his guilt to you. That's what he deserves. He betrayed all of us."

"The matrons ordered us to bring—"

Jumping Badger shifted, turning just enough to target her uncle, and let fly.

The arrow struck Blue Raven in the belly, knocking him backward. His mouth dropped open in shock, and his eyes flared as he fell to the ground.

Wren screamed, *"No!"*

Elk Ivory shouted, "You fool! You just violated your clan matron's orders!"

Wren ran for her uncle, throwing herself over his chest, crying, "Don't hurt him! You don't understand! You don't know . . ."

Blue Raven twined a hand in Wren's hair and yanked her ear down to his lips, whispering, "Don't say anything! You can . . . go home now. I want you . . . to go home."

"No, please, Uncle." She grabbed his wrist. "I can't let them think—"

Blue Raven's arm went slack, and thumped to the ground.

Wren cried, "No! Please, gods, no!"

Jumping Badger stalked by her, saying, "He's not dead." Then to his warriors, he said, "Bring him. Before he dies, we must find out where his accomplices have taken the False Face Child."

"*Shh!* Keep your head down!" Sparrow shoved Dust Moon's head under the log.

She watched through the weave of deadfall. They had spotted the woman warrior long before she'd called out to Blue Raven, and had taken cover. The woman, Elk Ivory, now stood over Blue Raven and Little Wren, shaking with what appeared to be rage. Little Wren's cries had stopped, but she clutched at her uncle's clothing as if she would never let go.

Four warriors gathered around Blue Raven, each picking up an arm or a leg. The arrow pierced his belly just below his ribs. The burly warrior with the Thornbush Clan haircut said, "Little Wren, you must move."

The girl dragged herself to her feet, and looked up at Elk Ivory with imploring eyes.

The woman warrior put a hand on Wren's back, and guided her down the hill.

"They look like they're heading for the ruins of Paint Rock Village," Dust whispered.

"Yes, what better place to threaten a wounded man and a little girl than surrounded by people you killed only a short time ago. If I were—"

"No one sane would camp with a crowd of angry ghosts."

"Jumping Badger is not sane, Dust. He—"

He took a faint sharp intake of breath, and Dust froze.

"There are more coming," Sparrow said.

"How do you know? Do you see—"

"Five or six men."

Dust could feel the hand resting on her head clench to a fist.

In the moonlit silence, the threat seemed almost palpable. Perhaps her souls could hear footsteps that her ears could not.

"Dust, as quietly as you can, stand up. We're going to have to try to get out of here before they come any closer."

Slowly, she rolled over, and got to her knees beside Sparrow.

Something indeed stirred in the darkness up the hill. The wind, blowing into their faces, carried a strange scent—a queer, fetid odor like moldering meat. She didn't see men, she saw . . . a luminous blur, swaying.

Sparrow whispered, *"Quietly. Run!"*

She felt the familiar strength of his arm go around her waist, and he half pulled her up the hill through the boulders and fallen logs. He'd always been able to see better in the dark than she. She'd often accused him of being part wolf.

"Crouch down, Dust! They may have seen us!"

She instantly obeyed, and glanced back toward the trail. Shapes materialized before her eyes, men walking in single file. One carried a long staff with a mask on it. The wood reflected the moon glow like polished silver, appearing to shine from its own inner light. The warrior didn't seem to relish his duty. He held the staff out as far from his face as he could, and Dust suddenly understood why. The reek of rotting flesh followed him as he wound down the hillside.

"Don't watch them, watch your feet!" Sparrow hissed. He dragged her toward the top of the hill.

Dust slipped and put her hand on his broad shoulder to steady herself. A thick carpet of damp leaves covered the ground here. They had entered a stand of sugar maples.

She did not know how long they scurried through the smoke-colored trunks, and rocks, but by the time they reached the hilltop, the cold, the fear, the fast for most of the long day, all had left her nerves overwrought.

She released Sparrow and stepped away from him. Her throat ached with the urge to cry, which angered her. She needed to think about Rumbler, to try to figure out where he might be, and instead she stood here with her hand to her mouth, gazing out across the vast silver-blue of Leafing Lake. Cloud Giants massed to the north, drifting toward them.

Sparrow walked to her, and his gaze examined every detail of her face. The wind gusted across the hilltop, blowing his white hair around his face. "Are you all right?"

She jerked a nod.

Sparrow's mouth quirked. "You're certain?"

Tears stung her eyes. "I'm fine, Sparrow."

"Oh, yes, I can see that."

He slipped his arm around her shoulders and slowly led her to a sheltered spot beneath a huge maple. The ceaseless wind coming off the lake had blown this spot clear of snow and dirt, leaving only thick roots and flat pieces of rock. Sparrow lowered her to sit on a wide slab of stone and sank down beside her.

He removed his pack, and tugged on her shoulder straps. Dust shifted to let him pull them from her back. Sparrow set both packs in the roots of the maple.

For a time they sat in silence, their bows on their knees, watching the lake, and enjoying the fact that blood still coursed in their veins. Miracles did happen, but they'd never happened to Dust before. She set her bow aside, leaned back, and stretched out on the rock, staring blindly at the bare branches soaked in moonlight. She took deep breaths just to feel her lungs work.

Sparrow stretched out beside her, placed his bow on top of their packs, and propped himself on his elbows.

She kept looking at the sky, but said, "Sparrow, there's so much to think about. What are we going to do—"

"Not tonight."

Dust turned to look at him, and he hesitated just a moment, peering deeply into her eyes, before he bent and kissed her.

His lips moved tenderly against hers. She told herself that she didn't have the strength to pull away, but, in truth, she didn't want to. It felt comforting to be kissed again. A warm tingle spread through her body, and all the day's weariness seemed to fade into the background. Sparrow pulled her against him, and Dust let herself drown in the soothing feel of his arms around her, and the—

He drew back of a sudden, and Dust looked up, frightened. "What?"

He gazed down at her with tears in his eyes.

"I love you," he said. "I never stopped loving you. You know that, don't you?"

"Yes." She put a hand behind his head, pulled him down, and kissed him again.

As the white veil of his hair tumbled around her, his tears landed warmly on her cheeks.

"I never stopped loving you, either," she said. "I just didn't like you very much."

Sparrow smiled against her lips. "We've shared so much, haven't we?"

The storm rolled over their heads, trailing gray tentacles of snow. Flakes landed silently, sticking in Dust's eyelashes, and sheathing Sparrow's hair.

She kissed him harder.

# Twenty-Seven

Blue Raven lay on his side at the outskirts of Paint Rock Village, his legs drawn up, his tied hands around the blood-slick arrow that pierced his stomach. The stench of torn intestines rose from the wound. He had seen enough gut shots in his life to know what was inevitable.

Wren sat twenty hands away, her wrists and ankles bound, as his were, with rawhide straps. Her terror-filled eyes had not left him.

Snow had been falling for about a hand of time, coating the branches and the corpses in the village. The faces of the dead had vanished. The burned lodges had transformed into pure white mounds.

Something inside him twisted, like a rope uncoiling, and the pain left him gasping, and clutching weakly at his belly. He knew how it went. Every breath that swelled his lungs squeezed poison into his stomach cavity. But it might take days for him to die.

Involuntarily, he writhed, his back arching, and a scream built at the back of his throat, pressing against his teeth, fighting to get out.

The warriors had laid him down atop an old flint-knapping site, and sharp flakes of stone glittered all around him. He concentrated on them, trying to conquer his own body.

While the warriors went about setting up camp, building fires, throwing out bedding, preparing food, Elk Ivory, Acorn, and Jumping Badger shouted at each other. They stood at the base of a huge oak tree to the south. Blue Raven had to tip his head back to look at them.

Elk Ivory said, "You stupid fool! Frost-in-the-Willows is the new head matron of our village, and you just murdered her only son!"

"The old woman will be glad to have the traitor gone!" Jumping Badger yelled. "And so will everyone else!"

Acorn made a calming gesture with his hands. "Please, screaming does no good. Let us sit down and speak of this quietly. Look. Buckeye has a fire going. Perhaps we can share it."

But neither Jumping Badger nor Elk Ivory made a move toward Buckeye's fire. They stood nose to nose glaring at each other.

Blue Raven digested the information. His mother could not have ascended to the position of head matron unless

Starflower, Beadfern, and Bogbean were dead. All were older than Frost-in-the-Willows, and better respected. If the clan had been given a more palatable choice, they would not have voted for his mother. Which meant they'd had no choice.

Had there been war? An attack on Walksalong?

Another wave of pain struck him, and Blue Raven hunched into a ball, his eyes clamped tightly shut, and his teeth gritted so hard his head shook. He had to stay quiet for as long as he could. Any sounds of anguish would affect Wren like knives plunged into her heart.

He prayed she would hold to the story he'd told Elk Ivory. If she did, she might actually make it out of this alive.

Jumping Badger lowered his voice and whispered hoarsely to Elk Ivory. It sounded like a threat.

She leaned toward him, her eyes like daggers. "I will fight you any day. Name the moment!"

Acorn put his hands out to separate them, pleading, "Enough! We should not be at each other's throats! We still have duties to our clan! We must find the False Face Child!"

Elk Ivory threw off Acorn's hand, and tramped away, toward Blue Raven.

Jumping Badger strode toward the murdered babies that scattered the ground on the north side of the plaza.

Elk Ivory knelt beside Blue Raven, her jaw working.

Blue Raven said, "Tell me what happened. At home."

Elk Ivory removed her buffalo coat and spread it over him, then took off her pack and water bag. "Springwater caught us this afternoon. He said there has been a storm. The longhouses collapsed. Many people were killed." She shook her head. "That is all we know. Your mother—"

"Yes. I—I heard."

Elk Ivory unlaced her pack and pulled out a red and blue strip of cloth that she often wore as a headband. She soaked it with water from her water bag, and mopped Blue Raven's forehead.

The coolness felt like a gift from the Earth Spirits. His shoulder muscles eased. "Thank you."

"Don't thank me." Emotion turned her voice thick. "I came looking for you to prevent this. I did a poor job."

"I should have guessed my cousin would wish me dead."

"You did not help matters," she said and gently washed the rest of his face and throat, "when you claimed guilt for something you didn't do."

Blue Raven lifted his tied bloody hands and gripped her wrist tightly. When she looked down at him, he whispered, "I had to save Wren. Please. Let me . . . let me do that."

Elk Ivory put her cloth aside and took his hands in both of hers. She heaved a deep breath. "I will do everything in my power to make certain she receives no blame in this affair. But I do it for you, Blue Raven. Not for her. She—"

"Is young." He forced a smile he didn't feel. "Remember how righteous you were at twelve winters? I do."

A bare smile touched her mouth. "Yes, I'm sure you do. And perhaps you are right. Once my anger and frustration fade, I may feel differently."

He squeezed her hand with as much strength as he could muster, then another fiery torrent of pain shook him to the bones. He didn't make a sound. When the burning eased, he fell back, panting, and stared up at Elk Ivory. Her shoulder-length hair had fallen forward, framing her brown eyes and flat nose. From the cant to her jaw, he could tell she'd clenched her teeth to fight her own pain at seeing him like this.

"I had forgotten," he murmured, "how pretty you are."

She gazed at him nakedly. "Do you . . . wish me to pull the arrow out?"

It would hasten death. While it remained inside him, the arrow partially blocked the flow of gut juices. Removal would also bring unbearable pain as the contents of his torn stomach and intestines filled him up inside, eating away at his liver, kidneys, and lungs.

Blue Raven said, "Are you certain Jumping Badger won't kill you for it? I suspect he wishes me to live as long as possible."

"If I do it now, before he gives an order to the contrary . . . then it's done." Her eyes implored him.

Blue Raven nodded. "Yes. Hurry."

Elk Ivory lifted her buffalo coat, and laid it aside, then gripped the bloody fletching on the arrow and cracked it off. Rising, she went around behind him, and snapped off the flint point.

"Are you ready?" she asked.

"As much as I—I can be. Go on."

In one swift clean move, she yanked the arrow all the way through his body.

Agony blinded Blue Raven. He cried out.

Wren screamed, *"Uncle? Uncle!"*

It took some time before his senses returned. When he opened his eyes again, he found Elk Ivory sitting at his side with her water bag open.

"You must be thirsty," she said.

He nodded, feeling as if he hadn't had a drink in a moon. She lifted his head up and tipped the bag to his lips. He drank greedily. The water would add to the blood and other deadly fluids draining out inside him, but it didn't matter. Already he could feel himself starting to bloat.

He turned his mouth away, and Elk Ivory pulled up the bag, and lowered his head to the ground again.

"Promise me," he croaked.

"What?"

"Promise me that . . . you . . . you will end this for me before I shame myself."

She slowly lifted her eyes, and he could see her paling.

He said, "I—I don't want Wren to remember me . . . begging."

Elk Ivory closed her eyes, and turned away.

They had both witnessed suffering that lasted for days. At the end, a man or woman would do anything, say anything, to end the pain.

Blue Raven weakly touched the fringe on her moccasin. "I ask this of you as more than a friend. We once loved each other."

"I will end it," she said, and turned back to look at him.

It was the first time in his life that he had seen tears in her eyes.

He drew his hands back to clutch at his belly. The pain had turned to hammer blows, stunning, rhythmic, timed to his breathing. "I have always trusted you," he said, and hunched up, fighting the sobs that constricted his throat.

Elk Ivory moved, sitting between Blue Raven and Wren to block Wren's view.

Blue Raven leaned his forehead against Elk Ivory's leg and wept silently.

She smoothed his hair with her hand. "I could do it now," she murmured. "Do you—"

"No. No, you can't. Jumping Badger . . . he would kill

you. He wants to question me. You . . ." He groaned softly, breathing hard. "You must let him. If you killed me now, he would take it out . . . on you and Wren. Wait. Wait until tomorrow. After he . . . he has . . ."

"Yes. I will," she answered, and laid a cool hand on his hair. "Now, try to rest. I know you will not sleep, but you must—"

"Elk Ivory? Could I speak with Wren? Has Jumping Badger forbidden it?"

She glanced over her shoulder, then looked back, and said, "He has not. But—"

"Please. It will be easier . . . for both of us . . . if I speak with her tonight. Tomorrow . . . I don't know if I'll be able to. Not without . . ." His strength faded with the words.

"I will try. But your cousin may try to stop it."

"I understand."

She rose to her feet, and slowly, as if without thinking, walked toward Wren. The other warriors did not seem to notice. They sat around their fires, talking and eating. Blue Raven searched the camp for Jumping Badger, but didn't see him. Thank the gods, this might work.

Elk Ivory crouched, slipped her knife from her belt sheath, and cut Wren's ankle bonds, then dragged Wren to her feet and shoved her toward Blue Raven.

"Don't run," he heard Elk Ivory order.

Wren walked calmly, her face a sculpture of desperation.

She dropped to her knees at Blue Raven's side, and said, "Uncle, I'm sorry. I love you. I didn't—"

"Shh, Wren," Blue Raven hushed her. "This is not your fault. None of it. Do you understand me?"

She nodded, but the tears leaking down her face said otherwise.

"Wren, we can't talk very long, and this may be our only chance to speak. Elk Ivory is risking her life to give us this chance. Please. Listen carefully."

"Yes," Wren sobbed. "I will."

Pain blazed through him. Blue Raven squeezed his eyes closed. His belly felt as if it were turning itself inside out. He couldn't stop the shuddering, but he kept the groan locked behind his teeth.

When the torment eased, he looked into Wren's horrified face, and fought to find the strength for words. "Wren . . . no matter what . . . happens. You must repeat the story you heard me tell Elk Ivory. Do you . . . do you remember it?"

"Yes, Uncle."

"Tell me. I want to—to hear you say it."

Wren gestured feebly with her bound hands. "I went to Lost Hill, and found you gone and Rumbler—"

"The False Face Child."

"The False Face Child. I found you both gone, and I followed you. I only caught up with you . . ." She blinked back her tears and shook her head. "When?"

"Yesterday. And you were with me when I . . . I sold . . . the boy."

"I was with you when you sold the boy to Matron—"

"No!" He shook his head violently. "No. You do not know who the two people were. They were from the . . . the Turtle Nation. That is all you know. It happened fast. We met them . . . they paid me . . . they left. You do not know where they were going."

She licked her lips nervously. "Yesterday, we met them, they paid you, and left. They didn't say where they were taking the False Face Child."

Blue Raven nodded. "Yes. Good. Good girl. Now . . . come here."

Wren leaned closer, her face a handbreath from his. She bit her lip to keep her tears at bay.

Blue Raven said, "I love you. Go home. Become clan matron"—he smiled—"and make me proud of you."

Tears streamed down her cheeks. "I love you, Uncle. I wish I could go back—"

"You can't," he said. "None of us can. We can only go forward. I want you . . . to look ahead. Never—never back. Wren, if you . . . if you start looking back, it is all you will ever be able to do. The past can swallow you whole. Don't let it. Remember that I—I said this to you."

"I will, Uncle. I will remember everything you've ever taught—"

"Quiet!" Elk Ivory turned suddenly. "I think he's coming back to camp."

Elk Ivory threw her coat over Blue Raven, jerked Wren to her feet, and dragged her stumbling back to her place twenty hands away. She shoved Wren down, retied her feet, and stalked across camp . . . but it was not Jumping Badger. Shield Maker walked out of the forest.

Blue Raven could hear Wren crying, but some of his fear had gone. She would be all right now.

He fumbled his shaking hands around until he could grasp one of the chert flakes that lay shining in the moonlight. About the size of his index finger, it had one sharp translucent edge.

He did it quickly, slicing his hide pants, then cutting deeply through the big arteries that ran along the insides of his thighs.

He looked up at the sky. Snow fluttered down, swaying and spinning.

Another spasm gripped him, clawing at his internal organs.

. . . But he could stand it now.

As his blood pumped out onto the frozen ground, a peaceful sensation came over him.

Jumping Badger would not have the pleasure of watching him die. Of torturing him in front of Wren.

Hot blood soaked the lower half of his body. He counted his heartbeats. When he reached one hundred, the pain started to dim. At two hundred, it vanished, and relief flooded him, leaving him light-headed. He could no longer move his hands. A smile brushed his lips.

*So this is what it feels like.*

He closed his eyes, and let go . . .

. . . and he found himself back in Walksalong Village. Dawn streamed through the trees, dappling the plaza with bright yellow. The scent of roasting fish and wild rice filled the air. Joy expanded his chest. He heard Skybow laugh, and turned to see the little boy running across the plaza with Trickster barking at his heels. His sister trotted behind Skybow. When she saw Blue Raven, she stopped, and smiled. She looked so much like Wren, her face slender, her eyes large and dark. Long hair draped the shoulders of her fringed doeskin dress.

"Well?" she said. "Are you coming?"

Blue Raven took a deep breath. "Yes," he said, and walked toward her. "I'm coming."

While Elk Ivory tended her dying lover, Jumping Badger searched the scattered remains of the dead children. The bodies had been ravaged by animals. He kicked the chewed head of a little boy. It tumbled over the snow, and stopped, the face up, peering at him through hollow eye sockets.

Shadows flittered in the trees to his left. He jerked to

look. Ghosts pranced and spun, their dark willowy arms up, their hair flying.

*The Death Dance! They were doing the Death Dance! For him.*

He could feel their presences. Heavy, and cold, like slabs of granite piled on his chest. He couldn't breathe.

If he didn't do something quickly they would kill him! He had to kneel and put a hand on the ground to steady his shaking legs.

And there, beside his spread fingers, lay the gnawed bones of a baby girl. A tiny ground-stone bracelet encircled her wrist.

He pretended to examine it while he glanced at his warriors. Occupied with unrolling hides, building fires, and muttering about the day's events, no one paid him much attention.

He looked at Elk Ivory again. She had her back to him, bent over Blue Raven.

Jumping Badger grabbed the foot of the little girl, tucked her chewed body inside his beaver-hide coat, and ran into the depths of the forest.

*I'll be safe if I stay at the edge of the light. They can't reach for me if I'm in the light!*

But they crowded around him, whispering and swaying as he crouched to build a fire.

Rumbler tugged up his hood, and huddled inside the fox-fur cape. He had crawled into a cocoon of low-hanging pine boughs. Through the cracks in the branches, he could see waves lapping the shore, and beyond them water and more water.

He was too afraid to sleep. As he'd climbed the hill, he'd heard shouts and a scream.

The trees shrieked at him and flung their arms.

"No," he whispered, and tucked the lower half of his face inside the cape.

Breath warmed his chest. He rocked back and forth, shivering.

Snow-covered rocks scattered the lakeshore. They were all dead Spirits. Cloaked in white burial blankets. But they shouted at him to run.

"No. Wren said morning."

Her name tasted bright and shiny, like sparks.

He wanted her badly. The longing had turned to a great darkness.

He wished he could swallow her name into his aching stomach where the darkness breathed. Maybe the sparks would shoot out in all directions, and the darkness would leak from the holes, and drain away.

He tucked his hurt hands between his knees.

Wind Mother wiggled through the pine boughs and shoved Rumbler hard.

"No!" He swallowed his tears. "Wren said morning. She'll be here in the morning!"

# Twenty-Eight

Snow fluttered down around Elk Ivory, landing in the fire to spit and sizzle. She plucked another strip of dark meat from the duck Acorn had given her. He sat to her right, eating his own duck, his bristly hair glimmering orange. Buckeye squatted to her left. A giant of a man, he made two of Acorn, with bulging muscles stretching his hide pants and cape. He wore his black hair in two short braids.

Jumping Badger sat across the fire from them. He had four new stilettos tucked into his belt. The freshly ground tips gleamed, sharpened to deadly points. It did not require great ability to discern where he'd gotten them, but she wondered at their utility. Made from the frail leg bones of a child, they would snap instantly if plunged into a human enemy. What possible use . . .

A log broke in the fire, and light splashed the camp. Jumping Badger jerked and yipped as shadows fluttered through the trees.

Jumping Badger pointed, and whispered, "Do you see them?"

"I do not see anyone, War Leader," she answered. "Whom do you see?"

His eyes narrowed. He clamped his jaw and turned to the staff with the masked head, two paces away. The crow's beak shone orange. "I can kill them now!" he shouted at Lamedeer. "Tell them! You tell them, they'll believe you!"

The mask seemed to be peering at the warriors wandering the camp. The eyeholes glimmered with hate.

Elk Ivory pulled off another greasy strip of duck and ate it. Lamedeer had every right to hate them tonight. They had brought him back to his old village, and slapped him in the face with the annihilation of his clan and those he loved. If a soul did inhabit that rotten head, it had undoubtedly been conversing with the unhappy ghosts that roamed these woods. She wouldn't be surprised if the ghosts sneaked out of the forest tonight and sucked all of their souls out through their ears.

She glowered at Jumping Badger.

He apparently sensed her eyes upon him—he whirled and glowered back. Every day that passed, she longed more to kill him. Tonight, the urge nearly overwhelmed her.

Blue Raven lay curled beneath her buffalo coat. The feel of his blood-drenched hands gripping hers had been like a lance in her heart, twisting.

She looked over at Little Wren. Her hands and feet bound, the girl had slumped against an oak trunk. No sounds came from her, but Elk Ivory could see the sobs shaking her shoulders.

She tore off a chunk of duck with her teeth and ate it slowly, thinking about the girl. By stealing that wicked child, Wren had doomed the one person she loved more than any other in the world. How would she be able to live with that fact? That she had caused her uncle's death? Despite Blue Raven's assurances that it wasn't Wren's fault, surely the girl knew better.

Blessed Spirits, what an awful burden for a girl of twelve winters.

Someone laughed across the camp, and Elk Ivory looked up. Rides-the-Bear and Shield Maker had gotten into a playful shoving contest. The other warriors around the fire grinned.

She ate the last bite of meat from her duck and tossed the remains into the fire. Flames licked around the carcass, scorched the bones, and sent up an acrid black smoke.

Rides-the-Bear, a member of Beadfern's longhouse, had watched Skullcap and Mossybill die. He hated Blue Raven for defending the False Face Child. But no Headman could be worshiped by every member of his clan. Headmen made decisions that benefited most of the people, most of the time. Which meant that a few people always stood on the fringes, grumbling.

Still . . . she didn't know how anyone could laugh tonight, and she despised Rides-the-Bear, and his friends, for it.

Acorn nudged Elk Ivory with his elbow, and murmured, "Are you well?"

She shook her head. After giving Blue Raven her coat, she had pulled her extra buckskin shirt from her pack. Knee-length, with a band of yellow porcupine quillwork across the shoulders, it barely kept the cold at bay. She'd been on the verge of shivering for a hand of time. She knew she could rise, go over to her bedding and pull out a blanket to wrap her shoulders. But she needed to feel the cold and snow. On a night filled with death, it let her know she was alive.

"Blue Raven hasn't moved in a while," Acorn said. "He must have passed out from the pain."

"I pray you are right."

"What are you whispering about over there?" Jumping Badger growled.

Elk Ivory glanced up. Only a few days ago he'd been a handsome young man, but not any longer. His once lustrous black hair now clung to his cheeks in filthy strands. His dark confident eyes had turned suspicious and wary, like those of a hunted animal. Even his perfectly chiseled jaw canted at an angle, as if he kept it perpetually clenched.

Around a mouthful of meat, Acorn answered, "I was just saying that I think Blue Raven passed out from the pain, War Leader. He hasn't moved—"

"Then go and wake him," Jumping Badger ordered. "Now!"

"Yes. All right." Acorn bit off another mouthful of duck, and lowered the rest to his bowl. After wiping his greasy hands on his pants, he rose, and headed for Blue Raven.

Elk Ivory lifted her teacup and sipped from it. The fragrance of spruce needles filled her nostrils. Jumping Badger smiled at her. A malicious grin, as if he got almost as much pleasure from her pain as he did from Blue Raven's.

She smiled back. A promise.

Jumping Badger's grin faded to a scowl. "What shall we do with the girl?"

"Take her home. She's innocent. You heard Blue Raven say so yourself." It hurt to speak the words, but she added, "Blue Raven is the one who stole the child, and sold it. He is the traitor, not Little Wren."

Jumping Badger's grin returned. "*I* told you so, did I not? You didn't wish to believe me, but I knew the truth all along." He tipped his chin toward the masked head. "Spirits do not lie."

Buckeye shifted uncomfortably. He glanced at the head, then at his half-eaten wild-rice cake. He threw the cake into the fire. "If you do not need me, War Leader, I think I will find my blankets."

"Go." Jumping Badger waved a hand. "You can do nothing more tonight."

Buckeye rose, bowed, and tramped away.

Jumping Badger said, "You and Acorn will guard the prisoners tonight. Two people should be enough. Then, in the morning, after Blue Raven's had a night to think on his errors, we will begin—"

"War Leader?"

Elk Ivory and Jumping Badger turned to face Acorn. He had an odd expression on his face, almost elated.

"Well?" Jumping Badger said. "What is it? Did you wake him?" He stared around Acorn's legs toward Blue Raven.

"I tried, War Leader," Acorn explained. "But he's dead."

Elk Ivory leaped to her feet and ran, flying past Little Wren to get to Blue Raven.

Even before she fell to her knees at his side, she saw the blood that soaked her coat, and pooled around his legs. He stared at her through half-open eyes.

"Blue Raven," she whispered, and threw her coat from his body.

The chert flake still rested in his open palm. He'd slashed both femoral arteries. It couldn't have taken more than a few hundred heartbeats for him to die.

Elk Ivory hung her head, suddenly more weary than she had ever been in her life. "Rest easy, old friend," she whispered. "I will make sure Little Wren is safe. Just as you wished."

Shouts rose around the camp, and feet pounded the ground. Warriors leaned over Elk Ivory, muttering and pointing.

Jumping Badger pushed through the crowd, carrying a torch, which he lowered to examine the slashes in Blue Raven's pants.

"He cheated me!" Jumping Badger snarled. "The filthy traitor!" He kicked Blue Raven in the head, and waved his torch wildly. "He knew I was going to burn him alive, and he couldn't stand it! The cowardly, stupid—"

"Enough." Elk Ivory rose to her feet. Warriors stared at her, their faces filled with unspoken questions. "We must still find the False Face Child. Which means we have to track down the two people Blue Raven sold him to. Acorn and I will stand watch over Little Wren. I suggest the rest of you go to your robes and get a good night's rest. It may be the last you have for a time."

She shouldered through the onlookers, went to her bedding and pulled out a blanket. As she threw it over her shoulder, and collected her bow and quiver, men be-

gan to trickle past her, muttering to each other. Some
went to finish supper. A few headed for their robes.

Acorn came up beside Elk Ivory and said, "He may
have betrayed us, but he served our clan faithfully for
twenty winters before that. I think he deserves a decent
burial. If you will help me—"

"I will help you."

"Tomorrow? After breakfast?"

She nodded, and looked back toward Blue Raven.

Only Jumping Badger remained standing over the dead
body. He held his torch high, and yelled, "You criminal!
You dirty traitor! You did this on purpose!"

He drew his foot back, and began kicking Blue
Raven—in the belly, the legs, the face.

Then, in a fit of laughter, he threw the torch down,
and drew his knife from his belt sheath. The gray blade
glinted as he gripped Blue Raven by the hair, and lowered the blade to his throat.

"No!" Elk Ivory shouted, and a dozen voices joined
hers as warriors leaped to their feet.

Acorn stood with his breast heaving. "For the sake of
our ancestors, Jumping Badger! Blue Raven's head is not
a trophy! He was the Headman of our clan!"

Voices rumbled assent, and Jumping Badger lowered
his knife, kicked Blue Raven in the mouth, and tramped
away.

Elk Ivory's gaze shifted to Little Wren.

The girl had stopped crying. She knelt, her bound
hands clenched to fists, watching Jumping Badger with
blazing eyes.

Spotted Frog grabbed Cornhusk's shoulder to steady himself while he wheezed. "Blessed—gods—is this the camp? Tell me we're stopping. I can't believe—we stayed on the trail—well past dark!"

"This is it," Cornhusk said, and gestured to the clearing where a fire burned, surrounded by the packs of nineteen warriors.

Each man had been assigned nightly duties. Four gathered wood, four set up camp, digging fire pits and laying out cooking tools. Six hunted or fished, four kept guard, and one man tended to Spotted Frog's numerous needs. The "tender," named Flying Skeleton, stood three hands taller than Cornhusk and had a lean feral face with slitted light brown eyes.

Cornhusk wasn't sure he liked the man. But he loved Silent Crow Clan's organization. He'd never seen anything like it.

By the time they reached camp each night, less than a finger of time after the lead warriors, most of the work was done. Spotted Frog's people built the fires, caught the food, prepared the food, cleaned the pots. It made evenings very pleasant.

"Come along, Spotted Frog," Cornhusk said, and gripped the clan patron's fat right arm. Flying Skeleton took his left.

Spotted Frog's meaty legs wobbled as they helped him into the clearing and set him down atop one of the five logs that had been drawn up around the fire pit. Flames crackled, sending up coils of blue smoke, and pots already hung over the coals, heating.

Guards stood at the northern and southern ends of camp, but the other warriors hiked through the trees, finishing their tasks.

"I had no—idea—the trails would be—this muddy!" Spotted Frog fanned his bloated face with his hand.

Sweat drenched his smoked moose-hide shirt and beaded his nose and forehead.

"Well," Cornhusk said as he slipped off his pack and let it fall to the ground at the base of the log. "This moon is unpredictable. Hot one day, ice storms the next."

Flying Skeleton slipped out of his pack, and knelt before Spotted Frog, saying, "Let me put on your dry moccasins, Patron."

"Oh, yes, please." Spotted Frog held out his right mud-caked moccasin.

Flying Skeleton unlaced and removed it, then reached into the pack for a dry one—lined with buffalo fur—and slipped it on Spotted Frog's foot.

Spotted Frog held out the left foot, and Cornhusk watched the process repeated.

He had to admit, it made him a little nauseous. He stayed away from his wife as much as possible precisely because he hated being "mothered." Women never treated a man like a man. They all seemed to think men were children in extremely large bodies.

He pulled his buffalo-bladder water bag from his pack and took a long drink, while he watched Spotted Frog from the corner of his eye.

The patron sighed when Flying Skeleton finished tying his moccasins.

"Do you wish me to comb out your hair now?" Flying Skeleton asked, scowling at Spotted Frog's tangled braids. "Or would a cup of tea be more to your liking?"

"Why don't you bring me a cup of tea, and I'll drink it while you comb my hair."

"Yes, Patron."

Flying Skeleton pulled a cup from the pack, and went to the large cone-shaped pot tucked into the coals at the edge of the flames.

Cornhusk pulled out his own cup and followed Flying

Skeleton. After Flying Skeleton had dipped Spotted Frog's cup full, and started back toward the log, Cornhusk peered into the soot-coated pot. The delicious fragrances of dried strawberries and pumpkin blossoms rose. He dipped his cup full, and looked around the camp. What an excellent location! He couldn't have done better himself. Twenty paces away, to his right, a small creek flowed down the hillside, burbling through a crust of ice. In a rough oval around the meadow, maples and oaks grew to unusual heights, towering above them. Acorns scattered the ground. Around them, the heart-shaped tracks of deer dimpled the old leaves and mud.

Cornhusk walked back to Spotted Frog's side, and sat down on the log. As he leaned forward, his black braid fell over his right shoulder, and the few gray strands shimmered in the firelight.

Warriors had started coming in, some with armloads of wood, which they added to the already substantial woodpile. One man carried seven squirrels on a cord. Another had a string of fish. Cornhusk's stomach growled.

"The efficiency of your men astounds me, Spotted Frog," Cornhusk said and sipped the fruity tea.

"You may thank Pup Woman for that. There are no shirkers in Silent Crow Village. Any child caught being lazy has to perform twice his or her normal chores. By the time our children are young men and young women, they know the cost of lethargy and the rewards of hard work."

"That is obvious." Cornhusk took another drink of tea. As it filled his belly, warmth spread through him. "Ah, it feels good to sit down."

Flying Skeleton removed a wooden comb from the pack, tucked it into his belt, and started unbraiding Spot-

ted Frog's hair. The tall skinny man touched Spotted
Frog's hair as if it might break.

The warrior who'd brought in the fish scooped mud
from around the fire pit and applied a thick coating to
each trout. Cornhusk loved trout cooked this way, sealed
in clayey mud and cooked slowly over the coals. The
process kept the juices in, making for a delectable supper.
When they were pulled out of the coals, the hardened
mud came off in chunks, taking the skin with it, and
leaving succulent white meat behind.

Another warrior knelt before the fire with a stick and
a pot. He carefully scooped ashes to the side of the fire
pit, then dipped spoonfuls of dough from the pot, and
dropped them into the ashes. Ash cakes! Cornhusk wondered what kind of dough he'd made, but he'd find out
soon enough. Ash cakes cooked quickly. They would be
done in half the time of the trout.

"I'm gratified that you decided to come with us, Cornhusk. You know this country so much better than my
clanspeople."

Cornhusk smiled, showing his missing front teeth. "It
was the least I could do, Spotted Frog. Your village has
been very kind to me."

And they'd offered him his weight in copper beads and
rare marginella shells.

"I just wish we had some way of knowing where the
children and Blue Raven might be."

Cornhusk grasped his teacup in both hands, letting it
warm his fingers. As warriors added more wood to the
fire, the flames leaped and swayed, and their heat grew.
His broken nose tingled. "The last I heard they were
headed north, as we are. If we follow the main trail, we
will soon arrive at Sleeping Mist Village. They may have
heard something. We can ask."

Spotted Frog's brow furrowed as Flying Skeleton went

on combing the tangles from his shoulder-length hair. "Those poor children. I pray we reach them before the Walksalong war party does. I'm sure that the patron, and elders, at Sleeping Mist will commit warriors to our search, but even if they don't, we mustn't stop until we've found Blue Raven and the children. They have been so brave. They deserve our help."

Cornhusk nodded gravely. His talent for storytelling often brought rewards, but he couldn't figure out how he could have misjudged Silent Crow Clan's response this badly. He'd expected people in the Turtle Nation to moan and groan, but he'd have never imagined such an outpouring of sentiment, particularly one backed by warriors.

Flying Skeleton finished combing Spotted Frog's hair and said, "Would you like your cape now, Patron?"

Spotted Frog considered a moment. "Yes, I think I've cooled off enough."

Flying Skeleton untied the rolled cape from the pack, shook it out, and draped it around Spotted Frog's shoulders. "Will there be anything else?"

"No," Spotted Frog said. "You may go about your personal needs. Thank you, Flying Skeleton."

The tall skinny man bowed, and headed for the trees.

It fascinated Cornhusk. Apparently, Flying Skeleton could not even empty his bladder until he'd taken care of Spotted Frog. A curious arrangement, to say the least.

The camp bustled with warriors now. Cornhusk counted eighteen. Everyone had returned except Flying Skeleton, and Cornhusk could see him in the trees just beyond the firelight. Soft conversations filled the air.

Spotted Frog gazed down into his tea. "Confidentially," he murmured, "I'm worried."

"I'd be worried, too. Forgive me, but your meager war party is no match for Jumping Badger."

"I know. But we must try."

Cornhusk slid back on the log and braced his elbows on his knees, watching the fire. Despite the fact he'd told Spotted Frog that Jumping Badger's warriors numbered at least two hundred, he'd been there when Starflower ordered Jumping Badger to take no more than twenty. Spotted Frog's war party already equaled Jumping Badger's. If he succeeded in gleaning more warriors from Sleeping Mist Village, the truth was that Jumping Badger might not be able to stand against Spotted Frog.

The thought comforted Cornhusk.

"I'm also worried about something else," Spotted Frog murmured, clearly not wishing to be overheard.

"And that is?"

"I don't know how to fight Lamedeer."

"That is a concern, I agree, but if I were you I would be more worried about the number of warriors Jumping Badger has."

Spotted Frog swirled his tea in his cup. "Warriors, my dear friend, can be killed. How do I fight a desperate ghost? Lamedeer was one of my relatives. I am fearful that when we catch up with Jumping Badger's war party, Lamedeer may take out his vengeance upon us."

Cornhusk lifted his cup and drank, then wiped his mouth on the sleeve of his mangy buffalo coat. "If you can get the head back and care for it, clean it and massage it with oil—"

"Yes, perhaps my uncle's cousin's son would forgive us if we put his ghost to rest, but we cannot do that until after the battle. How will I fight him during the battle? Or before? What if Lamedeer foresees our coming, and tells Jumping Badger? He could set up a devastating ambush."

The scent of roasting fish and cooking ash cakes wafted toward Cornhusk. He inhaled deeply, before answering, "Too bad we don't know a good soul-flying witch. She could fly to Lamedeer's head, and tell Lamedeer that we are coming to rescue him as well as the children and Blue Raven."

Spotted Frog's brows lifted. "I know some witches to the south, down around Going Wolf village, but I know of none in these northern territories."

"Perhaps the patron at Sleeping Mist will know someone. Witches cost a fortune, but—"

"Before we left," Spotted Frog said, a fond gleam in his eyes, "Pup Woman told me to save the heroic children and the Walksalong Headman even if it cost the wealth of our entire village."

"Admirable," Cornhusk said with due reverence, "but witches are even more distrustful than Traders. They demand instant payment. How much did you bring with you?"

Spotted Frog's lips tightened. "Some."

"Some?"

"Enough, I think. Pup Woman tried to plan for all possible needs."

Cornhusk drummed his fingers on the side of his cup. "You don't trust me, do you, Spotted Frog?"

He smiled, and watched Flying Skeleton as the skinny man walked out of the trees and back into camp.

Cornhusk said, "You could save yourself a good deal if we knew where Silver Sparrow was. He soul-flies. And he hates Jumping Badger. He'd probably do it without charging you a single copper bead."

"Yes." Spotted Frog sighed. "I regret that we didn't have time to send a runner to Earth Thunderer Village, but—"

"I'm not certain he went home."

Spotted Frog turned. His mouth slowly opened. "Do

you think he and Dust Moon decided to try and track down the False Face Child?''

Cornhusk blew on his tea, and frowned at the tiny whirlwinds of steam that rose. "What would you do if a child you loved was on the run from a horde of vicious warriors?"

Spotted Frog grimaced at the fire.

Flying Skeleton knelt before the ash cakes. A stack of bowls and spoons rested near the fire pit. Flying Skeleton took a spoon and lifted several ash cakes into a bowl, then rose to his feet, and walked toward Spotted Frog. The man reminded Cornhusk of a very tall weasel.

Cornhusk said, "I realize you do not trust me, but—"

"I did not say that."

Flying Skeleton handed Spotted Frog the bowl. "The fish will be done soon. Do you require more tea?"

"Yes, thank you, Flying Skeleton." He handed the man his empty cup, and Flying Skeleton returned to the fire pit.

Spotted Frog bit into an ash cake and a look of pleasure spread across his fat face. "Here," he said and held out the bowl. "Try one of these."

"Gracious of you to offer." Cornhusk took one. Made of acorn flour mixed with roasted marsh-elder seeds, the cakes melted in his mouth. "Delicious. Truly, your people are master cooks and brewers." He added, "Even if you don't trust me."

Spotted Frog smiled. "Cornhusk, my friend, I trust you as much as any Trader."

Cornhusk thought about that, then sighed.

Flakes of snow drifted out of the sky, frosting the trees, and sizzling on the hearthstones.

Cornhusk shielded his eyes and looked up. "There's

a storm pushing down from the north. We had better prepare for a long day tomorrow, too.''

Spotted Frog finished his ash cake and wiped his hands on the hem of his cape. "I pray it snows heavily, and for many days straight.''

''And covers each moccasin print the children and Blue Raven leave?''

Spotted Frog gazed up into the falling snow. It stuck to his hair and fat cheeks. "And our trail, too, my friend. Just in case we're being followed.''

''Us? Followed?'' Cornhusk sat up straighter. "Who would follow us?''

Spotted Frog bit into another ash cake. "Many villages from the Bear Nation. If word has reached them that we set out with a war party looking for Jumping Badger, there is no telling what they might do. They are a violent people.''

''Hallowed . . . ancestors.''

Why hadn't he thought of that! Great Badger Above, if *anyone* in the Bear Nation discovered that he had led the Turtle Nation war party that fought Jumping Badger, and rescued the ''traitors'' . . .

Spotted Frog handed the bowl of ash cakes back to Cornhusk. "Would you like another?''

Cornhusk took three. "Thank you, Patron,'' he said and stared morosely at the cakes. He had better start enjoying every meal he got. No telling which one might be his last.

# Twenty-Nine

Sparrow woke in the middle of the night with the elk hide pulled over his head. He lay with his legs curled against Dust's, and his arms around her. Her head rested beneath his chin. The fact that he'd given up hope of ever holding her this way again made it even more glorious. He lightly kissed Dust's hair.

"Are you awake?" she whispered sleepily.

"Yes."

"Should we rise?"

She slid back against him, snuggling into the curve of his body.

Sparrow tightened his hold around her. "Probably. The snow is still falling. If we leave now, it will fill in our tracks."

But neither of them moved. Dust pulled his arm closer, and Sparrow nuzzled his chin against her hair. The feel of her lithe body tucked against him, the warmth of her breath on his hand, filled him with a sudden anguish.

"Dust?"

"Umm?"

"I'm sorry."

She turned, and in the light that streamed beneath the elk hide, he could see her eyes shining, her face framed in a glistening bed of silver hair. "What for?"

"I'm the one who wounded our love."

For a time, she didn't move, then she said, "Sparrow, there is no unwounded love—"

"No, Dust. Just listen. It was my fault, and I've never admitted it. I am sorry. You needed me, and I wasn't there."

"Yes, I did need you. Very much." A pained expression creased her wrinkled face. "Sparrow, do you realize that everything would have been different if you'd just wakened me that night and told me what had happened?"

"Would it, Dust?" he softly asked. "Are you sure?"

Her brows lowered. "I hated you for leaving me alone, Sparrow. But, to tell you the truth, I don't know which was worse, the hurt you gave me, or the one I gave me. It's not easy hating someone you love with both your souls."

Sparrow lowered his eyes. "Do you still hate me?"

She pulled a lock of his hair across her throat, and stroked it. "No, I haven't hated you for a long time, Sparrow."

He pressed his forehead against hers. "There are so many things I want to say to you. But they all come down to just one thing: I want to wake up with you in my arms every morning, Dust."

"Sparrow, I . . . it will be . . . difficult. There was a time when I thought my heart would die without you. But it didn't. It kept beating. The rains kept coming. The wind still blew." She pushed back, and studied his face. "I love you. But can I depend on you?"

The tone in her voice struck him like a physical blow. He had abandoned her once; she wanted to know if he'd do it again. Sparrow thought about his Spirit Helper, about the needs of the world that often outweighed his own needs . . . and her needs. *Could* she depend on him? What if he had another vision like the one about Paint Rock Village, and had to leave immediately to go and warn the people—and she needed him at the same time? Could he stay with her?

His forehead lined. "I can promise you that I'll try, Dust. That's all."

She turned away, and exhaled hard. "Will you promise me that you'll tell me what's happening to you? Or at least send me word that you'll be away for a time, so I don't worry my souls loose from my body?"

"If I can, Dust, yes."

Her eyes examined the underside of the elk hide for a long time, before she turned back to him. "Then I promise you that if we survive this journey I'll try to trust you again. And if we don't survive at least we'll have had this trip. Do you agree?"

"Yes." He smiled.

"Good, now let's forget about us, and start thinking about Rumbler."

Sparrow pulled the elk hide down, exposing their faces to the falling snow. Moonlight gleamed through the thin layer of clouds, reflecting from the lake below. "I don't know if this storm is going to last much longer. We'd better pack up and start walking. I just wish I knew which direction we should head."

Dust sat up. "I've been thinking about that. Sparrow, when Little Wren broke and ran last night, do you think she could have been trying to draw us away from that shelter?"

She pulled her hair over her shoulder, divided it into three parts and began braiding it.

He held her gaze. "You mean you think Rumbler is still there? Gods, I pray not."

"Why?"

"That shelter is visible from Paint Rock Village. When Grandfather Day Maker rises, that's the first place Jumping Badger will look."

"Then shouldn't we look first?"

Sparrow sat up. "It's too dangerous, Dust. There will be guards stationed all around the village, watching for any movement, and they are definitely hunting us. You heard what Blue Raven told the woman warrior last night. About selling Rumbler to us."

"Yes, that was quick thinking on his part." She finished her thick braid, and searched the snow for the cord she'd removed last night. As she tied it to the end of the braid, she said, "I certainly misjudged him, didn't I?"

"Well," he said softly, "it isn't always easy to know what people will do when pushed."

"But it did not even occur to me that he might be willing to sacrifice himself to save Little Wren."

"He surprised me, too, though I should have expected what he did."

She pulled the elk hide up to her chin and looked at Sparrow. "What do you mean?"

"What would you have done, Dust? If Rumbler had been accused of betraying his people, and you knew that he believed he had done the right thing, wouldn't you offer your life for his? To keep that innocence alive in the world?"

A white cloud of exhaled breath condensed before her. "Yes," she whispered. "Yes, I suppose I would."

Sparrow brushed the snow from his hair, and his bushy brows drew together. "Dust, we need to start thinking about how we're going to escape. Thus far we've been concerned solely with finding Rumbler. But he can't be far. We *will* find him, and once we do, we have to know what comes next."

Her gaze flitted over the hilltop, skimming the trees, and rocks, trailing down to the lakeshore. A thin band of scalloped sand separated the water and the snow. "You don't think the war party will be satisfied with capturing the 'traitors'?"

"No. At first light, they'll begin torturing Blue Raven, trying to find out where Rumbler is—where *you and I* are taking him, and then they'll be on our trail like a pack of wolves after a wounded deer."

"But Blue Raven knows we don't have Rumbler, and even if we did, he has no idea where we might take him."

Sparrow straightened the hide to shield their exposed feet. When he spoke, he couldn't keep the fear from his voice. "He'll lie, Dust. He'll tell them whatever he thinks they want to hear. Maybe not today, but surely by tomorrow night. And even if, by some miracle, he doesn't, Little Wren will be watching. When she sees her uncle suffer, she will tell Jumping Badger anything he wants to know."

Sympathy creased her face. "Poor Little Wren. Sparrow, maybe—"

"*Stop* thinking about it. The task ahead is difficult enough without attempting to take on an entire war party."

Dust jerked a nod, and brushed at the snow on the hide. "You're right. I don't like it, but I know you're right."

Dust shook out the elk hide and began rolling it up.

Sparrow picked up his bow and quiver—he'd slept with them next to him under the hide—and slung them over his right shoulder. Then he reached for their packs. As he handed Dust's to her, he said, "I know the girl risked her life for Rumbler, but—"

"Every instant we spend worrying about Little Wren is one less instant we will have to think about Rumbler. We have to concentrate, or none of us will make it out of this. So . . .'' She slipped her pack on. "What is our escape plan?"

Sparrow took the rolled hide and tied it to the top of his pack. "The closest village is Sleeping Mist. If we find Rumbler, I think we should—''

"But they were just recently attacked, Sparrow. Their foodstores may have been raided. They will be drowning in grief. If I were one of the elders there I'm not sure I would appreciate strangers running in out of the darkness and asking me for shelter."

Sparrow shrugged into his pack, and adjusted his bow and quiver so he could reach them easily. "They have the best reason of all to help us, Dust. They hate Jumping Badger and his warriors more than we do."

He got to his feet and extended her a hand. Dust took it, and rose.

She picked up her pack, and slipped her arms through the straps, saying, "They may hate him, Sparrow, but are they willing to risk every last surviving member of their village to protect us? That is the question. *I* wouldn't be."

"Well, let's hope their clan patron is more generous than you are." Sparrow licked his finger and held it up to the wind. "Wind Mother is gusting down from the north. I'd much rather walk with the wind in my face, than blowing up my back."

"I suppose it's a coincidence that it also happens to be the direction of Sleeping Mist Village?"

"No," he said, and stuck his thumbs in his pack straps. As he started down the hill toward the shore, he added, "Who is the patron there, now? Do you know?"

"We heard that old Mouse Bone was killed in the raid, and that Hungry Owl took his place."

"His son?"

"Yes, he's barely twenty-five, but I hear he's highly respected."

Dust's voice grew fainter and fainter. It occurred to Sparrow that she wasn't following him.

He stopped, and called, "Dust—"

"You don't have to come with me," she called back. "In fact, it would be better if you didn't. That way if the war party sees me, only one of us will be captured. That will leave the other to continue searching for Rumbler."

He expelled a gruff breath and walked back up the hill. "I'm the one who was a warrior. I know how they think. I'll check the shelter. But I want you to wait up here for me. Agreed?"

The jagged line that cut down around her right eye pulled tight. "I'll agree to wait near the shelter. That way I can see—"

"Yes!" He threw up his hands. "Fine. I know that look on your face. There's no way I'm going to convince you to stay in a safe place, so let's just go!"

Sparrow trudged across the hilltop and down among the trees. Deep drifts piled against trunks and boulders. He did his best to work around them, but occasionally he sank up to his hips.

They made it to the main game trail that cut across the front of the hill overlooking the ruins of Paint Rock Village. Sparrow stopped for a moment's rest. Dust came up behind him and grabbed his shoulder to steady herself.

"Do you see it?" she whispered.

"Yes. The shelter is down there. *You* stay here."

"I will. Sparrow? Please be careful." She crouched down behind a pile of deadfall.

Sparrow slowly made his way along the trail. He took three steps, then stopped, surveyed the forest, and listened, before taking another three steps. Snow fell around him, but through the white haze he could see faint crim-

son glows near the outskirts of Paint Rock Village. . . .
Fires burned down to coals.

Sparrow scanned the forest. Where would Jumping
Badger have posted guards? Probably along the trails
coming into Paint Rock. One near Calling Hawk's pinioned corpse. Another at the opposite end of the village.
He didn't see anyone, but he wouldn't. Warriors standing
guard went to a lot of trouble to be invisible.

Humps scattered the area around the fire pits—snow-
covered sleeping warriors. He counted about fifteen people, but there could have been more. The falling snow
obscured a great deal.

The closer he got to the shelter, the stronger the scent
of smoke became.

Sparrow trudged through the snow to the slender poles
leaned against the boulder's face. They had constructed
a snug resting place.

Sparrow whispered, "Rumbler? It's Silver Sparrow.
. . . Are you in there?"

Only the pattering of snow on the poles answered.

Sparrow knelt and peered through a gap in the poles.
They'd thrown dirt over the fire, but some of the coals
beneath had survived. A dull red sheen lit the interior.
Strips of cloth lay on the hearthstones. Sparrow frowned.
He reached in and pulled out the pack that lay against
the wall. Dishes clattered. As he slipped the strap over
his shoulder, he saw the folded cape on the floor . . . then
the opening in the poles on the other end of the shelter.

*She did draw us away. Blessed Spirits, how many times
has that little girl risked her life to save Rumbler? While
we were chasing her, Rumbler was running in the other
direction.*

Sparrow rose to his feet and cautiously examined the
ground. Any tracks Rumbler had left had long ago filled
in with snow. But where might he have gone? Not down-

hill. They would have seen him. Not across the face of the hill. Too much deadfall. The only clear path led from the top of the boulder up the hill.

Sparrow squinted, thinking, then headed back for Dust.

By the time he reached her, the snow had diminished to a few big flakes.

Dust stood up, her face shining within the frame of her hood. "Rumbler wasn't there?" Disappointment laced her voice.

"No, Dust, but I found this." He pointed to the pack. "And I think I know what happened to Rumbler."

Dust clenched her jaw, as if steeling herself. "What?"

"There were two openings in their shelter. One on this side, the one we saw Wren dash out of, and one on the opposite side of the shelter. I think Rumbler went out that one right after Wren caught our attention."

She searched his face: "But where did he go?"

"As best I can figure, up the hill."

Dust turned and looked, then started back up the trail they'd come down. Sparrow followed her in silence.

When they had cleared the drifts and reemerged on the hilltop a short distance from where they'd slept, Dust stopped and tried to catch her breath.

"Do you think," she asked, "that they talked about a meeting place?"

"I don't know. They didn't have much time after we found them. But they might have. Little Wren must be a smart girl. They managed to avoid the war party longer than most adults would have."

Dust touched the pack. "This must have belonged to her. It's too big for Rumbler to carry."

Sparrow nodded, and let his eyes trace the undulating line of the hill to the spot where he thought the trail from the boulder might come out. "Do you see that grove of pines to the northeast? Down near the water's edge?"

Dust looked into the wind. Gusts flapped her hood around her face. "What about it?"

"The trail I told you about? The one I think Rumbler may have taken? It would come out on the hilltop just above that grove of pines."

Moonlight shot through a gap in the lines of the marching Cloud Giants, and ignited the snow. It blazed like blue-white fire.

"Do you think he's hiding there somewhere?" Dust asked. "Waiting for Wren?"

Sparrow gripped her hand, and led her down the hill. "Let's find out."

Freezing, her dark blue shirt and pants soaked with melted snow, Wren leaned against the oak tree, staring at Uncle Blue Raven. He lay on his back twenty hands away, his eyes half-open.

She kept expecting to see him move.

To take a breath.

For a full hand of time after Acorn had found him, and said he was dead, Uncle Blue Raven had moved. His fingers had clenched. His feet had jerked.

A disoriented numbness filled Wren. He must be dead. Everyone said so. But . . .

She clutched the rawhide strip on her belt.

Elk Ivory sat on a stump a short distance away, a blanket around her shoulders, and her bow across her lap. Wren didn't know where Acorn had gone. The other warriors, including her cousin Jumping Badger, lay rolled in their blankets, snoring.

She had to think. She knew it. But her brain had stopped working.

Elk Ivory stood up, stretched her back, and walked toward Wren. "Are you cold?"

Wren nodded. She didn't want to open her mouth. Her teeth had been chattering uncontrollably. She tried to remember to keep her jaw clenched, but sometimes she forgot, and her mangled tongue filled her mouth with blood.

Elk Ivory draped her blanket around Wren's shoulders, and the warmth struck her like a splash of boiling water. She shivered wildly.

Elk Ivory knelt beside Wren. "You should try to sleep."

"Elk I-Ivory," she stammered. "Is—is h-he dead?"

She frowned. "Yes, Wren."

"But he m-moved. After you s-said he was."

Elk Ivory sighed. "Sometimes the body doesn't know it's dead. It fights. I have seen men's legs try to run after they've fallen. I have seen dead hands reach for bows. But there is no thought behind the movements, Wren."

"His afterlife s-soul is gone?"

"Yes. I give you my pledge that it is."

Wren gazed at her uncle, afraid to take her eyes from him for fear that he might blink, or sit up, and prove Elk Ivory wrong.

"Can I go . . . t-to him?"

Elk Ivory put a hand on Wren's shoulder. "Wren, he is gone. Do you hear me? It happened very quickly."

Wren tightened her hold on Trickster's rawhide toy. "C-can I go to him?"

Elk Ivory looked away and shook her head. Then she rose to her feet, took her knife out, slit Wren's ankle bindings, and hauled her to her feet. Gripping Wren's elbow, Elk Ivory led her to Uncle Blue Raven.

Wren looked down.

She saw the gashes in his pants, the blood soaking the

snow in an enormous circle around his legs.

"U-Uncle?" she called.

He didn't move.

Snow fell on his open eyes, and fell . . . and fell.

*"Uncle?"* she sobbed.

# Thirty

Sparrow reached the bottom of the hill and headed straight for the sand that had been washed clean by the waves. Dust's steps patted behind him.

"By dawn our moccasins will be soaked," she said, as she stepped onto the wet sand.

"Yes, but the water will have erased our tracks."

A stiff wind blew in off the lake, rippling the moonlit surface and pushing white-crested waves onto the shore. Sparrow inhaled deeply of the damp fishy air, and frowned at the night sky. Cloud Giants roamed the heavens, but between them, in broad patches of open sky, the lodges of the Night Walkers sparkled.

"The storm is breaking," he said. "This isn't good, Dust."

"Just keep walking. So long as we are getting farther away from the war party, it's good."

Sparrow concentrated on placing his feet as close to the water as possible without stepping in it. Their thick winter moccasins had been heavily smoked, and would repel a little water, but they couldn't stand being drenched.

"Sparrow, are you sure that Rumbler was with Little Wren last night? Maybe she hid him somewhere along the trail, and ran ahead—"

"Maybe, but I don't think so, Dust. I didn't see any tracks at the shelter. For that matter, I didn't see anything to indicate that two people had been in the shelter, but I think he was there."

"Tell me what you saw. Her pack. But was there anything else inside?"

Sparrow stepped around a rock and continued forward. "There was a deer-hide cape on the floor. But when we caught up with Wren she was wearing only a long blue shirt and pants, so I assumed the cape belonged to her. There were two pots over the coals. And something odd. Strips of black cloth lay over the hearthstones."

"Strips of cloth? . . . Like bandages?"

"That's what they looked like, yes."

Dust went silent, probably wondering, as he was, which of the children had been hurt. He hadn't noticed any wounds on Wren's exposed hands or face, but that didn't mean much. She could have been wounded in a place he couldn't see. Still, she had flown down the trail like a falcon, apparently in perfect health. If the strips of cloth had been used as bandages, the wound probably belonged to Rumbler.

This new information would be eating at Dust. The little boy needed her, and she didn't know how to find him to help him.

Wind whipped Sparrow's white hair around his owlish face, and tangled it with his eyelashes. He brushed it behind his ears.

While he couldn't shove his worry for Rumbler completely out of his heart, he had more pressing things to consider.

All night long he'd been thinking about Jumping

Badger. If he caught Sparrow and Dust before they'd found Rumbler, Jumping Badger could hold Dust hostage until Sparrow removed his curse, then he'd torture them to find out what they knew about Rumbler. Since they didn't know anything, he'd kill them.

If the war party caught them after they'd found Rumbler, Jumping Badger would hold Rumbler and Dust hostage until Sparrow removed his curse, torturing them, if necessary, in front of Sparrow. Then, after Sparrow removed the curse, he would kill them.

In any case, once Sparrow removed the nonexistent curse, they were all dead.

The solution, of course, was not to get caught, but Sparrow had the uncomfortable feeling that he'd better prepare for the worst.

He studied the shoreline. Five hundred paces ahead, it curved sharply to the left, the dark water rolling up to the grove of pines. The waves had been undercutting the grove for some time. Huge roots hung out of the bank, dangling into the lake like dark twisted arms.

The narrow strip of light sand widened, and Dust trotted forward to walk alongside him. Wind buffeted her hood around her face.

"Sparrow," Dust said and her mouth pressed into a line. "After we find Rumbler, and lose the war party, do you think we can take Rumbler home?"

"I don't—"

A wave splashed Sparrow's legs, drenching his moccasins and pants. He yelped and jumped out of the way. Dust ran. The wave missed her. When it had flowed back into the lake, Dust returned to his side.

"You were saying? You don't . . . what?"

His feet squished. "I don't know, Dust." He didn't really want to discuss this with her, though he'd been worrying about it for several days. "I suspect that stories have traveled far and wide by now. Dozens of villages must be talking about the False Face Child, and what happened at Walksalong Village.''

She gripped her hood beneath her chin. ''Gods, if Cornhusk is telling the story, those three corpses have grown to at least fifty.''

Waves curled over the sand in front of them, tumbling pebbles and squirrel-gnawed pinecones. As they neared the grove, the sweet tangy fragrance of damp pines filled the air.

''Do you want the truth, Dust?'' he asked, and gave her a sideways glance.

''Yes, of course I do.''

''Every member of the Bear Nation has already heard about my 'curse,' and is terrified that the False Face Child might survive.''

He saw the fingers tighten on her hood. ''You don't think Rumbler will be safe anywhere, do you?''

''No,'' he answered softly. Then he added, ''And the village that takes him in will be committing suicide.''

Dust blinked and lowered her gaze to the sand. She walked quietly, her face shielded.

Sparrow inhaled the pine-sharp breeze, knowing the paths her thoughts must be taking. If she couldn't take him home, then she had to choose between Rumbler, and Earth Thunderer Village. The Earth Thunderer Clan depended upon her. Her daughter and grandchildren lived there. But how could she leave a boy of nine winters, a boy she loved, in the hands of strangers?

''Where would he be safe, Sparrow?''

''A place where no one cares about the squabbles between the Bear Nation and the Turtle Nation.''

''Where is that?''

''A place that we've never been. The far north. The far south. Maybe out beyond the western mountains.''

The moon-cast shadow of a bird circled them. Sparrow looked up. The owl sailed over the beach, its eyes shining like polished shells, and landed in one of the pines. It fluffed its wings for warmth, observing them with mild interest.

A game trail cut across the face of the hill, disappearing into the pine grove just beneath the owl. Sparrow studied the bird, then the exposed tree roots. Rocks and cones glittered in the hollow carved in the bank. On the ledge above, ten hands away, pine boughs dipped mournfully. The heavy weight of snow had bent the branches until they touched the ground. The owl blinked at them.

"Dust," he said and put out a hand to stop her. "Wait."

She looked at him. "What do you see?"

"I don't . . ." He shook his head. "What I see is an owl, but my stomach muscles just clenched tight."

She peered at him from the corner of her eye. "Silver Sparrow, don't you ever again complain about my unruly hair, or my nose for the garbage midden."

"This is different, Dust."

She glanced at the owl again. "Really?"

"Yes." He unslung his bow, pulled an arrow from his quiver, and nocked it. The pain in his heart had returned, burning and throbbing. He winced. "I don't know what's happening, but Power is loose on the night. I feel as if every breath of wind is trying to tell me . . . something."

Rumbler lay on his side with his knees pulled up inside the fox-fur cape, his good finger tucked into his mouth. He'd been crying. The people standing on the shore below were blurry, like faraway mountains on a hot day.

The wind and waves gnashed at each other, eating the people's words, but he could hear their voices. . . .

He shivered.

The voices glittered inside him, like the skin of ghosts, or dead eyes underwater.

He reached over, and spread the pine boughs to see better.

Sparrow edged closer to the water-carved hollow in the bank. The owl watched him. Wind Mother gusted across the shore, rattling the exposed roots, and blowing a haze of moonlit snow down from the bank above. Sparrow closed his eyes briefly, then examined the ground. No tracks marred the sand. But the pain in his chest had turned fiery, as if his Spirit Helper . . .

Dust gasped, and Sparrow spun to look at her. She had a hand over her mouth, pressing as if to stop a scream, and Sparrow saw the veins in her temples throbbing.

"Dust!" He grabbed for her arm. "What—"

"Don't you see the face? His face!"

Dust threw off his arm, and ran back the way they'd come, along the game trail that led up through the pine grove.

"*Rumbler?*" she shouted. "*Rumbler!*"

From beneath the pine boughs, a snowy white figure emerged. He trotted to the edge of the bank. Chin-length black hair framed the round face in the fox-fur hood. Moonlight gleamed on the tears on his cheeks.

In a choking voice, he called, "*Grandmother? Grandfather?*"

Dust ran. She fell on her knees in front of him, and

clutched him to her chest, kissing his face and throat, murmuring words Sparrow could not hear.

Sparrow straightened. The pain in his chest had vanished. In an instant. The moment he'd seen Rumbler.

He glanced around the dark shore, expecting to catch a glimpse of his Spirit Helper, but saw no one.

Sparrow trotted to the game trail and climbed to join them.

When he knelt, Rumbler disentangled himself from Dust's grip, and threw his arms around Sparrow's neck. "Grandfather, Grandfather!"

"Shh, you're all right now." Sparrow hugged the sobbing boy, and patted his back. Rumbler had a bow and quiver slung over his shoulder beneath his cape. Wren's? "Everything's going to be all right."

He picked Rumbler up, and started down the hill.

Rumbler extended a tiny hand over his shoulder, reaching out to Dust, and she rushed forward to grab his fingers.

A small terrible cry came from her lips.

Sparrow blurted, "Dust?"

"Oh, Sparrow. His hands. He—he must have had frostbite. I need to look—"

"Later. Let's put distance between us and the war party. At dawn, we'll stop and eat, and you can take a closer look at his hands."

"Yes, you're right."

He felt Dust stroking Rumbler's hair and heard her say, "We're going to get you away from here, then we'll figure out what to do."

"Yes, Grandmother." Rumbler wept the words, and buried his face in the hollow of Sparrow's throat.

Sparrow led the way back to the sand, and headed northward as fast as he could walk.

It took less than a finger of time for Rumbler's body

to relax in Sparrow's arms, his breathing to slow in the deep rhythms of sleep.

Dust let go of his hand, and came around to walk at Sparrow's side.

A frown lined her face. "If we keep up this pace, we should make it to Sleeping Mist Village by early afternoon, shouldn't we?"

"Yes, Dust. We'd better."

Wren lay curled on her side with her cold hands between her knees, watching Dawn Woman wander across the meadow. The lavender hem of her dress dyed the snow as she moved. A weary breath escaped Wren's lungs, and floated away in white streamers. Her gaze clung to them as they drifted out over the meadow.

Acorn and Elk Ivory stood at the edge of the growing light, thirty paces away, digging a hole in the ground with wooden bowls. They had carried Uncle Blue Raven into the meadow and laid him in the snow. His blood-soaked hide pants sparkled the deep red-brown of old scarlet oak leaves.

Like shocked nerves awakening after a blow, a tingle spread across Wren's chest.

She remembered the love in his eyes the day he'd helped her bury Trickster. Uncle Blue Raven had gently lifted the spotted dog and placed him in the grave. After Wren had petted Trickster, filled the grave with precious toys and elk jerky, they'd covered him up, and Sung the Death Song. Wren had only been able to Sing part of the song, because she'd started crying. Uncle Blue Raven had put an arm around her shoulders, and finished the Song for both of them.

She remembered the pain on his face the last night she'd brought him food on Lost Hill . . . the sad way he'd gazed at Rumbler.

Rumbler . . .

*Ancestors Above, please help him.*

He would be looking for her right now. He must be freezing and hungry. Wren wished she'd thought to give him the pack with the food bags last night. At least he had her bow and quiver. He could hunt, maybe, if his hands allowed. But she prayed he wouldn't come out of his hiding place, wherever it was, until long after Jumping Badger and his warriors had gone.

Elk Ivory and Acorn set their bowls aside, and lifted Uncle Blue Raven into the shallow hole, four hands deep. They did it gently, with respect, then piled the dirt back over his body.

Elk Ivory stood, and began the Death Song. Her beautiful high voice rang across the camp.

Acorn's rich baritone joined hers.

Wren closed her eyes, and whispered the words, *Sky Holder, great Sky Holder, come walking, lift Blue Raven's soul . . .*

Several warriors walked away from their morning fires and shuffled around the grave in the Death Dance, Singing, their arms over their heads, their feet stamping the ground, sending up puffs of white.

Steps crunched the snow around Wren. She opened her eyes.

Jumping Badger stood over her, surrounded by Rides-the-Bear, Shield Maker, and Buckeye. The other warriors tended to their morning chores, rolling blankets, making breakfast, monitoring the fires.

Jumping Badger's breath puffed from his nostrils and twisted away in the morning breeze. He wore a heavy beaver-hide coat, and held the staff with the dead war leader's head in his right hand.

Wren had barely enough strength to stare up at the new mask that covered Lamedeer's face. Her eyes didn't want to focus. The mask might have been carved by a child of six winters. The crow's beak was crooked, one eyehole larger than the other, and set higher. But through them, Wren saw sunken pits filled with yellow crust.

Nausea clawed at her stomach.

Jumping Badger thrust the staff at Buckeye, who stood beside him, saying, "Hold this until I'm finished."

Buckeye took the staff and held it a distance, his head pulled back, as if to avoid the reek. Three hands taller, and twice as wide as Jumping Badger, Buckeye dwarfed the war leader. He had plaited his black hair into two short braids.

"Perhaps I could plant the staff in the snow," Buckeye suggested. The numerous scars on his round face twitched.

Jumping Badger replied, "You will hold it, as I ordered you to."

"Yes, War Leader," Buckeye said, but he grimaced.

The other warriors cast uncomfortable glances at Buckeye, as if grateful he'd gotten the duty instead of them.

Jumping Badger crouched before Wren, and smiled coldly. "Sit up, cousin."

Wren braced her bound hands on the ground, and tried to sit up, but her shaking arms wouldn't hold her. She struggled for a time longer, then slumped to the snow, trembling.

Jumping Badger gripped Wren by the shoulders, and pushed her back against the oak trunk. Her head thumped hard.

But she didn't make a sound. She just blinked at him.

Buckeye glanced disapprovingly at Jumping Badger, and his jaw locked.

The other warriors, Rides-the-Bear and Shield Maker, grinned. Though they were cousins, they looked like twins. Both had ugly triangular faces, with thin noses, and missing teeth. Rides-the-Bear wore a dirty buckskin cape. Shield Maker had on a bear-hide coat, and a necklace made from the toe bones of a dog.

Wren closed her eyes, longing for Trickster. She moved her bound hands to the right and stroked the chewed strip of rawhide. She tried to imagine him chewing it, his eyes bright, his tail wagging.

"Look at me, cousin."

Wren opened her eyes.

Jumping Badger stared at her from less than two hands away. Filthy strings of black hair framed his oval face. "Where is the False Face Child?"

Wren shook her head weakly. "Uncle . . . sold him."

"I know that. I heard Blue Raven tell his tale of his treachery. Who did he sell the child to?"

"People . . ." She swallowed hard. Her tongue had swollen, making it hard to talk. "Turtle Nation people. I didn't . . . know them."

"What did they look like?"

Wren did not know what to answer. Her uncle hadn't told her what to say. Could it hurt to tell the truth? "The man . . . had seen about thirty winters. He had some gray in his black hair. The woman . . . she was younger. Maybe . . . eighteen. She had deep black hair."

Buckeye said, "She just described half of the Bear Nation. What good does this—"

"Yes," Elk Ivory said as she and Acorn stepped into the circle. "What good does this questioning do, War Leader? The girl knows nothing. Blue Raven said so himself."

Jumping Badger slowly turned to look at her, then Buckeye's face and Acorn's. Hatred lit his eyes. "She may know nothing. But I have not determined that yet."

Jumping Badger smiled at Wren again, then slapped her as hard as he could.

The force of the blow sent Wren tumbling to the left. Her head struck a rock buried beneath the snow, and pain exploded. Blood filled her mouth from where she'd bitten her tongue again. She weakly spat the blood onto the snow.

"Jumping Badger!" Buckeye shouted. "This is madness! She is a child!"

Jumping Badger ignored him. "Sit up, cousin. Sit up!"

Wren dragged herself up, and Jumping Badger hit her again, knocking her back down in the snow. Sickness welled in her throat. Her stomach pumped until nothing more would come up. But the spasms didn't stop. Her belly heaved, and heaved.

Elk Ivory glared her disgust at Jumping Badger. Acorn and Buckeye turned away, looking ill.

"Sit up, cousin," Jumping Badger ordered. "Now!"

Wren struggled to do as he said, but her arms had turned to boiled grass stems. She made it halfway up, then collapsed in her own vomit.

Jumping Badger twined his fist in Wren's hair, and yanked her to a sitting position. "Where is the False Face Child, cousin? You must have heard something. Where did the Turtle Nation people say they were going?" He picked up a rock and tested its weight in his hand.

Light-headed, confused, Wren shook her head. "No, I—I didn't—"

The blow came out of nowhere.

She heard her skull crack, and found herself sprawling face first into the snow. She couldn't breathe. Jumping

Badger kicked her over onto her back, and shouted at her, but his voice sounded thin and faint, and his face above her kept diving close, then flying away.

"Blessed ancestors!" Elk Ivory shouted. "She is a little girl, Jumping Badger! Leave her be!"

Acorn knelt beside Wren, and helped her to sit up. Her brain pounded, trying to get out of her skull. Wren wobbled against him.

Acorn gently said, "Are you all right?"

"S-sick. Sick."

Jumping Badger drew back his fist and started to strike her again, but Elk Ivory caught his arm and shoved him backward. Jumping Badger stumbled in the slippery snow. When he caught his balance, he grabbed for his stiletto, but Elk Ivory pulled hers first. She stood poised on the balls of her toes, her arms spread, circling him. Fury blazed in her eyes.

"Let us end this," Elk Ivory said in a low deadly voice. "Here and now."

"I will enjoy killing you, old woman." Jumping Badger smiled.

"Stop this!" Acorn shouted, and leaped between them. "Are you fools? Half of our village is dead, and you wish to kill each other!"

Without Acorn to support her, Wren crumpled to the snow again. She lay on her back, blinking at the drifting Cloud Giants. They seemed to be dancing.

Jumping Badger spread his feet, bracing himself for the fight. Sweat beaded his upper lip.

"You are stupid, Acorn," he said. "If we do not find out where the Turtle people are taking the False Face Child, we will never find him, and everyone left alive in our clan will be dead."

Elk Ivory moved to the left, forcing Jumping Badger down the hill. She said, "Blue Raven told you that Little

Wren knew nothing. He said she'd caught up with him only yesterday. What good does it do to hurt her?''

"I hurt her because she knows more than she's telling! I can see it in her face. If Blue Raven sold the boy to people from the Turtle Nation, where is the payment he received? He had nothing on him. Did he hide it? I don't think so. He did not have time. The girl knows the real story!'' As Jumping Badger circled around close to Wren, he shouted, *"Don't you, girl?,"* and delivered a brutal kick to her shoulder.

The jolt flung Wren down the hill. She rolled twice, landing on her belly. Snow coated her eyelashes and long hair. Weak and bewildered, blood throbbing in her ears, she knew she couldn't sit up without falling. She lifted her head, and looked at Jumping Badger. "I hate you," she said wearily.

He moved toward her, but Acorn cut him off.

Acorn said, "If they are Turtle Nation people, won't they go to the nearest Turtle village for help? I would!''

Buckeye asked, "What is the nearest village?"

Jumping Badger's eyes narrowed. He glanced at Acorn, then back to Elk Ivory, and cautiously straightened up, lowering his stiletto. "Sleeping Mist," he said. Then, as if at a new thought, he roared with laughter. Every warrior went silent. "Sleeping Mist! Those fools! Do you think word has reached them that we are chasing the False Face Child? Could they possibly be idiotic enough to risk the pitiful survivors of their village by sheltering our quarry?"

Buckeye's nostrils flared. He thrust the staff with the head into the snow, planting it deep, then glared at Jumping Badger as if daring him to say anything. When Jumping Badger just scowled, Buckeye tramped away toward camp.

Elk Ivory lowered her stiletto, and stepped back, breathing hard.

She went around to Wren, slipped her arms under Wren's knees and shoulders, then lifted her.

As Elk Ivory carried her back into camp, she whispered, "Wren. Answer me. Is that where they said they were going? To Sleeping Mist?"

Wren lay limply in Elk Ivory's arms, her brain hammering against her skull. Thirst plagued her. She had never been this thirsty in all her life. Every muscle in her body cried out for water. "Didn't," she croaked. "Didn't . . . say. I d-don't know . . . where . . . really, Elk Ivory."

Her bound feet swung in time to Elk Ivory's steps, and the ropes cut deeper and deeper into her ankles. Blood ran warm down her feet.

Elk Ivory clutched Wren to her chest. As they neared the fire pits, the warriors gathered around them, peering worriedly at Wren, barraging Elk Ivory with questions:

"Is she all right?"

"Jumping Badger is such a fool! Striking a child from his own clan! Has he lost his souls?"

"You should have killed him, Elk Ivory. I wish you—"

"Little Wren needs tea and food," Elk Ivory said. "Who has these things ready?"

Buckeye rose from where he stoked his fire with a long stick. Hard muscles bulged against his cape and pants. He glared hatred at Jumping Badger, standing in the meadow arguing with Acorn, then looked back at Elk Ivory and Wren. His expression softened. "I do. I would share my meal with both of you."

Wren murmured, "Thank . . . you, Buckeye."

The big man's tight expression eased. "Come. Sit down." He gestured to the fallen log he'd pulled up beside the fire pit.

Elk Ivory sat down, holding Wren on her lap. "Can you sit up by yourself, Little Wren? Or would you have me hold you?"

Wren nuzzled her cheek against the soft hide over Elk Ivory's shoulder. Loneliness filled her up until she thought her heart would burst. Uncle Blue Raven was gone. Trickster was gone. Her parents and brother were dead. Even Rumbler . . .

She forced a swallow down her parched throat, and mustered the strength to say, "H-hold me. Please hold me."

# Thirty-One

Dawn light streamed across the lake, turning it into an expanse of glittering amethyst jewels. Dust Moon and Rumbler sat on the strip of sand between the water and the snow, tending their breakfast fire. The waves had calmed with the coming of morning. They shished and rocked gently, tumbling pebbles and bleached twigs before them.

Dust Moon checked the teapot and cook pot hanging on their tripods at the edges of the flames. They steamed, but not enough. She added more driftwood to the fire. Orange tongues of flame licked up beneath the soot-coated pot bottoms. Cups, bowls, and horn spoons nested near the fire pit. Sparrow had gone hunting right after they'd stopped, about half a hand of time ago, but hadn't returned yet.

Rumbler sat across from her, his unwavering gaze on Wren's pack. It rested beside the fire pit, the top unlaced. The corner of Rumbler's black shirt stuck up through the opening. It had been washed and carefully folded. Dust had searched the pack, found a number of empty food bags and one containing a small amount of cornmeal, but little else.

A thoughtful expression creased Rumbler's round face.

"That's your shirt, isn't it, Rumbler?" she asked.

Rumbler nodded. He drew his legs up beneath the fox-fur cape, and propped his chin on his knees. The white hood that framed his round face made his chin-length hair appear startlingly black. "It was dirty. Wren gave me one of hers to wear."

The love in his voice touched Dust Moon.

"She gave you that cape, too, didn't she?"

It had to be. Made to swing around a girl's waist, it hung to Rumbler's ankles.

"Yes," he said softly. "I was cold. Wren took the deer-hide cape for herself. Sometimes, she shivered all night long, Grandmother."

Dust Moon walked around the fire and sat on the sand beside him. The fragrance of pine-needle tea touched her nose.

"I'm glad Wren took such good care of you."

Rumbler rubbed his plump cheek against the fur over his knees. On the horizon behind him, yellow lances of light shot across the sky. The glimmers on the lake changed from amethyst to pale yellow. "Wren is my best friend."

"I thank the Spirits that you found such a friend. By the time we learned you had been captured, and the Walksalongs planned to kill you—"

"Not all of the Walksalongs, Grandmother. Wren's

uncle told his people not to hurt me and—and Wren sneaked me food on Lost Hill.''

Dust pulled a stick from the woodpile to her right and prodded the fire. Sparks flitted and popped. So that's how he had survived the bitter cold and wind. Hallowed ancestors, if anyone had seen Little Wren bringing a condemned child food, she would have been punished severely, maybe even killed.

A faint lake-scented breeze ruffled the gray wisps of hair on Dust's forehead.

"Wasn't Blue Raven watching? How did Wren manage to bring you food when—"

"Wren is smart, Grandmother," Rumbler said. "At dark, she gathered wood, then she built her uncle's fire very high, to blind him. She'd crawl through the snow on her belly to reach me. She always wore this cape. It was hard to see her coming, even for me.''

The worship on his face made Dust's heart ache. She tilted her head. "That took real courage."

Rumbler frowned at his mangled hands. "She's brave.''

Dust reached for Rumbler's hands, and gingerly turned them over. "Did Wren do this, too?"

"Yes." He slid closer to Dust, offering his hands for her inspection. "Wren sawed the black joints off with her knife. She was scared. But she did it."

Dust examined the work. "She did a good job, too. The tendons and ligaments were severed cleanly, and she sliced through the middle of the joint. Did she cauterize the wounds—"

"Yes, she—she said it would help to seal the flesh around the bones." Rumbler wiggled his fingers. "See? It did. Mostly."

"Yes, I do see."

The little fingers on both hands remained infected, but

Dust Moon would take care of that. She released Rumbler's hands, and reached for her pack. As she dragged it over, and searched around inside, she said, "Someday Wren will make a great Healer."

"I know. I—I love her, Grandmother," he murmured.

Dust found the folded bandages and Healing herbs, lifted them out. The laces on the leather herb bag had been gnawed in two.

"Mice!" she said. "They chew up everything. I wish the gods would wipe them all from the face of the earth."

Wind fluttered Rumbler's hood around his face. He tilted his head and looked away.

"What's wrong? Do you like mice?" Dust asked.

"They do chew on things, but . . ."

"What, Rumbler?"

"Well, they also listen, Grandmother. When I was on Lost Hill they came to me every night. I talked to them, and they listened. The mice made me feel better."

Dust stroked his hair. "I'm sorry, Rumbler. I won't say another bad thing about mice."

His black eyes glowed. "The mice might have been trying to tell you something, Grandmother, but they had to chew your laces to get your attention."

Dust shrugged awkwardly. "Well, if so, I didn't hear them."

"Mother . . . my mother," he said with a quaver in his voice, "she told me once that animals talk to humans all the time, but only our souls can hear them. She said that even though we have human bodies, our souls have wings and whiskers. That's why our souls hear the voices of the animals, and our ears don't."

Dust smiled. "Yes, that sounds like Briar. She was very wise."

Dust dipped up a cup of pine-needle tea, and set it on the sand beside her, then unfolded two strips of bandages.

Shadow Spirits fled from the scent of pine needles like cougars from the scent of humans. She tucked the bandages into the cup, and while they soaked, loosened the gnawed ties on her bag of licorice root.

Rumbler sniffed. "Is that licorice, Grandmother?"

"Yes, it is. Here, let me see your hands again."

Rumbler propped his right hand on Dust's knee, and watched as she poured a little ground licorice powder into her bowl. "I told Wren about licorice."

"She didn't know that licorice drives away Shadow Spirits?"

He shook his head. "I think her people have different plant Spirit Helpers."

Dust poured enough tea over the powder to make a paste, then stirred it with her finger. She dabbed the thick paste over the feeding grounds of the Shadow Spirits, then lifted one of the bandages from the tea. After wringing it out, she carefully coiled it around Rumbler's little finger and wrapped his palm twice. As she tied off the cloth ends, she said, "Let's take care of the other hand, then we'll have a cup of tea. How does that sound?"

"I'd like that, Grandmother."

Rumbler held out his left hand, and Dust glanced at him as she coated it with licorice paste. "What are you thinking, Rumbler? Your eyebrows just pinched."

He moved his bandaged finger, then in a barely audible voice, said, "I found my mother."

Dust hesitated, then finished bandaging his left little finger and tied it off. She touched Rumbler's chin, tipping his face to look into his eyes. Anguish and grief filled those black depths. Until this moment, it had not occurred to her that perhaps he'd seen Jumping Badger clubbing Briar, or watched her crawl from the lodge on fire . . . or heard her screams.

Dust murmured, "We saw her, too."

Rumbler tucked his freshly bandaged hands in his lap. "Grandmother? Do you think . . . I've been worried about Mother's afterlife soul. I asked a siskin to go and see if she was in the Up-Above-World, but it never came back. What do you think that means?"

Dust could see the terrible fear in his eyes, fear that his mother wandered the earth alone, a wailing homeless ghost. "Oh, Rumbler, I should have told you the instant we found you. Don't worry about your mother. Sparrow and I buried her."

Rumbler's mouth dropped open. Disbelief vied with hope in his eyes. "Did you Sing her soul to the Up-Above-World?"

"Yes, we Sang her soul to the Up-Above-World. I'm sure she's there this instant, laughing with old friends."

His head trembled. "Then—if I ever learn to soul-fly, I can go see her?"

"You certainly can."

He threw his arms around Dust's neck and hugged her. His hood fell back. "Oh, Grandmother, thank you."

She kissed his hair. "We couldn't leave her like that, Rumbler. We loved her, too."

His breath warmed Dust's ear for a time, then he whispered, "I miss her."

She hugged him tighter. "I do, too. There's something your mother wished me to talk to you about."

"You spoke with her? Before—"

"No, this was a long time ago, right after you were born."

He pulled back and frowned. "After I was born?"

"Yes." Dust smiled at the memory. "I had just cleaned you up, and wrapped you in a blanket, and your mother looked at me and said, 'Dust, if anything ever happens to me, I want you to take Rumbler. Promise me you will take him and raise him as your own son.' "

Rumbler toyed with the fringes on her cape, flipping them. "What did you say, Grandmother?"

"I told her that I could think of nothing more wonderful than having you as my own son."

For a moment, the joy of being loved and wanted seemed so great that he couldn't answer. His throat worked, and he tugged at Dust's fringes. "I love you, Grandmother."

"We love you, too. Very much. Sparrow and I want you to live with us. If you want to. You know you have other relatives, third and fourth cousins in Flowering Tree Village—"

"But Grandmother, first . . . I—I want to find my father."

"Your father?"

"Yes. Wren and I?" he said in a desperate voice. "We were on our way when her uncle came. But now you could go with us! You and Grandfather." He smiled as though she'd just answered a silent prayer. "If you were with us, we wouldn't have to be scared."

The shock coalesced into a hard knot beneath Dust Moon's ribs. "Rumbler . . . your father . . . I don't know where he is."

"But I heard my mother tell you! She told you my father had gone north to the Picture Rocks."

Dust felt as if a bolt of lightning had just struck her. Every nerve hummed. She remembered that conversation as if it had taken place yesterday. She and Briar had been huddled together in the lodge, whispering, trying not to wake Rumbler who slept in the back. He couldn't have been more than two winters old.

Dust said, "Blessed gods, you remember that?"

"Yes, Grandmother. My mother said that after my father discovered she was heavy with child, he decided to go far away. To the Picture Rocks. Don't you remember?''

"Well, yes, I do, but . . ."

Sparrow walked out of the elm trees that lined the shore, carrying a cleaned, plucked grouse in his left hand. Wind Mother had snarled his waist-length white hair into a mass of tangles. Damp curls bordered his cheeks, and draped the front of his elk-hide coat.

As he neared the camp, he held up the grouse and smiled. "It's not much, but it should put some fire back in our bellies."

The newborn light shadowed the hollows of his wrinkled cheeks and temples, making his dark eyes, and beaked nose, seem to jut from his face.

Dust gave Rumbler a serious look, and said, "Let's eat, then we'll talk more, all right?"

He nodded, but he didn't look overjoyed with the idea of waiting.

Dust kissed his forehead and said, "Sit down and I'll get you a cup of hot tea."

Rumbler stepped back, and sank to the sand.

Dust dipped up a cup of tea for him. "Don't worry, Rumbler." She handed him the cup. "Here, this should warm you up inside."

He took the cup in silence and balanced it on his knee.

Sparrow knelt at Dust's side and glanced between them. "You two look like somebody put water hemlock in your tea. What's wrong?"

"Nothing, Sparrow. That grouse looks wonderful. Instead of boiling that bird, why don't we cut it into quarters, and roast it?"

Sparrow grinned. "I like that idea."

He removed his knife from his belt, slit the bird around the middle, then cracked the spine in two. Next, he sawed along the backbone, splitting the two pieces into four, and handed them to Dust.

She pulled sticks from the woodpile, skewered the pieces, and stuck the sticks into the wet sand. Then she tilted the sticks to lean the grouse quarters over the flames to cook.

In only moments the sweet aroma of roasting meat filled the cold morning air.

Dust dipped up two more cups of tea and handed one to Sparrow. Their fingers brushed as he took it, and he seemed to feel her tension.

"Are you going to tell me," he asked, "or do I have to guess?"

Dust sipped her own tea. The tart flavor of the pine needles enlivened her flagging souls, and gave her the strength to pull the memories from the dark corners where she kept them. *I have held this secret in my heart for ten winters. Can I talk about it? Even with Briar dead? I gave her my promise I would never speak of it again.*

She looked up and found Sparrow staring at her intently.

Dust said, "Rumbler wants us to help him find his father."

"His father? You mean the Forest Spirit? The Disowned?"

Rumbler licked his lips, and rushed to say, "Yes, Grandfather. Wren and I were going, but then her uncle came."

Sparrow smiled. "But Rumbler, who can know where a Forest Spirit lives? They're very fickle. They ride whirlwinds, and fly on falling stars. I don't think we could ever—"

"Grandmother"—he sucked in a halting breath, and looked at Dust—"she knows."

Sparrow lifted his brows, and swung around to face Dust. "Do you? How?"

Dust ran her finger around the warm lip of her cup, frowning at the pale green liquid inside. Images flashed, faces half-remembered, others too clear to bear. The sound of Briar's cries floated through Dust. Her heart thudded dully. She lowered her cup to the sand.

"I know because—because I'm the one . . . I . . ." The words failed. She took a deep breath. "I'm the one who asked him to go away."

Sparrow sat immobile, but she could see the thoughts coalescing beyond his dark eyes. "Is this something we should talk about now?" He glanced at Rumbler.

Rumbler's eyes had gone huge. The cup on his knee trembled.

Dust reached over and brushed his cheek with the back of her hand. "I promised I would never tell you," she said, and the ache came through her smile. "But I think it's time for you to hear the story."

Rumbler whispered, "Did he go to the Picture Rocks?"

Dust let her hand fall. "Yes, at first. But I've heard through Traders since then that your father has moved several times. The last I heard he'd gone to a place called the Cove Meadows."

"Can we go, too?"

Dust laced her fingers in her lap, and held them tightly.

Sparrow didn't say a word. But he didn't have to. Kindness and patience shone in his face.

Sparrow asked, "What was his name?"

"Bull Killer."

Sparrow bowed his head, and closed his eyes for a long moment. "Lamedeer's father?"

Rumbler looked between them, then blurted, "Lamedeer's father? You mean Lamedeer is my brother? My father is *human*?''

Dust nodded. ''Yes, Rumbler, he is.''

''But—but I thought Lamedeer had killed his father? Red Pipe told me—''

''I know he did,'' Dust said gently. ''But Red Pipe did not know the truth. No one did. Except Briar, Lamedeer, Bull Killer, and me.''

Fear slackened Rumbler's young face. ''Did my father do something bad? Is that why you made him go away?''

Dust picked up her cup again and took a long sip.

A molten crescent of Grandfather Day Maker's face crested the eastern horizon, and a sparkling flood of light poured over the water. She admired the beauty for a time.

Rumbler frowned at his hands. ''Red Pipe told me that Bull Killer was a witch. He said that's why Lamedeer had to kill him. He—''

''He wasn't a witch, Rumbler,'' Dust said. ''He was a very good man. Just a man of poor judgment.''

Sparrow, his head still down, said, ''What you did was for the best, Dust. The scandal would have torn Paint Rock apart.''

Dust turned the four sticks holding the grouse quarters. Fat dripped into the fire and sizzled on the coals. She looked at Rumbler. He watched her like a dog waiting to be thrown a scrap.

''Rumbler,'' she said. ''This is a hard story to tell. It might take me a while to get it out.''

He said, ''You don't have to, Grandmother. I'll still love you.''

Dust bent forward and kissed his forehead. ''Thank you. You need to know the truth, Rumbler.''

She refilled the teacup, and held it in her lap. ''Your mother had seen eleven winters when her father died. Your grandmother, Evening Star, was very lonely. She took a second husband almost immediately. That's where the mistakes began, but it's not where they ended. Bull Killer's first wife had died in a raid only two moons before. He was lonely, too. When he married your grandmother, he wanted to move to Paint Rock Village. Your grandmother agreed, and he came to live with her.''

"And Lamedeer came, too?" Rumbler asked.

Dust nodded. "Bull Killer had seen thirty winters, ten less than Evening Star. He . . . he didn't love her. He tried, but they were very different people.'' She looked at Rumbler, and found him breathlessly waiting for her next words. "Bull Killer made a mistake in marrying her. But he made a bigger mistake . . . when he started to love Evening Star's daughter.''

Rumbler said, "My mother?"

"Yes. Your mother loved Bull Killer, too, Rumbler. It was wrong, and they both knew it. But it didn't make any difference to the way they felt about each other.''

Rumbler smoothed his left thumb over the bandage on his right hand. "That's when he went away?''

"Yes, but he didn't want to go, Rumbler. He wanted to divorce your grandmother and marry your mother.''

Sparrow said, "Blessed Spirits, if the Paint Rock elders had discovered the truth, that Briar was already pregnant with Rumbler, they would have cast out Briar and Bull Killer. Rumbler would have never had a home. No clan, no village.''

Dust turned her cup in her hands. "It was for your sake, Rumbler, that your parents decided Bull Killer should go away.''

Wisps of black smoke rose from the grouse. Dust leaped forward, pulling them away from the flames. Spots of the skin had charred, but the meat smelled wonderful. She turned the sticks upside down and dumped the pieces into their bowls.

She handed Sparrow his portion, and he took it without a word.

As she handed Rumbler his bowl, she said, "I know this isn't easy to understand, Rumbler. All I can tell you is that every winter, Bull Killer sent a runner to ask Briar how the two of you were doing. I think that's why she never married. She was hoping that someday he would return."

Rumbler blew on his grouse, and steam spun up around his contemplative face.

Dust wondered if he could grasp what she'd been saying. Adultery. Scandal. His mother, barely more than a child, loving her own mother's husband. In the depths of Dust's heart, she actually hoped that Rumbler didn't understand.

"Briar always planned on telling you, Rumbler, when you got old enough," she said.

He took a bite of his grouse. As he ate, grease coated his face and hands. He said nothing.

Dust bit into her own grouse. Neither she nor Sparrow had eaten since yesterday morning. At the first taste of the delicious bird, her stomach growled. She ate slowly, relishing each bite.

Sunrise blazed across the sky, and the Cloud Giants gleamed in unearthly shades of pink and yellow.

Rumbler finished his grouse, and pulled his arms beneath his cape. He watched the fire in silence while Sparrow and Dust finished.

Dust tossed her bones into the flames and cleaned her hands in the damp sand. "Rumbler? Are you all right?"

He sucked in his lower lip and chewed on it for a while. "Grandmother?" he said. "Do you think he cares about me?"

A pain lanced Dust's chest. "Oh, yes, I do."

Rumbler peered at her from the corner of his eye.

"Then, will you go with me to find him?"

Sparrow dumped the bones from his bowl into the fire, and said, "I will, Rumbler."

Dust jerked around.

Sparrow met her probing gaze calmly. He dipped his bowl in the sand, and began wiping it out, cleaning it. "We can't stay here, Dust. You know it. I know it."

"But . . ." Her voice came out low, pleading. "What about Planter and our grandchildren?"

"They'll be here when we get back. This may be Rumbler's only chance."

*For happiness.*

Dust collected the dishes, and tucked them into her pack, thinking about those long-ago events that had changed the entire world. If Bull Killer had not married Evening Star, none of them would be here now. Paint Rock Village would be thriving. Briar would have married someone else. Rumbler might not be alive. . . .

Unexpected tears burned her eyes. She grabbed for Rumbler, and clutched him to her chest. "I'm so glad you're here, Rumbler. We'll find your father. I'll send word to Planter that we'll be gone for a few moons, and we'll go."

Rumbler disentangled himself from Dust's grip, his eyes shining. "As soon as Wren comes."

Sparrow rose to his feet, and slipped his pack over his shoulders. "We should be on our way."

Rumbler craned his neck to look up at Sparrow, and smiling, said, "Are we going back now?"

"Back? Back where?"

"To the pine trees."

Sparrow frowned. "What pine trees?"

Rumbler blinked. "By the shore."

"You mean . . . where we found you last night? Why would we want to go back there?"

Rumbler put a bandaged hand on Dust's neck. "Wren said morning. It's morning."

Sparrow glanced at Dust.

Dust swallowed hard. Gently, she said, "Rumbler . . . Wren won't be there."

Rumbler stared at her. "She—she said she would try to come."

"I know, but"—Dust put her hand over Rumbler's—"do you remember when Wren ran out of the shelter?"

"Yes. She told me to wait down by the shore."

Dust squeezed his hand. "I know, Rumbler, but the war party captured Wren. They captured Wren, and her uncle, Blue Raven. Sparrow and I barely escaped. We—"

A high-pitched animal scream escaped Rumbler's throat.

Dust's souls froze. She reached for him, to hold him, but Rumbler tore free, and dashed away, racing back down the beach with his fox-fur cape flying around his legs.

*"Wren?"* he cried. *"Wren!"*

"Oh, Sparrow!" Dust lunged to her feet. "Hurry! Catch him!"

Sparrow ran, his long legs eating at the distance, calling, "Rumbler? Rumbler, wait!"

When Sparrow caught up with him, he grabbed Rumbler's hood, and pulled him backward. Rumbler stumbled, shrieking, "No! No!" Sparrow lifted Rumbler, kicking, into his arms.

"Rumbler, listen. Listen to me!" Sparrow shouted.

Rumbler punched Sparrow with his wounded hands, sobbing, "She needs me! Wren needs me, Grandfather!"

"Shh! Shh." Sparrow hugged him tightly, and found himself saying something he'd never intended to. "We're going to help Wren. All right? We're going to help her.

We just have to go to Sleeping Mist Village first. We need their warriors, Rumbler. The Walksalong war party is probably on our trail this instant. The three of us can't fight a whole war party by ourselves. If we tried, we'd all be killed. Then who would save Wren?''

Rumbler stopped fighting, but he sobbed, ''So . . . the war party will bring Wren to us?''

''Yes. I think so.''

''Grandfather?'' His mouth trembled. ''Make them come fast. Her echoes . . . Wren's echoes, they're getting harder to hear. We have to make them hurry.''

Sparrow nodded, said, ''We will, Rumbler,'' and carried the boy up the beach toward Dust Moon. She stood by the fire with her gray hair blowing in the wind.

When he reached the camp, Sparrow set Rumbler on the ground, and gave Dust an ironic smile. ''We're going to Sleeping Mist Village.''

Dust exhaled in relief. ''Good. How did you—''

''I told Rumbler we would go to Sleeping Mist and get help. Then we would save Wren.''

Dust looked down at Rumbler's tearful face and understanding dawned. She murmured, ''Yes. Of course we will.''

Dust slipped on her pack and kicked sand over the fire, then said, ''Let's go.''

As they headed north, Rumbler trotted up between them and tucked his hands into their palms. Sparrow's fingers closed around that tiny hand. A heartrending expression creased Dust's face.

They walked forward together.

But toward what, the Spirits alone knew.

# Thirty-Two

Sparrow and Dust Moon left the sandy fringe of the lake, and took the trail up the low rise toward Sleeping Mist Village. The three women working in the plaza hadn't seen them yet. Early afternoon sunlight streamed through the sour gum and dogwood trees, throwing a patchwork of light over the conical bark-covered lodges. Smoke curled from the roofs. The day had warmed and melted most of the snow. Sparrow counted seven lodges in the clearing, but he could see the dark circles where four more had stood. The burned debris had been hauled away, but the earth held their shadows.

"I wonder how many died," Sparrow said to Dust, who walked beside him, her long gray braid hanging down the front of her cape. Rumbler trailed a few paces behind.

"We heard that Jumping Badger slaughtered half the people."

"Then there should be more than three people in the plaza on a warm day like today."

Dust gave him a look. "Yes. On a warm day like today there should be fifteen or twenty people in the plaza, milling corn, knapping new arrow points, scraping hides from recently killed animals. Where do you think they are?"

Sparrow shrugged uneasily.

They crested the low rise, and five dogs raced from

the village, barking and snarling. Sparrow unslung his bow and waved it at them to keep them back, then he looked at the virtually empty plaza again. He pulled an arrow from his quiver and nocked it.

Dust turned around. "Hurry, Rumbler. Let me hold your hand."

The little boy ran forward in his stiff swaggering gait, his hand out, and Dust grasped it.

Rumbler whispered, "Is something bad happening, Grandmother?"

"I don't think so, but we aren't going to take chances."

Rumbler had removed his cape, and tied it around the waist of his long pale blue shirt. The shell beads across the chest shimmered. "I have cousins here," Rumbler reminded her.

"Yes, I know," Dust whispered. "But I want you to stay close to me anyway."

"Yes, Grandmother."

The dogs followed them into the plaza, barking and wagging their tails.

One of the women, pudgy and young, perhaps twenty winters, warily rose to her feet. Her black hair had been cut short in mourning. She called, "Who comes?"

Dust shouted, "Dust Moon! Matron of Earth Thunderer Village, and her family. Who are you?"

The woman wiped her hands on her brown skirt, and narrowed her eyes. "I am Redbud, sister of Hungry Owl. Are you alone? Just the three of you?"

Sparrow stopped, his nocked bow down at his side, and scanned the trees. "Yes," he answered. "We are alone. Are you expecting someone else?"

Like the Faces of the Forest stepping out at dark, dozens of people slipped from behind tree trunks. Each person had a bow or knife, even children barely old enough to walk. The villagers closed in, surrounding the new-comers. People whispered at the sight of Rumbler, and their eyes widened.

Sparrow released the tension on his bow, and slowly spread his arms. "We mean you no harm."

Dust called, "This is no way to greet your relatives. We have come to speak with Patron Hungry Owl! Where is he?"

A slender young man ducked from the lodge at the far western edge of the village, straight up the hill in front of them. He wore a red and black striped shirt, and had plaited his long black hair into a single braid. His turned-up nose rode over full lips.

"Forgive us, Dust Moon," Hungry Owl said as he hurried forward. "We can spare no sentiment these days." But he embraced Dust Moon and whispered, "It is good to see you. Come. Share the fire in my lodge."

"Thank you, Hungry Owl. We are probably being followed. You should post lookouts, just in case—"

"We already have lookouts posted, Matron, that's how we knew you were coming. But thank you for telling me. Please, this way."

Hungry Owl turned and walked back up the hill. Dust fell in behind, and Rumbler trotted at her heels, one hand holding onto her skirt.

Sparrow walked last in line, nodding to the warriors he passed. Many wore bandages on arms or legs. One had a broad swath of cloth wrapping his right shoulder. Blood dyed the fabric. Their visit must have forced him from his robes.

Sparrow recognized none of them. It had been seven or eight winters since he, Dust, and Flintboy had been here. In his fourth winter, everything had excited and delighted Flintboy. But much had changed. Children had grown up. The elders Sparrow remembered were gone. Flintboy was gone. . . .

He ducked beneath the door curtain into the firelit warmth. Buffalo robes covered the floor, and the scent of rose-hip tea filled the air. He knelt beside Dust, across the fire from Hungry Owl. Rumbler sat at the back of the lodge, between Hungry Owl and Dust, his hands on his drawn-up knees, his gaze taking in everything.

Sparrow shifted to a cross-legged position and set his bow at his side.

Pots lined the walls, globular in shape, with round bottoms. Rocks had been wedged around the bases to keep the pots upright. Unpainted, drab designs decorated the clay: checks, raised squares, and the markings from cord-wrapped sticks. In the final stages of shaping a pot, the potter slapped the exterior with the flat face of a paddle. To keep the paddle from sticking to the clay, the paddle was often carved into a checkered pattern, or ribbed with wood. Many people preferred to wrap the paddle with cord. A good potter usually smoothed over these impressions before firing the pot, but these had not been touched. Perhaps the pots had been made in haste? To replace those destroyed during Jumping Badger's attack?

The fire cast a flickering amber light over the soot-coated ceiling, and wavered from the finely woven baskets hanging on the walls.

Dust slipped out of her pack and lifted her cape over her head, revealing her yellow dress. The fringes on the sleeves danced long after she'd stopped moving. "I'm sorry we frightened you, Hungry Owl. We should have called out before we stepped into the plaza."

Hungry Owl reached for the dishes stacked beside the fire pit, and pulled out four cups. A cone-shaped teapot rested in the coals at the side of the pit. "We've been cautious since the attack. Perhaps too cautious, but we're afraid to relax our guard. We have lookouts posted on the surrounding high points. They report any strangers that come near.''

Dust smoothed the frizzy gray hair away from her face. Her braid hung down the middle of her back. ''I think that's wise,'' Dust said softly, then added, ''I was sorry to hear about your father. Mouse Bone was a great leader.''

Hungry Owl smiled sadly, and started dipping up cups of tea for them. He handed the first cup to Dust. ''Just before the attack, he was speaking of you and Silver Sparrow. He could never quite believe that you'd divorced. He said you always seemed inseparable.'' Hungry Owl handed the second cup to Sparrow.

He took it, saying, ''We are. It just took Dust a while to realize it.''

Dust's mouth quirked, but she didn't comment.

Hungry Owl handed the third cup to Rumbler. Awe tinged his voice when he said, ''You must be the False Face Child we have heard so much about.''

Rumbler nodded. He took the cup as best he could with his bandaged fingers. ''Yes. My name is Rumbler.''

''Rumbler,'' Hungry Owl said. ''I like that.''

As he filled his own cup, Hungry Owl's brows drew down over his turned-up nose. ''Is Earth Thunderer Village well?''

Dust frowned down into her tea. ''As far as we know. We haven't been there in more than a moon.''

Hungry Owl took a drink of tea, and waited for more. The red stripes on his black shirt shone orange in the fire's gleam. ''We heard that the False . . . that Rumbler had been stolen during the attack on Paint Rock. How does he come to be with you?''

Sparrow said, ''You mean you haven't heard the story?

I'm surprised. I thought that by now every village for a moon's walk would have—''

"We have heard a few things," Hungry Owl interrupted. "But only about Rumbler. A Trader came through two days ago, and said that the Headman of Walksalong Village had cut Rumbler loose, and escaped with him into the forest. We also heard that a war party was chasing this Headman, trying to get Rumbler back." His gaze slid to Rumbler, then back to Sparrow. "But we heard nothing about you two."

"Well, our story starts many days ago, when Cornhusk came to Earth Thunderer bringing a message—"

Dust put a hand on Sparrow's arm. "Let me tell Hungry Owl, Sparrow," she said. "The Headman, Blue Raven, sought us out on the trail to Paint Rock Village. He sold Rumbler to us. Right after that happened, Jumping Badger caught Blue Raven. We barely escaped with our lives."

Rumbler's mouth gaped at the errors in the story, but he didn't dare correct his grandmother in front of other people.

Hungry Owl didn't blink. He asked, "Is the war party hunting you?"

"Almost certainly. We haven't seen them today, but you should assume that they are behind us."

Hungry Owl nodded. "I feared as much." Leaning sideways, he pulled the door curtain back, and called, "Opposumback?"

The man immediately ducked beneath the curtain, and lowered himself on one knee. He must have been waiting just outside. Tall, with broad shoulders, and shoulder-length hair held in place by a braided leather headband, he might have seen twenty-one winters. A long healing cut slashed across his right cheek. "Yes, Patron?"

"I want you to take the elders, children, young mothers, and all of the dogs into the forest to the Hollow Rocks. Carry plenty of food and water. Tell them they may have to stay there for a few nights. And tell the war leader I wish to see him.''

''Yes, Patron. I'll go right now.''

''Thank you, Opposumback.''

He ducked beneath the curtain, and voices barraged him with questions. Opposumback shouted answers, and called, ''Bigtooth? Find Gull, tell him the patron wishes to speak with him.''

While he waited for his war leader's arrival, Hungry Owl looked at Dust. ''There aren't many of us left, but those of us who are able will help you protect the False Face Child.''

Dust reached around the fire and squeezed Hungry Owl's hand. ''Thank you. You are a generous leader.''

''No,'' Hungry Owl said through a long exhalation. ''I am just my father's son. He taught me well. Someday, I may need to ask your help.''

''When you do, you will have it,'' Dust promised.

The door curtain lifted and cold air streamed into the warm lodge, slapping at the fire, and blowing smoke into Hungry Owl's face. He squinted against it, and waved the man inside, saying, ''Please sit down, War Leader.''

Gull crouched between Hungry Owl and Sparrow. Around thirty winters old, he had a heavy brow, with fierce brown eyes and deep lines across his forehead. Silver streaked his long braid. He wore a knee-length buckskin shirt, and pants. ''Yes, Patron?''

Hungry Owl held out a hand. ''This is Rumbler, also known as the False Face Child''—Gull's face slackened. He nodded respectfully to Rumbler—''and this is Matron Dust Moon, and Silver Sparrow, from Earth Thunderer Village.''

Gull inclined his head to each of them. "We are honored to have you in our village."

Hungry Owl said, "They are running from a war party led by your wife's murderer."

Gull's eyes went hard. He looked at Sparrow. "How far behind you are they?"

"A few hands of time. If they picked up our trail, they could be here by dusk."

Gull grimaced at the flames. "Then we may have time to prepare. Patron, I would like to station scouts along the main trails. If they see anything, they can signal our lookouts."

"Yes, proceed."

Gull turned to Sparrow again. "Do you know how many warriors are in this war party?"

"We heard there were twenty. We saw around fifteen."

"You saw them?" Gull asked. "When?"

"Just after dark last night. Outside the ruins of Paint Rock Village."

"Paint Rock?" Hungry Owl said. "You were at Paint Rock last night? How did you get here so quickly? You must have walked all night."

"Most of the night," Sparrow agreed.

Hungry Owl said, "I should have known. You look exhausted. I will have my sisters prepare food and lay out blankets for you."

"I don't think either Dust or I could sleep, but Rumbler—"

"You should try to sleep," Hungry Owl said. "In a few hands of time, you will wish you had. And don't fear. Our lookouts will warn us if they spot anyone approaching."

Gull rubbed his heavy brow. "I promise you, if there

is danger, I will wake you myself. We need every bow we have.''

Sparrow studied the taut lines around the war leader's mouth. "How many warriors do you have left?"

"Real warriors? Eleven," Gull said. "The rest of our people know how to shoot, but they are hunters, not warriors. I don't know if they'll be able to hit anything when arrows are flying at them."

Sparrow clutched his teacup. Badly outnumbered. A battle would leave many more of their people dead. The fact left a bad taste at the back of Sparrow's mouth. Now he wished he'd listened to Dust, and avoided Sleeping Mist altogether. Though he doubted they would have survived on their own. He told Gull, "When you need us, we'll be ready."

Gull nodded, and said to Hungry Owl, "If you are finished with me, Patron, I would like to go and prepare my people."

"Yes, go. Thank you, Gull."

The curtain swung behind Gull, flashing sunlight across Hungry Owl's face, gleaming in his downcast eyes. He said, "Our chances are not good, as I'm sure you know. I have one important question. Do you wish to keep Rumbler close to you during the battle, or would you rather hide him in the forest somewhere? I would recommend hiding him. For two reasons: He will be safer away from the battle, and you will be able to fight better if you are not worrying about him. But it is your decision."

Rumbler lurched to his feet and ran to Dust, wrapping his arms around her throat in a choking hold. In her ear, he whispered, "Grandmother, please don't make me go!"

Dust grasped his wrist, and said, "We'll think about

it together, all right? We have time before we have to decide.''

Rumbler gazed at Hungry Owl as if the man had just proposed serving his liver for supper.

"Yes, you do," Hungry Owl said, "but not much time. Now, I should go and speak with my people. While I am away, I will have my sisters bring you food and blankets." He rose to his feet. "You really must rest."

"Yes, we will," Dust answered. "Thank you, Patron."

Hungry Owl ducked outside, and Dust gave Sparrow a desperate look.

He could read the tracks of her souls. "Yes," he said, "I know, but Rumbler's chances for survival have just improved tenfold. If we hadn't come here, we—"

"What about Wren?" Rumbler asked. He loosened his hold on Dust. "Can we save her now?"

Sparrow smoothed a hand down Dust's arm, trying to ease her guilt. She grabbed his fingers and held them.

Sparrow said, "The only way we're going to save Wren is by fighting to get her back, Rumbler. She may die in the battle, but her chances of living a long and happy life are much greater if we win."

Rumbler wet his lips, and solemnly repeated, "If we win."

"Matron Dust Moon?" a voice called from outside. "May I enter?"

"Yes, of course."

Redbud, the pudgy young woman they'd seen upon entering the village, stepped inside. Her black hair had been chopped off unevenly, leaving gaping holes in her hair. In one arm she carried three blankets. In the other, she had a basket filled with wild-rice acorn bread. She set the basket in front of Dust Moon, then handed the blankets to Sparrow. "If there is anything else you require, I will be by the village fire pit."

"We have more than we need, Redbud. You've been very kind. Thank you."

The woman smiled, said, "I wish you a good rest," then left.

Rumbler sat on the floor between Dust and Sparrow and reached for a piece of bread. Crumbs dropped down the front of his pale blue shirt. The boy ate as if he hadn't been fed in days, chewing and swallowing as fast as he could.

"Slow down, Rumbler," Sparrow said. "You can have another one."

"Yes, but I have to hurry, Grandfather. The sooner I go to sleep, the sooner Wren will be here."

Sparrow ate a piece, and watched Dust bite into hers. The wild rice added a rich nutty flavor. Rumbler gobbled half a piece more, then took a blanket from Sparrow's lap and dragged it to the back of the lodge. He finished the bread under his blanket, staring thoughtfully at the shiny layer of black creosote on the ceiling.

Sparrow ate another piece of bread, then rose and walked back toward Rumbler. He spread the two remaining blankets over the buffalo hides, and crawled underneath. His face rested about four hands from Rumbler's.

Dust remained sitting by the fire, eating slowly while she watched the flames.

Sparrow could sense her apprehension, but they had crossed over the river now. They had to fight, or die.

He closed his eyes, and did his best to rest.

Rumbler brushed the crumbs from his hands onto his blanket, and slid closer to Grandfather Silver Sparrow. Long white hair spread around his grandfather's face. It looked like a Cloud Giant's hair. Rumbler wondered if it could breathe. The higher you went on a mountain, the harder it was to breathe. Rumbler had always worried that maybe the Giants couldn't get enough air. He reached out and touched the glittering white.

Grandfather opened one eye. "Are you all right?"

"Grandfather, can your Spirit Helper come to help us?"

Grandfather Silver Sparrow tilted his head back to look at Rumbler. The wrinkles on his forehead deepened. "Well, I don't know. I'll ask, Rumbler, but usually he doesn't come to me unless I'm on a vision quest."

"Usually?" Rumbler poked his good finger into the thick white nest. A lot of air lived between the strands. Probably they could breathe.

"I've seen my Helper a few other times. But, frankly, I'd rather not have. I awakened once to find him chasing me like a rabid wolf, and I was running for my life."

"For your life, Grandfather?"

"That's how it felt."

"Um . . ." Rumbler sighed. "Maybe."

Grandfather Silver Sparrow frowned. "What do you mean, 'maybe'?"

Rumbler rolled onto his back and slid up until his ear touched his grandfather's. Smoke wings fluttered around the hole in the roof, batting at each other, trying to get out to fly in the open sky.

"I mean, were you running because he was chasing you, or was he chasing you because you were running?"

Grandfather Silver Sparrow's bushy gray brows pulled together over his beaked nose. "I never thought of it that way. Maybe I shouldn't have run, eh?"

"Spirit Helpers are faster than humans anyway."

"That's true. He always catches me." Grandfather put his hand behind his head. "Three or four moons ago, he knocked me flat, and sank his teeth into my spine. I—"

"Stopped running?"

The corners of Grandfather Silver Sparrow's eyes crinkled. He glanced around the lodge. "Yes."

"He must have really wanted you to stop, Grandfather."

Silver Sparrow rolled to his stomach and braced himself up on his elbows, peering down at Rumbler. The Cloud Giant hair fell across the buffalo hide like foam spilling over a waterfall. "Well, he got what he wanted, but he had to take extreme measures, didn't he?"

"I don't think you'd better run again. Next time he might leap for your throat, or chew out your eyes."

Grandfather scratched his ear. "That *would* be unpleasant. Where did you learn so much about Spirit Helpers?"

Rumbler yawned, a wide long yawn, and pulled his blanket up to his cheek. The cloth had been woven with strips of rabbit hide, and it felt soft and warm against his face. "My mother used to run. The last time she did it, her Spirit Helper leaped on her back, and tore out her windpipe. She told me wisdom was born standing still."

Grandfather Silver Sparrow stretched out on his stomach and rested his chin on his arm. He had an odd expression on his face.

Rumbler closed his eyes.

Grandfather Silver Sparrow whispered, "I wish you'd told me that two winters ago."

Rumbler reached out, and patted his grandfather's hand.

Wan sunlight penetrated the clouds and fell upon the glittering surface of Leafing Lake in veils of fallow gold. The wave crests glowed yellow.

Wren staggered along the sandy shore behind Acorn, her soaked moccasins like clumps of ice around her ankles. They had untied her feet, but a new rope connected her bound wrists to Acorn's belt. When they'd left Paint Rock that morning, she and Acorn had been at the head of the party, but her stumbling gait had pulled Acorn farther and farther behind, until they now brought up the rear.

Waves washed the shore to her right, pushing and pulling at the sand. Wet pebbles sparkled at the edge of the water. Wren concentrated on following the line of Acorn's moccasin prints.

Her head throbbed as if her brain had swollen and was trying to burst through her skull. She couldn't see out of her right eye. Her chest hurt, too. Stabbing pains climbed from her belly all the way up to her throat. His kick must have broken her ribs.

The bulk of the war party stood in a circle two hundred paces ahead, looking at something. Voices rode the afternoon breeze, but she couldn't hear their words.

Acorn muttered, "What are they looking at?"

Wren had no strength to answer. She shook her head.

Just after dawn, they'd discovered the two sets of adult footprints leading away from the lakeshore and up the snowy trail to the pine grove. She had seen Rumbler's prints under the tips of the lowest boughs, and thanked the Spirits that Dust Moon and Silver Sparrow had found him.

But they'd left a trail.

After picking Rumbler up, they'd walked down toward the water. Their steps had vanished the instant they'd stepped onto the sand, but they'd been headed north.

It was enough.

As she neared the circle of warriors, Wren could see a fire pit dug into the sand. They hadn't used all the wood they'd gathered. Several branches lay beside the pit, and charred grouse bones scattered the bed of ashes.

The tracks left no doubt. Three people had stopped here. One of them was Rumbler.

Jumping Badger walked around the pit, using the staff with the severed head like a walking stick. Matted greasy hair framed his slitted eyes. From the days on the trail, and the reflection of sunlight off snow, his skin had sunburned. The white scar across his throat stood out.

He pulled a stick from the woodpile and dug through the ashes.

"There is no warmth," he declared. "But here, on the edge of the lake, the wind would have cooled the coals quickly. I say they are no more than three or four hands of time ahead of us."

Rides-the-Bear grinned broadly. "So we will catch them today." His ugly triangular face and thin nose bore streaks of soot. Both of his canine teeth had been knocked out many winters ago. Since that time, his two front teeth had inched outward, until now they stuck out like a beaver's.

"Yes. Late this afternoon."

Elk Ivory said, "War Leader, I do not think it wise to approach a village we attacked only a half moon ago when they can see us coming. Perhaps we should rest for a time, eat and drink. Then we can approach under the cover of darkness.''

Buckeye came to stand behind Elk Ivory, adding his voice. "I think that is prudent, War Leader. I was not with the last party, but—"

"But you think you know what is best for the rest of us," Jumping Badger said in a low threatening voice, clearly upset that Buckeye had taken Elk Ivory's side. "I think that those of us who have already risked our lives here once know better than you."

Buckeye straightened to his full height, towering over the other warriors. "I don't wish to die, War Leader. I don't think anyone here wishes to. We want to accomplish our goals, and get out with the fewest losses possible. Attacking at night would seem the best way to do that."

Jumping Badger held the staff high, and called to the assembled warriors. "Buckeye and Elk Ivory think we should sit here cowering in our moccasins until we can sneak into Sleeping Mist Village after dark. What do you say? Shall we act like mice afraid of our own shadows? Which of you is a mouse? Call out!"

The warriors milled around, whispering sullenly, but only Acorn lifted his hand.

Elk Ivory said, "For the sake of your ancestors, Jumping Badger, listen to reason." The nostrils of her broad flat nose flared. She lifted her pointed chin, and tucked her shoulder-length hair behind her ears. "Being wary is not the same as being a coward. The survivors of Sleeping Mist Village must still be frightened and watchful. Do you want us to walk into an ambush?"

"I certainly don't," Buckeye said.

"You don't," Jumping Badger mocked. "Listen to the great Buckeye. He does not know what he may be facing and already he is recoiling from the fight. How many warriors do you think Sleeping Mist has, after our attack? Eh? What . . . ten? Maybe twelve?''

Rides-the-Bear folded his arms over the chest of his dirty buckskin cape. ''I would say ten, War Leader. They had no more than twenty to begin with, and I killed three myself.''

''Yes,'' Jumping Badger said proudly. ''You are a fighter. As is every warrior in your longhouse. If Mossybill or Skullcap were here, they would want to run to Sleeping Mist as soon as possible. To get this over and done with so we could go home to our families.''

Elk Ivory lifted a brow. ''That's why they're dead. Neither one of them had the judgment Falling Woman gave a mosquito.''

Rides-the-Bear shoved forward with his fists clenched, as if to fight Elk Ivory . . . until Buckeye stepped alongside her, and drew his stiletto. His massive shoulders rippled with muscles, and his gaze turned deadly.

Rides-the-Bear stopped, took a breath, and stabbed a finger at her. ''When this is over, I will settle with you for your insults, old woman.''

Elk Ivory looked at him blandly. ''Look around you. All of you! We are at each other's throats. We are tired, and disheartened over the news about our families. Do you think this is the time to rush into battle? Of course not! We need to rest, and consider how to proceed!''

Acorn dragged Wren up behind Elk Ivory, and said, ''What harm could it do to spend a few moments talking?''

Wren sank to the sand at Acorn's feet, and tilted her head to peer up at Elk Ivory. Until yesterday, she had never understood why Uncle Blue Raven had once loved her so much.

*Elk Ivory cares about people. She understands their souls. As Uncle did. She should be war leader.*

As Wren looked around the circle, she could see the same thought on the faces of many of the warriors. Jumping Badger apparently saw the same thing. His teeth ground beneath the thin veneer of sunburned skin.

Jumping Badger lifted his staff, and called, "Let us cast our voices! Who wishes to come with me to fight the cowards in Sleeping Mist Village who are protecting the False Face Child? Who wishes to help me kill the False Face Child?"

"We don't know they're protecting—" Elk Ivory began.

Jumping Badger shouted her down. "Who will follow me? Which of you is still loyal to the orders of the Walksalong matrons?"

Wren watched as men dropped their heads, shuffled anxiously, then walked like kicked dogs to stand behind Jumping Badger. But several also walked to stand behind Elk Ivory.

After sides had been chosen, Jumping Badger counted the men behind him, and said, "Twelve brave men stand with me, Elk Ivory. You have eight."

She nodded, but it was a cold gesture. "We will stand with our relatives, as we always have," she said. "But many fine warriors are about to die, Jumping Badger, and you are to blame."

"Yes, go ahead and blame me, old woman. What do I care? Just do your duty to your people. We must kill the False Face Child before the rest of our clan dies!"

Jumping Badger turned his back to her, and ran up the beach with a straggling line of warriors behind him.

Buckeye put a hand on Elk Ivory's shoulder. "Your words were true. I regret that so few people listened to them."

Elk Ivory looked around at the warriors who had stood with her. "We all cast our voices. Even if we do not like the outcome, our responsibility now is to help our relatives. Come. Let's catch up with them."

Elk Ivory led the group forward at a trot.

Acorn pulled Wren to her feet, and started to follow.

But, wobbly from sitting, her head in agony, Wren's feet didn't want to work. She weaved from side to side, staggering uncontrollably, then tripped in one of Acorn's moccasin prints and toppled to the sand. He dragged her for two paces, and stopped.

Acorn's mouth tightened, and tears filled Wren's eyes.

He glanced at the war party, pulling ahead fast, and bent over Wren. The ridge of hair that ran down the middle of his shaved skull shone in the light.

"My head," she said hoarsely. "It hurts."

"Little Wren, I cannot carry you. I must have my arms free to shoot my bow. But we also cannot lag hundreds of paces behind the war party. If we're attacked, you and I will be the first ones picked off. Do you understand this?"

"Yes."

"What am I to do with you?"

"L-leave me. Leave me here."

"I can't do that. And if I tell Jumping Badger that you can't keep up, he'll kill you."

Wren bit her lip, and struggled to her feet, but nausea overwhelmed her, and her knees buckled. She hit the sand retching. She sat there until she could muster the strength to try again. This time, she rose and locked her knees. "I can keep up," she said.

Acorn searched her bruised face. "Very well, but if you fall again, I don't know what will happen to you."

Wren nodded.

Acorn straightened, and started walking.

Wren focused her good eye on the backs of Acorn's moccasins. Grains of wet sand clung to the leather.

Her entire body hurt. But she couldn't let herself think of that.

Instead, she thought about Rumbler. About the way he had looked at her the night she'd rolled him onto her cape and dragged him off Lost Hill. About the sound of his cries when he'd found his mother.

And she thought about Uncle Blue Raven.

A thousand winters from now, when her lonely soul wandered the dark forests, she would hear his voice ordering her to lie, to tell people it had been his fault . . . and the hurt would have nowhere to hide in her ghost's body.

In the trees to her left, a branch cracked.

Wren pulled her head up.

He moved from tree to tree.

Dancing. Hiding and peeking out. A specter of blood and sunlight flashing between the dark trunks, his face luminous.

The crimson slashes across his chest had become streaks of fire.

His whisper seeped from the sand and sky, *I told you, Wren. I told you you would come.*

# Thirty-Three

Iron-gray light streamed through the smoke hole, waking Dust Moon with a start. Her heart pounded as she propped herself up on one elbow to look around. Had it gotten so late? The fire had burned down to coals. A soft red gleam coated the interior of the lodge, dyeing the baskets on the walls, and the black hair over Rumbler's face.

Sparrow lay on his side facing Dust, fast asleep. A wealth of white hair fell around him. Her gaze drifted over the deep lines in his face, the dark circles beneath his eyes, the sensual curve of his lips, his beaked nose.

In their entire life together, she had never longed to touch him more than at this moment.

But she didn't. The sight soothed her. Rumbler lay on his back with the top of his head touching Sparrow's, and his hand buried in Sparrow's hair, the embers in the fire pit behind them wavering redly, the rich scent of wood smoke blending with that of damp bark walls.

The innocence and stillness made the night to come seem unbearable.

If she died it didn't matter, but it was very important to her that they live.

The night of Flintboy's death, after Sparrow had left her, she had lain in their bedding, alone for the first time in her life, and screamed at the gods. And at Sparrow. His strength had anchored her to the world and, without it, nothing had seemed quite real. During the eighty-three days of his absence, she had wandered the village like a sleepwalker, only half-alive, caught in a terrible nightmare from which she could not escape.

Every instant she had feared Sparrow was dead, and prayed that the gods would give her the strength to stand it. Somehow she knew she would have to, for the sake of their daughter and grandchildren. For their clan.

But the thought of him being dead had left her longing for death, too.

She didn't ever want to feel that way again.

Sparrow's hand rested palm up on the warm buffalo

hide between them. Dust reached out and lightly touched his fingers.

An ache swelled her heart.

This might be their last day together, and she wanted to tell him a thousand things.

She let her finger trace the side of his forefinger down to the curve of his thumb.

His eyelids fluttered. He murmured, "Worried that by tomorrow we might be dead?"

"Death doesn't frighten me, Sparrow," she whispered. "The idea of living without you frightens me."

His lips twisted in a slight smile. "You've been reading the tracks of my souls."

She studied his closed eyes. "Have I?"

"Yes." He opened his eyes, and propped his head on his hand. "I've been thinking . . ."

She gave him a few moments to continue, but when he occupied himself smoothing his fingers over the curly buffalo hide, she said, "I already hate the idea, Sparrow, and I've only heard the tone in your voice. What is it?"

"It's practical." He sucked in a deep breath. "There's no reason for both of us to be in the thick of the fighting. I—"

"I'm staying here with you. I can shoot a bow."

"I know that, it's just that . . . well . . . Rumbler won't go to the forest unless one of us goes with him, and he will certainly be safer out there than in the village. Also, just as importantly"—he clasped her hand and drew it against his chest—"Dust, please, I don't want you here."

"But you need me here. Gull said they needed every bow—"

"I remember what he said." He clutched her hand more tightly. "But I also know that if you are beside me, I will be so concerned about you, I won't be much good to Gull."

He looked at her, and in those dark loving eyes she saw his fear.

Her voice quavered. "Sparrow, you are not a young man. This battle—"

"Has to be fought."

"Sparrow—please—just—I don't want you to die."

He gave her a somber look. "It makes me very happy to hear you say it, Dust, but you must realize that my chances of staying alive are much better if you aren't in the fight. I'll be able to concentrate, and you'll be able to protect Rumbler. You know as well as I that if you give Rumbler into someone else's hands, and stay here with me, you'll be worried sick about him the entire time. You'll be preoccupied worrying about Rumbler and me. I'll be preoccupied worrying about Rumbler and you. Rumbler will be worrying about both of us. This is a simple matter. We will all feel better if you and Rumbler are hiding in the forest."

Wind puffed beneath the door curtain and fanned the coals. The resulting flare of scarlet light lit his eyes. He lifted Dust's fingers and kissed them. "Pretend you're a clan matron," he said. "What would you advise us to do?"

She scowled. "I still don't like it."

"But Rumbler and I do, don't we?" He stretched to look at Rumbler.

Dust had been so involved in the discussion she had not even considered the boy might be listening.

Rumbler brushed his hair behind his ears and sat up. His round face had a rosy hue.

"I won't be scared if you're with me, Grandmother."

"I know, Rumbler, but . . ."

The door curtain lifted and Hungry Owl stuck his head inside. He had donned a dark moose-hide cape. With the hood pulled up, his young face looked very pale.

"A heavy mist has rolled in," Hungry Owl said. "Our lookouts can see nothing. You might want to get up."

Sparrow threw back their blankets, and got to his feet. As he picked up his bow and quiver, he said, "Thank you, Hungry Owl. Where are your people gathering?"

"We've built a fire in the trees to the north."

"We'll meet you there shortly."

Hungry Owl nodded, said, "Please empty the teapot over the coals before you leave. We're killing all the fires in the village." Then he let the curtain drop. His steps retreated quickly, and Dust could hear hushed voices outside.

Dust put her cape back on, and handed Rumbler's fox-fur cape to him. The boy took it, and slipped it over his head, waiting wide-eyed for directions from either one of them.

Dust said, "Rumbler, don't forget your bow and quiver." She handed them to him, and then picked up her own.

Rumbler clutched the weapons to his chest. Softly, he said, "Wren's bow and quiver."

"Oh. I should have known. Thank the Spirits for Little Wren. Rumbler, you still have a half-full teacup. It might be the last you get to drink for a time. Why don't you finish it."

"Yes, Grandmother," he said and reached for the cup.

While he drank, Dust locked gazes with Sparrow. He shrugged into his buffalo coat, and gave her a small confident smile.

"I trust," she said, "that you asked your Spirit Helper for a little assistance."

Rumbler answered, "I asked mine. They said they would come down from the skies." He set his empty cup by the fire, and pushed by Dust, trotting for the door. Before he exited, he added, "Grandfather asked his, too." He ducked outside, and they could hear him emptying his night water.

Dust gave Sparrow an uncomfortable look.

Sparrow spread his arms helplessly. "I don't know who he talks to."

"Did you ask for help?"

"Of course I did."

Sparrow reached for the teapot. As he poured the liquid over the coals, sizzling, spitting clouds of smoke erupted.

Dust picked up her pack, and headed for the door. She ducked out into the dreary afternoon, and held the curtain aside for Sparrow. As he ducked out, he looked at Rumbler, who had joined the people gathered by the fire pit ten paces away, and whispered, "When you get the chance, find out what else he knows."

"Like whether or not we win?"

"No, Dust. Like whether or not we live."

Cornhusk eased a low-hanging spruce bough aside and scanned the woods. Through the thick mist he could barely see five paces ahead. Red maples and sugar maples canopied the trail. Mist dripped from the bare branches, creating a constant patter against the forest floor. His mangy buffalo coat clung to his body like wet rawhide.

It unnerved Cornhusk. They couldn't be more than one or two hands of time from Sleeping Mist Village, and not even he, who had traveled this trail a hundred times, could be sure where they were.

As he shoved the bough aside, the pungent tang of spruce needles encircled him. He listened to the forest.

No wind whispered. No birds chirped.

He had learned from long practice that a man could not be too cautious when approaching a village that had been recently attacked. Some became overzealous in their pursuit of security. Three winters ago, he'd heard that Jumping Badger had attacked Grand Banks Village. The foodstores had been raided. Since starving people often traded rare and precious goods to feed their children, Cornhusk had loaded his packs with corn, marsh-elder and sunflower seeds, beans, squash, and other staples, and hit the trail. He'd blithely trotted into Grand Banks Village with a broad smile on his face. Before he'd reached the center of the plaza, dozens of bow-wielding people had surrounded him—many too young to realize the ill effects of killing a Trader.

He'd discovered soon thereafter that the Grand Banks Clan believed a Trader had betrayed them to their enemies, in order to profit from their needs.

He had genuinely been innocent. But it took a few very disagreeable days, and watching them eat all the food in his packs, to convince them.

He didn't wish to repeat that experience.

Spotted Frog edged alongside Cornhusk. Flying Skeleton had coiled the patron's black braids on top of his head and secured them with a wooden comb. The patron's bloated face glowed red from exertion. "What do you see?"

Cornhusk ran his tongue between the gap in his missing front teeth. "Thick mist, Patron."

Spotted Frog gave him an incredulous look. "Is this the way to Sleeping Mist Village?"

Cornhusk cocked his head, and scrutinized the trail. "Probably."

"Probably?"

Warriors crowded behind Spotted Frog, peering over

his shoulders, their bows nocked and ready. Murmuring broke out.

"I can't be sure, Patron. I could verify our position from any high point—if we could see. But we can't. The most I can say, then, is that I think this is the trail."

Spotted Frog wiped his sweating brow with his sleeve. "Are there no other landmarks on this trail? Boulders, lightning-struck stumps, oddly shaped trees?"

"Yes," Cornhusk replied. "There is a hillside of downed trees half a hand of time before reaching Sleeping Mist Village. A tornado ripped through two winters ago. It snapped trees in two, and flung them about like kindling. But I haven't seen that yet."

Spotted Frog inhaled and let out a deep breath. "Well, let us proceed. If we are on the wrong trail we will know it by dusk, won't we?"

"Definitely. Even with this fog, Sleeping Mist cannot be more than two hands of time away."

"Very well." Spotted Frog nodded. "Continue, Cornhusk. We will follow you."

Cornhusk shifted his weight to his left foot. If anyone out there had laid a trap, the first person in line would be a sacrificial offering to appease their uncertainty. He didn't particularly like the idea that it might be him.

He said, "Patron, are you certain you don't want your warriors to lead the way? After all, there are so many more of them, and they are far better—"

"Yes. I'm certain. My warriors have never been here. You have." Spotted Frog lifted his chin, and drummed his fingers on his bow, daring Cornhusk to display more spineless traits.

After glancing at the slit-eyed warriors, Cornhusk decided he'd better not.

He waved them all forward. "Yes, come along. Follow me."

Dust Moon, Rumbler, and Sparrow stood in the circle with fourteen members of Sleeping Mist Clan. Rumbler leaned against Dust's legs, his hands buried in the folds of her skirt, his white hood covering his short black hair. Sour gum trees towered above them. The fire sizzled in the shower falling from the branches.

Hungry Owl stood with his arms folded, looking down at Gull who knelt before him, his silver-streaked braid over his left shoulder. Gull wore a beautifully tanned buckskin coat, but it had no decorations, no beads, or quillwork, not even a fringe. Nothing to catch the eye, and reveal his position to an enemy warrior. He carried his bow and quiver over his right shoulder. Firelight shadowed the deep wrinkles in his heavy brow.

"We have advance scouts out, Patron," Gull said. "But I do not expect them to be of much use in this fog. At most, if they see someone coming, they may be able to give us a few hundred heartbeats of warning."

"I understand," Hungry Owl said. "Go on."

Gull drew a map in the mud with his finger. "Our eleven warriors will assume their former hiding positions." He made dots in the mud showing the locations. "The rest of you may join any warrior you wish. I assure you he or she will be glad for the extra eyes. And we should leave one person here to keep the fire built up."

Hungry Owl said, "To draw our enemies into the village?"

"Yes," Gull answered. "The closer we can get them to come, the more the blaze will blind them, and the more light we will have to shoot them by."

Hungry Owl's full lips pursed. "Keeping the fire will

be the most dangerous of all positions. Who did you have in mind for—''

''I will,'' Sparrow said.

Dust jerked around with her mouth open. ''But Sparrow, why you? Why not someone—''

''These people are risking their lives to help us, Dust. I will not have Patron Hungry Owl placing one of his loved ones in a position that I am best suited for.''

Hungry Owl said, ''Why are you best suited for this position?''

''I don't have time to tell you the whole story, Patron,'' Sparrow answered, ''but I think that if Jumping Badger sees me standing alone, he will want to speak with me, and his people will follow him into the plaza.''

Gull turned to look up at Hungry Owl. ''That is a good reason, Patron.''

Hungry Owl looked at the firelit faces around him, and asked, ''Does anyone have an objection to Silver Sparrow serving as fire keeper?''

All eyes rested on Sparrow's calm face.

Dust reached for Sparrow's hand and gripped it tightly.

Hungry Owl bowed his head, and the firelight accentuated the curve of his turned-up nose. ''You are brave, Silver Sparrow. You will be fire keeper.''

Sparrow inclined his head, and smiled.

He appeared tranquil and composed, but his hold on Dust's hand tightened until it hurt.

Gull's voice went low. ''Most of our loved ones are hidden at the Hollow Rocks. The rest of us must keep the Walksalongs here, and busy, as long as we can. The more we kill, the less likely they are to want to prowl the forests for missing members of Sleeping Mist Clan. Do we all understand this?''

Nods went round.

Dust Moon's throat ached at their expressions. They

had suffered greatly in the last battle, yet they stood here risking everything they had left to help her, and Sparrow, and Rumbler—distant relatives they had seen, perhaps, three times in their lives.

She lowered a hand to Rumbler's hood, and patted his cheek through the thick fur.

"Very well," Gull said, and rose to his feet. "Let us take our positions."

As people vanished into the mist, Hungry Owl came around the fire to speak with Dust Moon. Beads of water pearled his hood and cape shoulders. "What did you decide about Rumbler? Shall he be taken to the Hollow Rocks with the other children?"

Rumbler groped in the folds of Dust's skirt for her leg, and held on to it as if it were a raft in a raging ocean.

"No," Dust said. "Rumbler and I will go into the forest by ourselves. We both have bows."

Rumbler let out a relieved breath.

Hungry Owl said, "As you wish. There is much vine-covered deadfall all around the village. Any would make a good hiding place."

"Thank you. I think we'll hide somewhere to the west. I want to keep an eye on the fire."

Hungry Owl nodded. "Yes, I understand. I would suggest the berry hill. It is covered with vines. There are many tunnels inside. Most are too small for humans, but a few have been hollowed out by wolves. If necessary you could crawl through them on your bellies." Hungry Owl pointed. "That way."

Dust said, "Thank you. If you need us, that's where we'll be."

"And if you need me," Hungry Owl said, "I will be behind the snowdrift to the north."

Hungry Owl turned and silently walked north.

Dust looked down, and found Rumbler peering up at

her with sparkling black eyes. "Are you ready?"

"Yes, Grandmother."

She took Rumbler's hand, and looked for Sparrow. He had stepped away to talk quietly with Gull. When Gull saw her coming, he nodded politely, said, "May the Spirits be with you, Matron," and left, trotting off to the south.

Dust stopped in front of Sparrow, but couldn't get words out of her constricted throat.

Sparrow laid a gentle hand against her gray hair, and anxiously studied her face. "Where will you be?"

"That hill"—she pointed—"in the vines."

Sparrow nodded. "Good. I—"

Dust slipped her arms around Sparrow's waist and pulled him against her in a crushing grip, nuzzling her cheek against his chest. She could feel him smile against her hair.

After several moments, he said, "Go now, Dust. We may not have much time."

She pushed away, grabbed Rumbler's hand again, and headed for the hill.

Mist swirled before them, creating ghostly patterns. Dust squinted at the vague faces and undulating arms that drifted in and out of existence.

When they reached the hill, she saw mounds of vines fifteen hands tall. The berries had grown over fallen timbers, weaving up and around the branches, tying them together like thick ropes. But tunnels remained beneath the timbers, hollowed out by animals.

She climbed higher up the hill, getting a better vantage of the village plaza and the fire where Sparrow knelt. He faced the east, looking down the trail they had come up only a few hands of time ago. A pile of firewood rested to his left.

Rumbler let go of Dust's hand, got down on all fours,

and crawled into a tunnel beneath the berry vines. The opening spread about four hands wide.

"Come in, Grandmother," Rumbler called. "It's big in here. There's room for both of us."

Dust lowered herself to one knee, unslung her pack, and looked in at Rumbler. He sat in a hollow about eight hands high and ten hands wide. Vines as thick as her arms crisscrossed to form the ceiling and walls. Children played here. Cornhusk dolls rested to Rumbler's right. He smiled at Dust, and propped his bow and quiver across his lap. His fox-fur cape shone in the dim gray light. At the opposite end of the hollow, a tunnel barely two hands across led into the heart of the bramble. Rabbit tracks marked the dirt.

She said, "For now, I'll stay out here, Rumbler. I want to watch your grandfather. I—"

"Shh! We don't want him to hear us."

Dust stuck her head inside the hollow. Rumbler tucked a finger in his mouth, and stared at her with huge bottomless black eyes.

"Who, Rumbler? Your grandfather?"

He whispered, "Grandfather's Spirit Helper."

The prickle began at the nape of her neck, and crept down her spine. "He's here?"

Barely audible, Rumbler said, "Yes. He's been Dancing around the village."

Dust straightened, and looked across the plaza.

"Doesn't he want your grandfather to know he's here?" Dust asked, as she unslung her bow, and pulled an arrow from her quiver. "You'd think a Spirit Helper would notify his own personal Dreamer of his arrival."

Rumbler crawled to the opening to look out at her. "He says Grandfather's too fast a runner."

Dust frowned. "Then how will Sparrow get the message he brings?"

"He just said that Grandfather would, and that . . . I . . ."

A pine siskin fluttered down less than ten hands away. The little grayish brown bird had bright yellow on its lower back and tail. The siskin cocked its head to the side, peering at Rumbler quizzically. Then it fluttered closer, landing on the dark tangle of vines directly over Rumbler's head.

Rumbler eased from the hollow, breathing hard, his cheeks flushed, and knelt barely two hands from the siskin.

Mesmerized, Dust watched.

The siskin lifted its head and chirped.

Rumbler's fists tightened. Tears filled his eyes. He opened his mouth, as if he longed to speak to the bird.

The siskin seemed to sense it. It nervously hopped away, and perched on the highest vine in the bramble. An instant later, it flew up into the mist.

Rumbler grabbed onto a vine to steady himself, and sank to the ground.

Dust whispered, "Rumbler?"

In a choking voice, he said, "They're coming. My mother sent the bird to tell us."

# Thirty-Four

The echoes of sunset blushed color into the mist, giving it a milky pink radiance.

Jumping Badger stopped at the heavily trodden trail that led from the lakeshore up the hill. Twenty or thirty people had walked this trail today, including the two people from the Turtle Nation and the False Face Child. He held up his staff to halt the warriors behind him. Voices murmured, transferring the unspoken order to those who couldn't see him in the glittering haze. Feet shuffling to a stop competed with the rhythmic shishing of the waves.

A light breeze blew in off the lake.

Jumping Badger lifted his nose and sniffed the air. The scent of smoke filtered through the fog.

The ghosts had grown bold. One swooped down from the sky and batted at his hair, while another slithered from the ground and clawed at his legs with icy hands. Jumping Badger cried out, and leaped sideways. Claw marks raked the sand where the disembodied hand had disappeared.

"Leave me alone! All of you!"

He hadn't slept in so long that he kept forgetting things. Only a hand of time ago, he'd ordered Buckeye to bring Blue Raven to him so he could question him. When Buckeye's mouth had dropped open, he'd realized his cousin was dead.

But not gone. Blue Raven's carefully placed steps echoed his own, close, less than a body's length away, and he could smell the man, the odor of torn intestines overpowering. Blue Raven suddenly ran at him, his steps shaking the ground.

Jumping Badger shoved the staff into the ground, and jerked out one of the stilettos made from the murdered baby's leg bones. Panic seared his veins. He screamed, "You joined the army of ghosts, is that it?"

Voices hissed at him, coming from the waves, and the wind. Laughter and shrieks.

There were so many of them now! Hundreds!

He clenched the stiletto in his sweaty fist. "Well, come

on! Come after me. I'm here! Right here! Let us end this!''

Elk Ivory came up beside him. She wore the heavy buffalo coat. Its lower half, once painted with green hawks, had turned solid black from Blue Raven's blood. Her eyes bored into him as she gripped Jumping Badger's shoulder and shoved him backward.

"Have you lost your souls?" she demanded to know. "Or did you just decide to tell everyone in Sleeping Mist that we are here and about to attack them again?"

Jumping Badger blinked and stumbled. The ghosts had vanished. His eyes searched the sand and sky.

Elk Ivory's fist slammed his shoulder. The nostrils of her broad flat nose flared. "Are you able to lead this attack, Jumping Badger? Do you wish me to—"

"I wish you to shut up, old woman!"

Jumping Badger sucked in a breath. All day she had found things to slow him down, nonexistent tracks in the woods, fire pits days old, snapped twigs and white fox hairs that she claimed must have been left by the Turtle Nation people. Each required attention. Each cost him time.

When all this was over, he promised himself, he would find a way. He couldn't kill her outright. Not and maintain his position as war leader. The matrons wouldn't stand for it. He needed a reason. Rides-the-Bear and Shield Maker hated her, too. Together, they would concoct something. Plant evidence of treason in her bedding.

Elk Ivory turned, and her gaze affected him like a blow to the head, numbing his senses. "The village is close," she said. "What now, War Leader?"

Rides-the-Bear moved up behind Jumping Badger. Sweat beaded his ugly triangular face. He ran his tongue through the gaps created by his missing canine teeth, and glared at Elk Ivory.

In response, Acorn and Buckeye came forward to stand at Elk Ivory's shoulders. Little Wren, her hands tethered to Acorn's belt, immediately dropped to the ground, trembling from fatigue. Long black hair fell around her face.

The burly Acorn looked diminutive next to Buckeye. The giant towered over them all, forcing Jumping Badger to look up into his squinted eyes. Two short braids framed Buckeye's heavily scarred face.

"They can't see us," Buckeye whispered, "but they know we are here. Should we abandon the attack?"

Acorn rubbed the bristly ridge of hair that ran down the middle of his head—a nervous habit that irritated Jumping Badger. Acorn said, "Something's wrong. The dogs should have scented us long before the . . . the noise. We haven't even heard a bark."

"No, we haven't," Elk Ivory whispered, and her face tensed. "War Leader, I suggest—"

Rides-the-Bear interrupted, saying, "We should spread out, War Leader, and surround the village as we did last time."

"No," Elk Ivory said. "We can't risk thinning our forces. We don't know what we might be facing. If we divide—"

"We can cover more ground," Jumping Badger said. "The weak survivors of this village can't put up much of a fight, old woman." He looked up at the masked head of Lamedeer, and frowned. The dead man had been strangely silent for the past few hands of time. The crow's-head mask shimmered wetly in the diffused light. "I think we should send out warriors in groups of two. That will give us six groups to surround the village, plus one larger group to enter from this trail."

Acorn tugged on the rope fastened to his belt, and Little Wren glanced up. Misery twisted her dirty face.

"What shall we do with the girl, War Leader?"

The useless prisoner bit her lip, waiting as if for a sentence of death.

Jumping Badger said, "Elk Ivory will guard her."

Elk Ivory peered at him with dark sober eyes. She knew as well as he that with the girl around her neck, and no warriors at her shoulders, she had meager chances of surviving. Jumping Badger smiled.

Acorn said, "Why can't we just tie the girl to a tree somewhere, and come back for her later? Wasting Elk Ivory's skills is—"

"No." Elk Ivory nodded to Acorn. "Untie the girl. I'll take her."

Acorn gave Elk Ivory an imploring glance, but did as she'd instructed, drawing his knife and cutting the rope from his belt. He handed the frayed end to Elk Ivory.

She took it, and tied it to her own belt.

Jumping Badger ordered, "Rides-the-Bear, organize the warriors into groups of two. Once you have them assembled, we will send three groups around to the south." He demonstrated, drawing an arc with his left hand. "One group, as well as you and Shield Maker, will come with me. The others will go to the north." He drew another arc. "At my first signal, all southern groups will begin closing in around the village. My second signal will tell the northern groups to move in. If we . . ."

*Laughter. Soft. Insidious.*

Jumping Badger jerked around to Lamedeer. "Why are you laughing!" He lunged for the staff and shook it violently. The mask slipped, revealing a grisly hairless scalp and one rotted eye. It peered at Jumping Badger malevolently.

"Answer me! Is something happening that I do not know about?"

The inhuman laughter faded into nothingness.

Behind Jumping Badger, the warriors shifted, and muttered darkly.

He swung around to glower at them, and they backed away. Most pretended to have found something fascinating on the toes of their moccasins.

Rides-the-Bear stood with his fists clenched, glancing between Jumping Badger and the severed head.

Jumping Badger said, "Didn't you hear me? I told you to organize groups!"

"Yes, War Leader." Rides-the-Bear hurried away, and Jumping Badger heard him whispering orders.

The mist spiraled in his wake, twisting up and blending with the glittering grayness. Grandfather Day Maker must have sunk below the western horizon. A dusky pall had settled over the shore. The waves lapped more softly. Wind Mother had gone still and silent.

Elk Ivory, Buckeye, and Acorn stood in a knot to his left, staring at Jumping Badger with cold eyes. Little Wren sat with her head down, but he could see the miserable wretch watching him. Hate oozed from every pore of her young body. She would never forget that he had killed her uncle before her eyes. When she got older, Jumping Badger would have to watch her carefully, or he might awake some night with an arrow in his own belly.

Rides-the-Bear trotted back. "We are ready, War Leader."

"Good," Jumping Badger said, and his gaze traced the trail that led up the hill. "Dispatch the groups."

But he did not move. Instead, he cocked his ear to the mist, straining to hear what the ghosts were saying. Their voices had gone almost too soft to . . .

He screamed, *"What are you saying? Tell me!"*

The others had gone. Elk Ivory stood with her bow in her hand, her eyes narrowed, as if seeing something in the mist that Wren did not.

Through the thick twilight fog, Wren could *feel* Rumbler. He hid somewhere close. His souls wavered at the edges of hers, the touch feathery and soft.

*Oh, Rumbler, stay hidden. They're coming.*

"Stand up, Wren," Elk Ivory murmured.

The ropes had cut deep gashes in Wren's wrists. Pain shot up her arms as she braced her hands on the sand and struggled to her feet.

"I'm r-ready, Elk Ivory."

Elk Ivory's head did not move, but her eyes lowered to look at Wren.

Wren stood shaking, her lungs heaving.

Elk Ivory pulled her knife and cut the rope tied to her belt, then sawed through the ropes around Wren's hands. Wren watched the bloody ropes fall to the ground and looked up in disbelief.

"I can't protect either of us unless I'm free to move," Elk Ivory said. "And you can't protect yourself with your hands bound."

"Protect . . . myself? You're going to let me?"

"Yes, I want you to stay close to me for as long as you can, but if things start looking bad, you are to run."

Wren wet her chapped lips. "Elk Ivory, why don't you just tie me up somewhere, like Acorn said. Or—or let me go."

"I can't do that." Elk Ivory exhaled. "Jumping Badger will come back, see my actions written in the sand, and have the reason he needs to kill me." She pulled an arrow from her quiver, and nocked it. "But if your tracks part from mine in the passion of the fight, no one will blame me."

Wren forced a swallow down her aching throat. Had she heard right? Had Elk Ivory just told her how and when to escape?

"I don't understand . . . what are you saying?"

Elk Ivory gave Wren a hard look. "And don't come back, Wren. I know your uncle told you he wished you to go home and become clan matron . . . but you must trust me that that was bad advice. I tell you this as one woman to another. If you come home people will go crazy, they'll start asking questions and, someday, the truth will come out." She tested the tension on her bowstring, pulling it back and releasing it. "I promised your uncle I would do my best to keep you alive. If you wish to help me keep that promise, you will never return to Walksalong Village."

Wren locked her knees. All the thoughts she'd had of home, the warmth of the longhouses, the soft sounds of people moving about in the morning, their laughter, her grandmother's voice . . . gone? All gone?

Wren's head trembled as she nodded. "I will. Help you keep it."

Elk Ivory put a hand on Wren's shoulder. "Then I will tell you when to run. When I do, you mustn't hesitate. I don't care what's happening, what you see, or hear. Your duty is to run away as hard and as fast as you can. You understand?"

"Yes."

Elk Ivory started to walk away.

"Elk Ivory?" Wren called softly, and the warrior looked at her. "Thank you."

Elk Ivory's face remained expressionless. "In a few moons, you may not feel such gratitude, Little Wren. The road that lies ahead of you will not be an easy one to walk.''

Wren bowed her head, and rubbed her sore wrists to get the circulation going. ''At least I'll have the chance to walk it.''

Elk Ivory studied Wren a long moment, then slipped her knife from its belt sheath and handed it to Wren, hilt first. ''You will if you live through this night.''

Wren took the knife, and gripped it tightly.

Sparrow, crouched between the woodpile and fire, could no longer see Dust, or the lodges in the village. A swimming sea of fog separated him from the rest of the world.

He tossed another log onto the fire. Flames leaped and crackled, and the mist gleamed with an unearthly brilliance. He felt as though the Spirits had spun a glittering cocoon around him, encasing him against his will. He reached down, pulled his stiletto from his belt and tucked it into his coat pocket.

The people hiding in the forest must be feeling the same anxiety. They couldn't see more than three paces in front of them. When the battle came, it would be invisibles fighting invisibles. Warriors would be afraid to move, lest they snap a twig, and catch the attention of an attacker cloaked in mist. Not even the bravest . . .

*Peent! Peent!* The sharp nighthawk's call rang through the trees.

Sparrow silently rose to his feet. He saw nothing. No one. But he sensed movement in the mist. He slowly turned around in a full circle. A few tree trunks slipped through the fog, then vanished again. Less than one hundred hands away Hungry Owl and several of his people hid behind a snowdrift, but the fog had swallowed them whole.

*Peent! Peent!*

Sparrow unslung his bow and pulled an arrow from his quiver.

Waiting.

# Thirty-Five

Jumping Badger walked the trail a step at a time. Waves washed the shore, and water dripped from the trees. A hundred paces ahead, he thought he glimpsed dark branches wavering through the fog. But as the twilight deepened, he couldn't be sure of anything. They might be ghost legs, running to surround him.

The dead had been waiting for this moment. He had no torch. No light to keep them back. His knees shook.

Behind him, that accursed Rides-the-Bear whispered, "Elk Ivory wanted to attack in the darkness. It looks as if she will get her wish. Unfortunately, we can't see them any better than they can see us."

Jumping Badger held up a hand and clenched it to a fist, ordering silence.

He took another step.

Rides-the-Bear, Shield Maker, and the two other warriors moved with him, the sound of their moccasins too faint to be heard from more than three or four paces away.

Out on the lake, a goose honked, a distant, haunting

cry, as if the bird called to a lifelong mate who could suddenly no longer answer.

Jumping Badger stopped, slipped his pack from his shoulders, and let it down easy onto the sand. He gestured for his warriors to do the same. In a dangerous situation, the weight of a pack could unbalance a warrior and make his arrow go awry. None of them would take chances tonight. Especially him. He would be fighting for his life against the living and the dead.

His breathing now came in shallow gasps.

The warriors did as he'd instructed, and Jumping Badger continued up the trail.

He knew this village. When they attacked before, he'd memorized the layout and the trails that led into the plaza. Most visitors approached either from the lakeshore, or from the inland trail that ran east from Silent Crow Village. Massive piles of deadfall bordered the village in a number of places on the southern and western margins. They provided excellent hiding places—and the warriors who had been with him on the first attack knew it. Most of their losses had come from people lurking in those intricate hives.

Jumping Badger stopped when the first conical lodge came into view. Four paces across, it stood around twelve hands high at the peak. No smoke curled from the roof.

He walked closer. Two more lodges appeared out of the mist. Both stone-cold.

Jumping Badger scanned the plaza. He saw nothing that would indicate people had used it in days. No hides lay staked out on the ground. No pots or baskets cluttered around the fire pits in the plaza.

The voices began again, high-pitched, like the keening of dying rabbits. The shrieks blasted his ears.

Jumping Badger tightened his grip on his stiletto and braced his legs. If they came at him from the shroud of mist, he could kill several before they knocked him down.

Rides-the-Bear and Shield Maker eased up on either side of Jumping Badger. The two young warriors who flanked them, Earth Diver and Bald One, remained behind.

Rides-the-Bear whispered, "The village looks abandoned. Perhaps they packed up and left after our last attack."

Shield Maker answered, "Perhaps, but more likely they are hiding in the forest."

Jumping Badger cautiously walked into the middle of the empty plaza. An orange glow took shape on the northern perimeter of the village, and relief flooded his veins. A fire!

"Look!" Rides-the-Bear said. "There's someone there!"

Jumping Badger spread his arms, holding his staff out to one side, and his stiletto out to the other. He ordered, "Lower your bows." He had his own bow and quiver slung over his shoulder.

The warriors exchanged a horrified glance, but did it.

Jumping Badger walked forward.

Through the glittering haze, the man took shape. He stood tall, silhouetted against the fiery orange halo.

Jumping Badger squinted, and thought he could make out flowing white hair.

As recognition dawned, Jumping Badger froze.

Rides-the-Bear asked, "Who is that?"

"That . . . is Silver Sparrow."

"Silver Sparrow!" Rides-the-Bear backpedaled, and swerved to aim his bow at the old man, bracing himself as if to battle one of the Faces of the Forest.

"Don't shoot!" Jumping Badger hissed, and batted Rides-the-Bear's bow down. "I must speak with him first! Shield Maker, come up on my right side. Rides-the-Bear, you guard my left. You two youths, guard my back!''

Jumping Badger walked to within forty hands of Silver Sparrow, well into the halo of firelight, and tucked his stiletto back into his belt. "Lower your bow, old man."

Silver Sparrow cautiously bent over and placed his bow and quiver on the ground. He rose with his hands up.

"So," Jumping Badger said. "You and Dust Moon were the Turtle people traveling with Blue Raven."

Silver Sparrow nodded. "I'm surprised you didn't figure it out long ago, Jumping Badger. Surely Cornhusk returned to Walksalong Village and told you that we were coming, as you requested, to complete our 'bargain.' "

Rides-the-Bear gave Jumping Badger a puzzled look.

"I don't know what you're speaking of, old man," Jumping Badger said, and shifted nervously.

The ghosts chittered nearby.

"I think you do." Silver Sparrow spread his arms, exposing his vulnerable chest, and walked toward Jumping Badger. "We accepted your offer. I agreed to come and remove my curse from you, and you agreed to kill Blue Raven and give us the False Face Child, alive and well."

Shield Maker's mouth fell open. He spun around to stare at Jumping Badger. The other two warriors gaped.

Jumping Badger said, "He's lying, you fools!"

He could feel the world shifting around him, Sleeping Mist's warriors, the ghosts, his own people. In the dense fog, none of them would rush. Fear would keep natural inclinations at bay. No one wanted to blindly walk into the arms of the enemy.

Jumping Badger walked closer to Silver Sparrow, his steps light, careful.

Silver Sparrow's bushy gray brows lowered. He said, "What took you so long? I expected you much earlier."

The comment unnerved Jumping Badger. Had the old Dreamer foreseen his coming? He held the staff with Lamedeer's severed head like a shield before him as he approached.

Silver Sparrow grimaced at the rough-hewn crow's-head mask that covered half of the face.

The odor of putrefying meat almost gagged Jumping Badger, and he'd grown used to it. He saw Silver Sparrow swallow the sickness that burned the back of his throat. Jumping Badger planted the staff in the ground, and lowered his fists to his sides. He saw Silver Sparrow glance at the five stilettos in his belt, four tiny, one large and deadly.

"I was detained killing your friend Blue Raven. What did you pay him to betray his people?"

The mist stirred at the edges of the village, swaying and spinning. Jumping Badger flinched. Had it been touched by a breeze or the cautious movements of ghost warriors?

Silver Sparrow spread his feet. "I gave him what he wanted most."

Jumping Badger's chin lifted. He peered at Sparrow through one eye. "And what was that?"

"You."

Jumping Badger didn't blink, or breathe.

Sparrow calmly walked toward him.

"Stop!" Jumping Badger said when Sparrow got to within three paces. He unslung his bow and nocked an arrow in it.

Sparrow raised his empty hands. "I thought you might wish to talk. Obviously, I haven't had time to carry out my part of the bargain." With a smile, he added, "Or you'd be dead."

Jumping Badger's eyes flared. "What do you want?"

"I want you to leave. Call in your warriors and go home. Now. This instant. Before it's too late."

"Too late? Too late for what, old man?"

But Jumping Badger already knew. A cold wave of air prickled around him, and he could hear them. Closing in . . .

Acorn tiptoed along the game trail, his bow up. The fog had started to freeze on the tree limbs and twigs that lined the trail, sheathing them in a glittering layer of ice. Buckeye walked behind him. They had come in from the north, drawn by the bubble of the orange light. A lodge stood in front of them, perhaps twenty hands away. Though they couldn't see Jumping Badger or Silver Sparrow, they'd been listening to their voices.

Acorn swiveled to look at Buckeye.

The huge man's skin glowed faintly orange. Rage did hideous things to the scars on his face. They twitched and jerked. Buckeye clutched his bow as if his hands were around Jumping Badger's throat. He opened his mouth to speak.

Acorn put a hand to his lips, and shook his head. If everything Silver Sparrow had said turned out to be true, Jumping Badger would never make it home.

He might not have had the chance to betray the Walksalong Clan, but he'd planned to.

Silver Sparrow said, "Too late for any of your people to survive this night, Jumping Badger. Surely you wish some of them to go back and tell the Walksalong matrons what happened when you faced me and my army of ghosts."

Jumping Badger let out a hoarse cry, then laughed breathlessly.

Acorn tried to swallow the sourness that tickled the back of his tongue. Ghosts? His eyes darted around the mist.

"Tell your ghosts to stay where they are!" Jumping Badger shouted. "I am alive, and my warriors are alive"—he raised his voice to a shriek—"because my Power is greater than yours!"

Acorn could envision Jumping Badger shaking the staff with the rotting head, and it made him want to retreat and let Sleeping Mist Village have his war leader.

Buckeye's face had gone bright red. Acorn could see the splotches on his cheeks even in the dim glow.

Buckeye used his blunt chin to gesture to the lodges, and Acorn nodded. They would make a perfect hiding place.

They bent low, and eased forward.

Acorn had taken three steps when a bloodcurdling shriek tore the air less than fifty hands to his right, and an arrow whistled past his ear. He felt the wind of its passing.

Acorn swung his bow in the direction from which the shot had come.

An arrow took him in the thigh, spun him around, and sent him stumbling backward. He tripped and fell, rolled, and dragged himself behind a massive tree trunk.

Buckeye staggered toward him with blood bubbling from his lips. The arrow had taken him squarely in the chest. Buckeye shivered, lost his balance and fell.

"Acorn!" he called out. "Acorn!"

Acorn snapped off the arrow in his thigh, slung his bow over his shoulder, and scrambled forward on his belly.

Buckeye clutched at Acorn's sleeve as he tore open

his shirt. The wound around the arrow sucked and blew. Blood had started to pour from Buckeye's lips.

"Oh, Buckeye, don't do this!" Acorn cracked the fletching from the shaft, then rolled Buckeye to his side and cracked off the point. Before he could take hold of the blood-slick shaft to pull it out, several arrows thudded into the ground around him.

He grabbed Buckeye's arm and dragged him two paces. With his third heave, Buckeye shuddered suddenly, and went limp. Acorn looked into Buckeye's wide dead eyes, then let his friend slide to the ground.

An arrow hit the tree over Acorn's head, sliced through a dead branch, and sent it crashing to the ground beside him. Icy splinters flew. He ripped his bow from his shoulder and nocked an arrow.

From the depths of the gray sparkling night, a man emerged, his bow aimed at Acorn's head. He screamed as he charged.

Acorn shot him in the chest. The man stumbled, twisted around and fell. His hands clawed at the ground until his screams gurgled into stillness.

Acorn crawled toward the closest tree, dragging his wounded leg, and slumped against the trunk. He nocked another arrow.

He heard a shout, then a din of voices. The ground shook with pounding feet. Three Turtle people, two men, and a woman, dashed headlong up the game trail for the village. Behind them came four Walksalong warriors.

The twanging of bows split the air. One of the men pitched forward, and his face plowed into the trail. The woman took an arrow in the back, but didn't fall. She forced her weaving feet onward. A *thock—hiss!* and another arrow lanced her chest. She slumped to her knees, and braced a hand on the ground, fighting to stay upright.

The last Turtle warrior turned, saw her fall, and fired

a wild shot at his pursuers. It sailed over the heads of his enemies. In less than a heartbeat, three arrows pierced his chest, and knocked him backward. He was dead before he hit the ground.

The Walksalong warriors leaped Buckeye's body, and raced by. One paused long enough to kick the dying woman in the face. She flopped over, coughing blood, and slowly went still.

Acorn blinked the stinging sweat from his eyes. Screams filled the forest, coming from every direction.

The war party needed him.

He set his bow aside, looked at the shaft in his leg, and gripped it with both hands. He tugged. It wouldn't come out. Shaking, he tried again, gritting his teeth, and yanking as hard as he could. The pain blazed through him like white-hot fire. Finally, his hands shook too badly to maintain his grip. He let go, and sank back against the dark trunk, groping for his bow.

He dragged it over his lap, and prayed.

Wren lay on her stomach next to Elk Ivory, the knife in her right hand, her heart thumping in her throat. They hid behind a jumbled pile of rocks to the south of the village. All around them, people crashed through deadfall, yelling, and cursing. So far, Elk Ivory had made no attempt to join the battle.

She lay prostrate, her eyes furiously scanning the mist.

Branches cracked behind them, and Elk Ivory leaped to her feet with her bow drawn.

Wren could make out a line of people coming toward them. Their bodies wavered in the mist, sometimes visible, sometimes not. She couldn't tell whose side they belonged to.

Elk Ivory reached down, grabbed Wren by the collar, and jerked her to her feet. "Go down to the lakeshore and run north along the sand," she whispered. "Now. *Run!*"

Wren flew down the hill, her legs pumping, and arms flying.

Two men stumbled into the village, fighting, and Jumping Badger spun to look.

Sparrow took the opportunity. Pulling his stiletto from his pocket, he took two running strides, and swung for Jumping Badger's chest. Jumping Badger caught his arm, pivoted, and threw Sparrow to the ground. Sparrow's foot shot out, catching Jumping Badger behind the knees. He toppled, but came up quickly and leaped for Sparrow's stiletto. Sparrow bellowed, grabbed Jumping Badger around the neck, jerked him sideways, and rolled on top of the young war leader. He gouged at Jumping Badger's left eye, trying to tear it from its socket.

Jumping Badger writhed like a dying animal. He slammed a fist into Sparrow's throat.

The flash of pain stunned Sparrow. He couldn't breathe. Jumping Badger flung Sparrow to his back.

As the two men rolled and thrashed across the ground, the village exploded around them. Warriors streamed in from both sides, shouting, and firing their bows from less than four paces. A melee of running, screaming people ensued.

Sparrow heard Dust shout hoarsely, then saw her racing across the plaza with her long gray braid flying. Two warriors tackled her, bringing her down hard.

Sparrow roared, and threw all of his strength into the fight. Dust had been right about his age. Jumping Badger had managed to get on top, and Sparrow couldn't seem to get the leverage to escape. His muscles were tiring fast, his grip on his stiletto weakening.

Jumping Badger glanced at Dust, then peered down at Sparrow with blazing eyes, and smiled. "I'm going to kill your wife while you watch."

Jumping Badger jammed his thumbs into Sparrow's wrist, and Sparrow's fingers began to open. The stiletto shook. Jumping Badger banged his hand on the ground, and the stiletto flew from Sparrow's grasp, landing six hands away.

Jumping Badger dove for it. Sparrow rolled to his knees and leaped for Jumping Badger. He reached around the man's head, grasped his chin, and twisted Jumping Badger's neck until he could hear bones cracking.

Jumping Badger cried out hoarsely, rolled under Sparrow, and came up with the stiletto.

He plunged it once, twice, into Sparrow's vulnerable throat and the opening in his coat collar. Blood spurted, covering Jumping Badger's face and eyes.

Sparrow tried to get to his feet to run, but three warriors hit him at once, and sent him sprawling. Two leaped for his arms, while a third struggled to keep his thrashing legs down.

Sparrow lay on his back, rasping, blood running hotly over his neck and chest.

From somewhere close, he heard Dust mew, "*Sparrow.*"

Jumping Badger staggered to his feet, and stood over Sparrow. Covered with Sparrow's blood, and with his own blood draining from his nose and left eye, he looked almost as bad as Sparrow felt. Not that it mattered. If the stiletto had struck the large artery in Sparrow's throat, he'd be dead very quickly.

Jumping Badger's eyes narrowed, as if he'd heard Sparrow's thoughts. Panting, he gestured with the bloody stiletto. "Rides-the-Bear . . . bandage his throat . . . I want him alive."

*"If you want him to live, let me do it!"* Dust cried. "I'm a Healer. Let me take care of him!"

Jumping Badger glared at her, then waved to the men who held her. "Let her do it."

He turned, and tramped down the trail that led to the lakeshore, vanishing into the swirling fog.

Dust dropped on her knees at Sparrow's side, and pressed the heels of her hands over the wound above his coat collar. As she looked up, fear tightened her eyes, but she whispered, "These are bad, but not lethal. Hold still."

She removed the heels of her hands from the first wound and jammed them down hard against the side of his throat. Blood from her fingers spattered his face.

Sparrow closed his eyes, and tried to concentrate on breathing. He heard someone retching, followed by a groan. Then voices closed in around the village.

He opened his eyes to see Gull, Hungry Owl, and six other members of Sleeping Mist Clan being herded into the village at arrow point. Hungry Owl had his chin high, but Gull walked like a man going to his own execution—which was very probably true. Walksalong warriors converged from all sides, forcing the eight captives into the center of the plaza.

Sparrow silently counted the numbers of the enemy. Twelve warriors, including Jumping Badger. Where were the others? Dead? Wounded? Or still out in the forest?

Dust ripped a strip of cloth from the bottom of her

dress and wrapped it around Sparrow's throat. "Can you breathe?"

He nodded, glanced at the two warriors standing close by, and mouthed the word, "Rumbler?"

Only Dust's eyes moved. They slid to the berry bramble, and came back.

Gods, Rumbler must be huddling in terror. That's why Dust had run. To draw the warriors away from the boy's hiding place.

Sparrow weakly reached up and clasped her forearm. She looked down into his eyes.

He murmured, "Will he stay?"

She glanced at the warriors, and shook her head, indicating she didn't know.

A cold gust of wind blew up from the lake, shredding the mist and tumbling it over Sparrow's head.

They would not truly lose until Rumbler came out, or the Walksalongs found him.

Either would mean death for all of them.

Sparrow exhaled wearily. He had no particular fear of death. He had been looking death in the eye for a long time. Most people did. They just didn't realize it. Death was the mirror that people held up to their faces every day. It reminded them of what they really faced, and how little time they had to appreciate it.

Tonight, finally, he fully appreciated it. He only wished he'd—

A wrenching scream split the darkness, coming from down near the lakeshore. Jumping Badger shouted, "Hold still, or I'll kill you!"

The wind picked up, gusting over Sparrow's hot body, and tousling his white hair. He took a deep breath. The scents of damp earth and wood smoke thankfully overpowered the smells of blood and death.

"Oh, Spirits, no," Dust whispered.

Sparrow turned his head, looking down the trail to the shore.

Jumping Badger marched from the mist with several packs slung over his shoulder, and his fist twined in the dark blue fabric of Little Wren's shirt.

# Thirty-Six

As Jumping Badger dragged Little Wren into the village, he dropped the packs on the ground, and shouted, "Elk Ivory! Elk Ivory, where are you?"

Wren kicked and slammed her fists into his stomach and legs, but Jumping Badger barely felt it. Euphoria fired his veins. He had beaten the ghosts! He lived, and they had vanished into nothingness! He held tight to the collar of the girl's shirt.

*"Elk Ivory!"*

Everyone in the plaza went quiet. The eight captives who sat together twenty paces away, surrounded by ten Walksalong warriors, whispered and shook their heads at the sight of Wren. As if they didn't know her. But Silver Sparrow and Matron Dust Moon appeared worried, frightened for the girl. Dust Moon sat on the ground with Silver Sparrow's head in her lap. Fresh blood speckled his wrinkled face and white hair, and soaked his coat. A thick bandage encircled his throat. Jumping Badger gave the old man a smug smile, but Silver Sparrow looked past him, to Little Wren's face, noting each bruise and cut, and the curve of Silver Sparrow's mouth went hard. Dust Moon's eyes glowed darkly.

Jumping Badger threw back his head, and bellowed, *"Elk Ivory, you treacherous . . . !"*

The words died in his throat when Elk Ivory slipped from between two sour gum trees on the hill to Jumping Badger's left. Tall, her expression cold, she held her bow down at her side, but her arrow remained nocked.

"What is it, War Leader?" she asked with deadly softness.

Jumping Badger shoved Wren to the ground, and stood breathing hard, his fists clenching and unclenching. "Why is this girl free?"

"She escaped during the fight. I did not even realize she was gone, until I—"

"Do not lie to me! You let her go! Do you think me a fool?"

One of Elk Ivory's brows quirked, and several of the Walksalong warriors laughed.

Jumping Badger swung around, his face twisted in fury. "Who laughed? Who was laughing!"

When no one owned up to it, Jumping Badger glowered at Wren, then backhanded her hard across the mouth.

Wren hit the ground spitting blood. Tears blurred her eyes. She rose on her hands and knees and tried to crawl away, but Jumping Badger kicked her down. Her chin skidded over the dirt, and she started crying.

"Oh, Wren," Dust Moon whispered.

Jumping Badger's eyes widened. "Do you know this girl? How long have you known her?"

As if suddenly realizing the implications of calling out to Wren, the woman shook her head. "I don't know her."

"But she *was* with Blue Raven when he sold you the

child? Isn't that so? That's what he told me.''

Wren looked at Dust Moon pleadingly, as if terrified the old woman might say the wrong thing.

Jumping Badger grabbed her by the hair, and said, ''Do you know Dust Moon and Silver Sparrow?''

''No, I—''

''How long have you known them?''

''I *don't* know them!'' Little Wren sobbed the words.

Jumping Badger shoved her face into the ground.

''Now, old woman,'' he said to Dust Moon. ''You will answer me. How long have you known this worthless girl?''

When Dust Moon's jaw clamped, he stepped toward her, drawing back his hand to wipe that expression from her wrinkled face.

''That is your way, isn't it, *brave* War Leader?'' Elk Ivory's voice stopped Jumping Badger in his tracks.

He turned to glare at her.

''Ever since you were a boy,'' Elk Ivory said, ''you've enjoyed hurting the helpless. Women, children, animals. We have all seen it. But when it comes to leading a war party, you often insist on walking in the rear, where you are safe. You are so cowardly you won't walk after dark unless we make torches to light your way. You refuse to discuss your strategy with any of your warriors. Instead, you talk to a rotting head! You are unfit to be war leader!''

Jumping Badger looked from Elk Ivory to Dust Moon, and then down at Wren. He sensed a strange undercurrent here, one he didn't understand.

He kicked Wren. ''What is it that they know about you, girl, that I do not? Eh? Perhaps Elk Ivory was right in the beginning. Do you remember?'' Jumping Badger shouted to his warriors. ''How many of you recall when Elk Ivory insisted that Blue Raven had had nothing to do with the theft of the False Face Child? She claimed that Wren had stolen the boy, and that Blue Raven was merely tracking his niece! Eh? How many of you recall those words?''

Nearly every Walksalong warrior in the village nodded.

''Well,'' Jumping Badger said. ''Perhaps she was right. Maybe this wretched girl did steal the False Face Child. I want answers!'' he shouted. ''Was this girl responsible?''

He crouched before Wren, breathing hard, his face awash in firelight, and hissed, ''I will have the truth, girl. And *you* will give it to me.''

''But I—I don't know anything. I only found Uncle a few days ago, and he—''

Jumping Badger grabbed Wren by the front of her blue shirt and dragged her face up to less than a handbreadth from his. He shouted, ''Where is the False Face Child?''

''Please, d-don't hurt me,'' she pleaded, and clutched at his fists. ''I swear I don't know anything!''

''Where is the False Face Child? Did you help him escape? Where is he!''

Jumping Badger shook Wren with all his strength, and she broke down and wept like an infant.

Without taking his blazing eyes from her, he called, ''Rides-the-Bear! Shield Maker! Set fire to the lodges. I am going to need light.''

''Yes, War Leader.''

The two men ran to the bonfire north of the village, pulled long branches from the woodpile, and thrust the tips into the flames. When the wood blazed, they trotted to the first lodge, threw up the door curtain, and stuck the fiery brands inside, setting fire to the dry interior walls. They went down the row, setting fire to all seven lodges.

At first the roofs steamed, then smoked, and finally lurid orange tongues leaped through the smoke holes. The lodges burst into fire, and sparks shot across the plaza.

As the flames built to a roar, a gaudy fluorescent halo expanded over the village. It glittered from the fog, and danced on the stark upturned faces of the Sleeping Mist captives.

Jumping Badger stood and yanked Wren to her feet. He shouted, "Tonight, even the Night Walkers will hear this girl's screams! She will tell me the truth, or I will blind her, and then . . ." He nodded, and smiled. "Then the real pain will begin. I never heard your uncle beg me to kill him. But you, girl, you *will*."

He gripped Wren's rope-burned wrist and hauled her across the dirt to the base of the staff. The sunken, crusted eye that peered from beneath the canted mask sparkled with evil.

Jumping Badger pulled his knife from his belt, and stood up, smiling at the people who watched him. "Now, witness the wrath of the Walksalong Clan."

He turned, and sprang for Wren, slamming her shoulders to the ground and pinning them with his massive left arm, while his knife pricked the corner of her eye.

Wren trembled like a dying fawn. "Jumping B-Badger, please. You are my cousin! Don't—"

*"Stop this!"* Elk Ivory's voice rang out. "Leave her alone!"

He swiveled his head, and saw Elk Ivory easing up behind him, her bow leveled at his back. The red chert arrow point shone in the flameglow.

"We do not kill our own people, Jumping Badger," Elk Ivory said. "All of you—look! Do you wish to see a little girl tortured? A member of your own clan? What have we become that could even think—"

Rides-the-Bears' war club cut through the mist with the silence of a bird. It struck Elk Ivory in the back of the head, and she crumpled to the ground.

Jumping Badger smiled approvingly at the ugly man. "Good work. We will finish her later. Watch them!" He pointed to Dust Moon and Silver Sparrow.

Silver Sparrow had managed to get to his feet, and stood with his legs braced. Blood flowed over his neck bandage and down his chest. His eyes had a strange savage glitter.

Jumping Badger turned back to Wren. He lifted and turned the black stone blade before her eyes, letting her see its long sharp edges.

"I have heard the pain is terrible," he whispered to Wren. "The knife slices through the eyeball, and as it twists inside the skull, there are flashes of light, and—"

"I don't know anything!" Wren screamed. "Please, I tell you, I don't—"

"*Where* is the False Face Child?" Jumping Badger shouted. "Where is he? He came into this village. We saw his tracks down on the shore. Where is he!" He pressed the knife into the fold at the top of Wren's right eye. "Tell me now. Tell me where the False Face Child is, or I'll—"

"*No!*" a small terrified voice cried. "*Leave Wren alone!*"

"Rumbler, no!" Wren sobbed, and fought against Jumping Badger's arm. "No! *Run!*"

A bizarre sound echoed across the village, and Jumping Badger went rigid.

Deep-throated, it resembled the low moaning growl of a cougar surprised when its prey suddenly turns to fight. The muscles in Jumping Badger's arms contracted. He sat up and scanned the faces in the mist.

"What is that?" he demanded to know. He rose to his

feet, clutching his knife tightly. "Who's making that sound?"

Shrill high-pitched laughter rang through the mist, then a deep inhuman voice said, *"I did, big man."*

Gasps and cries rose from the people in the village. Several of his warriors spun around with their bows up.

Jumping Badger turned slowly.

The False Face Child stood on the hill. In the garish firelight, his white cape glittered, and his eyes shone like huge black moons.

Jumping Badger glared at his warriors, shouting, "What are you waiting for? Kill him! He's the False Face Child!"

Flickers of light danced through the forest, and for a moment, Jumping Badger thought that sparks from the burning lodges had caught in the dry winter grasses.

No. No! Had the ghosts returned?

His warriors spun around, their mouths open, watching the lights.

"Rides-the-Bear!" Jumping Badger yelled. "Shoot the child!"

A streak of light, like a fiery falcon, swooped over Rides-the-Bear's head, and he hit the ground, shrieking, "What was that? What's happening?"

Fear congealed like ice in Jumping Badger's veins. He ripped Elk Ivory's bow from her unconscious hands, and reached for the arrow that lay on the ground—

Four lights cut through the mist above him, unfurling burning streamers, as if the gods were playing a game of catch with ball lightning.

"What is this?" Jumping Badger cried, gaping at the mist-shrouded sky. "These are not ghosts! What's happening?"

*"You are about to die, big man,"* that strange echoing voice said.

He jerked to look at the False Face Child, not quite able to believe the boy could make his voice sound that way. "Boy? Did you say that? Who said that!"

Jumping Badger took a step backward, and bumped into something. He whirled, and the severed head toppled forward, bashing him in the face. The overpowering stench struck him first, then he felt the half-melted flesh clinging to his forehead, and trickling down his temple. He twisted away, and wiped frantically at the putrid slime. The mask had fallen off when the head hit the ground. Bone gleamed on the rotted head where once there had been scalp.

Loud, gleeful laughter. The hideous cackle mixed with the roaring fires, and rose like a shriek inside him.

Jumping Badger cried out, aimed his bow, and shot Lamedeer through the mouth.

*I'm so glad you brought me along. I've been waiting for this.*

"Shut up!" Jumping Badger flung his bow aside, reached for the staff and slammed the head into the ground, shrieking like a madman. "Don't talk to me! I can't stand it!"

He gripped the staff, swung it round and round and cast it into the forest, then stumbled to a stop, breathing hard.

His warriors gaped. The captives watched him in shock.

A huge ball of fire danced through the mist over the plaza, as if it had flown very high, and now plunged downward toward them.

Little Wren whimpered, and curled into a ball.

Jumping Badger turned on her. "I'm going to kill you first, girl! Do you hear that, boy? I'm killing the girl first!"

He reached for Wren's throat, and she screamed.

And another scream shredded the night, hoarse and chilling, as if being torn from a child's stomach by a stone fish hook.

Jumping Badger turned and saw the dwarf child running as fast his short legs would carry him, dashing across the plaza with his pitiful child's bow up. The boy's mangled hands could barely steady the nocked arrow. A horrified cry of determination tore from his throat.

Jumping Badger laughed. "You think you can kill me with that, boy? That arrow is not even long enough to—"

The boy fired.

And from all around the child, rolling fireballs flared, seeming to come from the ends of his hair, his hands, his eyes.

An incoherent cry escaped Jumping Badger's mouth as, first, the boy's little arrow struck his chest, then the balls of fire. Like claps of silent lightning, each knocked him back until he collapsed on his knees, his clothes ablaze.

"Put it out!" he shrieked. "I'm on fire, put it out!"

None of his warriors moved.

The boy ran past Jumping Badger, his white cape flying around his malformed legs, threw down his bow, and wrapped his arms around Wren, breathlessly sobbing, "Wren? Wren, are you all right?"

Jumping Badger rolled on the ground to put out the fire, tearing at his clothes. . . .

*"Don't move!"*

The order came from the dark hill where the False Face Child had first appeared.

The fire out, Jumping Badger sprawled on his back, and weakly clutched at the five large arrows, and one small arrow, that pierced his chest.

Warriors began to emerge from the misty shadows,

their faces drawn, bows aimed. Several carried torches.

The Walksalong warriors looked around, assessing their odds, and began to mutter to each other.

"Lower your bows!" a corpulent man with a bloated face ordered as he waddled from the trees. "Do it now! Do you wish to die?"

Jumping Badger felt as if a granite boulder weighted his chest. He couldn't get air. He blinked wearily as he watched his men drop their bows and lift their hands over their heads. "No . . ." he rasped.

*Breathless, triumphant laughter.*

It filled the village, loud and raucous, the insane hilarity of victory.

Jumping Badger's face contorted.

Mist spun around him, spawning bizarre monstrous creatures three times the height of a man. Thousands . . . there were thousands! Dancing. Leaping. One face formed clearly. The face of a little boy with glowing ember eyes. It swayed above him. The boy leaned over, his undulant arms made of swirling fog, his mouth a hollow of firelight, and he smiled. Then he reached for Jumping Badger. . . .

Dust Moon inspected the corpulent man who waddled into the plaza. "Blessed Spirits, that's Spotted Frog."

"Yes," Sparrow said. "Dust, help me to walk."

She slipped her arm around his waist. "Put your arm over my shoulders."

As Spotted Frog's warriors closed in around the plaza, Cornhusk came running from the trees with his arms wide, calling, "Please, everyone be calm. You're safe! Everything's all right!"

The Silent Crow warriors collected weapons and searched the Walksalong men.

Gull rose from the circle of captives. Tears filled his eyes. He looked at Spotted Frog, and said, "Where did you come from? We thought we were dead."

Spotted Frog smiled, and walked forward. "We came from Silent Crow Village, my friend. When we saw the fires here, we feared the worst. We've been shooting flaming arrows for half a hand of time, to tell you we were coming. Didn't you see them?"

Gull bowed his head, trying to hide the tears that ran down his cheeks. "Yes." He nodded. "In the mist, we didn't know what they were. But . . . yes. Thank you. We owe you our lives."

Spotted Frog waved the thanks away, and looked at Rumbler and Little Wren, who sat crying with their arms around each other. He said, "Are those the hero children?"

Gull turned. The lines in his forehead deepened. "The boy is the False Face Child from Paint Rock Village. The girl is from Walksalong Village. We do not know her, but her name is Little Wren."

Spotted Frog's face slackened with reverence. He waddled toward them.

Sparrow said, "Let's join them, Dust."

They gradually made their way across the plaza.

Cornhusk trotted up to join them. Tall, and lanky, his buffalo coat looked even more mangy than the last time they'd seen him. The silver strands in his black hair shone. He grinned, showing his missing front teeth. "Look!" he said. "I saved you again!"

"Really?" Dust lifted a skeptical brow. "Do we have you to thank for this?"

"Well," Cornhusk said with mock modesty, "I told Spotted Frog and his village the story, but they are the ones who decided to mount a war party to help you. I guided them here, though!''

''Then we are in your debt, Cornhusk,'' Dust said. ''Thank you.''

Cornhusk bowed, and grinned.

Just before they reached the children, a man staggered from the forest. He had a walking stick propped before him, and wore his hair in the cut of the Thornbush Clan, with the sides shaved and a ridge of hair down the middle of his skull. Blood drenched his left leg.

''Don't shoot!'' he called. ''I'm unarmed!''

Spotted Frog gestured to two of his warriors. ''Let this warrior join the other captives.''

The young men trotted forward, their bows aimed at the man's chest, and gestured for him to enter the plaza.

He swung his wounded leg forward stiffly, propping his walking stick as he came. When he saw Jumping Badger's dead body, and Elk Ivory lying on her back, he gritted his teeth, let out a hoarse roar, and began kicking Jumping Badger with all the might he could muster.

Other Walksalong warriors saw him, and walked forward, escorted by Silent Crow guards. They stood around the body, kicking Jumping Badger, spitting upon him, and cursing him.

The sight made Sparrow feel cold to his bones.

Dust pulled him forward, toward the children. They arrived in time to see Spotted Frog kneel beside Rumbler and Little Wren.

In a gentle voice, the patron asked, ''Are you both well? Do you need food or water?''

Rumbler rubbed fists in his wet eyes, and studied Spotted Frog for several moments. He murmured, ''Are you the man with the silver gorget shaped like a wolf?''

Spotted Frog straightened, and blinked. He pulled the pendant from his cape. It glimmered in the dwindling firelight. "My great-grandmother gave this to me. How did you know I had—"

"I saw you," Rumbler said. "In a Dream. You had a hundred Spirit Helpers crowding behind your shoulders."

Spotted Frog's warriors glanced at each other, and looked upon their leader with new awe.

Spotted Frog smiled. "Well, I am glad to know that. Thank you."

Sparrow tightened his hold around Dust Moon's shoulders, and said, "I can't tell you how glad we are to see you, Spotted Frog."

Spotted Frog grunted to his feet, and glanced fondly at them. "For a time, I feared we weren't going to arrive soon enough. Cornhusk lost the trail."

The Trader shoved his hands in his coat pockets, and shrugged. "Well, I found it again after we lit torches, Patron. In this mist, no one—"

"At any rate," Spotted Frog said. "We made it."

The patron lowered his gaze to Rumbler and Wren, and his brows drew together. "What will happen to the children now? Will you take them?"

Dust tightened her arm around Sparrow's waist. "Yes," she answered. "Though I don't know where we will go. Wren betrayed her people by stealing Rumbler. She can't go home, and I—"

"I do," Wren whispered. She got on her knees, and stood up, wincing as if every rib in her body had been broken. "We need to go north."

Rumbler rose beside her, and tucked his hand into her palm. When he looked at her, his eyes shone like stars.

"Grandmother," Rumbler said, and glanced uncertainly at the people standing around. "Wren and I, we want to go find my father."

Wren held his little hand tighter, and nodded. "He

needs to find his father. If he doesn't go now, he may never have another chance.''

Dust smiled, but uncertainty invaded her chest. She turned around. "Cornhusk, have you ever been to the far northern islands? A place called the Cove Meadows?"

"Why, yes!" Cornhusk said. "I've been there once. There isn't really much there. Why?"

Dust tenderly tucked Sparrow's blood-spattered hair behind his ears, and gazed up at him with her whole heart in her eyes. She said, "We have a message we want you to carry to a man there, named Bull Killer."

# Thirty-Seven

Grandfather Day Maker had not yet risen, but a golden gleam arched over the eastern horizon. The tufts of mist glimmered in the treetops, and drifted along the lakeshore. A cool fish-scented wind tousled Wren's long hair around her face.

Wren took a breath and winced. She sat cross-legged before the plaza fire, her hands braced on her knees, while Matron Dust Moon wrapped her chest with bandages. Rumbler sat beside her, holding tight to her pant leg, but his dark eyes studied the movements of the warriors in the plaza. His plump cheeks and chin-length black hair gleamed from the thorough scrubbing Dust Moon had given him a hand of time ago.

Dust Moon ripped the ends of the strip of fabric and

knotted it. "Now take a deep breath, Wren. Can you feel your ribs shifting?"

Wren cautiously obeyed, filling her lungs. Tendrils of pain flashed across her chest, but nothing like the fiery lances that had tormented her throughout the night. "No. They feel better. Thank you, Dust Moon."

"Good, let's slip on your shirt."

Wren squinted against the pain as she lifted her arms, and allowed Dust Moon to pull her blue shirt on. Then Dust Moon draped a red blanket over Wren's shoulders, and said, "I was thinking I'd comb your hair for you."

Wren turned to peer up at her kind, deep-wrinkled face, and the golden fleck just beneath the pupil of her left eye. She wore her hair in a long gray braid. "Yes," Wren said and gave her a tremulous smile. "I'd like that."

Dust Moon smiled, and pulled a wooden comb from the open pack beside her. As she started gently running the comb through Wren's hair, Wren sighed. No one had combed her hair since her mother's death. Warmth grew in Wren's heart and filtered out through her tired body.

Rumbler shifted beside her, and Wren turned. He frowned at the ring of prisoners who sat twenty paces to his right, their hands and feet bound. Many had untended wounds. Elk Ivory lay curled on her side next to Acorn. She had yet to sit up this morning, and after the blow she'd taken to the skull, Wren suspected she wouldn't until someone forced her to. She probably felt violently ill. Turtle Nation warriors surrounded them, their expressions grim. Occasionally one of the Silent Crow warriors would kick one of the Walksalong Village warriors. It hurt to watch.

Silver Sparrow stood near the prisoners, talking to Spotted Frog and Hungry Owl. They made a strange sight, Silver Sparrow with his wrinkled face and long white hair, beside the young dark-haired Hungry Owl. Both men towered over Spotted Frog. The patron of Silent Crow Village stood with his hands laced over his large belly, and his head bowed. He wore his black hair in a series of intricate braids, coiled on top of his head, and pinned with a shell comb. He kept nodding at Silver Sparrow's soft words.

Finally, Spotted Frog said, "No, it's too dangerous. Who is to say what will happen if we let them go?"

Hungry Owl said, "I agree. They may decide to attack other Turtle Nation villages on their way back to Walksalong Village." His eyes narrowed as he scanned the burned lodges, and the dead bodies that lay in a row at the edge of the trees. "I don't want to see other villages slaughtered the way we were."

Spotted Frog nodded. "I think it would be best if we just killed them here and now. It would certainly send a scare into the Walksalong matrons—"

Sparrow interrupted, saying, "Or maybe make them decide to dispatch the rest of their warriors for Silent Crow Village, Spotted Frog."

In a forlorn voice, Rumbler whispered, "I can't stand to see anybody else die, Wren."

She clamped her jaw. Tears had sprung to Rumbler's eyes.

Silver Sparrow said, "Listen to me, please. This insanity has to stop somewhere. I—"

"It could stop," Wren said in a strong voice, "if we established an alliance."

"A—a what?" Hungry Owl scoffed. "An alliance with your people? We can't trust anyone from the Bear Nation! You are all murderers and thieves!"

Wren lowered her eyes, and blinked at the ground. Her heart had started to pound.

Rumbler shouted, "No they aren't! They are just people. Like us. Can't we talk with them?"

Spotted Frog looked at Wren and Rumbler with a strange respect.

Wren had never had an adult look at her that way, and it scared her a little. She groped for Rumbler's hand. His good finger went tight around her thumb.

Silver Sparrow and Hungry Owl followed Spotted Frog across the plaza. They stopped a pace away, and Spotted Frog said, "Do you truly believe this might work?"

Rumbler nodded with a lot more certainty than Wren felt. "Yes," he said. "It might."

Wren added, "My uncle . . . he always wanted to establish an alliance between the Turtle Nation and the Bear Nation. He said that if we agreed to stop raiding, and to help each other, that we would all be better off."

Spotted Frog fingered his triple chin. "If it worked, yes, but—"

"How can we ever trust them?" Hungry Owl demanded to know. "After what they have done to us?"

Silver Sparrow's bushy brows lowered over his beak nose. "Well, let's ask what would happen if we could Trade would definitely benefit. And if we agreed, as Wren suggests, to help defend each other's villages, our alliance would be virtually invincible."

"It would certainly make the Flicker Clans think twice about attacking us, wouldn't it?" Spotted Frog asked.

Hungry Owl scowled down at Wren. "The Bears might agree to an alliance, and then turn around and attack us when our defenses are down."

"Yes, it's possible. I agree," Spotted Frog said, "but if Little Wren and Rumbler think it might work—"

"It *will* work," Elk Ivory called. She lay curled on her side, and squinted at Spotted Frog through one eye.

The village went quiet as people turned to peer at her. Spotted Frog said, "And what makes you so sure?"

Elk Ivory squeezed her eyes closed, and weakly sat up. "I am not war leader yet, Patron," she said. "But I think I will be when I arrive home. *If* you allow me and my warriors to return to Walksalong Village, and if my people cast their voices for me . . . I give you my pledge that I will talk with my matrons about this alliance. I have always believed, as Blue Raven did, that it would mean greater safety and prosperity for all of us."

Spotted Frog scanned the faces of his warriors, and said, "It cannot hurt us to try."

Elk Ivory nodded, and eased to the ground again. Her mouth pursed as if nausea tweaked her. She said, "Let us go, Patron. Give us the chance to work for this alliance together."

Spotted Frog appeared to be considering, then he looked at Silver Sparrow, and Hungry Owl, and saw each of them nod in turn, though Hungry Owl did it reluctantly.

Spotted Frog waddled toward Wren and Rumbler. He peered down at their twined hands, knelt, and put his over the top of theirs. A light shone in his eyes as he smiled. "You two children may have just changed our world forever."

The Cove
Meadows

NORTH

Sleeping
Mists

Earth
Thunder
Village

Walksalong Village

Going Wolf Village

GREEN SPIDER LAKE

THE
JOURNEY

# Epilogue

"Are you ready?" Cornhusk said. "They are almost here."

Bull Killer put down the arrow shaft he'd been smoothing with his chert spokeshave, and rose to his feet. He turned to look westward. Thick stands of conifers covered most of the island, their fragrant boughs so dark green that they appeared almost black. Through the middle of that vast forest, a tiny tan trail wound. Four people came down it.

Bull Killer touched Cornhusk's arm, and said, "Are you certain it's them?"

Cornhusk grinned, showing his missing front teeth. "I just came from speaking with them. I ran all the way to tell you they were coming. I thought you might wish a little time to prepare yourself."

"Yes," Bull Killer said, and nodded. "Thank you."

"Do you wish me to go with you? To meet them?"

His voice came out a whisper. "No."

Cornhusk inclined his head and trotted toward the villagers gathered in the trees to the north. For almost six moons they had been watching the ghost people build their stone houses on the beach. They had proven to be fierce warriors, shooting arrows that flashed like lightning.

Cloud Giants drifted through the elemental blue sky over Bull Killer's head, casting shadows across the land, but warm bright sunlight fell upon the trail where the people stood.

Bull Killer wiped his hands on his knee-length brown shirt, and sucked in a deep breath. Sweat beaded his pointed nose, and soaked the silver-streaked black hair that framed his oval face, and hung down to his broad shoulders.

He was afraid, and he had not been truly afraid in a long time.

He smiled wanly to himself. The last time he'd felt this quivering in his belly he'd been standing before Dust Moon, listening to her tell him he had to leave—he had to give up everything he cared about if he wished to protect the people he loved. She'd told him he would eventually learn to live without Briar—but she'd been wrong. To this day, even though he knew she was dead, he still held her in his arms in his dreams.

He started up the trail to meet them.

A light breeze blew off the ocean, flapping his brown shirt around his long legs. The mixture of the salt air and spruce trees soothed him a little. He had lived here for seven winters, and come to love this northern country, and its people.

As he closed the gap with them, he could see Dust Moon clearly. Deep wrinkles creased her face, and her hair had gone all gray. She wore it in a long braid. Silver Sparrow looked virtually the same, with long flowing white hair, and a beak nose. The slender young woman who walked with them had a lean angular face, as if her features had been carved from a fine golden brown wood.

. . . He looked at the boy.

And the boy looked at him.

Bull Killer's eyes blurred. Who would have thought eleven winters ago that a Power child could come from his joining with Briar?

The boy had short arms and legs, and a beautiful round face with lustrous black hair. He wore a dark blue shirt with tiny white spirals across the chest. Much too big for him, it hung to the ground.

Dust Moon bent down and whispered something to the boy, and he stared at Bull Killer with shining black eyes. Dust Moon gave the boy a shove.

Rumbler walked toward him, his steps slow and deliberate.

Bull Killer knelt in the trail, and opened his arms.

A tremulous smile touched the boy's lips. He broke into a run, reaching out for Bull Killer.

"Oh, gods," Bull Killer whispered as he embraced Rumbler, and clutched that small body to his chest. "My son, my son, I never thought I would see you." He kissed Rumbler's hair. "I love you. I've always loved you."

"Let's give them some time alone," Sparrow said.

Wren nodded, and led the way around them and on down the trail. But after five paces, she turned to look back at Rumbler. He had his chin braced on his father's shoulder, and a broad smile on his face. He lifted his stubby half-fingers to her, and Wren waved back.

They started down the trail again, and Wren asked, "Where are we going, Sparrow?"

He came alongside her, and put an affectionate hand on top of her head. "Well, there are people down there at the edge of the trees. I see Cornhusk with them, so they must be friendly—"

"So far," Dust Moon said. "They obviously don't know Cornhusk very well yet. We'd better get there before they do."

Sparrow laughed. "Wise idea."

Wren inhaled the rich scents of this new land. She'd always wanted to be a Trader, but she had never imagined the joy of the journey itself. Over the past six moons, they had walked, or canoed, all day long every day, and she had cherished every moment of it.

"Will we stay here for a while?" Wren asked, and looked up at Sparrow.

He gave her a serene smile. "Yes, at least until Rumbler decides what he wants to do. Why, are you so anxious to be off?"

Wren shrugged. Her hair danced in the warm sea breeze. "I could rest for a while," she answered. "It's been a long trip."

"Yes," Sparrow said with a deep sigh, "it has."

As they neared the trees, Wren glimpsed the pale blue ocean beyond. She could hear waves washing the shore.

Cornhusk trotted out to meet them, his ugly face alight. "Come on. Hurry! You won't believe this."

"What?" Sparrow's dark eyes narrowed.

"Just come! I'm not going to tell you, and spoil it."

Cornhusk gripped Sparrow's sleeve and dragged him around the crowd of onlookers to a space between the spruce trees that opened onto the beach.

Wren and Dust Moon followed at their own paces. Dust put an arm around Wren's shoulders as they walked. Wren had come to love them very much. She . . .

Sparrow halted suddenly, and Wren saw his mouth open. "What . . . is it?"

Wren and Dust walked around to Sparrow's right side, and followed his gaze.

A huge broad-beamed boat rocked in the water.

"Look!" Cornhusk said and pointed. "There they are!"

Sparrow turned to his left to peer through the trees, and Wren edged closer to him.

Cornhusk said, "The people here say they are the ghosts of Grandfather Day Maker's children. Look at the sunshine color of their hair, and their white skin. They look like corpses. See the stone houses they have built! They won't let anyone get close enough to really look. They're apparently afraid of humans."

"Blessed gods," Sparrow said hoarsely. "Grandfather Day Maker's children . . . they're h-here."

Dust said, "What are you talking about?"

Sparrow took a step backward, as if preparing to run. "I saw . . . millions . . . crying out for help."

Cornhusk's smile had frozen at Sparrow's words. He stood as rigidly as a man on the edge of a precipice, afraid to move.

The quaking began in Wren's legs and worked up through her body.

*They build houses because they are afraid of us . . . our world is about to end. We have to warn people, before it's too late. . . .*

"Wren?" Dust Moon said. "Wren! What is it?"

Dust Moon knelt and took Wren by the shoulders, searching her face.

Wren closed her eyes, and let the tears run silently down her cheeks. "Dust Moon . . . do you remember when I—I told you about the bloody boy?"

"Yes," Dust answered. Her wrinkled face had gone serious. "You said he was hurt."

*Yes, hurt badly. . . . Help me, Wren. I need your help.*

"Little Wren," Dust said, "what about the bloody boy?"

Wren opened her eyes and gazed upon the sunshine ghosts as they moved, stacking rocks to make their houses.

She answered, "I finally know what happened to him."

# Afterword

The Cove Meadows, where Rumbler meets his father, is a real archaeological site called L'Anse aux Meadows in Newfoundland.

From Norse records, we know that about A.D. 1000, Leif Eriksson set sail from Iceland in a broad-beamed open boat with one square sail, called a *knarr*. He landed on Baffin Island, which he called Hulluland, or "rocky land," then sailed for the southern coast of Labrador, and finally landed at a place he named Vinland, for the abundance of wild vines that grew there.

The L'Anse aux Meadows site is the only confirmed Norse settlement in North America, and is probably the place where Leif Eriksson and the other Norse explorers stayed for the winter of A.D. 1000.

There were other expeditions to Vinland in the years of 1003–1015. Leif's brother, Thorvald, led one of those expeditions. He was killed in Vinland. After that, Thorfinn Karlsefni led another expedition, which included one hundred and sixty colonists. Karlsefni and his colonists were terrified by the aboriginal peoples, whom they called *Skraelings*, and killed several. The Indians fought back. Karlsefni and his colonists left after about a year, and never returned.

Vinland practically disappears from the records after that. The only thing we can say for certain is that the aboriginal peoples *won* the first round.

The second round would not begin for another five centuries. It would have dramatic consequences, not just for the native peoples of North America, but for the world.

People today tend to speak in terms of the dispossession and "Americanization" of the Indian, but the reverse is equally, if not more powerfully, true. We have all been "Indianized."

We would argue, in fact, that without Indian contact there would have been no fall of the Berlin Wall, no collapse of communism. There would be no United Nations, no striving for democracy or human rights.

The average citizen in fifteenth- and sixteenth-century Europe survived under monarchies often indifferent to the needs of the common person, and sometimes willing to kill thousands in the pursuit of "proper" religious, economic, and political beliefs, as evidenced by the Crusades, the Inquisition, the suppression of the "wild" tribes of Ireland and Scotland, among many other examples. By contrast, the American Indian notion of democracy was astounding.

Thomas Jefferson, when fashioning the First Amendment to the Constitution of the United States wrote, "There is an error into which most of the speculators on government have fallen, and which the well-known state of society of our Indians ought, before now, to have corrected. In their [Europe's] hypothesis of the origin of government, they suppose it to have commenced in the patriarchial or monarchial form. . . . [Indian] leaders influence by their character alone; they follow, or not, as they please, him whose character for wisdom or war they have the highest opinion . . . every man, with them, is perfectly free to follow his own inclinations. But if, in doing this, he violates the rights of another, if the case be slight, he is punished by the disesteem of society, or as we say, public opinion; if serious, he is tomahawked as a serious enemy.''

From the first moment that reports reached Europe describing the lifeways of the aboriginal peoples, Europeans were intoxicated.

In fact, it became a real problem for European governments. To battle this fascination with the ''Noble Savage,'' the European elite proposed the ''theory of degeneration.'' According to which, the American climate debased all life on the continent, animals, plants, the aboriginal peoples, and, of course, any European who set foot there.

This only seemed to inflame the interests of the common people, and gifted writers like Benjamin Franklin and Thomas Jefferson made sure that interest did not wane. They genuinely *believed* that the Iroquoian form of government was superior to that of the monarchy, and encouraged all colonists to listen carefully to what the Iroquois had to say.

This began a chain reaction that has yet to end.

In 1744, the leader of the Iroquois League, Canassatego, met with American colonists at Lancaster, Pennsylvania. After hearing about their difficulties with the Crown, he told them that if they were wise, they would quickly establish a union like that of the Iroquois, so that they could defend themselves.

In Boston, in 1774, colonists dressed as Iroquois warriors dumped tea into the harbor to protest British taxation and the confiscation of gunpowder, which they equated with their right of self-protection. In 1775, battles broke out in Concord and Lexington. On August 25 of that year, approximately two hundred and fifty years after their first encounter, the colonists met with leaders of the Iroquois League in Philadelphia. The colonial commissioners told the Iroquois: ''Our business with you, besides rekindling the ancient council-fire, and renewing the covenant . . . is to inform you of the advice that was given about thirty years ago . . . when Canassatego spoke to us . . . Brothers, our forefathers rejoiced to hear Canassatego speak these words. They sank deep into our hearts. . . . We thank the great God that we are all united; that we have a strong confederacy, composed of twelve provinces . . ."

The first "united states," then, came about at least partly as a result of sage Iroquois advice.

In 1775, James Adair wrote a book called *History of the American Indians,* in which he described the Iroquoian system of government: "Their whole constitution breathes nothing but liberty . . . there is equality of condition, manners and privileges . . ."

On the eve of the American Revolution, in 1776, a popular account of "Americans" widely circulated in England read: "The darling passion of the American is liberty, and that in its fullest extent; nor is it the original natives only to whom this passion is confined; our colonists sent thither seem to have imbibed the same principles."

That would prove one of the greatest understatements in the history of the world.

In fact, it is out of that rich aboriginal democratic tradition that the political ideals of what would become known as the Free World emerged.

The government espoused by the League of the Iroquois was everything that European monarchies were not. The Iroquois refused to put power in the hands of any single individual, lest that power be abused. The league sought to maximize individual freedoms, and to minimize governmental interference in people's lives. The Iroquois taught that a system of government should preserve individual rights, while at the same time striving to insure the public welfare; it should reward initiative, champion tolerance, and establish inalienable human rights. Good government, they believed, provided for referendum and recall, assured for the common good by a one-person-one-vote system of election. They accepted as fact the equality of men and women, respected the diversity of peoples, their religious, economic, and political ideals, their dreams.

None of these principles were part of the European way of life. But no European who heard them could deny their power.

This is not to say that European civilization had no impact on the form American government would take. It had a profound influence. But it was the contrasting of these two governmental traditions that prompted transplanted Europeans to evolve a system of government which promoted democracy and freedom for all peoples.

In the final analysis, then, the democratic nations of the world owe the aboriginal peoples of North America a debt of gratitude for one very important thing:

Their existence.